"You'd better believe it." Reilly tapped a leather briefcase on the seat beside him. "It's all right here. Documented. Every last piece. Can't you tell from the stink?"

Forster sat staring at Reilly's briefcase. "Let me see what you have in there."

The SEC lawyer . . . took some typewritten sheets out of his briefcase. . . . When Forster began reading, a sudden sweat turned cold on his back. . . . For in page after page of sworn statements filed with the United States District Court, the case against the six accused bankers came into focus as complete, assured, irrefutable. . . . The evidence indicated that the profits from the group's illegal activities came to about $50 million per man. . . .

Forster finished the last of the transcript. . . . Considered in its entirety, the evidence against the six men was awesome. If less than half of it were true, they had to be guilty as hell.

Reilly looked at Forster. . . . "Believe it now?"

Forster drank his whiskey in silence.

Also by Norman Garbo:

Fiction:
CONFRONTATION (with Howard Goodkind)
THE MOVEMENT
THE ARTIST
CABAL
SPY
TURNER'S WIFE
GAYNOR'S PASSION

Nonfiction:
PULL UP AN EASEL
TO LOVE AGAIN

DIRTY SECRETS

Norman Garbo

FAWCETT CREST • NEW YORK

A Fawcett Crest Book
Published by Ballantine Books
Copyright © 1989 by Norman Garbo

Library of Congress Catalog Card Number: 88-21778

ISBN 0-449-21883-X

This edition published by arrangement with E. P. Dutton, a division of Penguin Books, USA Inc.

Manufactured in the United States of America

First Ballantine Books Edition: July 1991

For Rhoda.

*How perfect that she continues
to share it all.*

Every line of work had its dirty
secrets [thought the president],
yet his had more than its share
because more lives were affected. . . .
—from *Dirty Secrets*

Paul Forster opened his eyes in the gray dawn light and gazed out through the mist at the Hudson River and the ghosts of the Palisades on the far shore. Savoring the view from his apartment windows was part of his morning ritual. It gave him a sense of well-being. He had been raised by urban parents to whom four tenement rooms facing front spelled good times, and four to the rear said things were hard. Forster's mother and father were long dead, but he still carried parts of them, which meant he never took his view for granted.

Forster half-turned to look at the woman sleeping beside him and was instantly depressed. It was not the woman's fault. She was young, reasonably pretty, and her body, naked on the sheets, glowed with the pink delicacy of one of Raphael's more earthly Madonnas. There was just something sad about waking up beside a woman you didn't really care about, although after almost seven years, Forster supposed he should be getting used to this. It had been that long since he last woke up beside his wife. *Former* wife, he thought. Forster had never been a man easily given to change. A friend had once mockingly dubbed him Flexy because he was so inflexible. When he had married he had fully expected it to be for life. Annie, his wife, had expected the same thing. They both had expected too much.

Daylight touched the nondescript furnishings, the few dusty paintings on the walls, the overflowing rows of books on the shelves. Flecks of light fell on the typewriter and papers on Forster's desk, on the stacks of research cards and periodicals, on the jumble of pencils lying about like spent cartridges on an abandoned battlefield. There were reasons for everything in the room, but Forster had begun to suspect that they might very well be the wrong reasons.

Yet who was he to insist on being right? Being right was

mostly a matter of timing, anyway. Luck also helped. *Mazel*, his mother had called it, claiming that whatever you did, it never hurt to have a little *mazel* thrown in. But, sadly enough, luck was something his mother had found in short supply. Down to ninety-seven pounds and dying, she had nevertheless smiled as she whispered, "I'm leaving it all to you, Paulie."

"Leaving what, Momma?"

"The *mazel* I never had."

His legacy.

The thought was mocking, but that was more a matter of style than fact. Forster had no true complaints. Life had treated him well enough. At least, in his work. He was an economist who wrote and lectured with better-than-average success on a subject never famous for its long-term joys. So that at the still-buoyant age of forty-one, Forster not only found himself the author of two of the more definitive books on long-term market timing and effects, of debt default and deficit spending, but he also had received an equal number of Pulitzers for his investigative reporting on the current economic scene. In addition, he enjoyed a pleasantly loose arrangement with *Finance Magazine*, the country's most prestigious financial periodical, that allowed him to contribute half a dozen pieces a year on topics of his own choosing while retaining final editorial control over their content. Not too bad for a kid who used to steal hubcaps.

So was it *mazel*? Or was luck really just the residue of design?

He stared off at the Hudson once more. With the breath of the sleeping woman warm against his flesh, Forster went on taking stock. Was he a smart man or a fool? The fact that he was a recognized expert on the traditionally dismal science of economics and had been acclaimed for it, had nothing to do with the question. Neither did the fact that he was earning more money than he would have believed possible less than ten years ago. Still, it could not be denied that he had made an illustrious enough beginning in his Ph.D. thesis, *Changing Economic Patterns and Their Effect on Nineteenth-Century European Political Philosophy*. And at twenty-five he had begun an academic career of great promise with an assistant professorship at Yale. But he had soon become bored with academia and the scholarly life and quit. Or maybe he just lacked the necessary depth of commitment and stability for pure scholarship. In any case, he had an impressive enough background by then to get whatever research grants and consulting jobs he needed until his books were published.

And now?

Now, he thought dully, I write pretty much the same things I've written before, make love to women I don't love, and wait without particular joy for whatever's going to happen next.

Pleased with his own toughness, actually relishing the harsh, cynical judgment with which he had indicted himself, Forster turned to accept his reward from the dependably receptive body of the young woman who was just then stirring herself awake beside him.

The lovemaking was pleasant enough, but absent of surprise or passion. They undoubtedly were both to blame, but Forster chose to take it all on himself. You got out of this sort of thing exactly what you brought to it, and it had been years since he had brought anything more than a certain amount of lust, skill, and an increasingly complex need for distraction. When the act had finally ended with its obligatory crescendos of movement and sound, Forster could barely wait for the woman to shower, dress, and leave.

At eleven o'clock, Forster rose from his desk, lit a cigarette, and made his way a trifle stiffly to a window. The cigarette was his first of the morning. His latest plan called for no more than one every two hours, and so far he was sticking to it. So far meant eight full days, his best effort to date.

The sun had burned away the early mist and the Hudson was in full light. The view from ten stories up had a fine flow to it that carried you down the sweep of Riverside Drive with its new, spring grass and out across the water to the Jersey cliffs. His fix. Although he had a pleasant enough office at *Finance Magazine*, he preferred working at home whenever possible. There were always distractions at the magazine, and writing was hard for him at best. Even after so many years, he still labored over every thought, every sentence, every word. He knew himself to be an economist because he had the hard knowledge and the credentials to prove it, but he still found it difficult to consider himself a true writer. And the two Pulitzers were of little reassurance. Such prizes were nothing but the subjective judgment of people, and people could be fooled. What he had was a solid depth of feeling and enough perception to let him cut through to the heart of things. And when he was at his best and a little lucky, he was able to make others know it.

At the moment, Forster was not writing anything. His battle this morning was in trying to decide what to write about next. Freedom of choice could be a double-edged sword. You could be immobilized by it, impaled on it. You could end up staring at the river. It was not an absence of conviction that gripped him, but an overabundance. Nothing in the realm of economics was trivial to him. Since life itself was sacred, then surely the science that determined the daily nature of that life was equally so. Did people dwell in plenty or go to bed hungry? Did they lead productive lives or have to beg for charity? Poverty could murder God and strangle the soul, so fighting want was fighting the devil.

The phone rang behind him.

With a sigh, Forster, a tall, lean man with dark-bright eyes and a way of carrying his head tilted slightly to one side, turned away from the window and slowly walked back to his desk. The tilt gave him a look of perpetual questioning, but actually was the result of a partial loss of vision in his left eye that made him compensate by leading with his right. The damage had been caused by a blow from a lead pipe in the hands of a Riverside Drive mugger whom Forster had caught practicing his trade on an old woman with an arthritic hip. Forster had then beaten the man senseless. It was Forster's first realization that he was capable of murder.

Reluctantly—he never enjoyed telephone conversations—Forster picked up the receiver.

"What were you doing?" asked Marty's voice. "Staring out at your beautiful polluted river?"

Forster smiled. "Exactly."

"I need to talk to you. Can you get down here in the next hour or so?"

"It's that serious?"

"I'm not sure yet. It could be."

Forster stubbed out the remains of his cigarette. "What's wrong, Marty? Are you sick?"

Marty was Martin Jennings, his true friend and sword as well as the executive editor of *Finance Magazine*. Marty had suffered a near-fatal heart attack less than a year ago that had brought

about no change in either his compulsive work habits or the
purity of his Type-A outlook.

"If I were sick, asshole, I'd have called a doctor."

"I'll be there in half an hour," Forster said.

Finance Magazine occupied the top two floors of its own building, a glass tower on Madison Avenue that reminded Forster of
a giant missile about to take off. He took an express elevator to
the forty-seventh floor and came out onto the opulent red carpeting of the editorial area. A blond receptionist flashed a smile.

"Good morning, Mr. Forster. We haven't seen you all week.
Have you been traveling?"

"Fargo, North Dakota," he told her.

She laughed and handed him his mail in a large manila folder.
The question and answer were a long-standing joke between
them. The receptionist knew very well where he had been all
week. Indeed, she had called him daily with messages, few of
which he had enjoyed. Either good news was becoming a van-
ishing commodity, or else people were going out of their way
to emphasize the bad.

Forster followed the red carpeting, which ran between por-
traits of the magazine's featured writers. His own photograph
was included, with framed copies of his two Pulitzers hanging
directly below. If there was any public relations benefit to be
squeezed from such things, *Finance* got it all. There were also
pictures of distinguished guest contributors who had written
pieces for the magazine over the years. Four presidents were
among them. We're a very important publication, all this pro-
claimed, so attention should be paid to what we say here. Forster
was unimpressed.

Martin Jennings's office was at the far end of the corridor; his
secretary greeted Forster and passed him right through. The
room was huge and all windows, with a view to the north and
east that made you feel as if you were dropping down a long
slide with the breath going out of you and nothing waiting at the
bottom. When entering the place you sensed a change in the
atmosphere—almost as if you'd entered an imperial chamber
where you either produced the proper credentials or were instantly banished. Jennings himself seemed oddly out of place in
the room, a peasant intruder in rumpled, poorly fitting shirt and

trousers who appeared to have slipped in when no one was watching and had not yet been thrown out.

He was a small man, made smaller still by the loss of weight he had suffered during his recent illness. His expression as he greeted Forster was dour. It usually was. His voice, however, was deep and rich, an instrument honed for his use. When he chose, he could charm anything alive. At other times, he could throw dirt in your face, close you out, and never blink.

"Thanks for coming," he said.

In the silence that followed, Jennings came out from behind his desk and told his secretary to hold all calls. Then he closed the door and returned to his seat. Forster watched the small ceremony. There was purpose to it, as there was to everything his friend did.

"What's happening, Marty?"

"I'm not sure. Maybe nothing and maybe a lot. At the moment, what I'm really after from you is a bit of conversation."

"Why not? My talk comes even cheaper than my writing. Go ahead."

"To begin with, I'd like to hear some of your thoughts on Wendell Norton."

Forster just looked at him.

"Well?"

"I don't understand. Why Norton?"

Jennings leaned back in his chair. "I don't want your questions. I've got enough of those of my own. I want your *thoughts* about him."

"What's there to think?" said Forster. "Wendell's conservative, strong-minded, fair, an original thinker, and probably the single best chairman the Federal Reserve Board and the country have been fortunate enough to get in recent memory." He paused. "And if he had less integrity and more compromise in him, he probably could be president."

"You make me want to stand up and cheer. Okay. What else?"

"I'm not sure what you mean."

"You've known Norton a long time. He was your economics professor at Harvard. He guided you through the travails of your doctorate. He considers you one of his all-time favorite students as well as his friend. You're a frequent guest at his home. You talk economics over brandy. Tell me about him. Is he for real? Is he everything he appears to be?"

"Come on, Marty, I'm not his analyst."

"But you *know* the man, damn it!"

Forster fumbled for his cigarettes and a small silence developed that was like the silence at a wake. There was no joy in Jennings's face, but this meant nothing. Nor was there even a hint of anything to be found in his eyes.

"I think you'd better tell me what this is all about," Forster said.

Jennings left his chair, his brief, relaxed period apparently over. When he began pacing, it was with the mincing steps of a once-fat man who hasn't yet realized he's gone skinny as a lizard.

"I'm sorry," he said. "But I heard something this morning that was like a kick in the gut and I still haven't recovered."

"It concerned Norton?"

"Yes."

"What is it, for God's sake?"

"You won't believe it."

"Try me."

"How about a pending, seventeen-count indictment for the alleged violation of federal securities regulations?"

Forster stared at the editor. *"Wendell Norton?"*

"I told you you wouldn't believe it."

"Where did you hear this stuff?"

"I have a source at the Securities and Exchange Commission. About an hour ago, I got a call telling me that at ten o'clock tomorrow morning the SEC will be filing papers to that effect with United States District Court in Manhattan."

"How reliable is your source?" he said.

Forster's face felt stiff, strained with the effort it took to keep its composure, as if merely a flicker of concern would be a betrayal. It was not even a question of truth. Just the fact of such an indictment could be catastrophic for the economy and the country. As for the effect on Wendell himself . . . Christ! For the moment, Forster tried not to think about any of that.

"Very. That's what worries me."

"What were the alleged violations?"

"Insider trading. Illegally using confidential information for profit in buying and selling stock and stock options."

"That's insane. Do you know the kind of man you're talking about?"

"That's what I called you here to tell me."

"Wendell wouldn't take a paper clip without a legal bill of sale. Righteousness is his major failing. He often acts as if he personally invented integrity." Forster shook his head. "I don't care how reliable your source is. This is one time he's wrong."

Tiredly, Jennings returned to his chair. He suddenly looked sick, old, a man afflicted with more problems than he can hope to handle.

"There's more, isn't there?" said Forster.

The editor was silent.

"You may as well hit me with the rest. It can't be any worse than this."

"No? Wait till you hear. Norton isn't the only one supposedly being named in the indictment. There'll be five others listed along with him."

"You mean the president and the top part of his cabinet?"

Jennings did not come close to smiling. "I wish I could dismiss this as easily as you."

"Who are the others?"

"Tom Stanton . . . Alfred Loomis . . . Hank Ridgeway . . . Pete Farnham . . . Bill Boyer."

Jennings recited the names in a cold flat voice. He might have been intoning a roll call of the newly dead. The men named were the respective chairmen of Citibank, Bank of America, Manufacturers Hanover, Chase Manhattan, and the First National Bank of Chicago. Forster knew them all, personally as well as professionally. He had interviewed and written about every one of them.

Forster closed his eyes and opened them, an unstrung man expecting a host of fearful apparitions to disappear. They didn't. His face still blank, he felt, successively, stunned, sick, angry. And through it all was the beating of his heart, so strong, so insistent, that he wanted to quiet it with his hands.

"I don't understand this," he said slowly. "Apart from any questions of morality and ethics, these are all men with large personal fortunes. Why in God's name would they put their good names, their careers, their entire lives, at risk for money they don't even need?"

"I've been wondering the same thing."

"Do you have any more details?"

"All I know is what I've told you."

"Can't you call your source?"

"No," said Jennings. "Besides, if he knew any more, he would have told me."

"I don't suppose it would be possible to check with Frank at this point, would it?" Frank was Frank Reilly, the lawyer who headed the Security and Exchange Commission's enforcement division, and the man ultimately responsible for all of the Commission's indictments.

"Hell, no. Frank could never admit anything before an official announcement. And all I'd accomplish would be to let him know there was a leak in his division and endanger my source."

"Then we'll just have to wait for tomorrow, won't we?"

The editor considered Forster with hooded eyes. "What changed your mind? When did the idea stop being so unbelievable?"

"It's still basically unbelievable. But I must admit those five additional names do worry me."

"Why?"

"I'm not sure. But suddenly the whole thing seems too wild, too involved and too specific to have just been made up."

They stared at each other across the executive editor's crowded desk.

"What are you thinking about?" Jennings asked.

"The same thing you are. The crack in the earth that's going to open if this insanity somehow turns out to be true."

Late that afternoon, for the first time in months, Forster called his ex-wife, but she was out of her office. Annie ran a large, midtown travel agency, which she had built herself. Forster tended to blame her job as much as anything for destroying their marriage. Ridiculous, of course. Husbands and wives destroy marriages. But he remained human enough to need to blame something other than himself.

Annie rang him back twenty minutes later.

"You called," she said.

"You make it sound like something terrible . . . an accusation."

"It's all in your mind. When are you going to stop being so defensive?"

"When you stop attacking me."

They laughed, but it was less than a joke. Their pecking and scratching at each other had often drawn blood. When roused, Annie could be an artist with the needle and he could be pretty good himself. It all depended, of course, on her current mood and his latest insecurity. The harmless comment of one moment could cause an ulcerating puncture an hour later.

"How about dinner tonight?" he said.

"What's wrong?" Annie sounded instantly concerned. "The last time you asked me to dinner you were about to go into the hospital."

"It was only a sebaceous cyst."

"Yes, but I recall some uncertainty."

"Well, this time there's no cyst and no uncertainty. I'd just like to have dinner with you."

"I'd love to, but I have a date. I'm sorry, Paul."

His disappointment was almost palpable. He had to remind himself: she's no longer yours. Maybe she never had been. Untrue. She had been as much his as he had been hers, which was totally. They had drawn moods from each other, air circling in on itself. But that was history, although he still hadn't learned it.

"Of course," he said. "I know it's very last minute and all, but I thought I'd take a chance. Everything okay?"

"Terrific. What about you?"

"Fine. Everything is fine."

Annie must have heard something in his voice. "You're sure you're all right?" she said.

"Absolutely."

"Listen," Annie told him. "It's only a business dinner. I should be home by ten, the latest. How about stopping by for a brandy?"

"I'd love it."

Forster hoped he didn't sound overly eager, but he knew he did. He had never been able to fool her before. He obviously still couldn't.

Annie, lacking Forster's affection for the Hudson and the West Side's faded elegance, lived in a Sutton Place co-op whose cost made him swallow hard just thinking about it. Still, it was all her own money. Earning close to twice Forster's average annual income, Annie had asked for no alimony. *I'm* the one who should have asked for payment, he thought. It might have helped keep her with me.

The doorman knew him. "Mrs. Forster is expecting you, sir." His smile said that Mrs. Forster also expected others from time to time. Well, why not? She was not a nun. Or so Forster told himself.

The elevator sped to the twenty-first floor in a whoosh of gloom. There was a claustrophobic richness to the place that never failed to send something awry in Forster's mind. The poor-boy syndrome? He should be over it by now, but wasn't.

Annie had her door open as he stepped out of the elevator. She kissed his cheek. "You don't look so terrible."

"Compared to whom?"

Laughing, she took him inside. Her laugh never failed to astonish him. It was still that of an open, guileless twenty-two-year-old, and it was a long time since she had been any of these things. Wearing an obviously expensive designer dress with a single strand of pearls, she appeared the quintessentially urbane career woman. Her face, as she continued to study Forster's, was pretty, inquiring.

"And you," he said, "you look just plain wonderful. But then you always do."

"Thank you, darling. It's at this time of night that I most need to hear such things."

But it was not flattery. Annie had cornflower-blue eyes, pale blond hair worn straight and chin-length, and a midwestern face with the sort of perfect, clean features that you see in soap ads. Annie would be thirty-seven in two months, and in the right light she could pass for fully ten years younger.

"How did your dinner go?" he said.

"Marvelously. I'm almost sure I'll get the account. Imagine. A firm of almost four hundred lawyers who spend a million a year on first-class business travel and never quibble about a dime because it's all billed to their clients. As a group, they're probably just as smug and arrogant as they come, but right now I'd just love to sprinkle each of their fatuous little heads with holy water and wish them long, prosperous lives."

"God bless America."

"Amen," Annie said and led him through a marble-tiled foyer to a large living room with a fireplace, bookshelves along one side, and an open terrace overlooking the East River at the far end. Forster had been here a dozen times before, but still felt as though he were visiting a stranger. Right now the room was presenting him with a curious sort of woe.

"You hate this apartment, don't you?" she said.

"It's magnificent. I just don't know anyone who lives here."

"*I* live here."

He said nothing.

"Don't you think you know me?"

"Once, I did."

"No one stays the same forever."

"I do."

"I meant no normal person."

"Did you invite me here for brandy or for abuse?"

"You're really such a terrible reverse snob, darling. Money doesn't necessarily mean bad, you know. It doesn't *have* to stand for all the wrong things."

"Maybe not. But somehow it usually does."

Annie sighed and went over to the liquor cabinet. It was a long-suffering wife's sigh, exactly the sort of mark of tired exasperation that usually set Forster's teeth on edge and brought him out swinging. At such moments he hated her, although his hatred was also a cage that wired his love. But tonight he barely noticed it. He was unmoved either way.

Annie carried the Napoleon and two large snifters, plump as pigeon breasts, out to the terrace and poured them both full measures. Another change. She had never touched alcohol of any sort while they were married. But now she had the acquired tastes of success and liberation. Still, she handled them gracefully. Observing her now, one would have thought she had been born to such things.

She met his eyes. "Well?"

"Well, what?"

"Are you ready to tell me what's bothering you?"

"Jesus, I can't stand know-it-alls."

"I don't know it all, darling. But I do know *you*."

He left that one untouched, and they drank for a while without speaking. The night was hot for early June, with a close brackish smell coming off the East River and heat lightning flickering over Long Island. Closer by, the lights of an incoming tanker passed beneath the Queensborough Bridge. The wail of a siren sounded somewhere in the dark. The beast never sleeps, thought Forster.

"I guess I just didn't want to be alone tonight," he said quietly. "And there was no one else I could think of that I really cared to be with." He laughed but it came out more like a grunt of pain. "Pretty sad, huh?"

Annie was kind enough not to reply.

"I heard something earlier today," Forster said. "I can't tell you what it is and it may not even be true. But if it is true, it could be a national disaster. And it scares the hell out of me."

Her expression turned dark.

"No exaggeration? You do have an occasional tendency to go overboard on the side of catastrophe, you know."

"Not this time. Not if what I heard turns out to be true."

She believed him. "Since you're an economist, I have to assume you're talking economic disaster."

Forster sipped his brandy and said nothing.

"When will you know whether it's so?"

"Sometime tomorrow."

"Will it be public knowledge then?"

"Only if it's true. If it's not, there'll be nothing to know."

"Will you be affected personally?"

"We'll all be affected in one way or another. I appreciate being here, but there's nothing more I can tell you."

Like the warmest of friends, Annie doled out the brandy and did not press him. When Forster spoke again, it was out of his own need, not hers.

"I hope it turns out to be nothing," he sighed. "If it doesn't, there'll be a loss of faith, of basic trust in this country so deep and bloody it'll take a generation to heal."

Forster peered long and broodingly at his glass. When he looked up, everything he felt was in his eyes.

"I'm sorry you never knew my grandfather," he said. "He was a skinny little tailor named Duvid Forstersky, who came here from Poland at the age of nine, worked his eyes blind eighteen hours a day for sixty years, raised and educated his family without ever having more than two nickels to rub together, and died blessing this country with his last breath. He always kept a small American flag in a jar on his windowsill, which he kissed, along with his *mazuzah*, every time he left and entered his apartment. Our relatives used to make fun of his patriotism, but I never did. I still don't."

Forster paused. "Let me tell you something," he said. "I've always loved my grandpa's patriotism, although I've never had the courage to express it as openly as he. God help me, I'm much too clever, cynical, and educated for that. But I happen to feel exactly as he did about this country. With all its faults, I can think of no better place in this world to live. So anything that threatens that place threatens me, and right now I feel threatened. Do you understand what I'm saying?"

Annie nodded without looking at him. She took his hand and held it.

For the first time since their divorce, Forster stayed the night. But this time they came together less like lovers than as friendly animals. They made love gently and without self-consciousness. They had, after all, been husband and wife for eight years. In some obscure, deeply buried part of each, perhaps they always would be. It was all coolness in mood and for a while Forster was sure he could go on with it forever. As for Annie, she was as warm and exquisitely sensitive as he remembered her.

Yet approaching climax, his new sense of dread rose in him again, as if he were suddenly reminded that all this wonder would soon pass and nothing would be changed. In a rush of panic, he opened his eyes and found Annie glowing and golden beneath him. "Ah, love," she whispered, "it'll be just fine." And the best of her flew in and carried him away.

2

Forster slept fitfully and was up for the night while it was still dark. Annie lying beside him brought a measure of comfort inside the room, yet outside, everything was all wrong. Remembrance returned in fragments, oiled by a sudden sweat. He studied Annie's face, rendered visible by a patch of moonlight. He felt the need to talk, but lacked the heart to wake her.

Carefully, he eased out of bed, picked up his clothes, dressed in the kitchen, and wrote her a note.

> Even asleep you're beautiful. Thanks . . . for everything.
> Love ya.

He found a taxi on Fifty-seventh Street and was in his apartment fifteen minutes later, having decided that five-thirty in the morning had to be the only sensible time to drive around New York. Like a fever, the desire for a cigarette came over him, but he fought it off and stood under the shower until he considered it safe to come out. Naked, he paced the apartment, unable to find a place for himself. The odor of bad news rose from the wastebaskets, from the garbage can in the kitchen, from the memories buried in the walls of every room. He watched sunlight hit the river, but even that was of little help.

He put on fresh clothes, taking more care than usual with his dressing. Although he had no desire for food, he made himself some orange juice, toast, and coffee because it was something to do. Finally, when it was just eight o'clock, he felt hc could decently leave for the magazine.

Jennings was waiting for him, looking as though he had never gone home, except that he had changed his suit, which, even now, was as badly rumpled as the one he had worn yesterday.

"I was hoping you'd get in early," he told Forster. "Were you able to sleep?"

"About as much as you."

"I kept having these god-awful dreams," said the editor. "I kept seeing the faces of those six men. They were weeping like children."

"I don't suppose you've heard from your source since yesterday."

Jennings shook his head.

"Well, we'll know soon enough," said Forster. "In the meantime, I have some Jack Daniel's in my desk that should make the waiting a bit easier."

The editor stared at him. "Are you really as calm as you look?"

Forster held out his hand. There was a trembling in the tips of his fingers that might have belonged to an old man with an advanced case of ague.

The news came over the Teletype at exactly 10:23 A.M. The bulletin was brief, stating only that the Securities and Exchange Commission had filed charges in the United States District Court for the Southern District of New York against the chairman of the Federal Reserve Board, along with the heads of five of the largest banks in the United States. Subsequent bulletins gave further details as they became available.

Within half an hour, the picture that emerged was that presented by Jennings's source, plus a growing list of additional facts. The SEC was charging the six men with using confidential information illegally in a stock-trading scheme that had reaped more than $300 million in profits over the past four years. More specifically, the plan involved buying and selling stock and stock options in seventeen different publicly owned companies, based on sensitive information about pending mergers, acquisitions, and buyouts financed with heavy debt. The Securities and Exchange Commission requested and received an order from the Federal District Court, freezing the assets of the six men and authorizing a full inquiry.

The Commission, it was stated, had jurisdiction to impose civil penalties under the Insider Trading Sanctions Act of 1984, whereby it could seek to have all the illegal profits, plus penalties totaling as much as three times the profits, given to the government. Although the SEC routinely referred significant cases of this type to the Justice Department for possible criminal prosecution, it would not now comment on whether it would do so in this case because of its far-reaching implications.

Reached at their respective offices, the six men in the alleged ring declared themselves stunned by the indictment, denied any wrongdoing, and refused further comment until they knew more of the facts. Their lawyers, however, offered repeated assurances that grave errors apparently had been made by the SEC, and that an official statement to that effect would be issued at the earliest possible moment. In the meantime, it was hoped that a spirit of calm would prevail.

But a spirit of calm did not prevail . . . certainly not anywhere within range of a Teletype or financial ticker. Except perhaps in Martin Jennings's office, where Forster and the editor sat quietly and watched the news develop. Indeed, with their worst fears realized, they seemed almost tranquil. Like two prophets granted advance knowledge of an approaching cataclysm, they appeared to have made a kind of separate peace with it.

By noon on the New York Stock Exchange, trading volume had already soared past two hundred million shares, and the pace was accelerating. The Dow Jones industrial average had dropped 263 points. The per share prices of the five involved banks fell about 20 percent each before trading in them was halted at their own request. The bond markets plunged in sympathy, as did the value of the dollar against all major foreign currencies.

"What do you think?" asked Jennings at one point.

"What I think," said Forster, "is that Wendell better say something pretty good, pretty damned quick."

The Federal Reserve Chairman's statement came over the Teletype at 1:37 P.M.

"I have read the charges against me," he declared, "and I am innocent on every count. I say this before God, my country, and those who trust and love me. I have no idea how this entire charade has come to pass, or what its ultimate purpose might be. But I have enough faith in the judicial processes of these United States, to feel certain that my innocence will quickly be brought to light."

The other indicted men made similar declarations.

The markets were not reassured. By 2:00 P.M., the Dow Jones

industrial average, the most widely watched of all stock market indicators and considered a prime barometer of the country's economic well-being, had plummeted 427 points on a volume of more than three hundred million shares.

Forster rose from his position in front of the computer screen. His stomach felt frozen solid, and he could sense the blood pounding at the base of his brain. "I can't just sit here anymore," he told Jennings. "If we're really crashing, I want to be out where it's happening."

"I'm not that brave," said the editor.

To Forster, the vast trading floor of the New York Stock Exchange looked and sounded like a full-scale battle in progress. Shouting, arm-waving floor brokers, clutching fistfuls of sell orders, appeared to be physically attacking the fifty-two specialist posts that handled every trade listed on the exchange tickers. The noise level alone was overwhelming, the shifting crowds without any resemblance to what one might expect the largest and most important capitalist auction of stocks in the world to be like. Forster could all but smell the fear. Still, there *was* a certain order. Stocks *were* being traded, and the prices of the trades were being flashed on screens for all to see. Yet it was a battleground, and the feeling it gave you in your throat and chest was the same as when you were under fire in combat . . . except that here you were not risking your life, just everything you owned. And today everything you owned was suddenly sliding to hell in a handbasket. The selling pressure was unrelieved. Stocks were in a free-fall. There simply were no buyers, and the specialists themselves could swallow no more stock. They were choking on what they already had. It was pure panic.

Jammed into the sweating crowd that packed the visitor's gallery, Forster could feel the convulsions rising in waves from the trading floor below. How different were the two levels that selling panics existed on, he thought. There were the quiet, panelled boardrooms of the big banks and investment firms (several of which he had just visited), where the lights of the computers glowed and there was a sense of control and efficiency, where the top executives sat in their designer suits and prepared statements to the effect that the fundamentals of the stock market were basically sound and that the wholesale dumping of shares now taking place was just a temporary aberration. In these places, there were large graphs and charts standing on easels, and plans already were in the process of being worked out to cover every aspect of the current debacle. Many of the executives had studied from the same textbooks at Harvard, Yale, Columbia, and Wharton, and they all knew what Jay Gould and Jack Morgan had done in similar situations in the past and what the results had been in every case.

The brokers and clerks on the trading floor saw the exploding sell-off on a different level. They had no reassuring graphs, charts, and technical statistics in front of them. They lacked the time and serenity necessary for the formulation of long-term theories on market trends. They had not been present at the high-level meetings in which was discussed the spectacular buying opportunities that were certain to result when all the emotionalism had run its course and sanity had returned to the markets. They had no economics books to study on the floor of the exchange, no secretaries with whom to flirt, no computer projections in which their actions, multiplied by several million, were turned into clear, organized symbols suitable for publicity releases and the bar graphs of social historians.

The floor brokers and their workers saw pressing, shoving bodies; waving arms; pale, sweating faces; a confused shouting mob of men and a sprinkling of women that seemed to bear no resemblance to any of the things they had been taught to expect as part of the market's trading community. To the board chairman and top executives of the major investment houses, sitting before Quotron and computer screens in carpeted offices, with memories of Adam Smith and John Maynard Keynes and Milton Friedman drifting through their brains, things certainly were not good, but there was still a certain amount of logic to what was happening. No market could go straight up for five years without a major correction. But to the floor brokers and small investors, thought Forster, there was as much logic in what they were seeing as in watching the earth open before them.

"Oh Christ!" they wailed, watching IBM, General Motors, and AT&T lose more than twenty percent of their value in less than three hours. "Oh, Christ!" as almost every stock on the board plummeted under a growing avalanche of large block sell orders. "Oh, Christ!" they cried, unable to believe that most of the savings of a lifetime could actually vanish between breakfast and lunch. "Oh, Christ!" as long-planned security and retirement dreams became nightmares. "Oh, Christ, everything has turned to shit."

Shaken, feeling himself in the presence of hunted things, Forster left the exchange for what he hoped would be the comparative calm and order of the magazine's offices.

But even there the mood of shock and disbelief was all-pervasive as clerks, secretaries, writers, editors, reacted to events and numbers that none had ever witnessed until today. They clustered about Forster for answers, assurances. He was their noted economist, their guru. How could such things be happening. Where would it end? Forster offered them no pat replies. This was no time for economic platitudes. Panic defied reasonable explanations. The passengers on a suddenly sinking ship didn't want to hear theories on airtight bulkheads, water pressure, and maritime safety. They wanted to know if there were enough lifeboats. This was an aberration, Forster told them, a glitch brought on at a vulnerable moment by an unexpected and appalling piece of news. Markets always overreacted to the unexpected—both up and down, to good as well as bad. Time was needed for proper assessment. In a few days calmer heads would prevail. The damage would be sustainable. Forster told them what they wanted and needed to hear, and tried hard to believe it himself. It was not easy.

There was no escape today, no sanctuary anywhere near a radio, Teletype, television, or Quotron screen. The disaster was omnipresent. When the day's trading ended and most of the figures from a late-running tape were in, Forster and Jennings considered them in stunned silence. They were two experienced, high-ranking professionals, yet nothing in the history of their combined careers came close to preparing them for the awesome scope of the debacle as the numbers unfolded.

The Dow Jones industrial average had plunged a record 713 points based on calculations that were only preliminary at this time because of the overwhelming volume of more than eight hundred million shares traded. The drop represented a loss of 32 percent, a far greater percentage loss than the drop of 12.82 percent on October 28, 1929, that along with the next day's 11.7 percent decline preceded the Great Depression. It even exceeded the 22.6 percent loss suffered on October 19, 1987, when the DJI plummeted 508 points at the climax of a five-year, uncorrected bull market.

According to Devon Associates, which tracked more than five thousand stocks, this latest rout obliterated more than $800 billion in equity value from the nation's stock portfolios. Commodities prices also plunged, except for precious metals and especially gold, which surged $14.70 an ounce to a five-year high. The losses sent shock waves to markets around the world, and many foreign exchanges posted record drops. In Washington, the White House spokesman, Martin Alcott, issued a statement saying that President Hanson, currently in Europe, had watched with concern the market's collapse. But the nation's chief executive remained convinced that this was just an emotional reaction to the indictment of the six bankers and that the economy was sound. Mr. Alcott said the president had directed administration officials to contact leading financial experts over the past few hours. "These consultations," the spokesman added, "confirm our view that the underlying economy remains sound."

Forster shook his head in disgust. "Bullshit! The underlying economy has been sitting on a giant time bomb of bad debts, banking abuse, deficit spending, and speculative excess for seven years. The only thing the indictments did was light the fuse."

"Then I take it you're ready to accept their guilt?" said Jennings.

"It doesn't matter whether I accept it. Wall Street and everyone else does. And today's carnage was just six hours' worth. Wait till it filters down, spreads, and the real loss of faith sets in."

"What are you expecting? Great Depression Two?"

"Hardly. That was fueled by ten-percent margin and the collapse of the banking system. Now we've got the SEC and the Federal Deposit Insurance Corporation. But there's still no way to legislate against panic and loss of faith, and we've seen just the start of those today." Forster's gaze was off somewhere. "What worries me most about those six indictments is that the SEC rarely takes such action without good cause."

"At this point," said the editor, "it might not be too bad an idea for you to talk to Reilly."

Forster agreed.

Leaving Jennings's office, the day's events seemed to tail after him like a sour effluvium. He was stopped repeatedly on the way to the elevator. He was asked more impossible questions.

"You know every one of those six sons of bitches, Paul. How in the name of Christ could they have tried to pull anything like that?"

"If this was today, what's tomorrow?"

"I haven't a nickel in the market, so why am I scared half to death?"

Forster recognized the fear. He understood it. These were knowledgeable, sophisticated people who worked on the country's leading financial publication, yet they suffered an instant sense of fragility, of vulnerability, that was both new and unpleasant. A copy editor with pink-rimmed eyes behind thick lenses rode down in the elevator with Forster. "When you see the greatest market in the world get whacked out like this," he said, "it makes you realize how faulty and useless most people's thinking is. It identifies clearly how small we are, how powerless. It's very distressing."

The elevator starter grabbed Forster's sleeve and hung on as he passed his station in the lobby. "I'm gonna get a margin call for sure tomorrow, Mr. Forster. Should I meet it or sell out?"

"No one can tell you that, Charlie."

"If you were me." The voice was desperate, pleading.

Forster sighed. "If I were you, I'd sell."

He waved down a cab on Madison Avenue and sagged back into the seat. The driver had no idea who he was, but offered him his market views nonstop, along with his plans to pick up some good buys at the opening tomorrow. *Good buys*. Everybody's an expert, thought Forster, with the familiar mix of anger and despondency that the public's compulsive love affair with stocks always aroused in him. Forget that panic was the flip side of greed. Far worse was that stock players, jokingly called investors, idolized the greediest, clung to them and their fatuous pronouncements, and hoped a few easy dollars would be swept into their own pockets. Then they moaned bitterly when their greed-gods suddenly panicked and collapsed in sudden realization of their own inadequacies. No one had ever told them that those who chose to enter a no-limit game had to leave their moaning outside.

McGinty's was an old, unfashionable waterfront bar on the Lower West Side of Manhattan whose patrons were still mostly longshoremen or teamsters. It had kept its traditional aromas of stale beer and honest sweat, which, when blended by a row of slowly turning ceiling fans, made Forster feel unnaturally deodorized and sterile.

Frank Reilly was at his usual corner table, the only man in the place wearing a business suit. For the SEC's chief investigator, McGinty's was part history, part sentiment, and part affectation. His father, the last of a century-old line of Irish longshoremen, had brought him here for his first beer, and he had been coming back ever since.

Forster sat down next to him in a booth.

"What took you so long?" said Reilly. "I expected you at least half an hour ago."

It was a tough, New York Irish voice that neither college, nor law school, nor a successful career, had softened. The voice came out of a hard, clean, youngish face with the kind of pale blue eyes that lived for a contest. The face carried its own sense of authority, and let you know it at once.

"It took me a while to dodge the jumpers," Forster told him. "They were coming down like ticker tape on a parade."

There actually had been a suicide. Forster had not seen it, but the crowds and the ambulance had carried the message. Death was in heat.

Reilly sipped a double whiskey and signaled the waiter to bring the same for Forster. "Are you blaming me for the jumpers, too?"

"I'm not blaming you for anything."

"The hell you're not. I saw daggers in your eyes the second you walked in here."

Laughter broke out at the bar, the sound loud, deep, and warm in the crowded room. Forster suddenly wished he had become a longshoreman. The waiter brought his drink, and he took half of it down with one breath.

"And I'll bet you still refuse to believe it, don't you?" said Reilly. "Well, you're right. I made the whole damned thing up. I wanted to get my picture in the papers and be starred on the eleven o'clock news. I wanted the hate calls coming in so fast that they've swamped our switchboards. I wanted to be called everything from an Irish Papist prick out to destroy America, to a dirty crook who must have sold the market short, then created his own selling panic to insure his profits."

Forster smiled. "That stuff doesn't bother you. You thrive on it. And the louder the screaming, the happier you get. So spare me your noble civil-servant shit. It's not the public image you give a damn about. What excites you is the idea of catching these six moguls with their hands in the cookie jar." Forster paused. "That is, if you really have caught them."

"I knew you still didn't believe it."

"It's not easy to believe."

"Maybe not for you. But for me it is. I'm the one who's been collecting the evidence, who's been eating and breathing it for sixteen months. At this point it's like having a long-festering boil finally pop open."

Forster sat looking at him.

"What's the matter?" asked Reilly. "Can't you accept the idea of your six golden gods having smelly feet?"

"They never were my gods."

"One of them was. How about Norton?"

"Wendell Norton . . ." Forster began with quiet dignity, then stopped as he realized the futility of trying to defend a man without knowing the evidence against him.

"Okay. I'm a good listener. Tell me about your esteemed Wendell Norton."

Forster declined the bait. He felt the whiskey burn through his chest and into his stomach. "You have the advantage of knowing all the facts. I don't."

"I'll tell you what," said Reilly. "If you come down to Federal District Court tomorrow morning at eleven, you could end up knowing almost as much as I do."

"What's going to be happening?"

"You know I can't say anything about that."

"What *can* you say?"

Reilly glanced up at the stained, faded face of an old Seth Thomas clock. It read 5:36 P.M. "I think I can safely say that in about twenty minutes, Wendell Norton and his five friends are scheduled to appear at the United States Attorney's office in Manhattan, where they'll be arrested on criminal charges stemming from our SEC civil suit."

"Holy Christ!"

"Precisely." Reilly's eyes were like dirty-blue river ice. Then they softened. "Whatever you think, it gives me no joy to be doing this. Not that I give a damn about those six privileged lords. They had it all and threw it away. But I hate the idea of so many others having to pay for it."

"You have that kind of evidence?"

"You'd better believe it." Reilly tapped a leather briefcase on the seat beside him. "It's all right here. Documented. Every last piece. Can't you tell from the stink?"

Forster felt like a fighter who had taken a few too many. He sat staring at Reilly's briefcase. "Let me see what you have in there."

"You've got to be kidding."

"I want to look at it. I want to see your alleged facts. Maybe then I'll believe what's happening."

"You know I can't do that. Not before the arraignment."

"Don't give me that chicken shit, Frankie. We go back too far. And you do owe me a few."

"That's unfair as hell."

"That's how I'm feeling tonight . . . unfair as hell."

The SEC lawyer didn't look happy. He took some typewritten sheets out of his briefcase, slid them inside a folded copy of *The Wall Street Journal*, and placed the newspaper on the table in front of Forster. "If this ever gets out, it's my ass."

"Then let's not tell anyone, okay?"

"And for Christ's sake don't look at it here," said Reilly. "Take it into the crapper. That's where it's best read, anyway."

Forster carried the folded *Journal* into the men's room and sat down in a stall. When he began reading, a sudden sweat turned cold on his back.

My God, he thought.

For in page after page of sworn statements filed with the United States District Court, the case against the six accused bankers came into focus as complete, assured, irrefutable. According to the papers, the men had been carrying on their illegal insider trading for almost four years, during which time they bought and sold the stocks of seventeen publicly owned corporations involved in mergers or acquisitions of which they had advance knowledge. In all cases, the knowledge came from the fact that one or another of the banks they headed was involved in the huge, highly leveraged financing that such deals usually required.

The evidence indicated that the profits from the group's illegal activities came to about $50 million per man, with all of the monies held in six individual Bahamian bank accounts under secret code names. Only one person at the Bahamian Bank Streit, a man named Alec Borman who functioned as the group's account executive, had any knowledge of who the six men really were. It was when Borman, finally crumbling beneath the pressure of the SEC's accumulating evidence, agreed to turn state's witness in return for immunity from prosecution, that the indictments were made.

Feeling as though he were draining the poison from a near-fatal wound, Forster read on.

The major portion of the government's case against the six bankers rested upon the sworn testimony and corroborating material provided by three individuals. One of these was Borman. Another was Katherine Harwith, a longtime executive assistant to the Fed chairman, whom Forster had known for years and who probably enjoyed greater knowledge of Wendell Norton's professional activities than anyone else alive.

Katherine? More burning confusion and disbelief. Just seeing Katherine Harwith's name in this context set off sirens. The woman had been closer to Wendell than his wife. How could she be doing this to him? Another useless question, he thought, and went on reading.

The third major government witness was the investigator who originally stumbled onto the computer-traced, stock-trading pattern that aroused his suspicions and later set off the Security and Exchange Commission's full-scale investigation. This man's name was Peter Stone, and Forster had lately become aware of him as one of the toughest and brightest of the new crop of young lawyers who worked for the SEC's investigative chief.

Forster read through a series of statements from handwriting experts attesting to the fact that the false, code-name signatures used for the Bank Streit trading accounts were actually written by the six accused bankers. Additional testimony revealed how the indicted men tried to cover the trails of their occasional, secret, day trips to the Bahamas by paying cash for airline tickets and taking indirect routes. In such cases they never told their wives of their whereabouts and made certain they did not remain away overnight. Too, their buy and sell orders to Alec Borman at the Bank Streit were all handled from public pay telephones.

Forster finished the last of the transcripts and sat staring blindly at the closed door of McGinty's toilet stall. He had drained the poison, but the curse was on him anyway and he knew no magic incantation that would make it go away. Considered in its entirety, the evidence against the six men was awesome. If less than half of it were true, they had to be guilty as hell.

Reilly looked at Forster as he returned to the table and handed him his transcripts. "Believe it now?"

Forster drank his whiskey in silence.

He was home in time to hear the eight o'clock news. In the solemn tones usually reserved for announcing the deaths of major figures, the anchorman declared that the Federal Reserve Chairman and his five alleged coconspirators in the SEC indictment had answered a subpoena to appear at the United States Attorney's office in the Borough of Manhattan. Following the usual procedures in such cases, the six men were handcuffed and placed under arrest on the criminal charges that they had illegally obstructed and impeded an SEC investigation into their alleged insider trading activities. They were then remanded for the night to the Metropolitan Correctional Center to await arraignment in United States District Court at eleven o'clock the next morning. It undoubtedly was the first time in recent history, the newscaster said, that six individuals of such high national standing and reputation had been forced to undergo the humiliation of being treated as common criminals.

The phone rang moments later. Forster knew it was Jennings before he picked up the receiver.

"I've been trying to get you for the past hour," said the editor. "Where the devil have you been?"

"Where I was supposed to be. With the devil himself. Reilly."

"Why didn't you call me?"

"His kind of news, you've got time to hear. Unless you're in a rush to call your broker with sell orders for tomorrow's opening." Forster paused. He could hear Jennings's breathing, rushed and heavy across the wire. "I got Frank to let me see a transcript of the evidence."

"And?"

"Just from what I read, they haven't a prayer."

"I'm not really surprised. Reilly doesn't waste time on indictments that won't stick."

The wire hummed.

"Frank thought there was a chance the Board of Governors

might suspend trading on the Exchange for a few days," said Forster. "At least until the hysteria quiets. I told him that would be the worst thing they could do. That would really make for panic."

"Judging from what we saw today, there'll be panic anyway. Who's going to do the buying? The specialists already have eaten so much stock they're choking on it. Hell, we've been getting primed for disaster for months. Between the Fed deficit, the trade deficit, the bad debts, the overleveraging of the markets, the rising interest rates, and a runaway bull market without a major correction in years, the only thing missing for a worst-case scenario was a sudden loss of faith in the system. And we sure got that with this morning's indictments. I don't mind telling you, I'm petrified."

"Who isn't?" said Forster. "But our most immediate worry is still tomorrow. If we get two days back to back of seven hundred points down, there could be enormous breaks in the system itself. They can appear anywhere . . . in clearing corporations, across the board, and in member firms that have capital commitments on margin selling. All our markets will be having these stresses, and there'll be more from overseas."

"How about the banking system? Do you think this can spread there too?"

"I sure as hell hope not. But the Fed's going to have to be pretty damned good if we do get another big drop. They'll have to push people to come up with the needed liquidity in the dry spots. And the treasury's going to have to do the same. If they don't, God only knows where this free-fall will end."

Jennings's sigh came over like a whisper of pain. "Will you be in court tomorrow for the arraignment?"

"How could I not?"

"Well, keep in touch. We're in uncharted territory. I'm going to want to hear your voice."

Forster hung up and sat staring at the phone. When it rang again, it was Annie.

"Now I know," she said.

"You and the rest of the world."

"Imagine. Men like that. Do you really think they're guilty?"

"Haven't you heard? In this country you're presumed innocent until proven otherwise."

"Don't give me platitudes. I asked what you thought."

"I don't know. In my wildest dreams I couldn't conceive of their doing this. Still . . ." Forster stopped as though in spasm. "I also can't imagine such charges just being pulled out of the air."

There was a pause. Then Annie's voice came over, sober and troubled. "You were crying out in your sleep last night."

"Leftover passion?"

"You said, 'Don't . . . don't, please don't. . . .' You kept saying it over and over."

Forster frowned. "Really?"

"You sounded frightened. Which frightened *me*."

"I don't remember a thing." He rubbed his jaw. "The coward betrayed by the sleeping man."

She hesitated. "Would you like to come over again tonight?"

"What a nice woman you are. How in God's name did I ever let you get away? No," he added. "Don't tell me."

Annie didn't. Anyway, it was a purely rhetorical question. All the answers still were firmly embedded in their flesh, and there were a lot of them. Or so it sometimes seemed. At other times, Forster couldn't think of one that made any real sense. Not if there was love, and somehow he never had doubted that. Still, there were clefts and rents that had cut like geological faults between them, a conflict of egos and uncertainties that could turn abiding warmth into instant chill. Now they appeared to be getting along better apart than they ever had together.

"I appreciate the offer," Forster said. "But one night of brandy and sympathy is all I'm entitled to. I wouldn't want to abuse the privilege."

"You wouldn't be."

He felt curiously embarrassed. "I think you're just hungry for my body."

"I always was," she said.

The wire hummed between them.

"I know how you've always felt about Wendell Norton," Annie said. "I'm sorry."

"At this point I'm afraid it's a lot more than just Wendell."

"Do you think I should sell my stocks tomorrow?"

Forster laughed. "Incredibly, I sometimes forget your practical side. But I'm not smart enough to advise you on that."

"You're the smartest man I know."

"So how come I'm not rich?"

"We both know the answer to that one, don't we?"

Forster knew, all right. Their differing attitudes toward money, its accumulation, purpose, and use, had been one of their prime sources of conflict. Annie contended that with his specialized knowledge and brains, it was only his stubborn perverseness and reverse snobbery that kept him from being wealthy. With half the fools in the country building fortunes in the market, it had to be a rare sort of esthetic and moral superiority that kept him from joining the gold rush. While for Forster, stock speculation was like some sort of synthetic heart, pumping out the idea of success and achievement totally apart from any true concept of how it was being accomplished and what it stood for. He allowed himself no part of it.

"Do you have very much in the market?" he asked.

"Apart from my business," said Annie, "just about everything. And heavily margined, too. I admit I'm worried."

Forster gazed out at his river, black now except for a few reflected lights. "Frankly, I'd sell everything at the opening tomorrow. You'll take a beating from today's closing prices, but you'll be glad you did before the week is over."

"Then you're really expecting the worst."

"I don't know what to expect. But a loss of faith is the single worst thing that can hit any market. Especially when it's as high and vulnerable as this one."

"Maybe we'll be surprised," Annie said. "Maybe it will all just blow over."

Forster smiled and said nothing.

"Stop smiling at me," she told him.

"You're still a witch."

"Only with you."

This made him smile even more, and remember her, and made him sorry and tender for her and for himself and for all men and women who may once have known love and seen what finally could happen to it.

"You're sure you don't want to come over?" Annie asked.

"I never said I didn't want to . . . just that I wouldn't."

"All right." She was silent. "Thanks for the advice. I'll sell everything at the opening."

"Don't blame me if the market decides to go up."

"Of course I'll blame you. What else are ex-husbands for?"

There was a click as the connection was cut off. Forster slowly put the receiver down. He sat there thinking about her.

Later, trying to sleep, he thought of other things. He felt as if a vital part of his world was dying, and that he, a noted specialist in such ailments, was helpless to stop it. A vast human action was going on, yet death watched. What it came down to was that everything he had ever been taught was either an extraordinarily elaborate lie, or he simply had misunderstood his lessons.

But it also was personal. Deep emotions, close family ties, were involved. His maternal grandfather had been broken, permanently scarred by the collapse of 1929 and the Depression that followed. More than forty years later, the punishing stock slide of the early seventies had turned his father into a morose shell with the vacant eyes and haunted look of the battle fatigued. Forster had grown up with both men seeping through his veins, the suffering of two generations becoming a kind of bitter purification rite in a family so tightly knit that they all shared in the pain. The hurt was a continuum. Forster could still feel his father and grandfather inside it. From one generation to the next, he thought, nothing really changed except the jargon, the computers, and the ever-deepening price slides of the Dow.

Forster arrived at the Federal Court Building well before the scheduled 11:00 A.M. hearing time and found the crowds and police lines already jamming the sidewalks outside. There was a lot of shoving and angry shouting. If they had ropes, thought Forster, they could have been a lynch mob. Stockholders, no doubt. What they yelled was ugly, frightening.

"Give us the crooks!"

"Hang 'em!"

"Justice!"

"Let's get 'em!"

They were only words and no one was doing anything more than shout and push, but Forster still felt it in his gut. Waving his press card, he worked his way forward. An embattled police sergeant helped clear a path for him.

He went up to the third floor. There was a crowd in front of the courtroom, too, along with some policemen guarding the entrance. The lieutenant in charge greeted him by name and opened the swinging doors. "Looks like a big one, eh, Mr. Forster?" He grinned as he spoke. Definitely not a stockholder.

The immense chamber had a high, ornate ceiling and arched windows. The broad, mahogany seats reserved for press and spectators appeared full, but Forster made some space off the center aisle and squeezed in. The first several rows were occupied by the six defendants in the SEC case, along with their wives and lawyers. Except, of course, for Wendell Norton's wife, who had died some years before. Forster studied what he could see of the Federal Reserve Chairman and the five other bankers, undoubtedly representing more combined wealth, prestige, and power than any single group of defendants in the history of American jurisprudence. Sitting there in dark, conservative business suits and silk ties, smooth-faced and well-barbered, poised, controlled, and apparently at ease, they might have been about to call a meeting to order in one of their own board rooms. While I'm sitting here sweating, thought Forster, and tried to imagine what really was taking place inside them.

The presiding judge, United States Magistrate Matilda Langley, appeared to take no special notice of the six bankers who suddenly had transformed her ordinary court chamber into a center of international attention. A plump, middle-aged black woman with graying hair and tired eyes, she was focusing her entire attention on the two defendants in a drug-related case as she was denying them bail.

The SEC case was the next one called, and the six accused men stood before the bench with their lawyers. An Assistant United States Attorney charged them with illegally obstructing and impeding a Securities and Exchange Commission investigation into their alleged insider trading activities. The arraignment moved ahead routinely. None of the men spoke. Their lawyers did all the talking. Judge Langley set bail at $5 million apiece and declared a preliminary hearing would be held in four weeks. Several of the lawyers protested the high bail, deeming it unnecessarily stringent considering who the defendants were, but the judge held firm. The bail, in the form of personal recognizance bonds, was to be secured by $100,000 in cash along with the men's homes, personal property, and stock holdings. In addition, the six men and five wives were asked to surrender their passports. The United States Attorney announced that the government would seek the maximum penalty for obstructing an SEC investigation, which was five years' imprisonment and a $250,000 fine.

The magistrate conducted the bankers' arraignment exactly as she had handled those of the drug dealers who had preceded them before the bar. Nor did she show the slightest evidence, subtle or otherwise, that the men involved in the SEC hearing were any different from these others. Forster was impressed. He also felt as though something cold and bitter had been injected into his bloodstream. It was all over in less than twenty minutes.

Forster sat watching the group—bankers, wives, lawyers— move slowly down the aisle toward the exit doors. Two of the women showed signs of weeping, but the rest appeared composed, confident, virtually unaffected. People who looked like that, thought Forster, should be outside police jurisdiction, immune to all lower forms of wrongdoing and punishment. Indeed, Wendell Norton seemed amused by the entire proceeding, as if he himself was a disinterested observer rather than one of the principals. He was a big man, with the thickening body of a former athlete going to fat, and an indoor pallor to his skin. His bearing was erect, almost rigid, and he looked straight ahead as he walked.

But when he was nearly abreast of Forster, he suddenly turned and stared directly at him, his eyes meeting and holding Forster's with so deep an authority of feeling that it might have been an embrace. It was a clear and powerful emotion reaching out, made all the more moving because it was so uncharacteristic. Despite their closeness, Norton had never been a confiding or revealing man. Yet at this instant there was such a need for comfort showing, such a sense of himself as a man in pain, that Forster could almost feel it leap into him like a tracer of light.

"You sonofabitch, you've ruined us all!"

The hoarsely shouted words came from directly behind Forster and slightly to his right. Whirling, he saw the glint of metal as the man raised a revolver and pointed it at the chairman's head. Oh, Christ, Forster thought, and dove straight over the mahogany seat back just as the gun exploded. The muzzle flash blinded him for an instant, but his fingers had made contact with something . . . an arm, a hand, a wrist . . . and the man's aim was thrown off. There was shouting and screaming all around. Stretched facedown across two rows of seats, Forster was struggling to right himself when another shot exploded close above him and a great weight came down across his back. He pulled free, feeling a warm wetness on his neck and cheek, along with a sudden fear and funk and whiff of the grave. Then he stared into the man's eyes, which were as clear a blue as ice in moonlight—until the light went out in them because the man's second shot had entered his head and the blood was rushing down his face.

Forster turned and saw the six bankers being hurried down the aisle toward the exit doors. Norton glanced back, straining to see him, his face appearing even whiter than usual against the dark blue of his suit.

"Paul!" he called, and although Forster was able to read his lips, his voice was lost in the general uproar. Then he and the other five indicted men were pushed through the courtroom doors and were gone.

With his insides awash and his knees trembling, Forster groped for a handkerchief and stood numbly wiping the dead man's blood from his face.

"Why didn't you let him shoot the bastards?" someone yelled.

The dead man turned out to be an options trader named Ralph Michaels, who had been wiped out in the 713-point market plunge of the day before. A scrawled note was found in his pocket. It said:

> My Dorothy—
> I've lost everything. I love you. I hate these men. I don't want them to live. I'm sorry.

There was no signature.

The police lieutenant, who knew Forster, had showed him the note. "You sure moved fast," he said. "You saved lives."

The courtroom had been emptied of spectators and Forster stood staring down at the body where it lay in a patch of blood. There were six bullets in that revolver, he thought with a dull mixture of anger and despair. Maybe I should have done as the man said. Maybe I should have let him shoot them all.

The financial markets, already nervous and reeling from yesterday's losses, were hit anew by the aftershocks of the bankers' criminal arraignment and their attempted assassination. By noon, the Dow was off an additional 322 points on volume of 294 million shares.

Long lines of people formed to take turns in the New York Stock Exchange's spectator gallery. One of those present, a twenty-six-year-old woman named Marlene Carling, said she wanted to be able to tell her grandchildren she actually saw the crash taking place. Then she wondered whether the crash meant she would never have any children and grandchildren. It was hard enough to get a husband in the best of times. What chance would she have in the coming depression?

In the thirty-ninth-floor trading room of the Smith, Kelly & Broden brokerage firm on Wall Street, traders were shocked by the arrival of three uniformed security guards to protect them from violent clients. The same precautions were being taken by brokerage firms all over the country as news of the courtroom shooting spread. In Miami, a sold-out investor was arrested after attacking and severely wounding his broker with a hunting knife.

By 12:30 P.M., stocks on the American Exchange were gyrating so wildly that floor specialists, who normally bought and sold stocks when no one else would, ran out of cash. Trading stopped in eighty-seven stocks. Exchange Chairman Kemper considered shutting down the entire market, but a sudden rally made him hold back. When the market started to fall again, he changed his mind about closing it, fearing that a worse disaster might result when it reopened.

Thousands of telegrams were going out all over the country telling investors they must either put up additional margin or be sold out to cover the collateral deficiency in their accounts. As a result of these demands, it became a common sight to see people on their way from banks to brokerage offices, carrying stock certificates and bonds taken from vaults. Insurance companies had a rush of clients wanting to cash in or borrow on their policies.

In the trading room of Prudential-Bache's Broad Street office, glowing green figures on computer consoles traced the market's fall. "We're going underwater!" shouted trader Jeff Tepper as he swallowed three aspirin tablets without water. "Seventy thousand Coke to sell!" cried one trader. "A hundred thousand GM to sell!" shouted another. "Chicago wants to sell a hundred and fifty thousand Exxon!" yelled someone else. The cries did not stop. Long after lunchtime, a trader bellowed, "Hamburger in six figures to go!'' He wanted to dump a hundred thousand shares of McDonald's.

From Washington, Secretary of the Treasury John Gaynor assured the country and the nation's banks that the Fed, under the control of Howard Bloom, the just-appointed interim replacement for Wendell Norton, would provide whatever fresh funds might be needed to support the falling markets, the dollar, and the banking system. The market rallied for over a hundred points on the statement, then ran into fresh selling pressure.

Thousands of pink buy and sell orders littered the floor of the Pacific Stock Exchange. ''I surrender!'' shouted one overwhelmed dealer. Another broker slammed his fist into his computer terminal. Outside the exchange, an investor jumped onto the roof of a parked car and screamed, ''Fuck all bankers and brokers!''

By early afternoon the waves of index futures selling on the Chicago Mercantile Exchange were overwhelming. This selling created a strange problem. The value of the stock-index futures plunged sharply below the value of the stocks themselves and sent a new and strongly negative sign to traders. That huge difference in price created a chance for program traders to buy the relatively cheap futures contracts and then sell the actual stocks in a computer-assisted flurry of trades. It was a signal that there would be an intensified wave of stock selling. In reality, the market was moving much too fast to do any such program trading. But the worry itself did its own damage. Fearful that the program traders were about to jump in, many investors began dumping stocks even more heavily, forcing additional selling in a self-fulfilling prophecy of doom.

Demonstrating that the loss of belief and confidence was worldwide, the dollar also was being hard-hit, with the yen, the German mark, the British pound, and the French and Swiss francs all rising against it by 17 to 28 percent. It was estimated that foreign liquidation of the American dollar in the past two days of frenzied trading equaled close to $100 billion, and was still going on at the rate of $9 billion an hour.

A messenger struggling through the frenzied crowd on the trading floor of the NYSE suddenly found himself grabbed by the hair and all but pulled off his feet. The man who held him kept screaming that he had been wiped out, that he had nothing left. Half out of his mind, he refused to let the boy go. The frightened messenger finally broke loose, leaving the man with a fistful of his hair.

News reports began filtering in about doctors in every part of the country having to treat hundreds of cases of stroke and heart attack. The cases were judged as being directly related to the emotional stress brought on by the crashing market.

But like bright bunting on a hearse, the inevitable grim humor that seemed to surface instantly on the most trying of times began making its latest appearance. On Wall Street the rumor was that Merrill Lynch had adjusted its investment portfolio to 50 percent cash and 50 percent canned goods. In Hollywood, production was said to have begun on a new movie . . . *Rambo Gets a Margin Call*. And what do you say to an investment banker? "Fill 'er up." A stand-up comic told his audience: "An armored car was robbed of five million dollars in securities. The current street value was fifteen thousand dollars." One money manager in Boston described his present investment strategy as devout prayer. All agreed that it was better to laugh than cry, but not many were laughing.

At the magazine, Forster paced, conferred, worked, and anguished with Jennings in the editor's office as the bad news came across the Teletypes and computers. They might have been brothers helplessly watching the family home go up in flames with their parents trapped inside. When the 4:00 P.M. closing bell finally sounded on the floor of the New York Stock Exchange, the tape was running more than an hour and a half late, but preliminary indications were that the Dow had plummeted close to an additional 500 points on top of the previous day's plunge of 700. The volume of shares traded appeared close to reaching an incredible 900 million.

Shortly after 4:30, the editor's secretary came in to say that a call for Forster had been forwarded from the central switchboard and to ask whether he would like to take it here.

"Who is it?" he asked.

The secretary's face was blank. "Wendell Norton."

"Damned right he'll take it," said Jennings.

Forster felt a rush of pressure in his chest.

"I want to hear this," said Jennings. "Okay if I listen in?"

Forster nodded and picked up the phone on the editor's desk.

Jennings went to an extension. A moment later Forster heard
Norton's voice.

"Paul?"

"Hello, Wendell."

"Thanks for this morning. You undoubtedly saved my life."
The voice was the same . . . deep, resonant, confident. "Though
I doubt that many others would thank you. These have been an
insane few days. It's hard to believe it's actually happening."
Norton let several beats go by. "Before they rushed us out, I
thought I saw blood on your face. You weren't hurt, were you?"

"I'm okay. The blood wasn't mine. Sorry about . . . everything."

"I appreciate it."

The wire was silent.

"I'd like to talk to you, Paul."

"Of course," said Forster.

"Would nine this evening be feasible? I'll be getting chewed
up by my lawyers until then."

"Just tell me where."

"I'm at the Waldorf. It would be simpler if I didn't have to
go out. My face has become better known during the last thirty
hours than in the thirty years before. Besides, after this morning's incident the local police are a bit worried about security.
If I'm going to be shot, they'd rather it happen someplace other
than New York."

"I'll be there at nine."

"Room 1806," said Norton. "And thanks again."

Forster slowly put down the phone. Jennings was looking at
him curiously. "It's just occurred to me," said the editor, "that
you yourself might have had your head blown off this morning."

Forster was never especially comfortable at the Waldorf. Some
were born to such places and others acquired the taste, but for
Forster the hotel always carried the sterile air of an art-deco bank
vault that was home to rich, elderly widows. Indeed, one of
these did trail by him as he entered the lobby, a frail, blue-haired
lady wearing a set of diamonds whose glow seemed stolen from
the northern lights. The young man with her was gay. Forster
mentally wished them luck.

He took an elevator to the eighteenth floor, found the room
number, and knocked. Norton opened the door. He was fully

dressed and wearing the same dark blue business suit he had worn in court that morning. But he evidently had been napping because his eyelids were pink and one cheek was creased with sleep.

"I must have dozed off," said Norton. "I'm sorry. I haven't had much sleep lately. The nights have been terrible. Come in, come in."

They shook hands. Forster felt a strong urge to embrace him but fought it down. Wendell had never been comfortable with emotion. Still, he did look vulnerable tonight. Then, like an old repertory player slipping into a familiar role, he straightened his shoulders, firmed his back, and put on his mildly amused expression.

"It's been a lovely couple of days in the markets, hasn't it?" he said. "That's what I like most about our financial community. Its cool, considered reactions to any kind of news."

A bottle of brandy was on a Louis XIV table and Norton half filled two glasses and handed one to Forster. "Do you know the only redeeming feature of this entire nightmare? The fact that Emily isn't alive to have to go through it with me. I was watching the faces of those other men's wives at the arraignment this morning and it tore my heart."

Forster could think of nothing fitting to say. Two patches of color had appeared high on the Federal Reserve Chairman's usually pale cheeks and remained there like a permanent blight. Still, the vague half smile remained.

"You may as well know I'm submitting my resignation in the morning," he said. "As are the others. I just can't see any of us functioning effectively with this circus going on. I also want you to know that regardless of what you've heard so far, or may hear in the days and weeks ahead, I'm innocent."

Forster almost wished Reilly hadn't shown him the totally damning evidence.

"You didn't have to tell me that."

"The devil I didn't. Blind faith and friendship can be presumed on just so far. Especially with the kind of evidence they've got against me. But I've never lied to you before and I'm not lying now. I haven't the slightest idea how or why any of this has come about. And as far as I know, every one of the five men indicted with me are in the exact same position."

Forster lit his next scheduled cigarette, sipped some brandy, and waited.

"I'm actually not even certain you believe me now," said Norton, "and I wouldn't blame you if you didn't. But I'm going to presume on your loyalty and feeling for me anyway, because I have no choice. I need your help."

Wendell didn't need help, Forster thought bleakly. He was beyond that. Only a miracle could do him any good.

"What can I do?"

"Considering the circumstances, probably nothing. But I'm desperate enough at this point to want you to try anyway."

"Try what?"

"To find out what in Christ's name this is all about. It's hard not to say this without sounding hopelessly paranoid. But since I know none of us are guilty as charged, I can only assume we've been set up. And don't ask me by whom, because I haven't the vaguest idea. Nor can I even begin to imagine how the obviously substantial evidence against us was created, or where our alleged three hundred million dollars in illegal trading profits came from. Good Lord! Who would want to destroy us badly enough to invest that kind of money in the project?"

For the first time in two days, Forster felt a twitch of hope. Maybe Norton was innocent after all! Still, it was faint and quickly turned to doubt.

"But why the six of you?" he said. "Assuming all this has been staged. For whatever the reasons. Why would you and these five others have been chosen as targets?"

"I can't answer that."

"You can't think of a possible common denominator? That is, other than the fact that you're all bankers?"

Norton shook his head. "I'm afraid I'm giving you an impossible job."

Forster was silent.

"If you turn me down I'll understand."

"No you won't. You'll think I'm a shit."

"Perhaps. Though I'm sure I'd phrase it better."

They sat considering each other.

"What about your five codefendants?" said Forster. "Will they cooperate with me?"

"Completely. And gratefully. They not only know you personally, they know your reputation in this area. It's hard to argue with two Pulitzers.''

''And if I come up with even more damaging evidence?''

''Considering what they've already got against us,'' said Norton, ''that would be hard to imagine. But if you do discover more bad news, take it straight to the U.S. Attorney's office.''

''I'd need copies of all the evidence you've seen so far, as well as anything that comes in down the line.''

''You'll have it.''

Forster's mind was already at work. It moved in quick, tight circles. Finally, it settled where it had started.

''I still think there has to be something that ties the six of you together,'' he said.

''If there is, I don't know about it.''

''Have you ever kept a diary of any sort? Something personal?''

''Not really. Just my appointment calendars. And I believe my secretary gets rid of those every few years.''

The Federal Reserve Chairman sank back into his chair. ''There are times,'' he said softly, ''when I actually can't accept the idea that all this is happening. I know it is, yet I still can't accept it. I've never been an especially religious man. Except for when Emily died, I can't remember the last time I was in a church. Yet last night, lying awake in the dark, I literally found myself talking to God. During the war it was what we used to call a foxhole conversion. Get me out of this in one piece, Lord, and my soul is yours. And suddenly there I was, in a queen-size bed in the Waldorf, begging for the same deal.'' He smiled coldly. ''Your rational, thinking, modern man under pressure.''

Forster's brandy seemed to be turning bitter in his mouth. Why was he even sitting here and carrying on this conversation? The fact that Wendell was a trusted longtime friend suddenly was not answer enough. Lies annulled both trust and friendship. Especially in something like this, where the resulting havoc, actual as well as projected, was near to unthinkable. Yet if he's lying, thought Forster, I'm blind to the point of death. Or else he's a perfect invention of evil, and friendship itself is the art of the devil. The latter thought alone made him savage, murderous.

Something of it must have shown in his face, because Norton said, ''You really don't believe me, do you? You're trying to be as kind as possible, but it's just a little too much for you, isn't it? You still think I'm guilty.''

Forster was silent.

"For God's sake, Paul! You've known me for more than twenty years. How could you even begin to believe . . .'' The anguish, controlled till now, took over and Norton gave himself up to it. Still, he was a proud and private man and the hurt showed only in his eyes. Then even this was gone and the amused look was back once more. "If you think I'm guilty, what chance do I have with a jury of strangers?''

"I'll be honest. I saw a transcript of the evidence. Jesus, Wendell.''

Norton sighed. "Aah. Of course. How can I blame you for thinking as you do. The evidence is patently irrefutable. But it's all lies, every word manufactured. I swear it. On whatever sweet memory I have of my wife, I swear nothing is true.''

"But who'd want to do such a thing to you . . . to all six of you . . . to the whole damn country, as it's turning out?''

"I have no idea. That's why I need your help.''

"Do you realize what you're asking me to take on? I wouldn't even know where the hell to begin. There's not the hint of a clue. It would be like staring into the void and waiting to hear voices.''

"If anyone can do it, you can.''

"I'm not Jesus Christ, Wendell.''

"I know,'' said Norton. "But you're all I've got.''

They talked and drank until near midnight. Then Forster took a cab home, more confused, anguished, and exhausted than he could have imagined, and tried to sleep.

But sleep was somewhere else and it all came over him then, wave after wave, perilous waves as though something deadly was riding through the water and smashing the shore. And Forster lay in the darkness and felt close to nausea because there were all these questions piled on his chest and he had no answers. Then somewhere in the night, born out of anger and frustration and the sum of the day's lies and disasters, he thought of everything his father and grandfather and so many others had suffered in pursuit of the American dream, and he knew, like a gift he didn't deserve, that whatever he might be called on to do to keep such things from happening again, he somehow would do.

* * *

He was still staring up at nothing when the phone rang. A luminous clock read 3:37. In its glow, the phone was black, insistent. Forster picked it up as though it were a snake.

"Sorry to wake you," said Norton, "but I just thought of
something."

Forster shook his head to clear it. "What?"

"It was a long time ago. Certainly twenty years. Maybe
more." Norton's voice was rushed, excited. "We were all members of a special banking panel appointed by Congress. I'd completely forgotten about it. We only sat for about four or five
months."

"The six of you were on it?"

"Yes. But there were seven of us altogether."

Forster was fully alert now, pulse racing. "Who was the seventh?"

"Bradkin . . . John Bradkin. He was with Chase at the time."

"Where is he now?"

"Dead. Had a heart attack ten years ago on the tennis court.
I remember the date because for a long time afterward Emily
was after me to give up tennis."

"At least it ties the six of you together," said Forster. "But
what sort of panel was it? What was it supposed to do? What
was it called?"

"We were known as the Malcolm Commission, after the then-
chairman of the Senate Banking Committee. Our mandate was
to review the banking system and investigate complaints and
infractions of rules within the industry."

"And then?"

"We'd pass on our findings to the United States Attorney's
office for possible civil or criminal action."

"Was such action ever taken?"

"I believe so."

"What do you mean you believe?" said Forster. "Was it or
wasn't it?"

Norton took a moment. "It was."

"Do you remember any of the cases?"

"Not really. No."

Forster was silent.

"Well?" said Norton. "What do you think?"

"What I think," Forster said slowly, "is that it's quite a coincidence that all six of you should have served together on the same commission more than twenty years ago. And to tell the truth, I don't believe in coincidence.''

Was it possible?

First, there was just the fever, the excitement of any new, potentially explosive discovery. Then the rage came, a killing, trembling rage that left Forster sweating in his bed, as if a spasm of illness that should have discharged itself from his throat had lifted instead to his brain. Was this all deliberate then? Could these past two days of cataclysm, and God only knew how many more of the same to come, really have been part of some carefully conceived, insanely brilliant plan? And if so, what sort of creatures could be behind it?

Then the rage, too, was gone . . . it passed as quickly as that . . . and a curious joy took its place, a feeling that perhaps now there might be a proper villain in all this, some true cynosure of evil to be sought out and destroyed, a role for which the six indicted bankers had not even come close to qualifying. Even if guilty as charged, they would have been little more than victims of their own greed, merely pathetic. They certainly had not set out to cause a national catastrophe. Now there appeared to be a chance that someone might have done precisely that.

Eyes closed in the darkness, Forster had a fantasy. He saw his father and grandfather sitting morosely on a park bench. They were clutching bundles of stock certificates.

"What's wrong?" he asked.

"We're ruined," they said in one voice. "The market has crashed. All our stocks are worthless."

"No," he told them. "There's been a great rally. Every stock you own has shot up, soared out of sight. You're rich. The streets are paved with gold."

At first they wouldn't believe him. Then he showed them the latest quotes in *The Wall Street Journal*. The stock listings were in Yiddish for his grandfather and English for his father.

"It's a miracle," they said.

"No," said Forster. "It's America."

3

The receptionist, looking hollow-eyed this morning but still smiling professionally, greeted Forster with the message that the executive editor wanted to see him in his office.

"Well?" said Jennings, moments later. "Let's hear about Wendell Norton."

Forster told him everything, including the middle-of-the-night telephone conversation.

"Do you believe him?" said Jennings.

"Why would he lie?"

"That's not what I asked."

"I believe there was a Malcolm Commission more than twenty years ago and that all six bankers were on it. I believe, too, that it's too great a coincidence to simply ignore."

Jennings reconfirmed his loss of hair with his fingertips and waited.

"As far as their guilt is concerned," said Forster, "I admit I'm suddenly a little shaky. And I wasn't before I met Wendell."

"He's a forceful personality."

"True. And hearing him swear his innocence on the memory of his dead wife had definite impact. But it was more than just that. Why would a guilty man plead so desperately for an investigation that couldn't possibly prove an innocence that didn't exist, and might even add to the evidence against him?"

"To convince you he was framed, set up, an innocent man maligned by anonymous forces that will never be uncovered, but will still allow him to wear the proud mantle of a martyred victim."

"That's pretty damned cynical, Marty."

"Visit a prison sometime. You'll be hard-pressed to find an inmate willing to admit his guilt. Everyone there has been framed, railroaded. It's the nature of the breed. And it would be especially important for Norton to have *you*, in particular, believe him innocent. You've been one of his closest friends and disciples. You've just saved him from an assassin's bullet. He couldn't bear the thought of standing soiled and naked in your sight. Guilty or innocent, who doesn't want to be loved, admired, supported? And what better way to insure that from you than to get you to take on a hopeless quest that can't help but keep you locked in his orbit and believing in him?"

It was time for Forster's first cigarette of the day and he lit it gratefully. "You write some scenario. Nothing is straight. Everything ends up devious."

"I don't make it that way. I'm just not blind to it."

"And I am?"

"If not blind, then certainly myopic."

They sat in a silence broken only by the chattering of the Teletype.

"You've decided to do it, haven't you?" Jennings said at last.

"Yes."

"I think you're making a mistake."

"Why?"

"Because considering the evidence you saw, the odds are still overwhelmingly in favor of Norton and his friends being guilty. Because even the possibility of their having been set up in a conspiracy as complex and costly as this one would have to be, is so remote as to be nonexistent. And even if it were true, I can't see the slightest chance of your being able to uncover it. There isn't a clue. I don't know where you'd start to look. The whole idea is insane."

Forster smiled. "Is that all?"

"No," said Jennings. "I also don't think you're being honest about the real reason you're doing it."

"And what's the real reason?"

"That it's simply what you want to do."

Forster looked at the editor.

"No, it's more than just *want*," said Jennings. "It's what you feel *compelled* to do. Illogical as such an investigation may be, it at least lets you feel you're taking action, that you're not just sitting helplessly in front of a computer screen, watching the country slide to hell. I know you, Paulie. Maybe I should be grateful to Norton for dropping this whole thing in your lap. It could have been worse. Another few days like these past two and you might have been out hunting extraterrestials.''

Forster slowly rose and went over to check the Teletype. In New York the market was showing some technical bounce from its lows of the previous day, but the rally was limited to the blue chips and without conviction. Forster didn't expect it to last. Stocks already had fallen in Melbourne, Tokyo, Hong Kong, and London, although not as broadly and steeply as the two days before . . . which were now known as Black Tuesday and Terrible Wednesday. The dollar also was continuing to fall against the yen, the British pound, the French and Swiss francs, and the German mark. United States T-bills were trading at their lowest price in five years.

Forster turned back to Jennings. "I passed a little man with a beard on Madison Avenue this morning. He was carrying a sign that said THE END OF AMERICA IS NIGH. I didn't believe him.''

The editor was silent, his expression dour, his eyes cautious.

"I'll tell you what I do believe,'' Forster said softly. "I believe we see too much greed, hear too many lies, lose too much faith, and start forgetting what this country is all about. Until something like this happens and we see what we could be losing.''

Forster paused to light a second cigarette from his first, although it was nowhere near his scheduled time. "But you're right about my needing this. And it has nothing to do with logic or reason or anything close to feasibility. Because if there was even the faintest hope that Wendell Norton *was* telling the truth, and that he and the others somehow *had* been set up, and if there were just one chance in a million that I might be able to do something about it, there would still be nothing on God's earth that could stop me from going for it.''

Forster had the magazine's research department dig out and send to his office everything they could find on the Malcolm Commission. Then he spent most of the day going over the material. He had no idea what he was looking for, or even whether there was anything of significance there for him to find. But the Commission certainly appeared to be the only reasonable place for him to start looking.

He had been young and in school at the time, and without

particular interest in such things as banking panels. But from what he read now, the Malcolm Commission had been regarded as something of a bête noire by the more liberal segments of the press, with the term "witch hunters" used more than once to describe the less-appealing aspects of their activities. Indeed, a *New York Times* editorial of the period wondered whether the distinguished panel might not actually be doing more harm than good as far as the nation's bankers were concerned by washing their dirty linen in public.

"We are only too well aware," declared the editorial, "that the keepers of our financial house are not always as efficient, as ethical, or even as honest as we would like them to be. But since very few love a banker to begin with, it does seem dangerously counter-productive to wave the industry's shortcomings in our faces like a banner, and then do nothing about them."

Not entirely true. Forster came across a series of five cases in which something definitely had been done, with the Commission investigating, considering, and ultimately passing on three of the cases to the United States Attorney's office for possible prosecution, and the others to the SEC for civil action. Forster made a list of names, dates, and pertinent details, and had the research department follow them up. An hour later he had a complete printout of the results on his desk.

Of the three cases sent to the United States Attorney's office, one was subsequently dismissed for lack of evidence, another resulted in a three-year prison sentence that was later reduced for good behavior, while the third case ended up with a ten-year prison term that was terminated by suicide when the convicted man's final appeal was turned down. The cases referred to the Securities and Exchange Commission were settled out of court with consent decrees and modest fines.

The only situations that Forster considered worth following up were the two that had resulted in criminal convictions. Both of the individuals involved had been upper-management bank executives. The man with the three-year sentence was Alfred Kent, an officer with the First National Bank of Chicago. The man who killed himself in prison had been a vice-president of Chase Manhattan named David Berenstein—and, thought Forster, in what had become a conditioned reflex over the years, obviously a Jew. Neither name meant a thing to him, yet there was a sudden excitement in his chest that was near to a fever.

Even sitting down, his legs felt shaky. He exulted in the feeling. It was a beginning.

He wrote down the two names along with the key facts relating to each. Then he brought them in to Alice Renquist, head of the research department, a determined birdlike woman who had spent the past twenty-five years of her life proving she could find anything findable.

"I need a detailed follow-up on these two," Forster said. "Background, families, where they are now. The whole deal."

Renquist glanced at the material. "One of them is no longer alive."

"Get me his cemetery address."

"When do you need all this?"

"An hour ago."

"It's that important?"

"It could be."

"I'll do what I can."

"That's usually enough."

"I'll get you the living one first," Alice said.

"We don't know for sure whether he's still living."

"Maybe not." A rare smile broadened her thin face. "But we do know for sure that the dead one isn't."

Two hours later she brought a folder into Forster's office.

"Alfred Kent is alive and well and living in Chicago," she told him.

"What about Berenstein?"

Renquist looked mildly hurt. "It's after five o'clock. My cats are waiting to be fed. David Berenstein isn't going anyplace. Wherever he's resting today, he'll still be resting tomorrow."

Forster opened the folder and began reading. Released from prison but banned for life from the banking and securities industries, Kent had gone into the fast-food business and prospered. He now headed a chain of barbecued chicken outlets throughout the Midwest with annual sales of close to half a billion dollars. He had been married and divorced twice, had three grown children, and was currently living with a television actress in a ten-room penthouse overlooking Lake Michigan. He was a deacon of the Baptist church, belonged to two country clubs, was on the boards of several corporations, and apparently had political connections of some note in Chicago, Springfield, and Washington.

Forster carried the folder into Jennings's office and dropped it on his desk.

"Take a look at this."

The editor glanced at the name on the cover. "Who's Alfred Kent?"

Forster summarized.

"Which means what?"

"Maybe nothing. But I think it might be worth a trip out there to talk to him. I'll make a morning flight and be back tomorrow night."

"Better call first. He could be out of town."

Forster put through the call from the executive editor's desk.

"Food Enterprises," said a woman's voice at the other end.

"Mr. Alfred Kent, please."

"Who's calling?"

"Paul Forster. *Finance Magazine*."

In tandem, the names did their work. Several moments later, Alfred Kent himself was on the line.

"Mr. Forster?"

"Hello, Mr. Kent."

"I happen to be a longtime fan. It's nice to speak to you in person after all these years." The voice was brisk, cordial, confident. "What can I do for you, sir?"

"I'm going to be in Chicago tomorrow. I was hoping you might be able to spare me an hour or so of your time."

"Do you mean for an interview?"

"Nothing that formal. Just some conversation."

"Tomorrow seems to shape up pretty tight. But I'm free for lunch, if that would be convenient."

"That would be fine."

"Good. Then shall we say one o'clock, at my office?"

"I'll be there."

There was a pause. "Terrible mess we're suddenly in, Mr. Forster. What's the feeling up at the magazine?"

"Not an especially happy one. How do *you* feel about it?"

"I believe the next few weeks could be crucial. If total panic can be avoided for at least this period, the damage may be controllable."

"You could be right," said Forster. "I'll see you tomorrow at one."

He hung up and looked at the drawn, brooding face of the editor. "Our Mr. Kent believes it's important to avoid panic for the next few weeks."

Jennings was silent.

"I've been buried all day. What's been happening?"

"Nothing good. The market tried to stabilize in the morning but it didn't last long. Runs were reported at a few small banks in the Minneapolis–Saint Paul area, which set off a new wave of selling."

"Any of the banks have to close?"

"Thank Christ, no. The Fed flew in all the cash they needed and things calmed down. But the liquidation of American Treasury bills is still building, the dollar is still getting whacked everywhere, and foreign funds by the tens of millions are being pulled out of our biggest banks . . . particularly the five whose chairmen were indicted. That can give us the worst trouble yet, if it continues."

Forster could feel it all in his stomach. He had been worrying, writing, lecturing, about the banks for years, an unpopular prophet warning about famine in the midst of plenty. For decades, American banks had been lending billions to Third World countries that couldn't possibly pay them back in this or the next century. So they kept lending them more and more to keep them afloat, and to keep themselves from having to write off all those billions as bad debts and thereby destroy their own fiscal viability. They had the proverbial tiger by the tail. There was no safe way to let go.

It was after nine o'clock and dark when he entered his apartment and breathed the faint scent of perfume. Then he switched on the light and saw Annie lying on the living room couch. She had been asleep, but the light wakened her.

Forster kissed her where she lay. "What an absolutely lovely surprise."

"Not if you had walked in with another woman."

"How did you get in?"

"I still have my key."

"You've had it for seven years and never used it. Why tonight?"

"I just thought it might be nice to thank you in person."

"For what?"

"Your terrific financial advice. You've saved me more than ten thousand dollars."

"I've always suspected it, but now I know for sure," he said.

"Know what?"

"That you've got a Dow Jones ticker for a heart."

Annie's eyes were cold. "That's a lovely thing to say to me."

"Hey, it was supposed to be a joke."

"Well, it's not funny. Not when I know you mean it." She shook her head. "You can still get to me faster than anyone else alive."

"That's *your* problem. For God's sake, Annie, I hope you're not losing your humor at this stage."

They sat considering each other, carefully not saying anything. When they did speak at such moments, they invariably said the wrong things. They had learned at least that much. But the learning had come hard and late.

Forster finally broke the silence. It was a change. In the past, he had usually out-waited her. "How have things been at the agency? Has the fallout hit you yet?"

"With a bang. Although our corporate travel hasn't really been affected that much. Just some token economies, like switching from first class to coach. Good markets or bad, people still have to fly to stay in business. But in the vacation area we've already lost over a hundred thousand in canceled trips. People may not *be* poor in a falling market, but they think poor. And the first thing they cut back on are luxuries like expensive holidays."

"Will that put you in trouble?"

"Not really. Although a few years ago it would have, since more than seventy percent of my bookings were in vacation travel. But I've been gradually shifting the agency's focus and building up the corporate sector . . . air travel, hotels, conventions, sales meetings, car rentals. That's where the best profit margins are . . . and now these account for almost eighty percent of my net. So I guess I've turned out to be lucky."

"Not lucky," said Forster. "Smart."

"Does that mean I've got a cash register for a brain?"

This time they were able to laugh.

Annie took his hand; apology by touch. "It looks bad out there, doesn't it?"

"We've never been here before. Not like these past two days."

"The biggest shocker is that Wendell actually could have done something like this."

"He swears he didn't."

Annie showed surprise. "You've seen him?"

Forster went for some bourbon and poured two drinks. Then the need to talk, to share, prodded him and he told her what he was doing.

"Is there any hope?" she asked.

"There's always hope." Forster fell silent. "The saddest part is how few people really understand who and what Wendell is— what he might have been—what he could still be if things were different. Given the chance, he'd have been one of the best leaders this country has ever seen."

"You don't mean president."

"Why not? He's come closer to getting the nomination than hardly anyone outside of the highest political back rooms has ever realized. He just lacked the necessary machine backing and charisma. And it's happened at least twice over the past ten years. It's one of Wendell's major frustrations. He still gets worked up just talking about it."

"I had no idea he had such ambitions."

"He doesn't spread it around. It's not considered good form. Yet look at the stature of the man. He's built a reputation of almost mythical proportions as Fed Chairman, as the sage and master of the world economy. Just a few months ago, *U.S. News & World Report* designated him as the most powerful man after the president, and neither the White House nor Congress has challenged it."

"And look at where he is now," said Annie flatly.

"That's another reason I find it so hard to believe in his guilt. The five men indicted with him are all tops in their field, but Wendell is in a class of his own. The Fed isn't just a bunch of neutral economists using its best expertise on money and banking. It's also a high-ranking political institution, a unique power group inside the federal government, and Wendell was its autocratic ruler. Not even the president and Congress could influence him. He'd never jeopardize a position like that for mere money." Forster paused. "That's why I have to say there's always hope."

"Sometimes there's only a prayer."

"Then I'll settle for that."

Annie studied him for a long moment. "You do have your little tics, but you're really a very nice man."

She seemed to recline in shadow. Forster saw her in parts . . . the curve of a cheek, the tilt of her nose, the fine yet stubborn line of her chin. She had been formed with grace . . . tapering fingers, long, beautifully curved legs, a neck like a lily stalk. He knew she was aware of the effect she still had on him. Just as he also knew that he was still able, at moments, to break through to her.

"Ah, Paulie, it's been some couple of days. Such awful things are happening. I'm so low and tired I could cry."

Her voice was soft enough to be coming from another room. "Let's go to sleep," he said.

A frenzied battleground during the day, battered Wall Street had its nocturnal activity as well. When it was past midnight, and even the most desperately besieged traders, brokers, and clerks had finally abandoned their posts to snatch a few hours of sleep, the Street's night crews moved in. These were the men and women whose job it was to account for and settle the billions of dollars of stock trades carried out through the day.

In dress alone, they offered a striking contrast to the three-piece suits, button-down shirts, and conservative ties of the daytime hours. Jeans, slacks, sweaters, and sport shirts were more the uniform of the night, along with sneakers and warm-up suits. And instead of the earlier hushed conversation of the boardrooms, and the cries of the trading floor, there was mostly the pounding of rock and roll music from portable radios.

Brian Deitz sat at the very center of power for the financial night shift. As manager of systems and computing for the Depository Trust Company, he controlled the groups of computer technicians and operators who served as a central clearing house for New York's securities industry. Grave-faced, bearded, he took his responsibilities seriously at all times, but never more so than during the current market turmoil. He felt proud of what he and his nightside people were accomplishing. He felt a certain superiority, too. They were used to crises at night. They knew how to take pressure in stride and deal with it. The day-time crowd tended to shout, throw up their hands and panic. There also was another factor that fed his ego needs. Deep inside him, Deitz was sure there wasn't a brokerage house in the city, regardless of how large and powerful, that couldn't be broken by something going wrong with what took place behind the scenes here at night.

Yet few people outside the industry itself were aware that each night every Wall Street house sent the records of its day's trades by computer to the Depository Trust Company's mainframe computer, which settled the transactions. The computer trans-missions had to be made before a deadline set by the Depository Trust, and those companies that missed the deadline had to de-liver the information on computer tape before 2:00 A.M. With the volume and turbulence of recent days, more and more firms were unable to make the deadline. So that in the final minutes before 2:00 A.M., messengers were scurrying all over Manhat-tan's downtown streets with reels of computer tape, desperately trying to deliver trading records worth billions of dollars to the Pit, the area two stories underground where the tapes were re-ceived. Up on the twenty-first floor, a group of operators put the taped material onto cartridges, while David Lipschutz, a senior supervisor with Depository Trust, sat watching for pos-sible mistakes as the billions of dollars worth of trades scrolled past his eyes. He tried not to think about the dollar amounts of the money going by. But sometimes he did, and the weight it placed on him was enormous.

Way downstairs at Depository Trust, there were huge vaults where the actual paper securities were kept for brokerage com-panies. Here, at close to 2:00 A.M., platoons of clerks were struggling to handle the billions in stock certificates that were lying about in steel baskets, waiting to have a microfilm record made of their arrival. The clerks in this area were low-paid, overworked, and mostly black and Hispanic, yet their respon-sibility for the smooth functioning of the entire system was as great down here as anyplace along the line.

At 2:10 A.M., Deitz received a phone call from Ken Rawson, a senior vice-president for the brokerage firm of Conners, Smith, Barney.

"We're running way overtime," said Rawson. "I haven't even

been able to get my messengers out yet with the tapes. You're going to have to extend the deadline for me.''

Deitz had never liked Rawson and he had learned to like him even less since the crash. This was the third time the broker had called about an extension, and he always demanded rather than asked. "I don't *have* to do anything except die, and you're not the one who's going to tell me when to do *that*.''

"Don't be a fool,'' said Rawson. "I'll have the tapes over by three-thirty.''

"You're too late.''

"What are you talking about?''

"I've given you three extensions in as many days and you're still asking for more. You're not that special. If others can get their tapes in on time, so can you.''

"Do you know the kind of volume we're dealing with here?''

"Yeah. The same kind as every other brokerage house in New York. I'm cutting you off, Rawson. You've had your last extension.''

"You can't do that!''

"Don't bet on it.''

There was silence at the other end as Rawson regrouped. "I'll go over your head,'' he said at last.

"Good luck,'' said Deitz.

Smiling gently through his beard, the systems manager hung up. To hell with the arrogant bastard. In fact, to hell with all brokers, Deitz decided, blaming the entire stock-hustling, conscienceless group for what was rapidly turning into one of the most traumatic economic events of modern times. How long had they expected a runaway bull market to keep rising without a major fall? It was pure financial dementia, a disease chronically infecting the whole industry, but this time threatening to be terminal. It was a disease, too, based on the belief that your intelligence was measured by the amount of money you made, and what broker didn't want to be thought a genius?

Yet how few dared say such things, thought Dietz. The market had become the prime symbol of a new secular religion. To criticize its behavior or those responsible for it would be considered blasphemous. Who would dare attack the investment community by blaming their greed and stupidity for the current debacle? So they blamed the six indicted bankers instead, saddling them and their alleged shenanigans with the responsibility for the market's crash. In this way they effectively transferred blame from the high priests of their beloved religion to the universally damned agents of the devil himself—the bankers.

It had to be the public relations coup of the century.

The Chicago headquarters of Food Enterprises occupied the entire fifty-third floor of an ominous-looking, gray office tower with a spectacular view of the city and lake.

Forster gave his name to a receptionist sitting behind a semicircular desk. Prominently displayed were the three most recent issues of *Finance Magazine*. On the walls were framed photographs of barbecued chicken drive-in restaurants. The camera angles were low, the restaurants silhouetted against the sky. The overall effect was to give the buildings a look of stature and nobility. They might have been the temples of a new religious order.

A young woman with golden-brown skin and a soft, shy voice appeared and led Forster to a corner office at the far end of a carpeted corridor. There was no sound as they walked. Maybe it *was* a new religion, he thought. The young priestess opened the door but did not go in with him.

"Mr. Forster."

Alfred Kent, a short, plump black man with thinning hair and steel-rimmed glasses, came out from behind his desk to shake hands. His face looked soft and pliant and only his eyes, which were so dark as to be almost opaque, gave any hint of the strength and stubbornness that had brought him where he was.

He smiled. "You're surprised I'm black?"

Forster said nothing.

"I enjoy watching people's reactions when they meet me for the first time. I must admit you're nowhere near as obvious as most, Mr. Forster, but you'd still better not play poker with me. I'd bankrupt you in an hour."

"Half an hour. I'm a lousy card player."

Kent laughed. Taking Forster's arm, he guided him through an open doorway into an adjoining room where a dining table had been set up beside a window. Crystal and silver sparkled in the light.

"Come," said Kent. "Let's have lunch. I've found that good food in pleasant surroundings has a civilizing influence not only on trouble, but on even the most disturbing conversations."

"Which are you expecting from me?"

"A little of both."

Forster angled his head to look at him properly. "Meaning what?"

"That I don't believe you had any plans to be in Chicago before we set up this appointment. And that you're probably here to talk about the Malcolm Commission and me."

"You were right before," said Forster. "I'd be a fool to play poker with you."

Kent seated Forster at the table, then sat down facing him. "It really wasn't that difficult to figure out. You're a superb investigative reporter. If you called to talk to me just forty-eight hours after those indictments, there had to be a connection."

"Then why did you agree to see me?"

"Because I prefer to meet my ghosts head on. Besides, as I told you on the phone, I'm a longtime fan. You've earned my respect. You've never been one of those scandal hounds or sensation mongers. If I have to talk to anyone about this, I feel I'm better off letting it be you."

A waiter came in to take their luncheon orders. Forster had little desire for food, but accepted the waiter's recommendation of lamb chops and salad. Waiting, both men sipped chilled vodka martinis.

"All right," said Kent. "Since I'm sure you've already gone through all the material in your files, what else would you like to know?"

"Whatever you'd like to tell me."

Kent's eyes were two black holes. "Let's not be overly polite. Neither of us has the time. Exactly what do you want from me?"

"Human interest. There's some very bitter irony at work here. Maybe even a touch of poetic justice. The six men who sat in judgment of you more than twenty years ago, who were responsible for sending you to prison, are now being judged themselves. How does that make you feel?"

Kent gazed off at Lake Michigan glistening in the sun. "I'll tell you how it makes me feel. It makes me feel sick. But not for the reason you think. Those six men weren't responsible for sending me to prison. *I* was responsible for that. If they hadn't blown the whistle on me, someone else would have done it. I feel sick because they've been so stupid and arrogant, because they've set off a chain of events that could end up robbing me of everything I've spent the past two decades trying to build.''

"Then you feel no satisfaction seeing them go down?"

"Not when I see myself going down with them. Or do you think I'm wrong in expecting one of the worst financial panics of our lifetime to grow out of this mess?"

Forster ignored the question. "You've never felt that your being black might have had something to do with your indictment and prosecution?"

"Of course I have. I'm human. It's always easier to scream prejudice than blame yourself. And for a while I built a very strong brief for just such an assumption." Kent studied his drink. "I assume you've done all your homework on the Malcolm Commission."

"I have."

"Then consider the facts. Of all the cases they investigated only two resulted in criminal indictments . . . mine and David Berenstein's. A black and a Jew. And very few members of either group were making it big in banking at the time. So I naturally figured the old-line establishment was out to shove the kikes and niggers back in their places. I screamed so loud I finally forced the NAACP and the Anti-Defamation League to take up the fight. Unfortunately, poor Berenstein hung himself before they could do anything for him. But at least I got part of my sentence knocked off."

Kent fell silent as the waiter appeared and began serving their food.

"Taste the lamb chops," Kent said. "If they're not the way you like them, send them back."

"They're delicious."

The chops had a crisp, brown crust and were juicy and pink underneath, but Forster still had no appetite. Alfred Kent ate with pleasure. When the waiter had gone, he continued.

"I was guilty, of course," he said. "But that didn't stop the civil liberties crowd from making their usual noises. Luckily, I was too smart to fool myself for long. So I put the blame where it belonged . . . on me . . . gave myself a second chance, and got on with my life. Which is exactly why I have no damn patience with our whiners, who cry about race prejudice and no opportunity while they're boozing it up, shooting drugs, and chasing ass.''

Kent looked fiercely at Forster as he chewed his meat.

"What kind of people are they?" he asked. "They're supposed to be my soul brothers, but I feel no connection with them. Dumb animals have more sense of survival. And I know all their arguments. I was raised on them. We're angry, wounded, and in pain, so we strike back with knives and guns. Bullshit!"

Kent had suddenly stopped eating. Both his fists were clenched on the table.

"There are a lot of clubs I can't get into," he said. "So what? That doesn't make me bleed. How does that wound me? I graduated magna cum laude from Princeton. I got myself a good job in a big bank. I turned crazy and committed larceny. I went to prison, paid my debt, and got out. I started my own business. I became rich. If I felt wounded or suffered prejudice, I just worked harder."

Forster gazed at him across the table. Tough, Forster thought. And smart. Capable of anything.

Kent glanced up. "Have I upset you?"

"Why?"

"Because my attitudes do upset people. And because you obviously came here looking for a different reaction."

"Such as?"

"Shouts of joy and vengeance."

Forster was silent.

"I'm sorry to disappoint you," said Kent. "But it's hard to shout much of anything while your throat is being cut. During the past few days, I've watched nearly thirty percent of the value of my company's stock wiped away; lines of credit have all but disappeared, and a bond issue's been postponed indefinitely because every buyer in the world seems to have suddenly died. If things continue like this I'm not even sure how long we'll be able to go on meeting payrolls."

Kent dabbed his mouth with a monogrammed napkin. "I'll tell you a little secret. Do you know one of the first thoughts I had when you called and said you wanted to talk to me?"

"No."

"Knowing of your affinity for our esteemed Snow White Fed Chairman and his five dwarfs, I thought you might have been seeking me out on their behalf."

"For what purpose?"

"Damned if I know. Maybe to see whether I had planned all this as part of a long-deferred act of retribution."

"How could you or anyone else possibly have done something like that?"

Kent shrugged.

"You must admit that's pretty paranoid."

"Of course. It's epidemic among us poor black folk. Like razor slashing, dope dealing, and high school pregnancy."

If Alfred Kent had expected a laugh from his audience of one, he was disappointed. Forster just stared at him.

Forster was back at La Guardia by 8:30 P.M. and at the magazine shortly after 9:00. Almost everyone was gone, leaving only a small night crew at work. In his office, Forster found a folder lying across his typewriter where Alice Renquist had left it. Scrawled in black across the cover was the name David Berenstein. Forster took off his jacket and began immersing himself in the tragic life and times of the long-buried bank embezzler.

Almost from the start there seemed to be a chill, blue haze to everything in the folder, over the flimsy printout paper, over the letters and words themselves. In this light there was only bad news.

It began in a Nazi death camp and came to a close at the end of an improvised rope. In between, as if to point up the tragedy of what had gone before and would soon come after, were the few good years. For Berenstein, the classic Holocaust survivor, this was a period of hope and rebirth, of a new life in a new land, of love, marriage, and children, of undreamed of opportunity and success.

Yet for Forster, the chill blue light drained all pleasure from the good and left him dry. All he could think of were the gas chambers, the ovens, the living skeletons with their black, staring eyes. He had never been a metaphysical thinker, nor a believer in portents and symbols. He was an intellectual, a believer in the power of reason. Yet how did reason explain this man's survival of the century's ultimate horror, only to take his own life more than twenty years later in an American prison cell?

He looked at an old news photo of Berenstein, his wife, and two children . . . a thin, dark-haired girl of about ten or eleven; a blond boy, a year or two older. The picture had been reproduced from a snapshot taken at the beach. It showed the four

Berensteins in their bathing suits, smiling at the camera, in an instant of happiness and summer sun. Evidently found by an enterprising reporter at the time of Berenstein's trial, the photo-caption read THE BERENSTEIN FAMILY DURING HAPPIER DAYS. David Berenstein himself—plump, jovial, apple-cheeked—looking as though he had never suffered anything more threatening or unpleasant than an annual visit to his dentist. His wife was pretty, blond, and proudly wearing a bikini that showed off her still-youthful figure. The boy and girl, standing between both parents, appeared safe and confident, clearly certain that whatever the future might hold for them, they would be cared for and protected.

It would not be so.

Not long after the happy snapshot was taken, the Berensteins were struck by a barrage of events that left the parents dead and their children adrift and alone. No *mazel*, thought Forster dully. Except, of course, that it was Berenstein's own folly, rather than any absence of luck, that had brought on the carnage. Or was it some sort of sudden madness that had caused him to embezzle the more than half a million in trust funds that eventually led to his destruction? Had his five-year ordeal in Hitler's camps caused invisible clots to form in the passages of his brain? Worn thin by years of indescribable horror, had they finally exploded like long-delayed time bombs at the very moment when life was opening up for him?

Unfair, unfair, Forster thought. Yet what had fairness to do with anything? There were no checks and balances. No one kept score.

Reading, in mournful succession, about the investigation, the trial, the futile declarations of innocence, the rejection of all appeals, the suicide in his cell, the death of his widow by cerebral hemorrhage not long after hearing the news, Forster began to tremble. The tragic string of events, burning their way into him, a total stranger, twenty-odd years after the fact, made him wonder what they had done to the boy and girl who had suffered through them.

He found a follow-up news story that described Helen and Arthur Berenstein as the innocent victims of a family disaster with all the elements of classic tragedy. Titled "Orphans," the article told of how the young brother and sister, suddenly without father or mother, were deposited in a series of foster homes from which they regularly ran away. The sins of the father, thought Forster bleakly, and somehow found himself reminded of Ethel and Julius Rosenberg's children, who had suffered much the same fate while their parents were being tried, sentenced, and executed. How could they not end up scarred? Sad and desperate human actions were going on, yet no one saw them, no one cared.

Forster imagined all the miseries that might have befallen the two young Berensteins, each one worse than the one before. The thoughts brought a bitter fluid to his mouth. It had to be swallowed.

I must find out what finally happened to them.

But he was able to discover no further follow-up information about the two children, not in the Berenstein folder, and not in any of the other research files.

Tomorrow, he thought, tomorrow I'll get in touch with whatever social agencies are responsible for such things. Beyond that, he suddenly was too tired and depressed even to think.

Not wanting to go home, he put out the lights and lay sleepless on an office couch. In the dark, he saw the Berensteins smiling on the beach. Except that this time they were naked and skeletal, with protruding bones, and everything was bathed in a chill, blue light.

4

President Donald Hanson, returning from Europe, entered a White House that was close to chaos, with the head of almost every agency and department wanting to see him. Only four, however, made it into the Oval Office that first morning, the seventeenth of June, the fifth day after the breaking of the scandal. They were the secretaries of state, defense, and treasury, and the just-appointed interim replacement for Wendell Norton at the Federal Reserve.

Tension grew worse as the meeting progressed, although the president himself was careful to remain calm. The usual Washington syndrome, he thought. Attack, place blame, justify, and at all costs protect yourself. He thought it without particular rancor because he understood it.

He took pride in doing his job well, leaving moral judgments to history. Every line of work had its dirty secrets, yet his had more than its share because more lives were affected. Sometimes they became too much, and he felt oppressed. It was something beyond him, some eternal seepage from the nation's waste pipes, and at its worst it was everywhere . . . at work, on the golf course, even in bed with his wife.

Seated behind his desk in the Oval Office, the American flag proudly unfurled at his right, the presidential banner at his left, Hanson listened to the cacophony of voices arguing, accusing, attempting to vilify, and found his insides suddenly begin quivering like a dowsing rod, as if some invisible evil lay hidden in the sounds.

What vile spirits haunted these lords in their high places? he thought.

"Gentlemen," he said when he felt himself in control once more, "we're obviously in trouble. So please . . . no more recriminations. Let's just stay with the facts and go from there."

For several moments no one seemed able to speak. Group guilt? wondered the president. "How bad was yesterday's market for T-bills?" he asked, speaking to Treasury Secretary John Gaynor, a slender, sallow-cheeked man with restless eyes. "As bad as the day before?"

"Worse, Mr. President. A massacre. Custer's last stand."

"Well, I don't expect it to be *our* last stand," said Hanson. "There'll be no collapse in the markets for the securities of the government of the United States. Not as long as I'm president. I want that understood by everyone here."

Secretary of State Walter Wilson laughed, but it had a cold, hollow sound. "We understand it, Mr. President. But with every sonofabitch and his brother rushing to dump our paper, I don't know how much good it's going to do us. And our alleged allies are leading the pack. That includes the Japanese, the Germans, the Saudis, and the Swiss. That the French are dumping more than anyone else, goes without saying."

"Let's put the blame where it belongs," said Howard Bloom, the interim Fed chairman. "Right here on us. We got into this mess all by ourselves, and we're going to have to get out of it the same way."

"Which means what?" asked the president.

"It means doing exactly what you just implied we should do, Mr. President . . . support our treasury paper at all costs. If no one else is buying our T-bills, then we'll just have to keep buying them ourselves until confidence is restored."

"Do you know how many billions that's going to take?" asked the Treasury chief.

"I have a fair idea."

"And where do you propose to get it?"

"There's enough cash in the Fed system to carry us for at least another week or so."

"You've had half a dozen runs on your member banks during the past two days alone, and there's going to be a lot more. Where are you going to get the money to keep your banks from closing?"

"If we run out," said Bloom, "we'll just print it."

"Print it? Print how much?"

"As much as we need to keep our banks open and the market for our treasury bills from collapsing."

Gaynor's sallow face had turned bright pink. "Are you out of your mind? You're talking about printing billions and billions in new money that's unsupported by taxes, borrowings, or gold dug out of the ground. Do you know the kind of runaway inflation that's going to create?''

"I don't give a damn right now about inflation," said the new Fed chairman. "All I care about at this minute is keeping us in business long enough for everyone to remember that this is still the United States of America, and that we're no better or worse than we were five days ago, before this whole insane scandal hit the news."

"You're still talking fiscal suicide!" Gaynor's voice was almost a shout. "Have you forgotten Germany after World War One? They needed wheelbarrows to carry enough cash to buy an egg."

"I haven't forgotten anything," said Bloom softly, his voice becoming lower as the treasury secretary's rose. "But this is one time history is of no use to us. No one has ever faced what we're facing today. And if we don't act decisively, if we let this get out of control, we can also produce what may well turn out to be the worst financial disaster of all time . . . the total destruction of money as we know it today."

"We're frightened enough, Howard," said Hanson. "Don't frighten us more."

"I'm just telling it as I see it, Mr. President. Unfortunately, we have all the negative ingredients primed and in place. A loss of faith at the top, collapsing markets, bank runs, budget and trade deficits running out of sight, a world economy so tightly intertwined, so vast, so accelerated by the use of computers, that its vulnerabilities have soared to unprecedented levels. And instead of realizing we're all in this together and supporting us when we most need it, our trading partners dump our treasury bills and huddle behind their tariff walls. What I'm afraid I see here, Mr. President, is a group of industrial nations close to being out of control, tottering on the brink of calamity. And the key ingredient at this moment is the dollar. If it goes over the edge, everything else has to follow. So I say print as much money as we need, and to hell with inflation until we can breathe again."

"It's extreme," said President Hanson, "but I'm afraid we don't have an alternative."

The room was quiet. "There is one alternative, Mr. President," Defense Secretary Exely said at last.

Hanson looked at him. Tom Exely's manner was measured, even judicious. "What is it, Tom?"

"A military diversion."

There was dead silence, almost as if a vacuum had been created by an explosion. Yet a message came up out of the silence like the whispering of a forest and Exely picked it up and rode it.

"At most," he said, "I'd see it as a very limited action . . . probably somewhere in the Middle East, where Christ knows we've been given more than enough provocation lately. And, of course, it would be planned carefully enough to avoid any chance of involving the Soviet Union."

"And exactly what would it offer us," asked the president, "other than a great opportunity to start World War Three?"

"I can't see it escalating, Mr. President." The defense secretary offered his most disarming smile. "And the benefits to us would be instantaneous. First, your emergency war powers would allow you to freeze billions in foreign funds and assets, easing our capital drain. Second, the country would respond as it always does in time of war by closing ranks behind you and doing whatever has to be done, regardless of sacrifice. And lastly, our allies would have to respond the same way, ending their attacks on our financial structure and standing firmly beside us until the crisis eased."

You should stuff .30-caliber bullets up your ass like suppositories till they come out of your mouth, the president wanted to tell his defense secretary. But all he said was, "I don't think we're quite that desperate yet, Tom." He hesitated. "Though I certainly can't see any harm in exploring the possibilities a bit further."

During the past forty-five minutes, Forster had been shunted from the Social Service Center's Child Abuse and Neglect Office, to the Children's Placement and Accountability Section, to the Parents' Rights Unit, to the Children's Rights Unit, to Group Homes, to Children's Foster Home Care, with not a single person able to help him discover what might have eventually become of David Berenstein's orphaned son and daughter more than two decades ago. It was as if the two Berenstein children no longer existed. And if their old identities had for some reason been changed to new ones, Forster could think of no way to discover who they might be.

Finally, he did what he supposed he should have done in the first place. He put through a call to City Hall and asked a favor of a ranking deputy mayor who owed him a few. "Charley," he said, "I need some help."

Fifteen minutes later he was sitting across a desk from a wizened caseworker named Gumble, surrounded by a maze of steel file cabinets. Nicotine-stained fingers held a cigarette in the continental style, like a pea shooter, while dark, rheumy eyes squinted at Forster through layers of smoke.

"The commissioner himself called," Gumble said. "You must be important."

"Not really. Just tired of getting the runaround."

"One way or another, it doesn't matter to me. I'm retiring in six weeks. I'm beyond being impressed by big shots. You see before you an impregnable man, Mr. Forster. After forty years, I can no longer be touched."

"Congratulations."

Gumble peered at a soiled, dog-eared folder on his desk. "I'm told you're interested in an old case of mine. The Berenstein children?"

"That's right."

"May I ask why?"

"I'm trying to find out what happened to them."

"After twenty-three years?"

Forster said nothing.

The caseworker opened his folder and leafed through its contents. "I remember those two kids like it was yesterday. They'd sit right there, right where you're sitting now, big-eyed and still, and just stare at me. A pair of picture-book youngsters . . . beautiful . . . and they were in total pain, total trauma. We had them in therapy for five years and every second of it was wasted. They refused to accept their losses, refused to adjust. I put them in one foster home after the other and they ran away every time. God only knows what finally happened to them. Though I know it can't be anything good. Not with those scars."

Gumble plucked a paper from the folder and handed it to Forster. "Their father hanged himself in prison. This is a copy of the note he left. The kids kept the original. They were never without it. Carried it like a talisman."

Forster looked at the note. Written in pencil, in a shaky scrawl, it said:

> My dearests . . . my family . . . Please, please forgive me. I simply cannot face so many years in this terrible place for something I did not do. Never forget. I am innocent and I love you.

There was no signature and the writing at the end was so uncontrolled, so poorly formed, as to be almost illegible. Forster felt the same dull burning in his chest that he had experienced when reading the old media accounts of the case.

"What's the last record you have of them?"

Gumble read for a moment. "The last people I put them with were a Minnie and Sam Abelman of Brighton Beach. It was the best placement of all. At least they managed to hold on to them for almost four years . . . more than all the others combined."

"What happened then?"

Gumble shrugged, exuding age like an animal smell. "One day they simply disappeared for good, and that was that."

"You put out tracers on them?"

"We kept a national check going for three years."

"Have you used the Abelmans as foster parents since?"

"No. That was a hard loss for them. They'd had enough. Then a few years later, Sam Abelman died."

"Is his wife still alive?"

"So far as my records show."

"What's her last address?"

"The one in Brighton Beach."

"May I have it?"

Gumble scribbled on a sheet of paper and pushed it across his desk. "Good luck. But if those two still don't want to be found, my feeling is that you're not going to find them."

Brighton Beach is a small enclave of American and Russian Jews, abutting Coney Island, on the southern rim of Brooklyn. Forster had often gone there on summer outings with his parents. There were wide, sandy beaches and handball courts and a boardwalk where politics were loudly argued in varying com-

binations of English, Yiddish, and Russian. In the heat of one
such argument, Forster had seen his father punch a man in the
stomach for calling Franklin D. Roosevelt a warmonger, although the war was long over and Roosevelt himself long dead.
Forster, the boy, had been impressed. Thirty years later, he still
was.

Minnie Abelman lived at 307 Brightwater Court, on the top
floor of a six-story, art-deco building facing the ocean. It was
the same place she had lived when the Berenstein children were
with her, and Forster was not in the apartment five minutes
before she was showing him their rooms and the assorted memorabilia of their four-year sojourn. Included were blue-and-gray
Lincoln High banners, straight-A report cards, plaques and ci-
tations won in statewide essay contests, and the framed, hand-
written original of Arthur Berenstein's high school valedictory
address.

"In all your life," declared Minnie Abelman, "you've never
seen two such children. My Sam couldn't have loved, couldn't
have been prouder of them if they were his own flesh and blood.
The night they left without a word, without even a goodbye . . .
that night was when my Sam started growing his cancer."

Minnie sighed. "The doctors, the big professors might say
different, but I know better. Cancer starts with a terrible aggra-
vation, a terrible hurt, and for my husband it was like those two
had stuck a knife in his stomach."

"Weren't you hurt too?" said Forster.

"Sure I was hurt. How could I not, after four years? But I
was harder, stronger than Sam. Also, I had a feeling."

"What kind of feeling?"

Minnie considered Forster. They were sitting on overstuffed
chairs in a parlor crammed with more than enough furniture for
two such rooms. "Who knows what kind of feeling?" she said.
"Maybe it had to do with Arthur finishing high school. He said
he didn't want to go to college. That was crazy for a boy with
such brains, such a head. There had to be something else, something he maybe wasn't talking about."

"What about his sister?"

"Helen was a different person. As smart as Arthur, but not
the same. Her, I felt, I could sometimes reach. She had soft
eyes. You could look in such eyes and see feeling, goodness.

Arthur had goodness too, but also an iron gall, a coldness inside that could turn you blue. What he wanted Helen to do, she did."

"Did they ever talk about their parents?"

"Never. Not once. It was as if they never had a momma and poppa. And the big professor they had to go to talk to every week, the Social Service's own Sigmund Freud, told Sam and me not to talk about them either."

They sat facing each other, Minnie's orange hair ablaze with the late sun, Forster's head tilted to give his good eye a better view. A horsefly kept thudding against the window screen.

"Maybe you told me on the phone before," Minnie said, "but I forgot. I'd forget my head these days if it wasn't attached. So tell me again. Why are you so interested in my Helen and Arthur?"

Forster had not told her a thing. "I'm a writer. I saw some old news stories about them and became curious." He lit and savored his fifth cigarette of the day. "All these years, Mrs. Abelman, and you've never heard from them?"

"Not once. Not a single word. It ate up Sam. And they had it in them to be so good, so loving. You could almost feel it trying to come out. Yet this was what they did to us. And it was no accident, their disappearing like that. It was what they set out to do from the start."

"How do you know?"

"I just know. Then about five years after they went away, I saw Helen's picture in a magazine and knew I was right."

Forster straightened in his chair. "What picture?"

Minnie rose on arthritic legs, shuffled to a bookcase, and returned with an eleven-year-old copy of *Life* magazine. "This one," she said and pointed to one of a series of photographs taken at a benefit ball for the San Francisco Opera Company.

Forster saw a delicately beautiful, dark-haired young woman and a distinguished-looking older man in evening clothes. They were holding champagne glasses and smiling at the camera. The caption identified the man as Harold Luckner, the prominent West Coast real estate developer and philanthropist, and the woman as Melissa Luckner, his wife of less than a year.

"This woman is Helen Berenstein?" Forster said.

"Yes."

"You're sure."

"Sure I'm sure. She's five years older here than when she left us and her hair is different, but that's still her face."

"Have you ever written to her?"

"Three times. Three letters. They all came back unopened."

Minnie sank into her chair. "So what should I do?" she said. "Kill myself? They already killed my husband, those two. Me, they won't bury so fast. Everybody wants what they want, and I guess what they want isn't me. I've lived this long without them, I'll live a little longer."

"I'd like to borrow this picture if I may. I'll take good care of it. You don't have to worry."

"Of course. Why should I worry? It's only an old picture."

"I can use it," he said.

The 747 soared west, and Forster, in his gut, felt as though he were doing nothing less than carrying the two kids to San Francisco with him.

Jennings, of course, thought he was just wasting time; Annie thought he was becoming obsessed; and he himself, during the rare moments when he was able to consider it coldly, tended to agree with them both. Still, he was going; once he had Minnie Abelman's information, it would have been impossible for him to do otherwise.

"That's one of the things I've always adored about you," Annie had said. "You can fall more deeply in love with your own emotional and romantic vision of two children you've never even met than other men can with the most exquisite woman."

Marty Jennings had been far less sanguine about the entire affair.

"I just don't see any sense to this whole approach," he told Forster. "What's your rationale? I can certainly understand the appeal of a couple of tragically orphaned waifs and their struggle for survival. And I can also see a certain amount of curiosity about what may finally have become of them. But what has any of this to do with your investigation? Unless"—here Jennings had looked long and deliberately at Forster—"unless you can tell me you honestly believe those two youngsters might have had something to do with it as adults."

Forster remained silent.

"Well?"

"I really don't know *what* I feel, Marty. But I do know I can't just leave this alone without seeing where it leads."

"You mean you *won't* leave it alone."

"For me, that's pretty much the same thing."

Hank Pollard was waiting for him in his glass-walled office at the far end of the *San Francisco Chronicle*'s city room. Theirs was a deep, powerful embrace, for they had been roommates in college, had gone to bed with some of the same women, and had fought and almost died together in Vietnam. All unshakable bonds, although they met rarely these days.

"It's good to see you," the editor said. Pale, pouched eyes took a quick inventory that was more like a body count. "Not that you look all that great. Why don't you try sleeping once in a while?"

"You mean like you?"

The city editor laughed. He was a big, deep-chested, frenetic man, whose great rumbling laugh sounded as though he might have invented it. "Don't be nasty. Remember, you're here as a supplicant. People asking favors in this town have to do some pretty heavy ass-kissing."

"Before you start dropping your pants, let's hear what you've got for me." Forster spoke flippantly, but could feel the adrenaline pumping through his body like a mob in riot.

Pollard dug through a wasteland of papers on his desk until he came up with the few scribbled notes he was searching for. "Here we are. Melissa Luckner." He picked up several news pictures, black-and-white glossies, and looked at them gravely. "Beautiful woman. Though she actually was more girl than woman while she was with Luckner. They were married less than six months, and I can't imagine how she stayed even that long. The guy was richer than God, but old enough to be her grandfather and kinky. I mean, if it could be done, he did it."

"She divorced him?"

"In spades. And took him for a pile. Millions, as I understand it. The divorce was uncontested, never went to court, so it shouldn't be too hard to figure out the kind of stuff she had on him."

"Did you ever meet her?"

"A few times."

"What was she like?"

Forster tried to make the question sound casual. The effort failed, though Hank didn't seem to notice.

"Hell, it was a long time ago, and always at those big showy affairs that Luckner's philanthropic crowd enjoyed going in for. But I do remember she carried herself well. Quiet, but extremely confident. Lots of poise for a kid that age."

A phone rang on the editor's desk and he picked it up and spoke quietly for several moments. Forster used the interruption to glance through the photographs of Melissa Luckner. They were far clearer than the faded reproduction he had seen in *Life*. The girl was dazzling.

"Where is she now?" Forster asked when Pollard was finished with his call. "Do you have an address?"

Hank slipped on a pair of horn-rims and peered at his notes. "No, no address. Nothing. She left town after the divorce and there's no indication of where she went. I had the police put her name in the computer for me, but they came up with the same dead end." He took off his glasses. "You never said what you wanted with her."

"Background for a piece I'm doing."

Pollard looked amused. "You always were a secretive sort of bastard. What's the matter? Afraid I'll steal your story?"

"Exactly. What about the husband? Luckner. Would he know where she was?"

"He might, if he weren't dead. Drove his little Ferrari into a big tree about ten years ago." Again, the editor checked his notes. "There's still a sister living in town; the only family member left. Henrietta. I'll give her a call and try to arrange a meeting. Maybe she can tell you something."

Henrietta Luckner lived in a large house, still managing to enjoy the kind of opulence for which Nob Hill had been famous for over a hundred years.

A butler answered his ring and led him to the kind of graceful, domed observatory in which privileged, well-mannered people of an earlier time used to take high tea. The sole surviving Luckner sat in a wicker chair, gazing out at the city and bay in the distance. She had a narrow, attractive face, but the skin had gone taut and translucent and her forehead was knotted by veins at the temples. One pale hand held a cigarette in a long holder, the other, a tumbler of what looked to be straight whiskey.

"Sit down, sit down." She waved her cigarette holder at a chair. "Hank tells me you want to talk about that little whore-bitch who married my brother. Pour yourself some whiskey. Or are you one of those fairies who drink nothing but white wine and give themselves gout?"

Forster smiled as he sat down facing her. "Whiskey is fine," he said and splashed some into a glass.

"In case you're a little slow in picking up on these things, I happen to have despised my former sister-in-law. Does that disturb you in any way?"

"No. But may I ask why?"

"You may ask anything you please. I never made a secret of how I felt about Melissa, and I still don't. That is, if anyone cares and is interested enough to listen." Miss Luckner drew on her cigarette and coughed. "I'm the first to admit that my brother was a fool, a drunk, and had some strange sexual tastes. But Melissa knew all these things before they even met, so there's no excuse for what she did."

"What did she do?"

"The cruelest and nastiest thing possible. She married him."

Forster stared at her. Henrietta smiled coldly, muscles in her gaunt cheeks working like fine wires between the skin and bone.

"The bitch was clever, shrewd as they come," she said. "She must have researched everything. Whatever there was to know about Harold, she evidently knew before she arrived in town. And she didn't waste a minute. She wasn't in San Francisco two months before they were married. And less than six months after that, she filed for her divorce. I'm certain she'd have filed sooner, but it evidently took her that long to clearly document every piece of dirty evidence she needed."

Forster studied two bronze busts resting on pedestals among the plants. One obviously was of Henrietta as a young girl, the other was of her brother. The family resemblance was unmistakable: narrow heads, aquiline noses, cupid-bow lips.

"And that cunning little schemer walked out of here exactly ten million richer than when she arrived. That was her price for keeping the filth off the front pages, and that was what he had to pay her. Do you know what ten million was in those days? It was like fifty million today."

"Where did she go when she left San Francisco?"

"I hope straight to hell." Henrietta refilled her glass. "I have no idea where she went. Nor have I ever wanted to know. My brother was a weak, self-indulgent man, but the only one he ever hurt was himself. Melissa, young as she was, was pure predator. The coldest I've ever seen.''

"What about her family? Did you ever meet them?''

"She claimed she had no family. I believed her. I'm sure she murdered them all in their sleep when she was five.''

Forster laughed. "You paint a dark portrait, Miss Luckner. There had to be some brightness somewhere.''

"On the surface, yes. Melissa was an extraordinarily beautiful young woman, with all the charm to match. She could be irresistible when it suited her. Which simply made her that much more dangerous. No one suspected the range of her capabilities.'' She stared off toward the bay, shining in the late sun. "Except for me. I saw through her from the beginning. Not that it helped. She accomplished everything she started out to do.''

"She never mentioned a brother?''

"Not to my knowledge.''

"Where had she been living before she came to San Francisco?''

"Chicago, she said. But she also said she had lived in Boston and Philadelphia. I never believed any part of it. The fact is, I never believed Melissa was even capable of speaking the truth. I warned Harold about her more times than I can remember. But it's impossible to talk logic to a man with an all-consuming erection pressing on his brain. Particularly if he's at an age when he's worrying about each one being his last.''

"What was her maiden name?''

Miss Luckner gazed blankly at him.

"You *must* know it.''

"At one time I undoubtedly did. But that was more than eleven years ago.''

"Perhaps you have some record of it somewhere . . . old documents, news accounts, one of your brother's wedding invitations. Things like that.''

"Is it so vital a piece of information?''

"It could be.''

Miss Luckner summoned her butler and had him bring in a metal file box from her study. She pulled out a large, square card, obviously an announcement or invitation of some sort, yellow with age.

She held it to the light. "Kenniston," she read. "The little whore-bitch's maiden name was Kenniston."

Forster called Guido Castanzo, his Washington-based private investigator, from a phone in Hank Pollard's office. About an hour later, he had a complete print-out on Melissa Kenniston.

Whoever the woman was, she was at least blessed with all the trappings of a legitimate existence. There were birth and school records that established her as currently being thirty-six years of age, and as having attended elementary and secondary schools in Boston, and the University of Pennsylvania's Wharton School in Philadelphia. She had a social security number, a single-item police record for a conviction stemming from an antinuclear demonstration, as well as the standard list of official minutiae that generally served to establish the identity of a late-twentieth-century citizen of the United States.

In addition, Forster learned that Melissa Kenniston was living in New York, where she ran a small investment company called the Olympus Fund. The name Kenniston, Forster realized, in its proper context, was vaguely familiar to him . . . as was the Olympus Fund. Although nothing specific was brought to mind. Or was that just a glitch brought on by the power of suggestion?

At 8:10 P.M., too anxious and stimulated to wait until morning, Forster put through a call to Brighton Beach, Brooklyn, where the time difference made it 11:10.

A sleep-muffled voice came on.

"Mrs. Abelman?" he said. "I'm sorry if I woke you. This is Paul Forster."

"What? Who?"

"Forster . . . Paul Forster. I was speaking to you yesterday about Helen Berenstein?"

"What's the matter?" The voice had come awake. "Something's wrong?"

"No, nothing is wrong. I'd just like to ask a couple of questions."

Minnie Abelman sighed. "Then ask."

"I just want to be certain. You're absolutely sure that was Helen Berenstein's picture in *Life* magazine?"

"Of course I'm sure. I already told you."

"I'd appreciate it if you'd tell me once more."

"That picture was nobody but Helen."

"Okay," said Forster. "Now just one more thing. Can you remember any special marks Helen might have had? Like a scar of some sort? A birthmark? Something like that?"

The wire hummed for several moments.

"She had that cut from when she was slicing a bagel," Minnie finally said. "The knife slipped. It took fourteen stitches to sew it up. She'll always have the scar. She's lucky she has the finger."

"Which finger? Which hand?"

"The first finger on the left hand. That's the one always gets it."

"Thank you, Mrs. Abelman. You've been a big help. Sorry I woke you."

Hank tried to talk him into staying over, but Forster knew he wouldn't be able to sleep anyway, so he caught the red-eye and was back in New York by early morning.

5

Forster was at the door of his apartment well before sunrise. He had barely dozed on the plane, but he wasn't the slightest bit tired. His excitement gave him energy. Then he opened the door and picked up the scent at once.

Although very faint, it was unmistakably Shalimar. He walked softly into the bedroom and found his former wife asleep under the covers. A fragment of moonlight lent its special magic to her face.

A floorboard groaned under his feet, and Annie stirred. "Paul?"

"Yes."

"I hope you don't mind." Her voice was soft, sleep-clogged. "I didn't want you having to come home to an empty bed."

"How did you know I'd be back tonight?"

"I called Hank Pollard in San Francisco."

She could do things like that. Forster sat on the edge of the bed and touched her hair.

"Did you find out anything?" she asked.

"It's past four. Go to sleep. I'll tell you in the morning."

"No. Now."

Forster told her everything he had learned about Melissa Kenniston.

"So where does that put you?"

"I don't know yet. Maybe nowhere. But at least it lets me move on to the next stage."

"What's that?"

"Getting to meet her."

Forster went to shower. When he returned, Annie was asleep, her breathing soft, rhythmic. He slipped into bed without waking her, then lay there, feeling her at his back. What was she doing here? What did she want from him after so many years?

79

He knew, yet he didn't know. He had started it by going to her that first night, but now she was coming to him with needs of her own. Were they both afraid and reaching out? Were they both so alone? Evidently. A world was in flux, in disarray. You sought comfort where you could.

Yet how they once hurt each other, Forster thought. The rending, the bloodletting, had been rare at first, but then it became habitual. A chance remark, a wrong look, would set the demons loose. Jealousy, vanity, doubt, anger echoed against the walls. Inadvertently, he had been the one to start that, too. He had fooled around, and Annie found out. Stupid. It meant nothing, he assured her, a purely physical act without ties or feeling. Their history, everything he felt for her, was intact, unsullied. Fine, she declared, and paid him back in kind with a man she met at a party and never saw again.

Nothing was the same after that . . . not for Forster anyway. Annie tried. *He* was too macho. The double standard was too deeply ingrained. It manacled his balls, gnawed him each time he touched her and remembered what she had done to him. *To him*. He took refuge in vain rages and arguments. They belittled each other's attitudes. When Annie went to work, then into business, Forster felt even more threatened. This was not the girl from Battle Creek he had married. The jargon of the sexual revolution exploded about their heads like grenades. It tore open new wounds, and deepened old ones. Neither of them seemed able to resolve things. They couldn't put love and respect together where they belonged, in proper order, with the sweet coherence of which both secretly dreamed. "I'm liberated," she said. "Enjoy it," he told her. Separately, then together, they discovered the other road. They invented divorce all by themselves.

Forster wavered on the edge of sleep. Sadly, neither of them had any answers then. Now he felt he did. Now he began to understand that some were born to fight off the best in life until it was no longer there. Or else they perverted it into nightmares. He, somehow, had managed to do both.

Forster was in his office at nine o'clock on less than three hours' sleep. By ten, he had a complete report on the Olympus Fund in his hands.

It appeared to be an innocuous little mutual hedge fund that had quietly sprung into being no more than seven years ago, and remained all but lost among the hundreds of high-powered growth funds and performance-oriented money managers that had been dominating the financial scene for the past decade. Yet reading further, Forster soon saw that Olympus appeared to have enjoyed an exceptional performance, with its most impressive results coming in its latest quarter. During this period, the tiny fund had sold heavily on balance, while all the large, highly publicized funds were still buying into a rising market. Which, thought Forster, considering what had been happening to the market all of this past week, made Melissa Kenniston's sense of timing seem phenomenal.

For the first time, Jennings showed signs of genuine interest. "Your lady is either a lot smarter than everyone else, or she's clairvoyant."

"We don't know for sure yet whether she's really my lady."

"What will it take to convince you?" said Jennings.

"A scar on the first finger of her left hand."

At about eleven o'clock, Forster put through a call to the Olympus Fund, then changed his mind and hung up. If he called for an appointment, it might be days or even weeks before Melissa Kenniston would see him. And if she had something to hide, she might well refuse to see him altogether. He decided to just appear unannounced at the fund's headquarters and take his chances.

The Olympus Fund was located a short walk away from the magazine, in one of the newer midtown office buildings. Like the company itself, the fund's offices were modest in size, with a single secretary working at a desk in the reception area and a corridor going off to the right. The place appeared to have been recently decorated and was pleasantly bright, with pale green walls that were as light as a new leaf, pastel-colored lithographs, and several vases of freshly cut flowers. Everything seemed removed from the traditional gloom and shadowy dankness of finance.

"Good morning," he said.

"Good morning, sir." The secretary was studying his face. "You're Paul Forster, aren't you?"

He nodded.

"I've seen your picture in *Finance*. You look much better in person, much less menacing. Why are you always scowling in your pictures?"

"I'm an economist. Economists are supposed to scowl. We've been doing it for a thousand years. It lends added weight and authority to our pronouncements."

"You also look much younger and handsomer."

"In that case I'll never scowl again as long as I live. Not even at funerals."

The girl's smile was as bright and pleasant as the decor. If I had money to invest, thought Forster, my first reaction would be to invest it here.

"I guess you want to see Miss Kenniston."

"If she's available."

"I'll tell her you're here," said the girl and all but flew down the corridor.

She was back in a moment.

"Please go right in. Just turn left at the end of the hall. You can't miss it."

Forster thanked her. Could it really be this simple? Feeling as though he had charged a locked, barricaded door only to find it swinging open, he proceeded as instructed. He passed two rooms and saw a man at work in one and a woman in the other. Both were young, and their offices were as appealing as the reception area. Even the computers looked cheerful, as though programmed to produce only up-ticks on the tape and consistent bull markets. If Norman Vincent Peale had ever decided to run a fund, thought Forster, he could have moved right in here and not had to change a thing.

Apparently, he had seen the entire organization, because as he turned left as directed, there was only the one large corner office ahead.

Melissa Kenniston came from behind her desk to greet him.

"Well, Mr. Forster. You seem to have made Peggy's day. She was almost incoherent with excitement at seeing you in person."

Melissa was taller than Forster had expected. Perhaps because Henrietta Luckner had kept referring to her as that *little* whore-bitch. Well, she was not little. And although eleven years had passed since the last photographs he had seen of her were taken, Melissa Kenniston remained as strikingly beautiful a woman as Forster could remember standing this close to. Even now, her face had the stillness of a lovely photograph. She appeared that composed, that self-possessed.

"I appreciate your seeing me without an appointment," he said. "I promise not to take too much of your time."

Her smile was bright, open, and disarming. "That's quite all right, Mr. Forster. I'm more controlled than Peggy, but no less delighted to meet you."

"You're embarrassing me."

"Marvelous. Then perhaps modesty isn't entirely extinct. Sometimes I feel as though I'm literally drowning in a sea of arrogance. Or perhaps it's because I'm forced to spend so much of my time with lawyers, bankers, and investment analysts. Please sit down." She indicated a setting of chairs arranged about a glass table. "Would you like coffee?"

"Please. Black. No sugar."

My God, he thought, she could charm rats out of a sewer. But her former sister-in-law had implied as much. She went over to a coffee maker sitting on an antique chest, and Forster became aware of the room itself, which was actually an omnibus library, art gallery, and sitting room, with a computer and a desk the only visible indications that it also was an office. More than half a dozen paintings were arranged about the walls, all perfectly placed and lighted. Forster recognized a Renoir, a Degas, and a Pizzaro, and suspected that all three were nothing less than originals.

"If I had an office like this," he said, "I'd probably never go home."

Her laugh was a few octaves lower than her voice, and her voice was low. "I barely do."

She brought two mugs of coffee to the table. As she put them down, Forster saw the small white scar on the first finger of her left hand and felt a sudden weakness go through him. He was aware of the same shock an aging fighter might feel at the end of a bad, late round, when his legs are gone and his arms won't respond. Well . . . he thought, and for an instant would not even trust himself to look at her. She sat facing him, waiting, and there were new currents in the room.

"The reason I'm here," he finally said, "is that I'd like to do a piece about you and wondered how you would feel about the idea."

"You mean for *Finance Magazine*?"

"Yes."

She took a moment to drink her coffee. "I'm flattered, of course. But why me? Until you walked in here a few minutes ago, I would have assumed you didn't know I existed."

"To be perfectly honest, Miss Kenniston, until a few days ago, I didn't. Then our research department came up with some startling statistics, and I've been intrigued by you ever since."

"I don't understand. What statistics?"

"The ones that showed the Olympus Fund to have swung overwhelmingly to the sell side during the last quarter, while just about everyone else was still trying to buy. You even took a very large short position during this same period of time."

Melissa's shrug was eloquent. "Oh, *that*," she said, as if dismissing it. "Although after this past week's debacle, and with the added brilliance of hindsight, I suppose I do come out looking like a genius."

"Or a psychic."

"I'm afraid I'm neither. And the closest thing to a crystal ball I've ever consulted was this."

She took a book from one of the shelves along the wall and laid it on the table before him. It was Forster's own, *Market Timing in a Changing Economy*.

"You made it all clear for me in chapters fourteen through eighteen," she said. "That, and your repeated warnings that a mammoth, out-of-control debt, soaring interest rates, and a state of general euphoria, were sure signs of impending catastrophe." She smiled. "So you see? You're the one who's the genius. I did only what you told me to do."

"I'm sure a lot of other money managers read my book and heard my warnings. But you're the only one who bet millions on them, and that's what makes the difference. Too, you're a woman in what's still a male-dominated arena. You're part of the investment industry, Miss Kenniston . . . and a very attractive part, at that."

She was silent and Forster took the moment to light a cigarette and consider her through the smoke, seeing the really startling lavender eyes, the fair skin, the nearly blue-black hair, which she wore short and close to the head. A fine line had appeared between her brows, and she looked less composed than she had a few moments before. Then there was a flash, like sun reflected from water as she glanced up and her gaze crossed his.

"What if I didn't want you to do this article?" she said.

"*Do* you object?"

"I'm sorry, but I'm afraid I do."

Naturally, thought Forster, and had an instant whiff of the devil's own perfume. "May I ask why?"

"It's nothing personal. Your books are my professional bibles and I haven't missed one of your magazine pieces in years. It's just that I've always kept a deliberately low profile for myself and my fund, and a feature article by Paul Forster in *Finance Magazine* would just blow all that sky high."

"I respect your feelings, Miss Kenniston, but you and the Olympus Fund are still part of the American financial scene and you can't expect to stay anonymous forever."

"We've done it for more than seven years."

"Yes, but this is the first time you've come up with a set of statistics like these. If I don't write about you, someone else will."

Her hand rose and smoothed the back of her hair, which hugged her head like a well-fitting cap and needed no smoothing. Forster had noticed the small gesture several times. It was her only visible tic . . . certainly a minor one considering the dark and deadly currents she might well be riding.

"I can always refuse to cooperate," she said.

"Yes, but that would be foolish."

"Why?"

"Because the article would be written anyway, and couldn't possibly be as good or carry as much weight as it would if you worked with me. You would also be sacrificing any chance to shape the final result with your personality and intelligence, and that would have to be a considerable loss."

Her smile was sardonic. "I don't think I've ever been bludgeoned into submission with quite such grace."

"Does that mean you'll cooperate?"

"It means that you seem to have left me with very little choice."

The room, to Forster, was suddenly an oven of burgeonings.

"If you'll let me take you to dinner tonight," he said, "I'll try to make up for it."

"I certainly think you should try to do *something*," she said.

* * *

They met as they usually did in New York, with Castanzo picking up Forster on a midtown street corner in the rented car he had just driven in from La Guardia. Then they swung through Central Park to the West Side Highway and headed north in the light, early afternoon traffic. It was less than two hours since Forster had left Melissa Kenniston's office.

"Well?" Forster said. "Were you able to come up with anything on my six friends?"

"Don't I always?"

"How bad is it?" Forster asked.

Castanzo's face showed nothing. After twenty years with the FBI and five more as a private investigator, there were few surprises left for him. "Not too terrible," he said. "But still nothing to run full-page ads about in the *Times*."

He took out a small, black notebook, flipped through several pages as he drove, then put the book back in his pocket.

"You're not interested in the nonsense," he said, "so I'll just give you the heart of it. To begin with, William Boyer has been giving quiet but substantial backing to a couple of extreme, right-wing hate groups for years. More significantly, one of the groups was responsible for that Mississippi church bombing a few months ago in which three black kids died."

"Lovely. Go ahead."

"Then there's Pete Farnham of Chase Manhattan, who was twice bailed out of trouble by Mafia money and muscle."

"What kind of trouble and how long ago?"

"He made a couple of bad, personal investments and some loan sharks were squeezing him. It was almost twenty years ago, but there could still be one or two connections."

"Okay."

"Al Loomis, you're going to love. He's got a thing for Jews that could turn a strong man's stomach. The big surprise here is mostly that he's been able to cover it so well. Only his analyst knows."

"And us," said Forster flatly.

"Exactly. As for your allegedly tight-assed buddy, Wendell Norton, he just happens to be paying fairly substantial blackmail over some hot love letters he once wrote to a junior senator's wife."

Castanzo grinned . . . in itself, unusual.

"That's funny to you?"

"The junior senator is now president of the United States."

"Terrific." Forster allowed it time to settle in. "What about the other two . . . Ridgeway and Stanton?"

"They seem to be clean. Which should help restore a bit of your sagging faith in the species."

Forster glanced at Castanzo's face in profile: dark, even-featured, handsome, an uprooted Florentine prince transplanted and thriving in the New World. Some of the things he routinely carried in his head would have given most men ulcers. Still, even he was not always immune. Once, having dinner in a Chicago restaurant, he had told Forster, he heard a voice from an adjoining table that he was sure he knew. He studied the man speaking but had never seen him before. Then he realized the voice was one he had listened to for several weeks while monitoring some wiretaps. It gave him an odd sensation. He knew the man's most intimate secrets, yet he was a stranger. A leaden anxiety settled in his stomach, his food tasted sour, and he broke into a sweat. He paid his check and fled.

Occupational hazard, thought Forster.

"I have a few more beauties for you," he said, and gave Castanzo the names and addresses of Alec Borman, Katherine Harwith, and Peter Stone, the three key witnesses in the government's case against the bankers.

About six hundred miles west of Manhattan, in a shopping center near Gary, Indiana, Charles Lewicki stood seventeenth in a long line of depositors waiting outside the doors of the Midwest National Bank. Lewicki, a drill press operator for the Ebco Tool Corporation, had been waiting more than four hours to reach his present position.

The people surrounding him were mostly second- and third-generation Americans whose ancestors had come from the towns and cities of Poland, Hungary, Russia, Italy, Germany, and Austria. Their bodies were well fed and they were prosperously dressed. Yet there were shadows beneath their eyes that made them look as though they lacked enough sun or sleep.

Lewicki saw several people he knew, but was as careful to avoid their eyes as they were to avoid his. There were no friends and neighbors on line, only antagonists. Every dollar delivered by a teller into someone else's hands meant one less dollar for you. And none of the periodic assurances from the bank president himself—that there was enough cash on hand to satisfy everyone's needs—soothed Lewicki's fear.

At a few minutes before 3:00 P.M., the bank's closing time, Lewicki had advanced to sixth in line. He was third when the big doors were closed in front of him. A groan rose from the depositors still crowding the sidewalk. People shouted for the doors to be opened. Finally, the doors did open and Neil Benton, the president, again appeared and begged for quiet.

"You all know me," he said. "I've never lied to you before and I'm not lying now. Your money is safe. The Midwest National will be open as usual at nine o'clock tomorrow morning. The Chicago Federal Reserve is supplying us with all the cash we need. There's nothing to worry about. The bank is fiscally sound. Please go home and come back in the morning if you still want to withdraw your money."

"And lose our places in line?" shouted Lewicki. "We've been here half the day. Open the damn doors and let us wait inside. Let us in!"

Others took up the cry. "Let us in! . . . Let us in!"

"That's against the law!" Benton cried. But his words were lost in the rising clamor.

Lewicki stood there, the crowd pressing at his back. He felt like a wrecked sailor in the lull between two storms.

"Come on," he yelled. "Let's go in. That's our sweat and blood they've got in there. We can't just walk away from it."

The crowd once more took up the chant, all of them pushing, flowing toward the doors.

Lewicki pressed forward, the crowd behind him. The bank president pleaded again for everyone to go home and come back in the morning. No one heard. Or if they did, they were not about to obey. At the last moment, Benton slipped back inside the bank. A pair of guards struggled to close the doors behind him, but it was too late. People shoved past them into the lobby. A solid line of helmeted police, holding nightsticks, stood waiting.

Lewicki knew some of the cops by sight. But he saw only their clubs as they started to swing.

Then he heard the flat, awful noise of wood hitting bone. Bodies slammed into him and the spurt of someone's blood, hot and slippery, went into his face. There was a confused flailing of arms and the black gleam of nightsticks flashing against the vaulted ceiling. One of the clubs whacked against the side of Lewicki's head, stabbed into his neck, and kept beating at him. He tried to move away but there was no room to budge. Blood ran down his cheeks and he began to feel dizzy.

Oh, Christ, he thought . . . oh, Christ, the sonofabitch is trying to kill me.

When he opened his eyes again he was lying on the cold, marble floor of the bank and everything was strangely quiet except for the weeping of women, soft and far away.

Forster took Melissa Kenniston to dinner that evening at Chez Vincent, a small French restaurant on East Fifty-fourth Street.

"I may as well warn you in advance," he said to Melissa earlier, "eating is not a theology to me. So if you'd like to choose the restaurant, I won't be offended."

"Burger King will do just beautifully," she told him.

Forster judged it a good beginning.

In the restaurant, they were shown to a corner table lit by a small orange candle. They gave their drink orders, then sat considering each other over chilled vodka martinis.

"This is a first for me," said Melissa. "I've never gone to dinner before as the subject of a magazine article. I'm not quite sure how to perform. Is there an accepted procedure for such things, or do we just wing it?"

Forster laughed. "Just think of me as a man taking you to dinner. Forget the article."

"That's all very well for you to say. But I'm the one whose image is going to be projected for a few million readers, and I'd be lying if I said I wasn't self-conscious about it. Or are you telling me that all your impressions are off the record tonight?"

"Actually, I never thought of this as a working dinner."

"How *did* you think of it?"

"As being with me, not the magazine," Forster said. "As an evening I looked forward to with a beautiful, intelligent, utterly fascinating woman."

"That's precisely the image I was hoping to project."

They beamed at each other like two diamond merchants considering a major sale.

"In any case," said Forster, "it's not my style to bludgeon my subject. So I hope you'll feel relaxed about that part. Too, you'll have a chance to see whatever I've done before it goes to press. And if there's anything you don't like, you won't find me unreasonable."

There are times, thought Forster, when I can get my mouth to say just about any damn thing.

It was over their second martinis that he asked, "Have you ever been married?"

"Of course. Hasn't everyone?" She allowed several beats. "Haven't *you*?"

"Yes."

"What happened?"

About to say something glib, Forster changed his mind. If he expected to get considered answers, he had to offer a few of his own. "I made one stupid mistake, my wife made another to get even, and things deteriorated from there. Then if you throw in a touch of acute male syndrome, mixed with a large dose of women's lib, you should have a fair idea of what happened."

"Was there love?"

"From beginning to end. Which was probably the saddest part of all." Forster looked at her eyes. "And you?"

"My standard lie is that I was too young, my husband was too old, and neither of us really knew what we were getting."

"And the truth?"

"Not for publication, I assume."

"Naturally."

Melissa took a deep breath. "The truth is that we both knew precisely what we were getting. Except, of course, that my husband didn't expect me to be getting anywhere near as much as I finally got."

That much, thought Forster, was undoubtedly true. He looked at her across Chez Vincent's ridiculously tiny table, studying the quiet softness of her face in the candlelight, the saucy way she wore her hair, the casual, understated elegance of her clothes . . . all in marked contrast to a suddenly intruding image of a thin, ten-year-old Helen Berenstein, standing with her brother and parents and smiling happily in a moment of summer sun.

"At least you had love," Melissa said flatly.

"You didn't?"

"Just a brief pretense. At the end, there wasn't even that."

The owner, who also functioned as the maitre d', took their dinner orders. Forster had known him for years as the quintessentially bright, charming Frenchman, but there was little of his usual Gallic cheer visible tonight.

"Bad day, Vincent?"

A philosophical shrug failed to come off. "The worst, Mr. Forster. I should have stayed with what I knew. My wife kept telling me I didn't belong in the market, but I didn't listen. I was greedy."

"I'm sorry," said Forster. "Are you margined?"

"On everything. I got two calls from brokers this morning. If I don't cover in the next couple of days, I'll be sold out." Vincent sighed. "I might be able to borrow on the restaurant, but if the market keeps falling I could lose that too. I hate dumping on you, Mr. Forster, especially when you're out with such a beautiful lady. But do you think there's a chance things could start turning around soon?"

"No one can answer that. But I think you'd be crazy to risk your restaurant."

"That's what my wife says." Vincent looked glumly at Forster. "I read in the paper where you saved those bankers from getting shot. I know it's an awful thing to say, but I wish you hadn't."

The restaurant owner walked away and Forster took advantage of the opening. "What about you?" he asked Melissa. "Do *you* wish I hadn't saved those bankers? Or do you feel more generous toward them?"

"How could I feel generous toward men like that? They've set off an earthquake with their greed."

"You don't think there's any chance that they're innocent?"

Melissa sipped the remains of her martini. "Do you?"

"I don't know, but they all swear they are."

"When has an indicted person ever admitted being guilty?"

"They do have the right to a trial."

"And they'll have it," she said. "But I did a little computer punching the other day and came up with some interesting statistics. Of the last hundred criminal cases that came to trial as a result of evidence gathered by the SEC and the U.S. Attorney's Office, ninety-seven resulted in convictions, two defendants died before a verdict was brought in, and one plea bargained for a reduced sentence."

"Not a very encouraging brief for innocence. Maybe they

should just be tossed in jail and save the taxpayers the expense of a trial.''

She offered a silvery smile. "Now you must think I'm a red-neck fascist.''

"Are you?''

"No. But where those six men are concerned, I'm ready to cry out for capital punishment.''

"Have you ever met any of them?''

"No.'' She looked at Forster and this time seemed to be mostly cat . . . cat's poise, cat's gold and lavender eyes, cat's perceptive, all-knowing mouth. "But *you* probably have, haven't you?''

"Yes.''

"Of course. Being who you are, I'm sure you know every one of them.'' She paused to light a cigarette. "How well do you know them?''

"Well enough to have been badly rocked by their indictments. I still find the whole thing hard to believe. Wendell Norton is an old friend and teacher. He helped me through my doctorals.''

It was the first real bait he had put out. Yet watching her face, he could see no reaction.

"Then this must be an especially difficult time for you,'' she said. "I'm sorry if I appeared unfeeling. Had I known you were that close, I'd have been more sensitive.''

The apology carried warmth, sincerity. She's either very good at what she's doing, thought Forster, or she hasn't done a thing and I'm wasting my time.

"If they're guilty,'' he said, "my knowing them doesn't make them less so.''

"Yes, but if you're a friend, there has to be unquestioning belief . . . rational or not. I can appreciate that.''

"There's also anger—a sense of betrayal.''

"Maybe. But with you, I can't help feeling the unquestioning belief would come first.''

Then their food was served—salad and stuffed breast of veal—and they ate for a while in a silence broken only by Melissa's comments on the excellence of Vincent's cuisine and her hope that the Frenchman would not be foolish enough to mortgage and lose his restaurant to the plunging stock market. Through dinner Forster found the former runaway waif almost like one of those beautiful, phantom women lonely men invent for themselves in the long, solitary stretches of their nights . . . interested, attentive, and so effortlessly poised that her very manner seemed like an exorbitant gift she had brought to the table to share as one would a rich dessert.

"Tell me about your family," he said over coffee. "Is it a large one?"

"I wish it were. It's always been one of my fantasies to live in a sprawling house surrounded by noisy brothers and sisters. But my parents are dead and I'm quite alone."

"No noisy brothers and sisters?"

"Not even quiet ones. Although I do have a cousin that I feel close to." She smiled, her eyes deeply set in the oval of her face. "My fantasy brother."

Her *real* brother, thought Forster. "Does he live in New York?"

"Yes, but he travels a lot. He's in London right now."

"It must be lonely for you."

"I have my work. And I do see people. I do go out."

"But no thought of marrying again?"

"That takes more than thought. With time, it gets harder and harder to make the required commitment. You begin judging too much and feeling too little. I was never a mad, romantic, impetuous girl. My early marriage was carefully planned and thought out, and dissolved the same way. So I'm certainly far from a mad, romantic, impetuous woman." She looked at Forster. "What about you?"

"In the sense that I'm alone, not too different from you. Except that I *was* a mad, romantic, impetuous boy, and I'm even more so as a man. I seem to learn nothing as I go along." He paused to consider it. "Although I suppose I have learned one thing."

"Which is?"

"That it gets more and more depressing to wake up beside someone you don't really care about."

Melissa invited him to have a brandy in her apartment, which looked out high over Central Park from Fifth Avenue and was a gracious continuation of everything Forster had admired in her office. Not everyone with money knew what to do with it, he thought. Melissa obviously did. Her late ex-husband would be pleased to know his generous divorce settlement had not been tastelessly squandered.

They sat quietly drinking, looking out over the darkness of the park and the lights beyond.

"I hope the evening wasn't too uncomfortable for you," he said.

"You know it wasn't."

"You don't mind the probing, the having to talk about yourself?"

"Who doesn't enjoy talking about themselves? Besides, I did a fair share of probing myself."

"I hate to press," said Forster, "but I do have a deadline. So I'd like to get together again as soon as possible for a real working session."

"I'm free tomorrow evening."

"Good. I'll pick you up at eight."

Walking back through the living room and foyer, Forster looked for her telephones as well as suitable cover for any additional listening devices Castanzo might decide were needed.

6

Forster walked into his office at shortly after nine the next morning and found his phone ringing.

"I've been wondering all day and all night." Annie's voice came over the wire: anxious, eager, full of energy. "Have you called her? Have you met her yet?"

Forster saw a collection of papers and messages on his desk but did not pick them up. "Yes."

"Yes, what?"

"Yes, I called her. Yes, I met her. I'm allegedly doing an article on her for the magazine. We had dinner last night."

"Then you're sure she's the Berenstein girl? She has the knife scar?"

"Yes."

"Oh, Paul!"

"That doesn't mean I know anything . . . or ever will."

"Don't be so negative. It's a beginning, isn't it?"

That much, it was, he thought.

"I have some people waiting," said Annie. "But I had to call and find out. God, this is exciting. I'll be in touch."

Forster slowly put down the phone, thinking about her. He glanced through half a dozen message slips and found that only one required immediate action. Wendell Norton was in town to confer with his defense lawyers and wondered whether it was possible for Forster to meet him for a drink at the Plaza at five. There was a number to call and Forster left word he would be there. Then he picked up that morning's copy of *The Wall Street Journal* and briefly scanned the latest litany of his country's afflictions.

In the familiar, dignified print of the *Journal*, which always reminded Forster of the speeches of elderly corporation counsels, the dollar was still dropping against most foreign currencies; the stock and bond markets enjoyed a brief, modest rally before the gains turned into further losses by the close; the administration indicated it would continue to support its treasury bills with all the resources at its command; the president was calling upon America's allies to be more supportive during the current crisis; runs were reported at scattered banks throughout the country, with violence breaking out between angry depositors and the police in Gary, Indiana, but as yet there was no news of either bank failures or forced closings.

Jennings appeared in the doorway.

"How did it go yesterday?"

"Not too badly."

"What does that mean?"

"It means I met Melissa Kenniston, found out for sure she was Helen Berenstein, got her to agree to cooperate on a magazine piece, established at least the beginnings of a relationship, and told Castanzo to bug her phone and apartment."

Jennings lit a long, richly dark Havana. "How did she explain her shift to the sell side during the last quarter?"

"She said it was all in my book on market timing."

"Smart lady." Jennings's eyes were attentive, as if he half expected Forster to suddenly assume a different shape. "What about her brother? Did you find out anything about him? Right now he's the missing link in all this."

"She said she had no brothers or sisters. But she did admit to a cousin whom she's close with. I'm betting the cousin is the missing brother. And if he is, then he's going to be making his presence known very soon."

"Why?"

"Because if I'm right, then Arthur Berenstein—or whatever name he's going by these days—has to be playing a major role in this whole elaborate scheme. And with me suddenly buzzing around his little sister, I figure he's going to have to show up to check me out."

Jennings shook his head. "You do have a devious way of thinking."

"Personally, I prefer the word logical."

"Whatever makes you happy. But did it ever occur to you that if you do turn out to be right, Berenstein could very well prove dangerous?"

"Not logical."

"Why not?"

"Because if Berenstein did somehow pull this conspiracy off, he certainly wouldn't be given to violence. If he were, it would have been a lot simpler to have avenged his father by taking out contracts on those six bankers than by spending more than twenty years of his life plotting to send them to jail."

Jennings studied the ash at the tip of his Havana. "I'm getting a little worried."

"About what?"

"About there actually being moments when I'm ready to think you may be starting to make a tiny modicum of sense in all this."

Forster spent the afternoon struggling over the start of a piece in which he hoped to explain, in terms understandable to the layman, the whys and wherefores of the current fiscal crisis.

It was not easy. Even the experts failed to agree on the basics. Economics, like psychology, was still more of an art than a science, and frequently an art practiced by fools. Still, Forster felt that the salient fact in the existing situation, the one holding the key to fiscal panic of any kind, was the single word *belief*. In a very real sense, all money was a matter of belief . . . belief in the probity of its backing. The word credit itself came from the Latin, *credere*, to believe. When that belief ends—belief in the integrity of the banking system itself and those at its head—panic begins. And once started, it is difficult to stop.

Also, Forster noted, since nothing ever took place entirely in a vacuum, the broad economic realities of the times couldn't be overlooked. This was the age of OPEC and the Chase Manhattan Bank. Once it was steel and coal and trade that drove the engines of finance. Now it was dollars and oil and the whims and life spans of Arab potentates and religious fanatics.

Once, imprudent banks making foolish loans were punished by the marketplace, declared bankrupt, and closed down. Not anymore. Today's banks were so interdependent that the shutting of even one could cause the collapse of the system. In fact, if only a small part of all outstanding debts were ever called, there would not be enough money in the world to make them good.

Right now, of course, thought Forster bleakly, the Federal Reserve was shouting out its own loud cries of *credere. Believe* your money is safe. *Believe* that it will be there when you need it. *Believe* there is no reason to take it out of our banks and stuff it in your mattresses. And certainly *believe* there is absolutely no reason for panic.

Fat chance.

Depressed, Forster sat brooding over the less-attractive possibilities still ahead. It was almost time for his appointment with Wendell Norton, so he slid his disorganized notes into a drawer and left the office.

He entered the Plaza Hotel through the Fifth Avenue entrance and went directly to the Palm Court.

Wendell Norton was waiting at a table against the far wall. At a distance, he still looked imposing. Yet, closer, there was a lack of life in his posture, a blankness in his eyes, that reminded Forster of those dead and empty spaces that collect about a man who has suffered a grievous loss from which he knows he will never recover. Seeing Forster, Norton managed a fair enough smile as he rose to shake hands.

"I'm glad you were able to make it. After a day with my lawyers, I'm ready to jump bail and go into exile. And they're supposed to be on *my* side."

"It was that bad?"

"You can't imagine."

"Yes I can. Don't forget. I've seen the evidence."

Norton nodded. "And every last word is fiction."

A waiter arrived with two bourbons and placed one in front of each of them with soda on the side. Norton, having arrived early and finished one drink, quickly started on his second.

"I'll tell you this," he said. "Increasingly, I find something terribly wrong, even obscene, about a system of justice that allows lawyers to proliferate like maggots and grow rich while those they defend have to bankrupt themselves for life trying to prove their innocence."

Forster went to work on his drink and felt it slide down warmly. "Have you been able to come up with anything yet?" the former Fed chairman asked. "What about that possibility with the Malcolm Commission?"

"There's nothing specific. But since we know the evidence against you is based on the testimony of three witnesses, I'm trying to find out why these people would lie." He had considered mentioning the Berensteins, but then decided against it. The fewer who knew, the better. At least so long as it was nothing but conjecture. "What about you, Wendell? Would you have any idea what possible reason these three might have to want to destroy you?"

Norton shook his head. "I've never even heard of Alec Borman and Peter Stone. As for Katherine Harwith"—Norton's face turned suddenly, dark, anguished—"well, . . . I suppose you know about Katherine."

"You've never said anything, but I've always assumed you had an involvement of some sort going."

"For more than ten years. And I want you to know it had absolutely nothing to do with my feelings for Emily. I loved my wife from the day I met her until the day she died and never regretted a minute of it. But it doesn't mean I haven't been attracted to other women. Flesh is flesh, and I must admit I've indulged myself there. But always with discretion."

"Not always, Wendell. I'd hardly call writing love letters to a married woman discreet."

Norton stared evenly at Forster for several moments before he blinked. "You've been doing investigating, all right."

"Nothing personal. I don't give a damn about any of that. But if I'm going to help you, I've got to know everything there is to know . . . not just what you decide to tell me. And right now I want to know why Katherine Harwith would despise you enough to want to ruin you and send you to prison for something you didn't do."

"I can't even begin to imagine."

Norton's self-absorption was suddenly too much for Forster. "My God! What the hell kind of man are you? How could you have worked eight hours a day with a woman, had a continuing affair with her for more than a decade, yet have remained so insensitive to what she must have been feeling?"

Norton gazed miserably into his half-empty glass. "We haven't actually been that close for a while. That is, outside of the office. Not for almost two years, anyway."

"Why? What happened?"

"It wasn't too long after Emily died. Maybe that had something to do with it. In any case, we gradually stopped seeing each other after work."

"What did your wife's death have to do with it?"

"My condition suddenly had changed. One of my life's most important constants suddenly was gone. Everything I did was affected. Certainly my relationship with Katherine was. I suppose she wanted more than I found myself willing to offer her."

"You mean like marriage?"

Norton nodded, looking, Forster thought, as though he wished he could be anywhere else. As close as they had been over the years, self-revelation had never been one of Wendell's strong points. It still wasn't.

"Did you ever fight about it?" Forster asked.

"We never fought about anything. Katherine wasn't a fighter. When she was displeased or unhappy, she just withdrew."

"I guess that made it pretty easy for you?"

"Made what easy?"

"Dumping her."

"I didn't really . . ." Norton fell silent. Emotion showed itself briefly, then retreated.

"I've got some dirty news for you," Forster said flatly. "I'm afraid this is one time your unhappy little Katherine decided to do more than just withdraw."

"I can't believe that."

"Well, you'd better start believing it." Forster's voice was dry, without joy. "Because if Katherine's evidence against you is actually the lie you claim it to be, there would have to be an awful lot of hate and vengefulness squeezed into it. Or do you think you behaved so nobly toward her that such hatred would be unwarranted?"

"I never intended to hurt her."

"Face it, Wendell. You treated her like shit!" Forster took a long drink to calm himself. His anger surprised him. The man was his friend, a superb banker, and a brilliant economist, but he was turning out to be a real horse's ass where women were concerned. So who wasn't? Forster thought.

"That may be so," said Norton. "But I hardly think Katherine's capabilities—fiscally, intellectually, or otherwise—could even come close to conceiving and carrying out a conspiracy as complex and far-reaching as this one would have to be."

"Of course not. She, Borman, and Stone would be little more than messengers in the overall scheme of things. Though they're obviously crucial to the government's case. What *I'm* hoping to find—what I *must* find if we're to have any chance of unraveling this godawful mess—is whoever it was that hired them.''

They sat while the Palm Court's string quartet offered them something shrill, woeful, and pleading. To Forster, the sound seemed to match Wendell's mood, his expression, his entire sadly fallen state. It made Forster regret his earlier anger.

"It'll be all right," he said by way of atonement. "I suddenly have a good feeling about this. Whatever I have to find, I'll find."

"I hope so. I've given you one devil of a job."

"I figure you're worth it."

"There are more and more moments when I wonder."

Forster fiddled with his drink. "Enough with the humility. You've worked hard for your arrogance. You've earned it. Don't go losing it all just when you need it most."

"This has been a humbling experience."

"It'll pass."

"If it does, it'll only be because of you," said Norton.

Forster looked away from his former professor's face. It was still hard for him to deal with what he saw there.

"I'll never be able to pay you back for what you're doing."

"Yes you will," said Forster.

"How?"

"When you're finally clear of all this and get to be president, you'll make me treasury secretary."

Norton looked at him long and solemnly. "You'll be one of our best."

He found Frank Reilly sitting alone at his customary table at McGinty's. The only visible sign that the SEC's chief investigator had left the table at all since Forster had seen him there six days ago was that he was wearing a medium gray, rather than a dark blue, suit.

"Where have you been?" he said as Forster sat down opposite him. "I've missed you. The fact is I miss everyone these days. There's hardly a sonofabitch in town who'll talk to me since the Unholy Six."

"I'll talk to you."

"That just means you want something."

"I'm interested in Peter Stone," Forster said.

"So's everyone else." Reilly's tone was bleak. "Personally, I can't stomach the bastard."

"Why not?"

"Because he's young, smart as hell, drives a top-of-the-line Porsche, screws the most beautiful models in town, and makes sure you know about every last bit of it."

A waiter brought Forster's drink.

"You're the one who hired him," said Forster.

"Shit, we all make mistakes."

"Come on, Frank. This whole six-star, dog and pony show of yours never would have gotten off the ground without Stone. But what I'm curious about is his original lead. Was it a tip-off or did he have to really work for it?"

The investigator's tough face was unyielding. "Oh, he worked for it all right. It wasn't one of those deals where some hustler gets pissed off and blows the whistle. I told you he's smart. Brains aren't his problem." Reilly drank his whiskey, exuding resentment like an animal smell. "Actually, it was a classic case. He used the right investigative procedures in just the right way."

"Such as?"

"You know the drill. We're always running computer checks on the stocks of companies involved in huge takeovers or mergers. Then we work backward from the day the acquisition was announced, looking for blips or abnormalities in trading patterns and price changes. When we find one, we investigate further."

"And Stone found one?"

"The tenacious little prick found half a dozen. When he traced back the larger buy and sell orders, he discovered some of them had come out of the Bank Streit in the Bahamas. And in every case, Alec Borman was the account executive. Of course by that time we had a full investigation going and eventually ran the case-count up to seventeen. Then we came down hard on Borman, promised him immunity, and got him to tell us who the six accounts really belonged to."

Reilly considered Forster with eyes that matched the pale blue of his shirt. "I get the feeling you still don't really believe this."

"How could I not believe it? I was in court for the arraignment." Foster swirled the Jack Daniel's in his glass. "What was the deal with Borman?"

"I told you. Immunity from prosecution."

"No fines? No returning of whatever bribes and personal profits he may have realized from all those insider tips?"

Reilly shrugged it off. "Small potatoes, Paulie. Especially since the guy is the guts of our case."

"I can understand that. But what I can't understand is why Borman should have known the names of all six of his clients."

"What do you mean?"

"Those six moguls represent the ultimate in financial sophistication. I'd imagine that if they decided to do something illegal, they'd have been smart enough to at least cover their identities."

Reilly drew his head in like a fighter protecting his chin. He seemed to be enjoying himself.

"They did hide their identities," he said. "All six accounts were under false code names. The only person who knew who they really were was Borman himself."

"Exactly. And Borman finally crumbled under pressure, turned state's evidence, and was able to name all six men. What I'm trying to say is that not even Borman should have known who they were."

"How else could they have made the deal with him to act as their account exec? It could hardly have been done anonymously, over the phone."

"No," said Forster. "But they certainly could have limited their exposure to just one man, not all six. They might have drawn lots to see which one did the deal with Borman for the entire group. Or better still, they could have had the chosen man arrange things with Borman through someone outside the group entirely. Then if things went bad and Borman crumbled, the only man he'd know would be the hired intermediary, not any of the six principals. And if the intermediary himself finally caved in, he'd still only be able to identify the single man who had hired him."

Reilly clutched his thoughts like large diamonds in his fist and said nothing.

"Wouldn't that have made more sense to you," Forster asked, "than the way they allegedly did handle it?"

Reilly shrugged. "Maybe. But I'll tell you what doesn't make any sense at all to me. The fact that you could still be implying, subtly or otherwise, that those six supercrooks might actually not be guilty as charged.''

"Wild, isn't it?'' said Forster.

He arrived exactly at eight; Melissa still was not completely dressed when she opened the door.

"You may as well know this right from the start,'' Forster said. "I suffer the worst of all curses. I'm always on time.''

"That's nothing. Wait till you learn some of *my* problems.''

She had just come out of a tub and gave off the scent of soap and bath powder. Her hair was soft and damp about her face and she wore a long, white terry robe.

He breathed what smelled like chicken cooking and saw the gleam of silver and crystal on the dining room table.

"I thought it might be nice not to have to go out tonight,'' she said.

"My God! You even cook?'' His surprise was genuine. In seven years of dating, restaurants had become his natural habitat . . . stoves, to the women he took out, a curious anachronism.

"I hope you like chicken.''

"I love chicken. I worship it. I have this small, gold icon of Frank Perdue at home.''

She laughed. "For an economist, you have a wonderfully light touch.''

"It's all surface. Underneath, I'm deep, dark, and brooding.''

"Who isn't?'' Melissa led him to the liquor cabinet. "If you'll take care of the martinis, I'll finish dressing.''

When she had left, Forster glanced about the living room, wondering whether Castanzo had had the time and opportunity to place his bugs, and where they were most likely to be. A pair of silver wall sconces seemed a good possibility, along with a centrally located cocktail table and several baroque picture frames. But less than twenty-four hours had passed since he gave Guido the order, so in all likelihood the apartment was still clean, unpenetrated.

They had their drinks and hors d'oeuvres out on the terrace, with the air pleasantly cool and the city's lights glinting through the dusk.

"I love this time of day,'' said Melissa. "There's at least a hint of peace in it—something I don't find easily. In case you hadn't noticed, I'm not an especially relaxed, easy-going sort.''

"Achievers rarely are."

Eyes in shadow, she looked at him. "Are we officially at work?"

"From the moment you opened the door in your simple, terry robe, with your wet hair plastered about your face and smelling of scented soap."

"What did that tell you about me?"

"That you're secure enough to be seen without makeup or putting a comb to your hair. That you feel beautiful just as you are. That regardless of your success in the marketplace, you're never out of contention as a woman."

She smiled. "All this from that? And aren't you presupposing that it was deliberate, that I didn't simply fall behind schedule and get caught by the bell?"

"You're a working woman. You know how to get through a crowded calendar with split-second timing. My feeling is that you either consciously or unconsciously may have wanted to be caught by the bell."

"Well, it is a thought, isn't it?" Melissa glanced about. "Didn't you bring a tape recorder?"

"I can't stand them. They make people stiff and guarded, make them feel as if every word they say is being chiseled in granite."

"No notebook either?"

"Just as bad—sometimes worse if you have to stop someone in the middle of a thought so you can write it all down. I remember what people say. The important things, anyway. The rest doesn't really matter." Forster worked briefly on his martini. "I know there's no such thing as a single guiding principle in a person's life. But if I were to ask you to choose one above all others—a single, basic philosophical belief that you do your best to follow—what would it be?"

"Grace." She said it without an instant's hesitation. "I believe in trying to live in as pure and continuing a state of grace as possible. And I don't use the word in its religious sense, or as having anything to do with style. That's not what the word means to me."

"What *does* it mean to you?"

"It means that if something can't be done with grace, it's not worth doing. Grace is courage. It's not compromising with the tawdry, the cruel, the ugly, the indecent. It's walking through mud up to your ears and somehow staying clean."

"You set some standards."

"Unfortunately, I can't always live up to them."

"I don't know anyone who could."

"You could."

Forster laughed. She was a better liar than he.

"You think that's funny?"

"It's very flattering, but you barely know me."

"I know the important things. You forget. I've been reading you for years, and isn't a writer supposed to be very much what he writes?"

"You overdignify me. I'm only a financial writer."

"Don't say *only*. Don't put yourself down. Through your writing you've given me glimpses of your intelligence, your compassion, your humor, your politics, your handling of adversity. I've watched your reactions to world events and their effect on the human condition. I've seen your responses to the suffering of the oppressed and the greed and indifference of the powerful. Oh, I know you all right. It's you who has yet to learn about *me*."

"I'm trying," he said.

But he was, of course, already learning about her. Maybe not all the specifics of the Helen Berenstein she had taken such pains to cover, but enough about the woman she had chosen to become to allow him a fair glimpse of where the two merged. At moments, talking to her, he felt like a petty thief selling stolen jewels to the devil. At other times it was almost like listening to a child's whisper, to tales so lush with whimsy that they hid more than they revealed. Was there really no evil that could not be reconsidered as a source of good? Did her suffering as a child now give her the right to make others suffer? Or did the act of suffering become, in itself, a kind of purification? At particular moments, his heart racing like that of a trapped bird, he almost began to think so—but never quite.

"You said last night that your parents were dead," Forster continued. "Would you mind telling me a little about them?"

"Not at all."

But she just sat drinking her martini in silence for several moments while the traffic noises rose faintly from Fifth Avenue. Forster waited, feeling the two, long-dead, elder Berensteins begin to stir somewhere, and wondering what new lies Melissa was about to create to dispose of them.

"My father killed himself." She said it at last without change in either her voice or expression. "He was a Holocaust survivor. He managed to live through five years of the most indescribable horror, of the most unbelievable hell, then decided to die in what he considered to be the most wonderful country on earth. Imagine. He left my mother and me a note of apology. My mother never did survive it. She couldn't. I could."

Forster felt as though a rock had entered his throat and lodged there. He had never expected the truth.

Melissa looked at him. "Had you known I was Jewish?"

"No," he lied.

"I'm not an observant Jew. I haven't been inside a synagogue since my parents died. But I see with Jewish eyes, think with a Jewish brain, feel with a Jewish heart. I wasn't even born at the time of the Holocaust, yet I'm unforgiving of Germany and Germans and expect to remain so until I die. My father died in this country, but it was really the Germans who killed him as surely as if he had ended up in one of their gas chambers. They left their poison sifting through his system for more than twenty years. It destroyed his resistance to pain and betrayal. Finally, he died of it."

A coldness had settled over her that was like the first thin coating of ice at the start of winter.

"For some reason," she said, "I've always had the feeling you were Jewish, too. I suppose it was the warmth you brought to your writing. Was I wrong?"

"You were right. My grandfather's name was Forstersky."

"I knew it! My mother used to say Jewish hearts have their own way of speaking to one another, of making these things known."

The fact of it seemed to please her. The coldness was gone from her eyes.

"My father hanged himself," she said tonelessly. "But he may just as well have been lynched for being a Jew. The cause and effect were the same. In my dreams, he still hangs like an empty coat in my closet."

The rock was still in Forster's throat.

A buzzer sounded somewhere in the apartment.

"It's my chicken," said Melissa.

* * *

Forster kept at it all through dinner, aware of something cold and dark circling in on itself yet seeing nothing. He felt as though he were hunting, having to be very still and at the same time set out questions like bait to bring his prey within range. Dinner was wasted on him, although the chicken contadine was tender and perfectly flavored, the salad crisp, the chablis dry, and the coffee given added punch by just a hint of Irish whiskey. Taking brandy later in the living room, the surrounding objects—the furniture, the lamps, the paintings, the several pieces of sculpture—stood about like sentries guarding against the truth.

Yet what was the truth? Under what chair, behind which vase, did it hide? Some of the questions Forster asked he already knew the answers to, but the fiction of the interview had to be maintained. Besides, it was important simply to keep her talking, to let one word, phrase, idea, inspire another and see where they might lead.

"How did you start the Olympus Fund?" he asked.

"With the money from my divorce settlement. I seemed to have an instinct for trading and a gambler's luck. In retrospect, my investments were never that brilliant. They just kept winning. At times it frightened me half to death. I was just a poor, little, Jewish, orphan girl."

"How old were you when you lost your parents?"

"Ten. Sometimes it seems a thousand years ago. Then it can feel like yesterday, and I'm bleeding again."

"Who took care of you?"

"An aunt and uncle."

"The parents of the cousin you mentioned yesterday?"

She threw him a quick look. "You *do* remember things, don't you?"

Forster was tempted to ask about the cousin, but thought better of it. "How do you feel about the current panic? What do you see ahead for us?"

"Some wild swings in the markets, but not the end of the world. The real danger would be a gridlocked global economy, so the best escape lies in faster growth abroad. Other countries are going to have to make up for their loss of exports to the U.S. market, build demand for American exports, and ease pressure on the dollar."

"Do you think we'll get that faster growth abroad?"

"We'd better. What's at issue is one of the great conflicts of our time—the collision between sovereign states and stateless economic forces. No nation marches alone anymore. Interdependence is more than a cliché."

"What's the Olympus Fund doing these days? Considering your recent record, a lot of investors are going to be very interested in where your money is going."

"I'm afraid they'll have to wait for our next reporting period to find out," Melissa said.

The light from a lamp broke in her eyes. Night made her face paler, her eyes a darker lavender.

Forster felt himself wasting time and decided on another approach. Intellectually, he was getting nowhere. He might do better with emotion. "May I ask a few questions about your father? Off the record, if that's how you want it."

"You can ask whatever you'd like. There's nothing about my father I'm ashamed of."

"Why did he kill himself?"

"Because he was sent to prison for something he didn't do, and he couldn't live with it."

"You know for certain he was innocent?"

"As well as I know anything."

"Yet there must have been evidence that said otherwise."

"It was all false."

Forster sipped his brandy and waited. He had her primed. He doubted that she could leave it alone from here. If she could, then she wouldn't be as obsessed, or maybe even as crazy, as she and her brother would have to be if they actually had dreamed up this whole insane blueprint for disaster.

"My father was treasurer of a fine, old-line investment house," she said. "Their showcase Jew. Then one day some funds turned up missing from a major account and he was the one chosen to pay for it."

"Chosen by whom?"

"His three high-class, Presbyterian bosses. They did whatever was needed to cover their own defalcation and threw him to the wolves."

"You were only ten years old. How could you possibly know something like that?"

"Because my father told me before he went to prison."

Forster saw her eyes wet with anger. He could almost smell

the salt in them. He was amazed, yet he was not amazed. She had metamorphosed her father's bank into an investment house, and the six bankers into three Presbyterian bosses, but she was totally drawn into it now. In a manner of speaking, there might even have been a little blood on the floor.

"Told you what?" Forster asked, gently leading her.

"That regardless of what I ever heard or read, regardless of what they finally did to him, he had done nothing wrong. That these men were little better than the Germans who had put him in Auschwitz, because they despised anyone not of their own kind and didn't care what they did to them." Melissa stared hard at Forster. "I'm a quarter of a century older now and I've learned to know these financial Brahmins, this ruling class in our supposedly classless society. God help me, I even married one of them. And they still make me want to weep. Do you know why? Because it's all so barefaced. They sit there in their sanctuaries of privilege and do anything they want, anything that comes into their heads between martini time and dinner because they're so contemptuous of us. And I'm sure you know who the *us* includes."

Of course, thought Forster, and knew she had to have been part of it then as surely as it was possible to know such a thing without seeing the hard evidence.

Melissa put down her drink. Sitting on the couch, she seemed buttressed for the next question, the next assault, her head up and her back straight, her arms folded tight as a locked gate.

"I'm sorry about your father," said Forster.

She shook her head impatiently. "It's ridiculous. I'm a grown woman. You'd think after all these years—"

A house phone in the foyer erupted like an alarm bell and Melissa went to answer it.

"It's my cousin," she said when she returned. "He's coming up for a moment. He's just in from Europe and has some reports I asked him to bring home." Melissa's loveliest smile shimmered about her like a harbor light. "I told Robert you're here, so he won't stay."

So it's Robert, thought Forster, and knew he was about to meet the missing Arthur Berenstein.

When the alleged cousin did appear moments later, Forster felt himself gripped by some deep authority of feeling. It was more than simply excitement. Here at last was the other half of the team, a tall, slim male replica of his sister—his eyes, face, and aura of dark-haired good looks an almost perfect match to hers. They might have been twins. In a sense, thought Forster, they were.

"Robert Bennet . . . Paul Forster," said Melissa, and the two men shook hands as she made the introduction.

"Sorry to intrude like this," said Bennet, "but I'm really delighted at the chance to meet you. I've been one of your more ardent followers for years." He showed a line of perfect teeth. "But obviously no more so than my cousin."

Forster knew Robert Bennet's name, if not his face. Bennet was a shadowy, amorphous presence on the international financial scene. There were a number of such figures about, people without specific titles or positions, who never were part of large, well-known, clearly defined organizations, who rarely were quoted in financial journals, but who nevertheless managed to establish and maintain seemingly prosperous, high-level personas that somehow generated respect in often diverse political and economic circles.

"Surely you have time for a brandy," said Forster. He poured some Remy Martin into a snifter and handed it to him. "Melissa tells me you're just back from London. How did you find the money men reacting to our troubles over there?"

"With howls of glee," said Bennet. "Like a bunch of congenital idiots enjoying a raging fire that they haven't the brains to realize is going to incinerate them along with everyone else."

Bennet peered into his brandy snifter as though it held a secret vision. "I've been around the markets for a long time, but I've never seen anything quite like this kind of turmoil. There's not even a show of support for either our equities or our currency, and that's doing as much damage as the actual selling itself. We all know it's public show that tells the world there's still order enough in the financial markets to at least make a decent display, and during these past few days in Europe I haven't seen that."

Bennet's voice was a rich instrument; it seemed to purr with its own wry blend of humors. Listening to him speak, Forster felt sure he had the charm, like Melissa, to capture anything alive. Forster wanted to hold onto him for a while, keep him talking. He in no way believed Bennet had just happened to stop by. He was there because he must have spoken to Melissa, learned that Forster was interviewing her for a magazine piece she didn't want, and stopped by to check him out for himself. Yet his easy smile and manner announced that all he aspired to were a few brief words and a quick departure.

"Then you think the fear is that dominant?" said Forster.

"Hell, you can smell it in the air. It's in everything, even the haute cuisine of the best restaurants. If it weren't so serious, it would be fascinating."

"How?"

"I keep wondering what's in the heads and guts of those trading in the markets, exploding them into turmoil, driving themselves and everyone else crazy." Bennet opened a gold case, removed a cigarette, and lit it. "Consider the rationality we normally take for granted in economics—clashes with fear, the stuff of abnormal psychology. Trained, educated judgment battles with a panicky unreasoning need to just dump everything and save oneself. Who can be sure at this point which is the right guide to buying long, selling short, or simply staying liquid? I've talked to dozens of people these past days, and come up with almost as many different answers."

"You should try talking to your cousin. She's beat everyone in calling this market's turn."

"Melissa's system of figuring the market is time-proven and simple. It's called a Ouija board."

Forster laughed. "I'm buying one first thing in the morning."

"Don't laugh," said Bennet. "The concept isn't so wild. The whole stock market is a Ouija board, pure fantasy. It gives the impression it knows something, that something is there, when nothing is there at all. It pitches the idea that money can be made without producing anything, and if that isn't illusion I don't know what is. It's modern mythology at its most basic, gushing out the image of achievement, when nothing is actually being accomplished other than the daily shifting of billions of dollars in and out of computers."

"Pay no attention to Robert," Melissa told Forster. "It's simply his regular jet-lag bitterness."

"He's not that wrong," said Forster. "Other than for the capital furnished companies on their initial stock offerings, it's often hard to see what positive contribution stock trading offers the economy. It's almost like an enormous all-night poker game in which the money keeps changing hands until the sun comes up and everyone realizes they've got to go out and get to work."

"Exactly," said Bennet. "And the big losers not only must work twice as hard to recoup their losses, but take abuse from their wives as well."

"You sound like a married poker player."

"I'm neither. I'd never risk a nickel in a card game, and the thought of having to perpetually explain my mistakes to a woman would drive me up a wall."

"Then how do you get your daily ration of pain?"

Bennet's laugh sounded younger than it had any right to sound. "I just open my eyes in the morning. The rest is easy." He considered Forster. "This is the first time Melissa has ever agreed to an interview. How did you manage it?"

"I simply told her I intended writing the piece with or without her help, so why shouldn't she have some input. Happily, your cousin is a reasonable woman."

"Also," said Melissa, "smart enough not to want to antagonize a potential critic with an important voice and a large following."

"How is it going?" Bennet asked Forster. "Have you shaken any of our family skeletons out of the closet yet?"

Forster looked at him. Cute. He thinks he's figured out the whole thing, but it's evidently not as much fun unless he lets me know he knows. "We haven't come to the part about Melissa's cousins yet."

"When you do, I hope you'll be kind. We're all human." Finishing his drink, Bennet rose. "Enough intrusion. My only excuse is that I don't often get the chance to toss around fiscal profundities with the likes of a Paul Forster. I hope we can do it again sometime soon."

"Why not?" said Forster and decided to push it. "How about lunch tomorrow? Then you can guard your skeletons personally."

Bennet suddenly appeared seamless. Forster felt himself scratching at a smooth, unmarred surface. Strong, perfect features, blow-dried hair, custom-tailored clothes—they were all of a piece—controlled. That was a word Forster felt he had never used in this context before. No thought, no act, no movement, was haphazard. His skin was like his clothes—a perfect custom job.

"I'd like that," Bennet answered. "Shall we say one o'clock at the Four Seasons? I'll take care of the reservations."

He shook Forster's hand and Melissa saw him to the door.

She returned smiling. "You certainly impressed him."

"*He* impressed *me*. He's a very attractive and appealing man." Forster couldn't resist it. "There's certainly a strong family resemblance."

"I know. For years people were sure we were brother and sister."

I'm still sure, Forster thought.

He was home shortly before midnight and called Castanzo at once. "Did you place anything at Kenniston's yet?" he asked.

"No. The ear I wanted was on another job. He'll do it tomorrow for sure."

"I need something else—fast—no later than nine in the morning. The name is Robert Bennet—double *n*, one *t*. New York residency. A full background check with possible areas of contact, knowledge of, or relationships with, one or more of the three witnesses I gave you yesterday . . . Borman, Harwith, and Stone."

"It's midnight, for Christ's sake!"

"Computers don't sleep. Neither does the FBI. Put as many people as you have to on it. Pay them double."

"Give me till tomorrow night."

"The morning, Guido. You know I don't push unless it's important. I've got a lunch date with Bennet. I can't walk in with nothing but sweat on my palms."

"I could never get paper to you by then, but maybe I can call you."

It was 8:47 A.M. when Castanzo phoned in. "You gave us some night, but here it is."

"I appreciate it."

"Appreciate, hell. Wait till you see the bill. Anyway, I've just shoved together stuff from five sources and it's still rough and out of sequence, so hang with me."

"Go ahead."

"There's all the usual background shit," said Castanzo. "Birth and school records, social security number, academic degrees, religious affiliation, and the rest. You want that now or saved for the written report?"

"Save it. Get to the job and work area."

There was the sound of paper being shuffled and soft swearing. "Okay. His only real job seems to have been with Chase Manhattan. Hired right after an M.B.A. from Princeton. First in his class, incidentally. Did international banking and investments for about four years. Posted in London, Zurich, and New York. Left Chase to go on his own—mostly financial consulting and money management. Currently calls himself Capital Value Limited. Has offices in New York, Washington, London, Paris, Basel. Good addresses and a list of multi-national clients that include some governments."

"Which governments?" Forster cut in.

"Chad—Nigeria—Israel—Nicaragua—Brazil—Iran—Saudi Arabia—"

"Okay."

"Unmarried and no discernible living family. Registered Republican. Member, the New York Athletic Club, Mamaroneck Country Club, Washington League for Planned Parenthood, Basel Masters Bridge Society." Castanzo paused and again there was the shuffling of papers. "I couldn't seem to come up with any areas of possible contact with your Borman, Harwith, and Stone group. Not through Bennet, anyway. So I cross-checked his printout against the reports on the three witnesses that just came in, and found this. Katherine Harwith is a working board member of the Washington League for Planned Parenthood, Peter Stone is on the membership committee of the Mamaroneck Country Club, and Borman is a past president of the Basel Masters Bridge Society."

Forster could feel the excitement in him racing like a motor.

7

During the early morning of June twenty-first, President Hanson met in the Oval Office with Defense Secretary Exely and Charles Maynard, director of the Central Intelligence Agency.

Just two days before, he had gone on radio and television to try to calm the American people. He assured them that the nation's economy was sound, that the wild gyrations of the stock, bond, and currency markets had little to do with the production and use of the goods and services that still remained the lifeblood of a country that had given its citizens the highest standard of living in history. The president told his fellow Americans that all the panic of these past days was in no way justified by the facts, that the American banking system was strong and solvent enough to meet any emergency, that the unfortunate scandal which had precipitated the present crisis, while undoubtedly disturbing, could in no way be considered grave enough to warrant the wholesale loss of faith it had generated.

The talk was put together with care and deliberation. The psychology of faith, fear, and panic was recognized as a major factor in the mass psychosis that seemed to be taking place. And short of putting two hundred million people on the couch, this voice of reason, offering the calming sound of rational advice, seemed the best approach.

Unfortunately, it had not been enough to soothe the roiling financial markets, and not enough to convince the American people that they had nothing to fear. For they saw more than just six of the country's most respected and powerful money lords standing in handcuffs before a judge; they saw the entire system being arraigned along with them. Their feeling was that if something was this rotten at the top, it had to be a hundred times worse down below, where it could be more easily concealed. They looked at the plunging dollar on world markets.

They saw foreigners losing confidence in the United States and pulling their money out of its banks and equities. And increasingly, their anxiety and anger began breaking loose.

In a downtown Pittsburgh bar, Chuck Kenny, a reporter for the *Pittsburgh Press*, was trying to absorb atmosphere for a story he was doing on the blue-collar response to the banking scandal and the resulting market crash and financial crisis. He had been warned by his editor that when he wrote the piece the word *panic* was to be avoided. But what he saw and heard carried a lot more controlled fury than panic. Someone had blown up copies of the six bankers' photographs, tacked them to a board, and let the crowd take turns throwing darts at them. After the president's speech, his photograph was added to the others. When the pictures finally were ripped beyond recognition, they were set afire to loud cheers. Kenny had the unpleasant feeling that if the seven men themselves had been there that evening, they might have received no better treatment.

On the sidewalk in front of Levinson's Furniture Store in Chicago's Loop, Tom Kominski sat in a brand-new, red leather armchair, which he had bought at the store two days ago. He had just tried unsuccessfully to return the chair because he had been laid off that afternoon with fifty other mill workers and felt he no longer could afford to sit in such comfort and luxury. When the police arrived to physically remove him as a public nuisance, he quietly got up, raised the big chair over his head, and sent it crashing through Levinson's plate-glass window. "Send the bill to those fucking bankers," he told Levinson. It took four cops ten minutes to subdue him enough to finally get him into a patrol car.

In a predominantly Hispanic neighborhood of Miami, a crowd of angry Cubans surrounded and started beating two United States marshals who were evicting Estaban Ramirez, his wife, his mother, and two children from their apartment for nonpayment of rent. The Ramirezes' rent had not been paid for three months and had nothing to do with the current fiscal crisis, but the crowd either didn't know or didn't care about that. From everything they had been hearing, reading, and seeing on television for the past eight days, they were sure that whatever future they had in America was about to be taken from them—and the Ramirez family's eviction was visible proof that their feared losses had already started. By the time the Miami police arrived in sufficient force to restore order, the two marshals lay beaten and stomped unconscious, a dozen stores had been looted, and clusters of cars were burning in the streets.

In the Washington, D.C. headquarters of the International Brotherhood of Teamsters, Chauffeurs, Warehousemen and Helpers of America, Jim Kennedy, the general president, was fighting a losing battle to keep a hastily called emergency meeting of his steering committee from deteriorating into a shouting match. Rumor had it that a nationwide group of major industrial corporations, using the current economic crisis as a powerful persuading force, were about to demand unprecedented wage and benefit concessions in a series of contract talks that were due to start in less than a month. With 745 locals and close to two million members spread across the country, the union's very size made it a perfect target for a combination of political pressure and employer abuse. Kennedy had already been spoken to off the record by the secretary of labor, who hoped that in this time of crisis, the Teamsters would lead the way in making whatever sacrifices might be necessary to preserve the national welfare. To Kennedy, it was bad either way for the union. If they made the concessions, they would be giving up five years of hard-won progress, and the rank and file would be screaming for their heads. If they stood firm and finally pulled two million men out, paralyzing the whole goddamned country, they would be a gang of traitors, mobsters, and worse. Sonofabitch, he thought as his committee swore and shouted all the same arguments at one another, it's a no-win, fucking deal.

In a suburban shopping mall in Shaker Heights, Ohio, Tom Lincoln led a line of five pickets marching back and forth in front of the First Cleveland Savings Bank. The demonstrators wore blue armbands marked with the red double-headed eagle of the American Renaissance Party and carried signs accusing the First Cleveland and all American banks of being controlled by an international conspiracy of Jews. They also carried other signs that said JEWS! NOT THE SIX BANKERS! JEWS! The watching crowd, mostly Jewish, shouted insults at the pickets. Lincoln waited for the first signs of the violence he was sure would come. It was why the pickets were there, why they had chosen a Jewish neighborhood for their demonstration, why ten more of their group were doing the same thing at this moment in ten different cities. Then someone tripped Lincoln, and he fell to the pavement and was jumped on. Angry hands groped for the pickets' signs, found them, tore them to shreds. All the pickets were fighting now. Giving and taking punishment was their métier, and it was based on an inviolate set of rules. The picket line was a free-fire zone. The demonstrators, with the odds heavily against them, were always beaten first. If they were tough enough, they survived and got to clobber a few themselves. Lincoln survived. When the police, reporters, and photographers came, he made sure that he and the other pickets got the right exposure, made the right statements about the six bankers and the Jewish conspiracy. Millions would read it, hear it on the radio, see it on television. All they finally would remember was that Jews were behind everything.

The president struggled to deal with this growing calamity, this sudden nightmare that had sprung from nowhere and stubbornly refused to disappear with the daylight. He had stopped counting the billions in unsupported paper that the Federal Reserve, under his direct orders, was stacking like sandbags to prop up America's tottering T-bills and currency. Why bother to count? Regardless of numbers, it had to continue.

Despite cynics, Hanson believed there was more than just self-seeking and partisan politics in Washington. America was still the country that was looked to and depended upon in time of need. No walls or barbed wire kept its people in. Its currency had to be supported under any conditions.

Still, Hanson was a pragmatist. How else, after all, had he become president? Survival depended upon it. And if you wanted to survive, you made contingency plans.

"As we see it at this point, Mr. President," Defense Secretary Exely was saying, "there's no question but that our most logical targets would be Libya, Syria, or Iran. All three are in the business of training and exporting terrorists. All have given us plenty of reason to take action."

"When must we decide which one it will be?" asked Hanson.

"We're meeting with the Israelis at the State Department later today," said the CIA chief. "We should have all the required information for you by then."

The president nodded. He appeared casual, but he still couldn't quite believe he really was having this discussion. He felt stifled, as if the valves of his heart were not closing and the blood was backing up into his lungs. This was naked military action that was being talked about. Exely and Maynard kept assuring him it would be controlled and limited, but he was not a fool. Once something like this got started, control became a capricious thing, while limitations could turn darkly arbitrary. Nevertheless, Hanson was seriously considering it. Indeed, the operation already had taken on a strong measure of solidity by simply being granted the code name Falcon.

"What the final decision will hinge on," said Maynard, "is logistics for us and the proper intelligence situation for the Israelis. We're going to have to be able to move a carrier task force to within striking distance of our primary target area, and the Mossad must have enough long-term, undercover agents in place and functioning there to avoid having to introduce new people at the last moment."

"Give me details," Hanson told the CIA director.

"In essence, the operation will be triggered by the alleged terrorist bombings of American consulates and embassies in half a dozen Middle Eastern cities. The bombings will be set up to occur within hours of one another in what will give the impression of being a coordinated attack by Arab terrorists on the American presence in that area."

"What about casualties?" Hanson's throat suddenly was dry. "When bombs explode people die. And since these bombs are going to explode in American installations, the dead are going to be American men and women. And, God help us, maybe children."

"We hope to keep the casualties to a minimum, Mr. President."

"What the hell does that mean?"

"It means that although the damage will be kept as light as possible, a certain number of dead and wounded are still unavoidable." Maynard looked evenly at the president. "I might even say they'll be necessary. In a practical sense our losses must raise such an outcry that our ensuing action by the Seventh Fleet will meet little opposition at home."

Dear Lord, thought Hanson. Just hearing the words created a sudden burning inside his body. He felt as though he had swallowed a lethal dose of poison and was waiting for it to finish him. Yet he kept his reaction carefully hidden as he faced the

two men who had step by step actually brought him to the point
of planning to murder his own people. There were those who
believed humane feelings of that sort had no place in the emotional makeup of a national leader, that they could only be a
handicap when hard, practical judgments were to be made. And
perhaps they were right.

"Go on," he told the CIA chief, who was watching him
closely, still trying to measure his response to the briefing.

"The Israeli secret service will, of course, handle the actual
demolition work. The Mossad will also create, and later discover and publicly reveal, indisputable evidence that the attacks
were the work of terrorists based and trained in Libya, Syria, or
Iran, and under the direct orders of its leaders. Additionally, the
Israeli agents will guarantee that several bodies of known, clearly
identifiable terrorists will be found at the bombing sights."
Maynard smiled. "Glorious suicides in the holy service of Is-
lam."

He's enjoying this, thought Hanson, he's actually taking pleasure in planning this whole terrible thing. Which is precisely
the quality that makes him so good at his job, and me so often
bad at mine.

"What we come down to now, Mr. President," said the secretary of defense, "is the question of timing. We have to set the
clock in motion. We need specific dates."

"Understand. I'm still not committed to this. If I go with it
at all, it's only because every other recourse has failed."

"We all feel the same way, Mr. President. But we still need
a target date."

Hanson took a small personal calendar out of his desk drawer.
Early that morning he had drawn a bright red line across June
twenty-eighth, which lay just seven days ahead and was the arbitrary date his economic advisers had chosen as the possible
beginning of what they termed a full-scale financial alert. They
felt that if there was no promise in sight of a substantial turna-
round in the markets by this date, that if the pressure on the
dollar and the flight of funds out of the country did not show
signs of abating, then the United States could well be facing the
worst financial disaster in history, a collapse that would take one
interdependent nation after another down with it, and lead finally to a world out of economic control, perched on the edge
of randomness. It was an unthinkable prospect, yet Hanson had

thought about it. Later, needing desperately to be alone, he had taken refuge in the bathroom, gazed into the mirror, and been struck by the overwhelming sadness he saw reflected in his eyes. This grave shell, this poor, dark response to the fate of being human. Or was it merely his response to being president?

"June twenty-eighth," he told Exely and Maynard. "If we haven't started seeing some signs of recovery by June twenty-eighth, you can plan on going ahead with Falcon."

Forster arrived outside the entrance to the Four Seasons moments before his one o'clock appointment with Robert Bennet.

"Mr. Forster?"

He turned and found himself looking at what appeared to be a six-and-a-half-foot tackle in a chauffeur's uniform.

"Mr. Bennet is waiting over here, sir."

Forster saw a gray limousine parked at the curb. The windows were of dark, tinted glass, so it was impossible to see inside. But as the chauffeur opened the rear door, Robert Bennet's voice cheerily called, "Hi, Paul. Come on in."

The perfect, even teeth gleamed as Bennet shook Forster's hand. "I hope you don't mind, but I presumed to change the plans. I felt this would give us more privacy than a restaurant. It's roomy and comfortably air conditioned. And from what Mellie tells me about your taste in food, you'll probably enjoy the hot pastrami sandwiches I picked up at the Carnegie Deli."

Forster laughed. "You do have a certain indisputable style."

The dove-gray limousine's interior was plush, with a small refrigerator, a fully stocked bar, individually anchored tray-tables, and a soundproof, glass partition separating the passenger area from the chauffeur. The pastrami sandwiches were laid out on good china; sour tomatoes sat sliced and moist on their plates.

"What would you like to drink?" asked Bennet. "Martini? Bourbon? A soft drink? Everyone has different tastes when it comes to their pastrami. Personally, I prefer straight cream soda with mine."

"I'm with you."

"Good. We think the same on the basics."

The limousine glided smoothly away from the curb and headed east. Bennet poured their drinks and handed one to Forster.

"For the past few hours I've been looking forward to seeing

you with the excitement I usually reserve for a new woman," he said, "and I happen to be a confirmed heterosexual." Bennet chuckled. "The fact is, Paul, ever since I called Minnie Abelman this morning and learned you'd spoken to her just four days ago, I've been in something of a fever. Not an unpleasant one, mind you, but a fever nonetheless. It probably was pretty close to the way you must have felt when I walked into Mellie's place last night, and you suddenly knew you were face to face with your missing Arthur Berenstein."

Forster could feel his heart beating. He was about to pretend he had no idea what Bennet was talking about, but stopped himself. It was much too late for that. Instead, he sipped his cream soda.

"What made you call Minnie?" he asked.

"Part instinct, part reason, part my long-conditioned sense of suspicion. Your sudden strong interest in Mellie began it, of course. Not that Mellie isn't worthy of such interest in herself. But when I combined that with your well-known relationship with Wendell Norton, I decided it was worth a call."

Bennet's smoothly attractive face was a surprise to Forster at that moment. Instead of showing anger or concern; it was pleased, interested, aglow with its own assortment of secret amusements.

"You're the only one who had sense enough to make any connection at all with the Malcolm Commission," he said. "But, of course, you were the only one who was interested enough to investigate. Everyone else simply assumed all six were guilty, even their own lawyers. And if Norton wasn't such a good friend, if you didn't know him so well, I'm certain you too would have assumed they were guilty as charged. True?"

"Probably," said Forster dully.

They were on the FDR Drive now, heading north. To their right, the East River and Roosevelt Island slid past in a pale, midday haze. Forster felt like a fox trapped in a bog while hounds bayed all around. When had he suddenly become the fox? Until a moment ago, he was sure he had been the lead hound.

"I'm impressed with all you've done, all you've found out," said Bennet. "But only as an abstract exercise. Because in every practical sense, you're not going to be able to change a thing. Your friend Wendell Norton will still be brought to trial, the evidence against him will still be complete and incontrovertible.

He and his friends will still be convicted of insider trading as charged, and they'll still spend their prescribed, well-deserved terms in jail.''

''How can you call going to prison for something they didn't do, well deserved?''

Bennet spent a moment absorbed with his sandwich. ''Who said it was something they didn't do? Certainly not I. And certainly not the SEC, not the U.S. Attorney's office, not the world's financial markets, and not a single person I've spoken to. So what makes *you* think those six men are innocent? Do you know something the rest of us don't?''

''I thought for a moment you were going to be honest.''

''Honest? Did you also think I was going to be a fool? As far as I'm concerned those men are guilty as charged. Which doesn't necessarily mean I wouldn't be interested in hearing whatever evidence you may think you have to the contrary.''

Of course he'd be interested, thought Forster, and wished he did have something more solid on him than just a few open lines of conjecture. Still, Bennet didn't know what he had.

They rode in silence. The sun reflected off the Harlem River on one side of the car and rows of apartment windows on the other. Bits of light glittered from surrounding cars. Pools of silver lay like water on the road ahead.

''I'll tell you something that may sound insane,'' said Bennet. ''After I learned of your interest in Mellie—after I met you in person yesterday—after I spent a mostly sleepless night examining every facet of who and what you were—I actually found myself hoping my suspicions that you were sniffing around after us would be justified when I called Minnie Abelman this morning.''

''Why?''

''Because I felt it would add something special for both Mellie and me.''

''How?''

''I'm not really sure. Maybe it's because we'd spent more than twenty years obsessed with a fixed idea that we'd finally managed to pull off and not a soul knew about it.''

Bennet's smile mellowed his face to an all-embracing warmth, as if with even so vague an admission finally made, he and Forster had become blood brothers. ''Maybe it's because I'm just human enough to be so proud of what we'd accomplished, that I suddenly felt cheated because it couldn't be shared."

"You're *proud*?" said Forster flatly. "Of what? Of ruining the country?"

"*I'm* not ruining the country. If the country's being ruined, it's ruining itself, with its fiscal excesses, its stupidities, its raising of six venal bigots to positions of power and influence." Bennet picked up a phone and told the chauffeur to start back. "Have you spoken to those men lately?" he asked Forster.

"What do you mean?"

"I mean have you sat down with them?"

"No. But we've arranged to meet tomorrow."

Bennet took several moments, as though his thoughts were suddenly a tremendous weight on his will. The limousine exited the expressway at Yonkers, circled around to the southbound entrance, and started back toward Manhattan.

"When you do talk to them," Bennet said, "please do us all a favor. Ask what happened to David Berenstein twenty-three years ago. Then enter them through their eyes and test their responses. Sniff them with your heart. Feel them moving inside you. You'll find their meanness in your stomach, their dirty thinking in your blood. Then maybe you'll squeeze out a hint of what I'm talking about."

They were like two hunters, each tracking the other, in the midnight of some jungle. But when Bennet next spoke, his voice was warm and genial.

"I have tickets to a new production of *Uncle Vanya* at Lincoln Center tomorrow night. I was hoping you and Mellie might join me."

Forster looked at Bennet as though he were his first sighting of some exotic new species. "Are you serious?"

"Absolutely."

"Considering what you now know, why would you want to spend any sort of social evening with me?"

"Because I like and respect you. Because I want time to show you how wrong you are about certain things, including those six men."

"Even if I consider you and Melissa dangerous psychopaths who belong in jail?"

Bennet laughed. "You'll change your mind when you learn more."

"How does Melissa feel about seeing me at this point?"

"No differently than I."

Forster finished his soda and set down the glass. Obviously they considered it best to keep a close watch on him. Still, it worked both ways. He could watch the watchers. Yet how amazing, he thought, and was intrigued by the fact that of the approximately five billion human beings currently in existence, each a tiny microcosmos, each infinitely precious to him or herself, he had somehow managed to stumble over these two.

He called Melissa the moment he reached his office.

"So now you know all about me," he said.

There was silence at the other end. Then she said, "And you know all about me."

"No. Not everything." But I will, he thought.

"Robert wasn't really surprised," she said. "He pretty much expected it when I told him about the interview. Yet I expected nothing. I seem to be congenitally naïve about such things."

Forster didn't believe it for a minute. "If you can accept the new conditions, I'd still like to go on with the article."

"Why? My allegedly brilliant market timing is no longer a mystery to you. And you can't print unproven libelous allegations without my suing your magazine for at least a hundred million. So I think we'd best bury that."

"And bury me right along with it?"

"I admit that was my initial reaction. I felt betrayed. I know I had no logical right to such feelings, but emotion has nothing to do with logic."

"Now you no longer want to shoot me?"

"Less frequently, anyway. Only every other half hour. In between, logic prevails."

"What does logic say?"

"That you did what you felt you had to; just as Robert and I did. That you're as warm and decent a man as I've always sensed you to be. That despite your intentions, you're really no threat to Robert and me."

"You know I'll still be trying, Melissa."

"Yes."

"So?"

Her sigh came softly over the wire. "So Robert would like us all to go on trying to be friends."

"Why?"

"He feels an instinctive empathy toward you. He feels that if we spend time together, that if you have a chance to know more about us personally, as well as about the facts, you'll feel differently about the whole situation."

"Is that how you feel too?"

"I'm afraid I'm less hopeful than Robert. But I'm willing to give it a try," Melissa paused. "Are you?"

Forster took a deep breath and relaxed in his chair. His desk seemed strangely empty, his office colorless and airless. Melissa's voice came into the room like a fire into a closet.

"Why not?" he said.

Annie phoned a short while later.

"This is a concern and charity call," she said. "Concern that you're running yourself into the ground with all your crisis-worry, pressure, and work. Charity, in that I'm willing to donate a home-cooked, full-course Thai dinner to help keep you alive and performing."

"Why Thai?"

"Because it's the most trendy food currently available. And you know me and trendy."

"Of course," he said and remembered another old source of bickering—Annie's almost compulsive need to try the latest in anything, be it food, clothing, music, dance, theater, travel. While he, naturally, was equally compulsive about sticking to the time-worn grooves of the old and familiar. It suddenly seemed an inane thing to fight about, yet he had called her foolish, flighty and stupidly superficial over it, while she had used words like stubborn, dull, and tiresome.

"You'll love it," she told him.

This time he wasn't calling her anything.

Annie fed him his Thai dinner by candlelight. Forster finished everything on his plate like an obedient child. He told Annie about having met Robert Bennet and about their movable feast that afternoon. If I'm not drinking and talking, he thought, I seem to be eating and talking. Annie listened carefully. The candlelight revealed the deep concern she obviously was feeling.

"Why are you so worried?" Forster asked.

"Because *you* don't seem to be."

"I'm being careful. It's a lot more practical than simply worrying."

She wasn't soothed. "These are two obviously clever, desperate, dangerous people, Paulie. They know what you're after now. They could kill you if they felt themselves, and what they're doing, threatened."

"You're way off. They may be a little obsessed and crazy, but they're not killers. If you met Melissa and Robert, if you knew them as I do, you'd understand what I mean."

Annie lit one of Forster's cigarettes and watched the smoke rise. "Then maybe I should meet and get to know them."

"Sure."

"Why not? I may even be of help."

"How?"

"By bringing in another pair of eyes and ears—by providing fresh insights, new perceptions. There are two of them and only one of you. I might be able to even the odds a little. You know how well I do with people. I have an instinct for what they're feeling, for what's going on inside them. It's why I've done so well with the agency."

"Then stick to the agency," he said. "This is a long way from the travel business."

"The more I think about it, the more I—"

"Forget it, Annie!"

She glowed with sudden anger. "What's the matter? Don't you think I can be trusted with something as important as this? Don't you think I'm sensitive or intelligent enough not to compromise a delicate situation?"

Forster realized too late how it was going to be. Another old scab being picked at, he thought, and saw the dynamics of a hundred dimly remembered arguments leaking out. "Why must you always take these things so personally?"

"Because that's the way you always intend them. It's never the idea or the situation you reject, it's always *me*. Think about it."

Forster did. He offered no response.

Sensing a momentary advantage, Annie said, "Now think about this. The three of you will be at Lincoln Center tomorrow evening. Would it be so terrible if I accidentally ran into you during intermission and was introduced to Melissa and Robert? I'd smile. I'd be charming. I'd talk until the curtain went up.

And that would be the end of it. What harm can you see in that?"

"None," he admitted. "But I can't see any good coming from it either."

"Maybe none will. But at least I'll have met and spoken with them. At least I'll be able to have a little more understanding of what you're dealing with. And who knows? I may even pick up some small bit you've missed."

Forster looked at her. "It's that important to you?"

"Yes."

"Why?"

"Because this whole thing is so obsessively important to *you*. And I can't stand not having some part in it."

"All right. Then we'll do it."

It took Annie a long moment to respond. When she did, she appeared moved. "I think that's the first time you've ever done that."

"Done what?"

"Agreed to something simply to please me—simply because I asked it."

The five bankers were assembled in Forster's living room at ten o'clock the next morning.

"Gentlemen," he said, "thank you for coming."

Forster had considered using a hotel suite or a conference room at the magazine for the meeting, but the informality of his home seemed best suited to his purpose. The indicted bankers sat facing him in a loose semicircle. Citibank's Tom Stanton was at his immediate left, followed by Alfred Loomis of the Bank of America, Hank Ridgeway, chairman of Manufacturers Hanover, and Peter Farnham and Bill Boyer, the respective heads of Chase Manhattan and the First National Bank of Chicago. *Former* heads, Forster reminded himself.

These were men, he thought, who had held dominion over small empires, traveled exclusively by limousine and corporate jet, were sought after and entertained by presidents, prime ministers, and ruling potentates. They were—or had been until nine days ago—the new royalty. And they all had agreed, without question, to his request to be here this morning. Why? Because he had become their single hope of avoiding disgrace and prison.

"Getting right to it, gentlemen," said Forster, "what I'd most like to discuss this morning is David Berenstein."

He paused to see what effect, if any, the name would have. There was nothing dramatic, of course. These were all perennial high-stakes players in a world-class poker game. What they really thought or felt was rarely visible. But what Forster did see was a slight raising of brows, several vague frowns, a hint of genuine puzzlement, and a single blank stare.

"Is there anyone here who doesn't remember who David Berenstein was?" he asked, then sat listening to a full fifteen seconds of silence.

It was Ridgeway who finally spoke. "I'm a little perplexed, Paul. I remember who Berenstein was, but I don't see what connection he could have to the subject at hand."

"I'm coming to that," said Forster. "It all has to do with the Malcolm Commission, which is the only thing I've been able to find that in any way connects the five of you and Wendell Norton together. And since Berenstein's imprisonment and death were direct results of the Commission's work, I was hoping one of you might know of a possible connection."

Peter Farnham grunted and lit a fresh cigar in a small cloud of smoke. "What could there be to know? Berenstein embezzled some client funds, he was sent to prison, and he hanged himself. That's all there is."

Forster nodded agreeably. It was Farnham whom Castanzo's investigative report had identified as having possible long-term syndicate connections. "If I'm not mistaken, Pete, wasn't it you who originally hired Berenstein for Chase?"

"That's correct. One of the many outstanding decisions for which I've since become famous."

No one appeared remotely amused.

Tom Stanton said, "That entire Berenstein affair was terribly sad. I'm sure it affected us all deeply. I know it did me. It was the only time in my life that I've felt responsible for someone's death."

Boyer waved an impatient hand. "Come on, Tom. The man committed suicide. You can hardly blame yourself for that."

"Maybe not literally," said Stanton. "But I did help send him to prison." He sat studying his hands, a sober, dark-eyed man who seemed, to Forster, to have aged ten years in the seven days since he saw him in court.

"Prison was where Berenstein belonged," said Alfred Loomis. "He was given a fair trial and convicted. He was a crook. And as far as I'm concerned that was the end of it."

Loomis, a spare, almost gaunt man whose face held much controlled anger, turned to Forster. A general could have been related to that face, thought Forster, and recalled him as the one who had been tapped as the group's closet anti-Semite. "What's the tie-in here, Paul?" asked Loomis. "You obviously didn't bring up the Berenstein case just to make conversation. Are we to assume you think there's some relationship between Berenstein and our indictment?"

"Yes."

"Do you have any proof of this?" asked Farnham.

"Not a shred," said Forster. Which was true as far as it went. The existence of Robert and Melissa hardly constituted evidence. And Forster had no intention of bringing them up at this point.

Farnham blew smoke. "Then what's your line of reasoning?"

"My line of reasoning is that I have no other. Unless one of you knows something you haven't told me."

Forster waited for an answer he didn't really expect. Enter them through their eyes and test their responses, Robert Bennet had said. But it was not that simple. They were not simple men, these five gold threads in the tapestry of American wealth.

"I'll be honest," Forster said. "Despite my friendship with Wendell and long association with all of you, I found it hard to believe in your innocence after I saw the evidence against you. The only thing that put some doubt in my mind was that all six of you have served together on the Malcolm Commission. That's what convinced me to take on this investigation."

"Why?" asked Ridgeway.

"Because I don't believe in coincidence. Certainly not in something like this. So if you were set up, I figured it had to stem from your work on the Commission. And since Alfred Kent and David Berenstein were the only two who ended up in prison because of you, they're the ones I've been checking out."

"Then what about Kent?" said Loomis.

"I've spoken to him. He's now a successful businessman in Chicago. He lacks the necessary bitterness and sense of tragedy to think of something like this. He's too sane, too satisfied with what he owns, too worried about what your indictments and the resulting panic are doing to his business. Whoever created and executed a plan like this, has to be both brilliant and a trifle insane.''

"And Berenstein is dead," said Ridgeway.

"Yes. But according to the old news accounts he did have a son and daughter."

"If I remember correctly," said Stanton, "they were just children."

"They wouldn't be children any more, Tom," Forster told him.

Stanton peered quizzically at Forster. He was a man with thin hair combed straight back and narrow eyes that gave him the look of an angry ferret. "Then what you're in effect telling us, is that Berenstein's two grown children, after waiting for twenty-three years, suddenly had the means and ability to invest more than three hundred million dollars to avenge the imprisonment of a convicted embezzler. Would you call that a reasonably correct assessment of what you're saying?" His tone was polite, but mocking.

"Yes," said Forster. "But the convicted embezzler happened to be their father, whom they loved dearly and believed to be innocent with the blind, unswerving intensity of a permanent fixation."

"As I'm sure any children would," said Farnham. "As I'm sure we all hope *our* children believe *we're* innocent."

Forster nodded. "Except that we're not talking about just *any* children. We're talking about two tragically orphaned kids who ran away from one foster home after the other—who finally disappeared from sight forever as teenagers—who took on whole new identities complete with birth records, social security numbers, and educational backgrounds, and who reappeared almost twenty years later as world-class financial consultants with possible connecting links to the three witnesses whose sworn testimony currently represents the heart of the government's case against each of you."

The room was silent and the air hung heavy. Breathing it, Forster had the feeling it suddenly was polluted. It was more than just the cigar and cigarette smoke, more than the steadily brewing coffee in its big, electric pot. At that moment he might have been sitting in the soiled backroom of a century-old police station after a hundred years of thieves, pimps, whores, and murderers had passed through it, leaving nothing clean or pure behind. All five men, Forster noted, were staring at him with a fine mix of responses that ranged all the way from utter disbelief to suddenly burgeoning hope. He sat there, quietly waiting them out.

Tom Stanton said, "You stated this last as though it were factual."

"It is."

"You actually know who these two people are?"

"Yes."

"Good Lord!" said Stanton, which was about as close to an expression of religiosity as he had come in thirty years.

"You're incredible, Paul," said Farnham. "Wendell said that if anyone could get us out of this mess, it would be you. I don't know how you dug this up, but we're certainly grateful."

Loomis and Ridgeway broke into spontaneous applause and the others joined in. The humors of their relief, joy, gratitude, flowed. It enveloped Forster in its tide.

"You're celebrating prematurely," he said. "As I mentioned earlier, I still haven't a shred of proof. That's what I'm working on now, and that's why I've been asking you about David Berenstein. Are you sure there's nothing you might be able to add to what I already know from reading old news accounts of the case?"

Again, Forster waited for replies he didn't really anticipate. Which made him wonder why he even bothered asking. Unless it was Bennet and Melissa unconsciously prodding him into dead-end areas that offered no hope of reward. Indeed, that in itself began to irritate him to the point where he had to shake them off like a pair of intruding dybbuks. Beat it, he told them. Go attach yourselves to somebody else.

Chase Manhattan's Farnham answered, "The whole Berenstein affair was really nothing more than a straightforward case of misappropriation of funds by a bank official. Unfortunately, it happens all too often in the banking business, where great amounts of cash, personal need, and temptation tend to go hand in hand. What made Berenstein's case different was the double tragedy of his suicide and his having been a Holocaust survivor. We were all affected by it." Farnham studied the gray ash at the tip of his cigar. A vein in his temple pulsed. "Being the one who hired him for Chase, I was probably more affected than anyone else. To be frank, it was a time when not many Jews or other minorities held positions of trust in the banking industry, and I was trying my best to correct that. It was sad for everyone, but was, of course, the worst of all possible tragedies for Berenstein's family. I know his wife died shortly after his suicide, but I've often wondered what became of his two children. What a bitter irony that a mad, misguided need for vengeance should have somehow precipitated our present calamity."

"You mentioned a change in identity," Boyer said to Forster. "Since you said they're involved in finance, would we perhaps know them under their new names?"

"It's possible."

"You're not going to tell us who they are?"

"You'll know that when I have the evidence I need, not before."

"It's *our* lives that are at stake," said Loomis. "Surely you can trust *us*."

"It's less a question of trust than of loose tongues. You're all too involved not to be tempted to tell your wives, children, or lawyers. And I can't risk having everything blown by a careless word reaching a wrong ear." Forster lifted the percolator and poured some coffee. "Too, there's a lot more at stake here than your own lives. There's the country's life as well."

That much, he believed.

Half an hour after the five bankers had gone, Guido Castanzo picked up Forster two blocks from his apartment and headed north along Riverside Drive.

"The bugs you wanted planted in the Kenniston woman's apartment were put in yesterday," said the ex-FBI agent. "Three hours later, every one was swept out clean—telephones included. And I had my best man on it."

"She's a smart lady," Forster sighed.

"She's certainly not a very trusting lady. Do you want me to try again?"

"Don't bother. Since she knows where I stand, there's no point."

Castanzo took an envelope from his jacket pocket and tossed it in Forster's lap. "Here are your reports on Borman, Harwith, and Stone. Other than for those tie-ins with Bennet I gave you the other night, they seem fairly routine to me. But you never can tell about these things. You might find significance in details I don't know anything about. Anyway, I hope they're what you're looking for.''

Forster considered the plain manila envelope without opening it. After a moment he slid it into his pocket. His meeting with the indicted bankers had left him strangely depressed. Or maybe it wasn't so strange. All that sad, concentrated business about David Berenstein; all that muddled helplessness from the principal owners of the republic. These financial lords were not only the primary intelligence of a monolithic establishment, they were its fusion, the cement holding it together. They interlocked with other bankers, communicating in their own unique language. Now the cement was crumbling and the single massive structure was turning into a Tower of Babel. It was enough to depress anyone.

''I've got to move faster on this,'' he told Castanzo. ''I feel as though I'm spinning my wheels. I think I'd better let you tap their home phones.''

''Borman, Harwith, and Stone?''

Forster nodded. ''I should have had you do it sooner. If they're talking to one another, I want to know what they're saying.''

He looked across the Hudson, squinting at the sky over the New Jersey shore. It had been cloudy all day, but a streak of late sun had broken through, turning buildings pale orange.

''And while you're at it,'' Forster said, ''let's go for broke. Give me bugs on the six bankers as well.''

Castanzo glanced curiously at him as he drove. ''What do you suddenly expect from *them*?''

''If I knew that, I wouldn't need the bugs.''

Forster showered and dressed for the evening, then settled into a comfortable chair with a two-olive martini and Castanzo's three reports.

Here are your Three Graces—wrote the private investigator in the familiar type of his old Royal portable—to be taken straight or with tonic added according to taste.

Forthwith, Alec Borman—

Middle-level career banker and international monetarist with usual obligatory lust for money. Came up through various departments of equally greedy Swiss banking system.

Lived in Basel for most of exceedingly dull life—other than for succession of overweight mistresses and high-stakes duplicate bridge forays—where he worked for Bank Zeitung, a parent organization of Bahamian bank, where he's currently employed. Or *was* employed before confessing sins in Great Banking Scandal. As mentioned on phone, was member and past president of Basel Masters Bridge Society, which Robert Bennet joined five years ago. Now living with wife in house in Old Brookville, Long Island, provided by federal government at taxpayers' expense while waiting to lie under oath for U.S. Attorney. Has two bovine daughters—brown eyed and large uddered—living in Switzerland to whose support he contributes monthly. Transferred to Bank Zeitung's Bahamian subsidiary just three months before six bankers opened up secret, code-named accounts at that branch and made him account executive. Smells right there in case you're asleep and didn't notice. More stink in his having requested transfer himself, claiming wife's worsening arthritis—*what arthritis*? Medical records show her healthy as her two cow daughters—made it imperative she live in warm climate.

Another fishy bit. Robert Bennet's company, Capital Value Limited, not only has one of its four offices in Basel, but regularly does business with Bank Zeitung's stock-trading division, which for years was managed by Alec Borman.

On to Katherine Harwith—

Forty-eight-year-old unmarried lady. Worked for Wendell Norton, in and out of bed, for eighteen years with unswerving devotion. Squeezed herself into all aspects of his life but always with discretion. Never saw other men. Ran Norton's office and affairs with total efficiency and toughness. Could be hard lady.

Deeply affected by damaging testimony she gave against former lover and employer. Seems to have gone into virtual seclusion. Provided SEC with mountain of corroborating details—records of phone calls made by Norton to his five coconspirators—records of phone calls to Alec Borman—records of meetings held with bankers—records of meetings held with Borman in Bahamas—always day trips. Provided copies of coded correspondence with other alleged conspirators. When decoded, gave further documentation of bankers' illegal activities. Really stuck it to the guy. Some loving lady. Enough to make a man faithful to his wife. As per our phone conversation, was working board member of Washington League for Planned Parenthood along with your Robert Bennet. Also served on fund-raising committee that Bennet chaired. Good connection there. Harwith additionally set up and maintained close associations with executive assistants to Norton's five coconspirators. Important. It gave her informal record of everything the five biggies were doing. Brother! Hell really hath no greater fury—

And so, Peter Stone—

Real smart-ass, wise apple. Not even a mother could love this one. SEC lawyer whose computer checks first uncovered evidence of insider trading by six bankers—

Forster skimmed over several paragraphs of material he previously had been given by Frank Reilly, Stone's boss. Then he began reading again.

Hot-shot prick was Law Review at Yale, clerked for Supreme Court Justice Emerson, then went on to join top Wall Street law firm of Pritchard, Kelly, Deever. Starting salary seventy thousand. You could vomit, right? Now get this. Quit his job at Pritchard four years ago—then making a hundred and ten thousand per—to join the SEC's investigative division at a fucking forty-five thousand. Reason for this on employment application was the pure bullshit that he was more interested in performing worthwhile public service than in getting rich. The great bit here is that Stone joined the SEC less than two months before first of six bankers' alleged insider trades was carried out. Again, as per phone regarding Bennet—Stone on membership committee of Mamaroneck Country Club, which Bennet joined five years ago. Timing in all cases perfect. You're on track. Stay there.

Guido

Forster had finished his martini but was still brooding over Castanzo's reports, when the doorman rang up from the lobby to announce the arrival of Robert Bennet's limousine.

On the western rim of America, in the sea-coast town of Mission Hills, Irwin Tyler sat at the window of the single-room efficiency he shared with his wife and watched the predawn fog roll in from the Pacific. It was his eighty-sixth birthday, and the remains of his mostly uneaten cake still stood on the table, its single bright blue candle mocking and tragic.

When, he thought, . . . when did I suddenly get so old?

The pink, neon sign of the Palm Grove Apartments filtered into the room, its bright color looking ridiculously cheerful on the drab, cheerless walls. Patches of pink lit the combination kitchen-bedroom-living room, which had been the only home the couple had known for years, touched Mary Tyler's sleeping face, drifted among the potted plants, and settled, finally, on the collection of pain killers that had become as much a part of Mary's daily life as her rasping breath.

Tyler listened to her labored breathing. Then he slowly rose, went over to his wife's bed, and stood staring down at her. Not even in sleep did the pain leave her face; it was too deeply etched. Sometimes, coming upon her unexpectedly, his mind unprepared, there were flashing moments when she might have been nothing more than an elderly stranger. Her skin was wrinkled, her eyes faded, her bones jagged and frail.

Mary?

Tyler closed his eyes and thought of her at nineteen, with a face as smoothly perfect as a cameo and a body that made him tremble. Mary, unafraid and generous, never really interested in material things, caring only about their being together. And singing, always singing.

Irwin shook his head. Somewhere in the back of his mind, her voice sang, *All I do is see you and my heart starts smiling,* and refused to be quieted or shut out.

Sixty-five years together and time had done its best and its worst for them, and so had he. Whatever modest talents he may have had, getting rich had never been one of them. They had lost two sons, the first as a child, the second, in a war. But the war had been necessary, and they had still had each other and that had always been enough. Except that now, the way things had become, it no longer seemed so. Then to have this happen— to suddenly wind up busted, dead broke, wiped out clean as a whistle—was just too much. Tyler gazed, dry-eyed, at his wife.

"I'm sorry," he told her.

He had been angry at first, furious, mostly, he supposed, because he was more comfortable with anger than with despair.

How could he have done it? How many in their right minds, at the age of eighty-six, would put every cent they owned into margined common stocks? Not many. Only those who were desperate, he thought dryly. Only those who felt forced to either make a fast, solid killing, or risk losing whatever small fragment of financial independence they had left.

The medical bills had pushed him into taking the risk. With what they owed, social security and Medicare became little more than down payments. And at this stage, he was not about to see his wife treated as an indigent. So he had tried. And for a while, in a euphorically rising market, he had done well. Then the value of his stock holdings had plunged close to seventy percent in nine days, and his broker had to sell out what remained to cover his margin debt. Now he was an eighty-six-year-old pauper. *Happy Birthday, Irwin*. Don't worry, he had always told his wife, you can rely on me. And whom did she have to rely on now?

Earlier, tired of railing at himself, he had railed at the six banking titans whose greed had triggered the entire catastrophe. *Oh, you sons of bitches . . . oh, you miserable bastards! You didn't have enough? You had to steal more? You had to take mine, too?* At other moments he chose to blame the country itself, his anguish so sharp, so intense an ache in his head that he was sure it was taking away the last of his senses. This was the United States of America! How could this have happened to him here? He had fought for it in one war, given a son to it in another. He deserved better. It was unjust, unjust.

He wandered over to the mirror over the sink and looked at himself. In the flickering pink light he saw an old man's head, face, neck, chest. How did such a thing happen? Was it one of God's less-sanctified jokes? Something to help keep him entertained when he wasn't busy creating some of his larger, grander catastrophes? If so, Tyler was not amused. All he saw in the mirror was this strange collection of decaying parts that would soon die. And inside them, suddenly, a kind of relief, perhaps even a rare sort of joy. Was death really that appealing?

Tyler slowly drifted toward the small stove standing in the kitchenette area. How simple, he thought. All he had to do was close the one open window, seal the crack under the door with a towel, blow out the pilot light, and turn on the jets. Then he would gently lie down one last time beside Mary and join her in a sleep from which they would never have to waken.

How well out of it they would be!

Tyler's wife sighed in her sleep, and the old man turned and looked at her. Apparently moved by a dream, her face in the uncertain light, suddenly seemed free of pain. Mary, he thought, and wondered what was wrong with him. How could he even think this way? Something surely was still left. Something inside him was still producing love, the way seeds produced flowers, the way trees produced leaves each spring.

He breathed deeply and took in a whiff of ocean air that was so clean, so clear that it was almost palpable. He felt himself moved by this sudden wealth. Something pure always survived. They were not solitary beings. Unseen lives recited their poems. If you didn't live, how could you hear them?

Tyler bent and kissed his wife's cheek. *All I do is see you and my heart starts smiling.* . . .

When he did go over to the stove later, it was to heat the coffee they would be having for breakfast.

8

The play was *Uncle Vanya*, and although Forster had seen it close to half a dozen times over the years, he still found himself as moved by Chekhov's vision of life as he was the first time. Perhaps more, he thought, because he was that much older.

With the first act completed, they left their seats for the champagne and caviar that Robert Bennet had arranged to have served during intermission.

"It's the only properly civilized way to enjoy Chekhov," he declared. "I despise Russians almost as much as I do Germans, but I love Chekhov. And perhaps most of all, I love the Chekhovian mood . . . that wonderful blend of gentle sorrow with the deep feeling that something of importance has been lost and will never be found again."

Bennet raised his glass. "To Anton Pavlovich Chekhov's gloriously gloomy heroes," he said and laughed. "A critic once accused Chekhov of avoiding true, positive, outstanding heroes as characters, and he replied, 'But where can I get them? Our life is provincial, our cities are unpaved, our villages are poor, our masses are abused. When we're young, we all chirp rapturously as sparrows on a dung heap. But when we're forty, we're already old and begin to think of death. Fine heroes we are.' And it's no different today," Bennet added. "The cynics rule."

Melissa said, "Stop it, Robert. You're absolutely depressing."

"It's not me, Mellie. It's just the way things are, one of the facts of life. Besides, it's the truth, and the truth should never be depressing."

"But it is," she said. "That's why I've always preferred pleasant fantasies."

"Then you certainly shouldn't be watching a Chekhov play."

Bennet appealed to Forster. "How do you feel about it, Paul? Do you prefer the sugary lie to the painful truth?"

"Not in art. Never in art. I don't think it's possible to lie in art. You can lie in love, politics, and business . . . in fact you can't survive if you don't . . . but it stops being art when you . . ."

Forster's voice faded off in midsentence. He had suddenly seen Annie approaching. She was right on cue, her timing perfect, yet he felt oddly unprepared for her, vulnerable. Or was it *her* vulnerability that bothered him? Yet, dazzling in a low-cut gown, there was nothing visibly defenseless about her as she worked her way toward him through the crowd.

"Paul, darling!" The false surprise in her voice was pure Hepburn. "How marvelous to run into you like this. When did you become a Chekhov fan?"

Smiling, she kissed him.

"Hello, Annie."

Forster went into the obligatory introductions. "I'd like you to meet Melissa Kenniston and Robert Bennet."

He watched everyone smile and nod.

"And this," he told Melissa and Robert, "is Annie Forster."

"Any relation to the celebrated economist?" asked Bennet.

"Only by former marriage," said Annie, offering Robert the full benefit of her eyes. "We've been apart seven years, and every time I see him I still don't know why I ever let him get away." Her laugh was soft. "Untrue. I know very well. He was a brilliant economist, a delightful man, a perfect lover, but an abominable husband. And if my life depended on it, I still couldn't get him to sit through a full evening of Chekhov."

Oh, God, thought Forster, hearing the light, playful approach she always used when she was at work on someone.

Bennet poured a glass of champagne and handed it to Annie. "I was just toasting Chekhov's gloomy heroes, which did nothing but depress Melissa. Perhaps you can think of something more cheerful to drink to."

"Why not?" Annie's eyes met and held Bennet's. Then she raised her glass. "Here's to never having to watch Chekhov . . . or for that matter, anything pure and beautiful . . . alone."

Solemnly, they all drank.

"That's not so cheerful," said Melissa.

Annie looked at her. It was a less than subtle appraisal. "It's cheerful enough if you're with someone, as the three of you obviously are."

"But you're not?"

"I was stood up at the last moment," said Annie. "And I must confess I hate it. Particularly with Chekhov. There's always so much to share, to talk about afterward. It makes being alone that much worse."

The warning bell sounded for the second act curtain and there was the sudden bustle of movement.

"It's strange," Annie went on quietly. "Most people seem to feel a greater need to share the bad than the good. I'm just the opposite. I'm better able to deal with the bad alone. It's when something wonderful happens that I really feel cheated if there's no one around who can share the way I feel."

"That's not so unusual," said Bennet. "I have much the same reaction. I find the good, unshared, is like a knife in the heart. So since I seem to have been left terminally alone, I'd be most grateful if you'd join us for supper after the show. It will give us a chance to share Chekhov and whatever else may please you."

"That's very kind of you. But I wouldn't dream of intruding."

"You would be doing me a great personal favor."

Carefully not looking at Forster, Annie considered it.

"I'm quite serious," Bennet told her.

"In that case, I'll be happy to join you all."

Terrific, thought Forster.

Annie batted her lashes at him.

The limousine was waiting to take them to a recently refurbished supper room at the Pierre. Bennet spoke briefly to the captain in flawless French and made him his for the night. Not at all bad, thought Forster, for a penniless, orphaned waif whose father died in prison.

Annie had thoughts of her own.

Resigned by now to her presence, Forster uneasily watched her perform. Lovely at any time, she obviously had gone all out for tonight. Her fair hair shone, her eyes gave off dancing lights, her smile was radiant. She had a deft, clever way with words, with the art of social conversation, that managed to include everyone in the group, yet made each feel singled out, special. And when it came to discussing Chekhov, she spoke as though she had been a student of his work for years.

"Chekhov was such a kind man," she declared at one point in the discussion, "that he once wrote to a friend that the most important thing was never to humiliate people. He considered it far better to make a person feel like an angel than a fool, although we were all more like fools than angels."

"Is that your philosophy too?" asked Bennet.

"I try. I certainly don't believe in deliberately hurting someone. There's enough pain around without our going out of our way to add to it. Don't you agree?"

"How could anyone not agree?"

"Watch the news any night at eleven," said Annie, "and you'll find out."

"I avoid the news these days. It's much too painful." Bennet smiled. "But if you're brave enough to dance with me, I'll introduce you to a whole different level of pain."

Forster gazed after them as they moved onto the dance floor. He should have known it would come to this, that it would never be enough for her to just meet Robert and Melissa during intermission, exchange a few words, and go home. But of course he *had* known. Which was precisely why he originally rejected the idea. On general principle, Annie hated being left out of anything—the perennial child wanting in at every party. Still, what harm could she do? No one had been fooling anyone even before she arrived.

"Your wife is really quite lovely and charming," said Melissa.

"My *former* wife."

"Of course." Her eyes were dark, hooded. "Whose idea was it to have her run into us at the theater? Hers or yours?"

I must remember never to underestimate this woman, Forster thought coldly. "Has anyone ever told you you're a very suspicious person?"

"I obviously wasn't suspicious enough where you were concerned. Especially since I found my apartment literally swarming with bugs just two days after you entered my life."

Forster felt tempted to apologize. Across the floor, he watched Annie and Robert moving gracefully together, her cheek against his, her fingers lightly touching the back of his neck.

"One of the problems with your being so damn smart," he said, "is that after a while you tend to think you know everything."

"Only a stupid person would ever think she knew everything. But I *am* beginning to know just a little about you."

He sat considering her. "Would you like to dance?"

"I thought you'd never ask."

It was strange holding her, feeling her physically close to him for the first time. Her body seemed fragile, oddly vulnerable. It reminded him of the faded news photo of her as a thin ten-year-old in a bathing suit. The image was disturbing and he missed a beat and stumbled over her foot.

"I'm sorry," he said.

"No. It was my fault. I guess I'm a little nervous."

"So am I."

"*I* have a reason," Melissa said against his ear. "*I'm* the prey. *You're* hunting *me*. But why are *you* nervous?"

Forster thought about it. "I suppose I don't want you to despise me."

"Why should that matter to you?"

"I don't know. But sometimes it does."

They danced without speaking.

"You really needn't worry about it," she said after a while. "I don't."

The remainder of the evening at the Pierre was a cautious, not entirely unpleasant blur to Forster. Four scheming people, he thought, with separate lines of velvet to sell and a calmly civilized way of doing it. Annie was utterly enchanting in her role of accidental guest, while Robert and Melissa graciously pretended to accept her at face value.

"Please extend my deepest appreciation to the idiot gentleman," Bennet told Annie in the limousine afterward.

"What idiot gentleman?"

"The one who so fortuitously stood you up at the theater and gave me one of the most delightful evenings I've had in a long time."

"Thank you. You're very kind." Annie looked at Forster, who sat facing her from a jump seat. "But I had the feeling Paul wanted to strangle me for intruding."

"He's an ex-husband," said Bennet. "I've yet to meet one who didn't feel rejected and resentful where their former wives were concerned."

The limousine stopped at Melissa's place and Forster saw her to the elevator.

"We haven't really had a chance to talk yet," she said. "I think we should."

"Yes."

"If it's not too late, how about coming up for a drink?"

Forster went out to say goodnight to Annie and Bennet. Then he rode up in the elevator with Melissa.

They sat on a large, sectional couch and sipped Remy Martin.

"There's a lot I have to explain," she said. "So if you don't mind, I'd like to go first. Is that all right with you?"

There was an uncertainty, a slight hesitation in her voice that he had never been aware of before. He found it oddly appealing.

"Of course," he said.

She looked at him, her eyes all but lost in shadow. "I want to talk about my father. I feel so foolish, having lied the other night when you knew the truth all along. But I lied about only two things—my father working at an investment house, not a bank, and his three bosses destroying him rather than the six bankers. Everything else was true—most importantly, the fact of his innocence."

As though fortifying herself, she took a deep swallow of the Remy Martin. "Would you like to hear how I know my father was innocent?"

Forster was silent. What could he say?

"Neither Robert nor I have ever told this to anyone," she said. "Whom could we tell? But I do feel the need to tell *you*. My father lived through almost five years in Auschwitz, which is something not many did. He lived because he was young, strong, able to work, and willing, finally, to debase his soul in order to survive and one day bear witness. As he described it, it all had to do with one little boy . . . something he never told us until the last time we visited him in prison."

She paused, tears welling. "The boy was very small, very young . . . probably not even two, and he was in a line of children waiting to enter one of the gas chambers. Of course, none of them had any idea of what was going to happen to them. Not even the adults knew. Everyone was told they were just going in for showers, and my father was one of those whose job it was to tell them that."

Melissa turned her shadowed eyes on Forster. "Please understand. If he had refused, he himself would have been killed and someone else would have done the job. Some choice. In any case, there was this little boy in line with the others. But when it was his turn to go into the building, he was too small to climb the steps at the entrance. So my father picked him up and carried him inside."

Gazing blankly, despairingly at Forster, Melissa took a long, deep breath.

"Then this little boy," she said, "who probably had been taught to demonstrate gratitude by offering affection, threw his arms about my father's neck and hugged and kissed him. As my father told it to us, by the time he finally put that child down, a large part of his soul was gone forever. But what remained kept him alive for two more years, remembering this one little boy among all those lost millions. 'Do you think,' he said to Robert and me, 'do you imagine for one second that with something like this carried inside me all this time . . . with no one else alive to know about this instant with this child . . . do you think I would defile his memory along with myself by becoming a thief? I swear on everything sacred, that I did nothing wrong.' "

A blush had settled on Melissa's cheeks. Incongruously, she tried to smile, but it turned sour.

"That was the last time Robert and I saw our father alive. He hanged himself two days later."

Forster sat there, not quite looking at her.

"I learned early to hate," Melissa said. "And what I couldn't learn by myself, Robert taught me. God, did we hate! All we wanted, all we lived for, was to get even." She sighed. "*Get even*. As if we ever could. But whatever we had to do, we did. All that time—all that effort—all that planning and scheming— all that dedication to a single, fixed idea. You've got to be demented. But if we didn't have that, I don't know what would have become of us. At times, it was all that held us together."

"And now?"

"Now we've done it."

"Yes," he said softly. "And torn the country apart in the process."

"I'm not happy about that."

Forster looked at her then and saw that she was weeping. She wept silently, without visible emotion, the tears simply sliding down her face unchecked. Forster dried her cheeks with a hand-kerchief. He knew he was being shamelessly manipulated. But he knew, too, that he didn't care.

When he held her, when he felt her clutching him fiercely, desperately, the pair of them rocking back and forth on the big couch like two people praying, Forster felt something in her burning so bright that it lit him as well. What am I doing?

Her thoughts were much the same. "This isn't why I asked you here. This isn't what I was after. Pity isn't what I want from you."

"Pity isn't what you're getting. I'm still going to put you in jail."

"Just keep trying," she whispered and kissed him.

It was a light, gentle, cautiously probing kiss, yet weighted with something so sweet and powerful that Forster felt as though he had taken a blow to the chest. When they kissed again, something seemed to be waiting.

Why not?—he thought, aware of that strange mixture of promise and respect that often came with such gifts. The reasoning, or the lack of it, could be held for later. Right now it was enough that there was a body next to his that seemed to be feeling the same sweet way he felt.

She was a prize in bed, wet at his first touch, a suddenly un-folding enigma. Neither shy nor bold, some cool sense of his needs lived in the turn of her flesh. She was exquisite. Yet at one point, something cold tore loose in him, as if he knew there was no such thing as a gift, that you got nothing for nothing and that one way or another, you paid. So that in a silent cry of dismay he wanted to pull free before it was too late. Then he saw her eyes, all bright lavender, all alive and shining with him, and the cry dissolved to a whisper.

Lying together, he watched her breast rise and fall with her heartbeat.

"Pure lust," she said softly. "Nothing else has changed. I still don't trust you worth a nickel."

He touched her flesh, so smooth it burned his hand. "You're right. You shouldn't trust me. But I think I've wanted you from that first moment in your office."

"Not before?"

"Maybe when I saw that old picture of you in *Life*."

"And not before that?"

He thought about it. "I didn't *want* you before that, but I may have loved you a little."

"When?"

"When you stood on the beach with your family at the age of ten, smiled into the camera, and absolutely broke my heart."

Forster unlocked his door in the early morning dark and entered his apartment. The air was thick, musty. Had he been gone for twelve hours or twelve months?

A floorboard squeaked.

"Annie?" he said and left the entrance hall for the living room.

He sensed rather than saw the blow coming, so that it just caught him glancingly above the eye. Stumbling, he spotted the figure close against the near wall, a bulky, light-haired man with a gun's butt sticking out of his fist like a deadly appendage. Instinctively, he dropped to his knees as the man started to swing again. Then Forster lunged for the man's legs and felt him come down on, and over, his back.

Whirling, Forster stomped hard on the man's wrist with one foot, kicked his gun free with the other, and watched it clatter across the floor and under a couch. Then the man was on him and they lay struggling together like two lovers, their faces inches apart. The man's eyes were yellow, an animal's eyes. Forster spat straight into them. The man blinked and Forster clubbed his jaw with his fist. Pressure was building behind his neck and all he could feel was a brain full of blood. His attacker was young, and clearly strong.

A knee like a steel bar suddenly rammed up between his legs, making him cry out. He saw a whole city of shimmering lights. Legs bent, he clutched his groin and desperately rolled away, gasping for breath like a beached fish. When he finally was able to let go of himself and stagger to his feet, the man was gone.

He groped his way to the house phone to alert the doorman. Then changing his mind, he hung up the receiver. The intruder had probably left the building through the basement and was sure to be blocks away. Besides, Forster wanted no involvement with the police. His right eye was blurring, and when he touched it his hand came away wet with blood. He suddenly felt terribly tired. His head and groin were separate centers of pain, and his flesh seemed old.

With great effort, he stretched out on the floor and felt around under the couch until he found the gun. It was a .38 caliber Smith and Wesson revolver with a silencer attached. All six chambers were loaded. He stood staring dumbly at the weapon for several moments. Then he slid it behind some books on the top shelf of an open cabinet.

In the bathroom, he took off his clothes, washed the blood from his face, and examined the wound. There was only a small break in the skin above his right eye and the bleeding had stopped. But there was a sizable lump on his forehead, and the flesh around the break was already turning blue from bruising.

Forster showered, washed the wound with peroxide, and covered it with a Band-Aid. Then he shaved and put on fresh clothing. It was only at this point that it occurred to him to check the apartment to see whether anything was missing.

Apparently, nothing was. The only visible signs of a search were in the study, where his desk drawers and file cabinets clearly had been gone through. Neatly and carefully. The mark of a professional. For now, at least, Forster chose to leave it at that. Otherwise, he would just find himself facing a new supply of dark intangibles, and he already was floundering among far too many of those.

At shortly after eight, he called Annie at home. She answered on the second ring.

"Are you alone?" he asked.

It took her a moment. "Don't be insulting."

"I'll be there in about half an hour," Forster said. "I want to talk to you."

Annie was dressed for work when he arrived—cool, fresh-looking white blouse; tan, summer-weight suit; sensible shoes. She stared at his forehead. The Band-Aid covered the cut, but the swelling and the blue-purple bruise were brutally visible.

"What happened?"

"I walked in on an intruder. Don't worry. It's nonfatal."

"My God! You might have been killed."

"But I wasn't."

"There could be a concussion. You should check with a doctor."

"How do you know I haven't?"

"Because it might—God forbid—confirm your mortality."

She took Forster into the kitchen and filled two coffee mugs. He waited until they were sitting at the table.

"Well, what did you think of them?" he said.

"Very attractive, very appealing. Which was the most frightening part." Annie took one of Forster's cigarettes and lit it. "I had to keep reminding myself of who they were and what they had done."

"Did Robert say anything?"

"About what?"

"The accidental meeting at the theater."

"Only that he was very glad it happened. He was quite flattering, of course. And he asked me out to dinner tonight."

"I assume you said you were busy."

"Why do you assume that?"

Forster looked at her, and her face stared back at him, piquant and painted for the day, inquisitive and suddenly a little rapacious. "Because all you asked for was a chance meeting and ten minutes of conversation, and you've already gone past that."

"I can't see any harm in having dinner with him."

"Don't tell me you accepted his invitation!"

"I did. And I see nothing wrong in it. We spent a pleasant evening together, we enjoyed talking, and at the end he really seemed to be opening up."

Forster felt a sudden heat rise to his face. "I knew I made a mistake when I agreed to this. You're as pig-headed and arrogant as you ever were. Well, you can call Robert up when you get to the office and break the date. What do you think you're fooling with? This isn't amateur night. You can do a lot of damage—not only to yourself, but to everything I'm trying to accomplish."

She said nothing, but Forster could feel her getting locked more deeply into it by the second.

"You never did fool him, Annie. He saw right through you—through us—from the start."

"How do you know?"

"Because Melissa very quickly figured it out. And if she knew, so did Robert."

Sun streamed into the kitchen and lit the anger in her face. "I'm not breaking the date. Talk about arrogance. You've been working at this for more than a week and getting nowhere, but you still refuse any help. You still think no one but you can do anything.''

"It has nothing to do with that."

"The devil it hasn't. Everything is ego with you. It always was. And when I'm involved, it's doubly so. That's exactly how you squelched me for years. But you're not stopping me in this. I don't care what you say. This time it's too important."

Annie poured her coffee into the sink and left the kitchen. Forster saw no point in going after her. After a while, he heard the apartment door slam.

At the magazine later, closeted with Jennings in his office, Forster brought the editor up to date. He held nothing back, not even the episode with the intruder.

Jennings sighed. "I would have preferred a simple story of intrigue, betrayal, and national interest." Lighting a fresh cigar, he considered the damage to Forster's forehead. "You could just as easily be lying dead on your living room floor, you know. Though I do think it may only have been a common burglary you walked in on."

"Really? And exactly how many self-respecting thieves go to work these days with silenced thirty-eights in their pockets?"

"If he wanted to shoot you, he could have done it easily enough. He wasn't there to kill."

"Maybe not," said Forster. "But he also wasn't there to steal my TV. What do you imagine he was searching for in my desk and files? All he obviously wanted was some evidence of how I was doing with my investigation."

"In that case, it would have had to be your two new friends who sent him. And I can't believe they'd send some half-ass housebreaker on such a long shot."

Forster studied the tip of his editor's cigar as if the answer lay buried somewhere inside the white ash. "What *I* can't believe," he said, "is that Robert and Melissa actually managed to handle this entire enterprise on their own. Do you realize the kind of money that was involved. "They *had* to have had outside help. Doesn't that seem logical to you?"

"If I was depending on logic to see me through what's been happening lately, I don't think I'd be able to get out of bed in the morning."

* * *

Forster pushed himself back to his typewriter that afternoon, trying once more to make the continuing fiscal crisis understandable. After several hours, he glanced over a few of the points he had covered so far.

If we learn anything at all from history it's that financial markets are nothing like markets in beef, hardware, or oranges. That's because they're affected far more by fear, rumor, reasonless hope, and equally reasonless depression, than markets in tangible products. So by their very nature, financial markets tend to be volatile and unstable. When this volatility becomes further blown up by a roulette wheel mentality, when the gambling drive takes over completely from the financial markets' original purpose of investing capital in an industrial or service enterprise, we shouldn't be any more surprised by today's panicky route than we would be to see the world's oldest traveling crap game flying in all directions after being raided by the police.

And—

Then we come to the experts—and there are as many unqualified experts in finance as there are in any other field. Borrow!—our prophets have been telling us for years. Borrow, and you'll have yourself a fine hedge against inflation. So that in time, because people like to listen to holy men, almost everyone was doing it. With the result that when our big banking scandal broke, the outstanding debt in the United States credit markets alone, was no less than eight trillion dollars . . . $8,000,000,000,000 . . . eight thousand billion. Written any way at all, the numbers defy rational comprehension.

Still, the numbers do include our car and mortgage payments, our credit card payments, corporations' bonds and commercial paper, and the borrowings of municipal and state governments. Then, of course, there's finally the ultimate Big Daddy of all borrowers, the boys in Washington themselves, who borrow to help the sick and poor, to support the farmers, to guard us from possible attack, to give aid to cities and states. All worthwhile deeds. But no one seems to have ever added up the cost. What would be the point? Everything had to be done anyway.

But we're not an isolated self-sufficient island here in America. As our debt buildup went on, we became more and more vulnerable to possible external as well as internal shocks—an oil crisis, a military catastrophe, the point at which other countries suddenly decide they no longer want our debased dollars. Without a shock, we might have gone on increasing our mountain of debt and climbed to an even greater fall. But the shock finally did come, in this case in the form of a top-level scandal. And the results we see are panic in the markets, foreign capital fleeing, and the even more frightening threat that the entire system might be facing a meltdown—

Forster's telephone rang, offering a reprieve. It was his private line, the one that did not go through the magazine switchboard.

"It's me," said Guido Castanzo. "Can you talk?"

"Yes. What's doing?"

"I've checked through the first round of tapes," said the investigator. "It's mostly garbage, but there's a brief stretch on one that I'd like you to hear."

"When?"

"How about this evening at six?"

"Fine."

They made arrangements.

Forster could feel his heart going at an accelerated pace. Easy, he told himself. Don't get your hopes up.

Traffic was bumper to bumper, but Castanzo still managed to appear at Madison and Sixty-sixth Street almost exactly on time.

Forster got into the car and they drove uptown then west to a parking area overlooking the Hudson. The water was gray and murky; some kids were throwing rocks at a floating bottle. Forster lit a cigarette, coughed, and tossed the thing out the window.

"Who slugged you?" asked the investigator.

Forster told him.

"It's finally getting interesting," said Castanzo. "What did you do with the gun?"

"I stuck it behind some books. Want to check it out?"

"No. It's not going to be licensed. At least not to the original owner. And whoever stole it probably filed off the registration numbers. But hold onto it, anyway.''

Castanzo had a small, battery-powered unit set up in an attaché case.

"This section was recorded at 9:32 P.M. of June twenty-second," he said. "Yesterday. It was taken from the home telephone of Citibank's Thomas Stanton. He's talking to Peter Farnham of Chase Manhattan, who initiated the call from an outside line of indeterminate location. The time frame puts it about eleven hours after your interviews with all five bankers.''

Forster felt an instant letdown. Since Castanzo's call he had been hoping . . . indeed, actually expecting . . . to hear something significant from Borman, Harwith, or Stone, the figures at the heart of the conspiracy. Without some specific evidence from them, he remained nowhere. Adrenaline leaked out of him and he closed his eyes.

"What's the matter?" said the investigator. "The bang on the head bothering you?''

"No. I'm fine. Just a little tired. Go ahead and roll it.''

Castanzo switched on the machine.

"Hello?" It was Stanton's blank, hollowed-out voice.

"Hello, Tom. Pete Farnham. How are you?''

"How am I?" Stanton's laugh was cold. "I assume that's a rhetorical question. Or are you expecting an answer?''

"Hardly. But I do still find myself going through the motions of polite conversation.''

"I'm afraid it's wasted on me.''

"I know.'' There was a sigh, then a brief pause. "What did you make of our meeting with Forster?''

"I'm not sure. But I'd have to say he's either a lot more clever or a lot more foolish than any of us thought.''

"It was just a fishing expedition. He couldn't possibly know anything.''

"Who knows? Do you? I certainly don't.''

There was a pause; the machine hummed.

"Wouldn't that be ironic?" said Farnham slowly. "It's far-fetched, of course, but wouldn't that really be the ultimate.''

"What's that?''

"The whole concept of Berenstein's grown children descending upon us like a pair of avenging angels. Of making us pay for something of which we were totally innocent, in precisely the same way we once did to their father. Wouldn't that be something?''

Stanton laughed. ''When did you last see an avenging angel fly into a courtroom?''

Castanzo turned off the machine. ''That's about it.''

''Give me the last minute again, please.'' Forster had heard it clearly enough, but it was too much to accept on one run-through.

The investigator rewound that part of the tape, then ran it forward. It made Forster feel no better the second time.

''What do you think, Guido?''

''The same as you. Your six pricks evidently did a real number on Berenstein.''

''I can't believe it.''

''You want to hear it a third time?''

Forster shook his head. ''Imagine,'' he whispered. ''How could they?''

''For Christ's sake! Are you a ten-year-old kid? You've been around for a while. Act it.''

Forster's heart and brain felt constricted, as though he had torn loose some promise of his soul and paid it over in ransom. ''Damn them . . . damn them all!''

''Ancient history,'' said Castanzo. ''It can't be changed. The only thing you can do something about is now.''

Forster breathed in something dead and rotten that seemed to come off the river. His mouth tasted dry as old leaves.

''The first thing I'm going to do,'' he said, ''is fly down to Washington and talk to Wendell Norton.''

''Good. When?''

''As soon as you get me out to La Guardia.''

''Call first.''

There was a pay phone at the edge of the parking area and Forster put in the call from there. Graffiti danced in front of his eyes.

''Wendell? It's Paul.''

''Paul! I've been thinking about you.'' The voice came instantly alive. ''Anything new?''

Forster took an instant to calm himself. Just hearing Norton's voice had set him off again. ''Yes. That's why I'm calling. I have to see you. Will you be home tonight at about ten?''

''You can depend on it.''

"I'll see you then," said Forster.

Back in Castanzo's car, the ex-FBI agent looked at him. "Well?"

"Let's go to the airport."

"Not so fast. First, you'd better open your shirt and let me wire you." Castanzo had all the necessary equipment laid out and ready; miniature mike, wires, and recording pack, adhesive tape to hold the unit flat against his body.

"I don't need that."

"The hell you don't. And if you can't figure out why, then you shouldn't be going."

"That's not my style, Guido."

"Don't be so fucking superior. You're going down to talk to Norton for only one reason—to confront and pressure him on this Berenstein business, to bluff him into thinking you've got real evidence, not just a bugged innuendo. What you've got to get from him is the whole story. Which won't be worth shit, if you should ever need it, unless you've got it down on tape."

Reluctantly, Forster unbuttoned his shirt. "I still don't like it."

"No one said you had to."

At 10:00 P.M. in the Wall Street area, small armies of back-office clerks were still at work. They were struggling to keep from being swamped by the average trading volume of the past week and a half of more than four hundred million shares daily. It had been another bad, though not cataclysmic day for the markets, with one failed rally attempt in the morning, another in the early afternoon, and the Dow finally closed down an additional forty-seven points. It was a mark of the prevailing mood that any drop of less than fifty points had almost become a cause for rejoicing. Among the margin clerks at Prudential-Bache who had been putting in fifteen-hour work days and sleeping in hotels was Lester Rosaro, who had not been home in ten nights. He was sorting through groups of accounts to check for those that would have to be tabulated for margin calls in the morning. Most were little more than numbers to him. But every once in a while a name broke through with its human history attached, assailing him with glimpses of an education fund wiped out, a retirement nest egg lost, a dream boat sunk at its dock, an Australian trip canceled forever. Rosaro felt himself torn,

then torn again. He envisioned the suddenly frightening glow of
his own computer screen multiplied by thousands more in banks
and brokerage houses all over the country, and his heart went
cold. Where would it all end?

In Springfield, Massachusetts, forty-two salesmen of the Dannico Sporting Goods Company sat in stunned silence as Frank
Hannauer, their regional manager, reported that the rumors they
had been hearing for the past several days were true. With their
already bad cash-flow problem brought to a head by the current
fiscal crisis, and the banks refusing to extend additional credit,
the company had been forced to accept a previously rejected
takeover bid from their chief competitor, Davidson-Heathe, In-
corporated. Which meant that fifty percent of all employees—
administrative, sales, and production—would have to be fired
immediately, and another twenty-five percent would be let go
over the next six months. Charlie Franklin, who had been with
Dannico Sporting for less than two years, stared blankly at the
manager's face as he heard his name read off the list of those
being fired immediately. He had moved to Springfield from Chicago for this job, had just bought a new house, and had reserves
of less than three thousand dollars in the bank. Until two minutes ago he had considered himself a young man on the rise,
with a good future and no money worries. Now he was out of a
job and without prospects of finding one. Then all he could think
of was how he was going to tell his wife.

At the brokerage firm of Baldwin, Conners and Williams in
Cincinnati, most of the employees had gone home for the night,
but the partners' room was crowded with the company's officers.
The liquor cabinet was open, and many of those present had
drinks in their hands. They were not celebrating. According to
the share prices posted at the close of that day's trading, the
company was technically insolvent, with the proportion of assets
to liabilities a full ten percent below the Securities and Exchange
Commission's minimum capital requirements. Tim Baldwin, the
president and managing partner, had just finished telling everyone what they had been fearing for days and already had sur-
mised—that unless the various banks that had loaned them
money were willing to postpone repayment of these loans and
lend them additional capital, they would have to seek an im-

mediate merger or face the prospect of closing their doors. Unless, of course, there was a substantial rally during the next few days—which no one really expected. There was little conversation in the room. Those who did speak did so in the hushed tones of the newly bereaved. Men stared appealingly at one another, seeking reassurances they knew they weren't going to get. Held together by a pack sense of despair, they didn't want to go home. For when they did finally leave the office, they'd have to be alone with their thoughts and feelings till morning. It was going to be a long night.

In Hong Kong, a government committee had been appointed to look into the operation of the Hong Kong stock and commodity exchanges, and was holding its first official meeting. There was fierce arguing among the committee members from the start. The Hong Kong Stock Exchange was the only major exchange in the world to suspend trading during the current global market upheaval, and the committee was divided between those who considered the five-day shutdown a proper move and those who didn't. Sir Henry Frobisher, the governor, said that the trading suspension was necessary because of the exchange's vulnerability to a complete breakdown during the first few days of emotional selling that followed news of the American banking scandal. His critics claimed that the closing weakened Hong Kong's credibility as a major financial center and that it would take a long time to rebuild the confidence that had been lost. Sir Henry's supporters declared that had the exchange remained open and degenerated into complete chaos, nothing would have been left to rebuild.

Japan's Prime Minister Osakida, in a widely covered policy speech delivered in Tokyo, said that what was taking place in today's markets was nothing less than a global monetary crunch, and that it really should not have surprised anyone. In placing their money, he declared, modern investors leaped from one country to another as though national boundaries didn't exist. From New York, to Tokyo, to London, to Paris, to Bonn—bankers, brokers, and money managers shifted billions daily at the quiver of a Eurodollar rate or the tap of an arbitrager's computer keys. But while the markets themselves were global, the politics of each country still ended at its own borders. Hence, the budget deficit and overconsumption had made the United States a debtor nation; the fear of inflation and urge to save had kept Japan and West Germany from spurring the consumption needed to add new power to the world economy; the ingrained resentment of America's power and leadership made France and Great Britain stomp on the dollar rather than support it during its time of greatest need. Since the United States, Japan, and West Germany produced half of the world's output, said Osakida, these three nations in particular would have to demonstrate an entirely new spirit of cooperation if there was to be any realistic hope of surviving the fiscal quagmire into which they had fallen. Unfortunately, these economic superpowers still refused to give up enough of their national self-interest to work together for the common good. If this self-destructive parochialism didn't change immediately, warned the prime minister, they could all wake up one morning and find themselves trapped in an economic meltdown.

Yet to the casual observer in New York the most likely epicenter of any such meltdown, life appeared to be going on very much as it usually did. The mayor was engaged in a nationally televised debate over the latest evidence of corruption uncovered in his administration. At Shea Stadium, the New York Mets were in the process of completing a three-game sweep of the St. Louis Cardinals before sellout crowds of screaming fans. A new Woody Allen movie had opened and been greeted by Vincent Canby's usual cries of "Genius! Genius!" At the Harvard Club, the vice-president of the United States was telling a gathering of Republican elite of the need for the Grand Old Party to regain control of the Senate in the coming elections. Calming, full-page advertisements had been placed in the morning's editions of *The New York Times* and *The Wall Street Journal* by two of the country's largest brokerage firms declaring that this was the time to buy common stocks, and that messages had been sent to their many thousands of clients informing them of this fact. The reassuring explanations being used in the advertisements, already polished to a minor art form through repeated use, was that a lot of paper profits had vanished, nothing more. It was a long overdue technical correction. Excess water squeezed out. A solid base had been established on which to build a fresh bull market. The fundamental business of the country, the production and distribution of commodities, remained sound and prosperous.

But no one was placing full page ads to tell about the more than one million layoffs that had taken place over the past ten days, or the production quotas for July and August that were being revised downward or cut back entirely until inventories were reduced to more comfortable levels. Nor was the general public aware of the fact that most of the money going into banks these days was from called-in and sold-out loans, and that fewer and fewer new loans were being made. The one statistic that the media seemed to keep accurate records on, and emphasize with relish, was the growing number of suicides.

Wendell Norton lived in an early-nineteenth-century Federalist house on a lamplit cobbled mews in Georgetown. The streets were quiet.

Wearing a short-sleeved sports shirt, Norton answered Forster's knock with a glass of brandy in his hand. His arms looked soft, loose-fleshed, aging.

"I'm glad to see you. Come in, come in." He saw Forster's wound.

"I walked into the bathroom door in the middle of the night."

"Happens to me all the time in the dark. Can't wait to have my prostate fixed so I can sleep through the night. But you're still a good twenty years away from that."

Norton took Forster's arm as though afraid he might suddenly disappear. "Come into the library. That's where the brandy is. I hope to hell you've got some good news for me. I can certainly use it."

The house, cool and silent, had the blank, airless quality of a bank vault. Nobody seemed to be living there, not even in the library, which had always been Forster's favorite room, but which now, as he entered it, felt suspended about him like a cave.

"The truth is, Wendell, I don't have good news for you. In fact, what I have to tell you is really quite bad."

In the act of pouring the brandy, Norton stopped and for a moment appeared immobilized. Then he finished what he was doing and carefully put down the bottle. Forster had to remind himself that he was furious. After so many years and so much feeling, it was not easy.

Norton managed a rueful smile. "How bad can it be? Everything's relative. After the kind of stuff I've been hit with lately, I no longer shock that easily." His hand was steady as he gave Forster his drink. "Well? What is it?"

"It goes all the way back to the Malcolm Commission and its handling of the Berenstein case." Forster paused for a sip of brandy. "I assume you remember David Berenstein."

Norton stared at him as though he were a suddenly risen presence in the room. "I remember Berenstein very well. He was a Holocaust survivor, a tragic figure who hanged himself after being sent to prison for embezzling some bank funds."

"That's right. Except that I've discovered Berenstein really never did embezzle those funds. For some reason he was framed, turned into a sacrificial piece of meat by you and your lovely friends on the Commission."

"You're out of your mind!" Norton's eyes widened. "How in God's name did you ever come up with such a patently mad idea?"

"Please, Wendell. We've been too close for too many years. Don't lie to me. *I've got documented evidence.* It turned me sick when I saw it, and it still does, but it's all there. You can't bluster your way out of this. All I'm asking now is why a man like you should have been party to such a horror story in the first place."

"I don't know where you could have picked up this incredible piece of misinformation, but it's simply not true. Admittedly, it was a painful case for all of us, for those of us on the Commission as well as for Berenstein. But the man was unalterably guilty. In fact if—"

"Stop, damn it!" Forster let the anger build and wash over him. It made things easier. "This was about as close to a sanctioned lynching as anything I've seen. And your trying to stonewall it now only makes it worse."

Norton stared into his glass as though there, indeed, were the entrails of a blood sacrifice.

"I don't care what you've seen, heard, or think you've found out," he said quietly. "It's just not true. And I'm deeply hurt you'd even consider believing something so ugly."

"Then you still deny it?"

"Categorically."

This time Norton's voice was so low that his tongue and teeth almost seemed part of his words. It was convincing enough to make Forster wonder whether he could have misinterpreted the tape. But the doubt lasted for only an instant.

"All right," he said. "Then I'm through with this whole stinking investigation. I'm taking whatever evidence I've found in the case to the United States Attorney's office."

It was all bluff. There was no evidence, only those few innuendoes on tape, which would mean little in a court of law. But Forster's anger was very real.

"Wendell, you sonofabitch. I could cut out your heart for this. Not just for lying to me, but for what you did to that poor, fucking family . . . that man, his wife, his two kids."

Forster put down his drink, abruptly rose, and stalked toward the door. At his back, Berenstein's death seemed to fly right along, like a beating of wings.

"Paul!"

Forster stopped and turned in the entrance hall.

"For God's sake, don't leave me like this."

Forster slowly came back. "Are you through lying?"

Norton stared hopelessly at him.

"I want the truth. All of it. Nothing left out. And I want it now."

"All right." The two words were barely audible.

A deep red flush surged up over Norton's collar and stained his cheeks, his ears. He chewed his lip in misery, then clenched his jaws until the muscles stood out in them. His eyes stared at Forster, wild, hopeless, full of guilt.

"We never expected such tragedy," he whispered. "We never dreamed Berenstein would end up killing himself. We planned it all very differently. I know that still doesn't make it right, doesn't morally excuse any part of it. But we did propose to have Berenstein released in a few months with the discovery of new evidence that would have cleared him. Please believe me. We never intended it to end up as it did."

"Congratulations. I'm sure the entire Berenstein family will be overjoyed to hear that." Forster sat down and lifted his glass once more. "Now I want the whole story from the beginning."

"But you already know it."

"I want to hear it from you. I want to hear how someone I've known for half my life, someone I've always admired, could have turned out to be such a bastard."

"I never really believed I was being so vile at the time."

"Jesus Christ, why didn't you?"

"I was convinced that what I was doing would be of some use to the country. By believing that the alternative of letting John Sterling be indicted would have sent some of the same shock waves through the system that are battering us today."

Forster remained silent. He remembered that John Sterling had resigned as chairman of Chase Manhattan to become secretary of state, which had to mean that Berenstein was made a scapegoat to save Sterling from prison, the administration from dishonor, and the banking system from attack. If true, it was a shocker. If untrue, then Wendell had more imagination than Forster had ever given him credit for.

"The irony of it," said Norton, "was that if Berenstein hadn't stumbled onto the fact that those trust funds were missing, Sterling would have replaced them and no one would have been the wiser. Sterling had no intention of embezzling that money. He had just extended himself into a temporary cash-flow problem. But once Berenstein noticed the apparent defalcation and brought it to Pete Farnham's attention, he doomed himself. Farnham traced the shift in funds to Sterling, and the old-boy network slid smoothly into gear."

"And you went along with it."

"You're damn right I did," Norton said harshly. "I and all my colleagues on the Commission. Not that we did it lightly or easily. Despite what you may think, and despite the palpable anti-Semitic overtones, we did weigh our choices very carefully. On one side was an innocent man who would be spending at most a few months in jail. While on the other, was not only a possible financial crisis, but a major embarrassment to the United States government with the indictment of its secretary of state on felony charges."

Norton's eyes sought Forster's. "You've always been a patriot, Paul. Without the brilliance of hindsight, what would you have done?"

"Not what you did."

The banker's expression was sardonic. "Then you're obviously a wiser and better man than the six of us on that commission. Because our decision was a unanimous one. If just one of us had had the guts to say no, if just one of us had said, 'No, this is not what justice in this country is all about,' the plan would have died right there. But when the White House chief of staff arranged a top secret meeting with us one day, when he told us in no uncertain terms that this was what the president himself was asking us to do, that duty to our country was a higher call, indeed, took clear precedence over the temporary pain of any single individual, there really was no contest.''

"I can't believe you bought that.''

"At this point, neither can I.'' Norton folded his hands in front of him, a parody of a man in prayer. "But this was a quarter of a century ago, and I wasn't then what I am today. In those days I was very big for the higher duty. I believed myself to be among the world's privileged. I believed myself to have been born, to have grown up, and to be living in the greatest, the noblest achievement of the human race on this planet. America.''

"You no longer feel that way?''

Norton shook his head. "I know that you do, but I'm afraid I don't.''

Forster said nothing. Outside on the cobbled mews two cats suddenly screeched, then became quiet. Forster felt as though he had entered a royal tomb, a dark repository of the dead that made all of living seem even more fragile, more transitory and meaningless than it actually was.

"I'll tell you why I no longer feel that way,'' Wendell Norton said. He was altogether calm as he spoke, but a vein in his forehead had begun to pulse. "It's because I'm frightened. And I'm frightened because we've become the most vain, the most hysterical, the most dangerous people on earth. We're as bad as the worst religious fanatics. We can't stand the idea that anybody anywhere else might be more advanced or more intelligent or closer to the one true faith than we are. And we're ready to mutilate and kill unlimited numbers just to prove it.''

"That's really not true, Wendell. If you—''

"The hell it's not. Read the newspapers. Watch TV. Listen to the radio. Everybody seems to be slavering to get his hands on the throat of everybody else.''

The banker studied the backs of his hands. "If I sound cynical,'' he said tiredly, "it's because I am. And a good part of my education in that area began with what we . . . the Commission, the president, the justice system . . . everyone concerned, God help us . . . were able to do to a poor, harmless sonofabitch like Berenstein. If my ambition to be president could have started at one particular instant in time, it was then. That's how badly I ached for the power to change things."

Forster looked at him hazily, as though Norton was far away, obscured in mist. He could feel his anger intensifying, rising to new heights. Where was all this garbage coming from? Having been part of an indefensible act that destroyed a man's life, did Wendell really expect him to believe his guilt should be shared by the entire country? It had to be the ultimate cop-out.

"Think whatever you will of me . . . of us . . . for what we did back then," said the banker, "and it may well be justified. But I swear on everything holy that we're innocent of the current charges against us."

"I know."

Norton showed the cautious surprise of a man who, having come to expect nothing but attacks, doesn't quite know how to respond to sudden support. His mouth quivered at the edge of a smile, hung there for a moment, then retreated into a grim line. "I'm astonished at your faith."

"It has nothing to do with faith," said Forster. "All six of you have managed to effectively destroy that."

Norton stared at him, trying to work through the implications. Almost painfully, his face tensed with anticipation. He appeared afraid to ask the obvious question. "Then—you've found something?"

"I know who framed you."

"Paul!" Norton's lips worked and he tried to say more, but emotion froze his tongue.

"Don't get your hopes too high. I still have no proof, no real evidence. And until I get some, it doesn't matter one damn bit what I know."

"My God!" Norton's speech was hoarse. "It matters to me. Who is it?"

"I'm not going to tell you."

"Why not?"

"Because I no longer trust you, Wendell. The fact is, if it weren't for the damage your indictment is doing to the country, I'd happily forget all six of you."

They sat there, not quite looking at each other.

"Now the only other things I want to hear from you," Forster finally said, "just to corroborate the evidence I already have, are the details of that Berenstein setup. I want to hear names, dates, places, and who said what to whom. Then I'll get out of your life, and you can get out of mine, until I have the evidence to exonerate you.''

Forster left a short while later. If Castanzo's recording device had worked as it was supposed to, he had every word effectively on tape.

9

The Israeli was a general and head of the Mossad, but to President Hanson he had the look of a middle-weight fighter in his prime. Seated between Exely and Maynard, General Aaron Yaacov made the two Americans appear soft by comparison. He also made Hanson feel uncomfortable. The man is here in my country, in my office, at my request, thought the president, yet he somehow manages to make me feel not quite in control. If I were, Operation Falcon would never have gotten this far to begin with.

This was the president's first meeting with General Yaacov, and they were just getting past the initial amenities. But his first reaction to the Israeli intelligence chief was one of gratitude that they were on the same side.

"As I understand it, General," he was saying, "it's Libya that's finally been chosen as our primary target. Was this a consensus judgment?"

"Completely, Mr. President. Qaddafi's despised. There's a worldwide antipathy toward him, and a general sense of fear, even among other Arab countries, that his peddling of terrorism is hurting everyone."

"How much preparation time will you need from your end?" asked Hanson.

"Six days from when you give your approval. We already have agents in place in seven prime target areas."

"Which are?"

"The American embassies in London, Paris, Bonn, and Rome. Also, your consulate offices in Damascus, Cairo, and Beirut."

Hanson felt as though he had stumbled into a newly dug grave. "I thought the targets were to be limited to middle-eastern cities."

"If I may, Mr. President"—Defense Secretary Exely cleared his throat, a man without happy news to deliver—"since the operation is our pretext for military action, we felt . . . all of us . . . that the stronger the provocation, the better. Especially since we need the support of our allies. With the bombings taking place in their own capitals, they'll have no choice but to share responsibility."

"Gentlemen, I'm awed." Hanson's tone was sardonic, yet he knew he had no right to sarcasm. If he did decide to go ahead with the operation, it only made sense to go all out with it. And London, Paris, Bonn, and Rome were as committed as you could get. Hanson addressed the director of the Central Intelligence Agency, Charles Maynard. "This was your idea to begin with, wasn't it?"

"Yes, Mr. President."

"I thought so. It has your personal stamp."

Maynard shifted uncomfortably under the president's steady gaze. "We're not locked into anything yet, Mr. President. We're still in the realm of conjecture, not action."

"Your idea is good," said Hanson. "It's strong. And we're getting closer to possible action by the hour. So I want everything on the table right now." The president turned back to General Yaacov. "Where are you going to plant the bodies of your Arab terrorists?"

"In London and Paris," said the general. "One will allegedly be shot by a guard. The other will be killed in the blast itself."

"Who will they be?"

"Abu Gamal and Bayed Shanti. They're both Libyan nationals, and both are high on our list of known terrorists."

"They're in your custody?" asked Hanson.

"Not yet, Mr. President. It's too soon for them to simply disappear. But we have people close to them and they'll be picked up a day or two before they're actually needed."

Hanson nodded. It was the age of specialization. Everyone had their own areas of expertise. And none were better at this sort of thing than the Israelis.

"Then I take it you're not worried," he said to Yaacov.

The general's stone face cracked into a smile. "I'm *always* worried, Mr. President. Almost every Israeli is." His eyes were cold. "But as far as Operation Falcon is concerned, I expect no real difficulty at our end. Nor do I envision any major problems for your own military. After that, of course, it's all politics. And it's always hard to tell exactly how that might go."

Hanson sat staring at the Israeli. "What's your personal opinion of this entire operation?"

"I'm not sure I know what you mean."

"It's a simple enough question."

Yaacov shrugged. "Excuse me, but that may well be one of the least simple questions that's ever been put to me. How do you mean it? Are you speaking morally? Politically? Militarily? Besides, I'm sure you've already had all the opinions you need from your own staff people."

"Spare me, General. Just tell me what you think."

Yaacov's smile twinkled about him like an aura. "I'm a Jew, Mr. President, living in a nation of Jews. So any answer you get from me has to come out of that."

"Agreed."

"So the answer is going to be long and complicated. And that's because as Jews we've learned more history more thoroughly than anyone else still around and like to think we've profited from it. We like to feel we know by now that virtue doesn't matter to history and that crimes against humanity go unpunished, but that every mistake in judgment is paid for in blood."

The general paused and looked piercingly at the three men listening to him in the oval room, as though he were hunting down any trace of mockery for his views.

"I tell you all this," he went on, "because we're not just your allies, but your friends. I daresay we're pretty much the best friends you have anywhere in the world. So when you're forced to act with violence—as you may be doing now—we're grateful for the chance to act with you and help. I say this knowing that innocent blood will be spilled and that if Israel's part in the operation is ever revealed, no one alive will ever forgive us."

Yaacov took a long, deep breath. "I also believe that this is the only practical course of action open to you in your present crisis. It's not easy to admit such a thing because . . . again as a Jew . . . I consider every human life to be sacred. I shudder to think how many times in the history of the Jews, our almost pathological concern for the possible loss of a few lives has finally resulted in the loss of thousands."

He looked straight at Hanson. "That's why you're not yet

committed to this operation, isn't it, Mr. President? The unavoidable loss of life."

"Do you blame me?"

"Not at all, sir. Since the final decision must rest with you, so must the responsibility. And what sane man could take that lightly?"

Bless you, bless you, thought Hanson, and once again was pleased to know that this stone-faced soldier would be standing beside him in whatever lay ahead. But surely this Israeli, this Jew, and his countrymen had no monopoly on humanism. Love also was the word of Christ, and it admitted no divisions, no slyness of calculation.

"Until now, I've been one of our lucky presidents," Hanson told the three men. "I haven't had to send any Americans out to kill and be killed. I've always been grateful for that. I still am, even though my luck seems to have run out." The president paused. "You'll have my decision on Falcon within forty-eight hours."

I'm entitled to two more days of grace, he thought. I deserve at least that.

Forster also was counting days.

At home, in his study, he had prepared a simple chart to help him keep track of things. Details tended to slip by him, and putting everything down on paper gave him a sense of orderliness and control that he did not otherwise feel. Strong natures, some philosopher once said, made themselves forget what they could not master. Not being a philosopher, Forster punished himself by writing things down. Today, according to his chart, was the twelfth day since the six money lords were indicted for acts they had not committed, the country was continuing to slide to its own fiscal hell, and he himself was faced with the need to make some significant decisions.

He called Robert Bennet at his office, gave his name to a secretary, and was put through.

"What a nice surprise, Paul." There was genuine pleasure in Bennet's voice.

"I hope I'm not calling at a bad time."

"Not at all. It's the only call I've gotten all day that I've been happy to receive. In fact, I've seriously been considering ripping out every phone and computer in the place. How do you think I'd manage without them?''

''More slowly,'' said Forster, ''but no less successfully.''

''I appreciate your confidence.'' Bennet took a moment. ''I enjoyed the other evening. And your Annie is an absolute delight.''

''You mean my *ex*-Annie.'' The correction was getting to be a conditioned reflex.

''Of course. For which I'm additionally grateful. I can't remember when I last met a woman who took me so completely by storm. How wonderful that she happened to run into you. Somehow, the best things seem to happen by accident.''

''The worst things, too,'' said Forster, and wondered just how much sarcasm Bennet's words carried. ''Something's come up that I'd like to discuss with you and Melissa.''

''You mean a three-way conference?''

''If you want to call it that. Can you possibly make it this evening?''

''I'm having dinner with Annie at eight, but perhaps we can get together earlier. Would six at Melissa's place be all right?''

''Perfect.''

''I'll call her right away.'' Bennet's voice turned slow, thoughtful. ''I hope you're not going to spoil things with any unpleasant surprises.''

''Why? Are you worried about something?''

Bennet laughed. ''I deserved that. I'll see you at six.''

Forster put down the phone.

When it rang moments later, he knew it was Melissa before he answered.

''I just heard about the big conference,'' she said.

''It's not really that big. Only the three of us.''

''What's it about?''

''Not anything to talk about on the phone. That's why I want the meeting.''

Melissa was silent for several seconds.

''Why are you doing this?'' she asked.

''Doing what?''

''Acting so portentous. Trying to make us feel on the verge of something cataclysmic.''

''Is that what I'm doing?''

''Paul!''

He relented. "Have no fear. I'm not sending you to prison."

"And that's how you're going to leave me?"

"You'll learn all about it at six o'clock."

When Forster arrived at Melissa's apartment, he found Bennet already there, stirring a pitcher of martinis.

"As you can see," he said, "I'm preparing for the worst. Nothing can beat a dry, properly chilled martini. It's to mourning what champagne is to celebration."

Melissa's welcoming kiss was warm, but abstracted. She had a lot on her mind.

"What happened to you?" she asked, frowning at Forster's wound.

"I came home earlier than expected the other night," Forster told them. "I walked in on your hired gun and got slugged."

Forster could tell very little from their reactions. Still, Melissa's eyes were hurt and angry. "You think we sent someone to search your place? Apart from everything else, we wouldn't be that stupid. What's the matter with you, Paul?"

"Probably a great deal. But in this case I know of no one else with as much reason to go through my desk and files."

"I can understand your thinking," said Bennet, pouring the martinis, "but you're wrong. And it's not even a question of trust. Because despite Mellie's obvious indignation, you really have no reason to trust us. Just as we have no reason to expect you to stop trying to nail us. And whatever feeling we may have for one another, has nothing to do with it."

Accepting his drink, Forster sat down opposite a Renoir woman he had first learned about in a high school art course. Melissa, he saw, was still angry; the emotion seemed a sincere response to his accusation. Was it possible that Robert knew about the intruder and she didn't?

She said, "Don't tell me that nonsense was the reason for this conference."

"No. But it bothered me and I thought it best to get it out in the open. What I have to tell you now is really far more important."

They sat down together on a couch, facing him. Neither of them said anything. Forster could almost sense the beating of their hearts.

"It's about your father," he said. "You were right. He *was* innocent."

They stared at him.

"What made you suddenly decide to believe us?" asked Bennet.

"It has nothing to do with you. I know your father was innocent because I now have actual proof."

Melissa's hand gripped her brother's so hard that her knuckles turned white. "*What* proof?"

"That your father was falsely accused, indicted, and convicted. I have names, dates, places, reasons . . . every last bit of it."

"You're serious?" said Bennet. "This isn't just some fanciful new ploy to . . ." He stopped as he saw Forster's face. "I'm sorry, Paul. It's just that after so many years it's not easy for us to even . . ."

Robert Bennet licked his lips and gazed blankly, almost despairingly at Forster. His jaws were tight. Melissa sat rigidly beside her brother, her hand still gripping his, her face set as though she had not been listening to a word. She wept in silence, sitting absolutely erect on the couch.

"We thank you," said Bennet. "Although thanks is really too feeble a word for what we feel, for what you've given us."

"If you'll let me," Forster said, "I'd like to give you something more."

"What's that?" asked Melissa.

"A chance for a deal."

Melissa and Robert considered Forster over their drinks. He could almost feel a wave of caution fly out of them and move across his face.

"What sort of deal?" said Robert.

"I'll have your father's name officially cleared by the Justice Department, I'll have you and Melissa paid suitable reparations for your father's false arrest and imprisonment, and I'll have you granted immunity from prosecution for any and all infractions of the law. In return, all I'm asking is your help in clearing up the indictments against the six bankers."

Other than for the hum of traffic far below, the room was silent. Forster felt his offer lying there like a rock upon which a ship has foundered.

"Let me give you the details," he said.

Bennet smiled. "Before I agree to anything, I want to hear about the evidence you discovered. I want to know why my father was sent to prison for something he didn't do, and who was responsible."

Forster hesitated. "I'd rather hold all that for another time."

"I'm sure you would," said Bennet. "But how can you expect us to consider a deal until we know exactly what happened and why?"

It was not to be avoided. Reluctantly, Forster told it all, told everything Wendell Norton had given him less than twenty-four hours before, and which still lay in his stomach like a badly digested meal. He told it as evenly as possible, trying to drain away his own feelings and leave only the facts.

"Dear, sweet God," Melissa whispered when he finally was through. "It was even worse than we could have thought."

Bennet's expression was amused. "You're being short-sighted, Mellie. You should be feeling better knowing it wasn't simply an accidental miscarriage of justice, that the president himself should have felt it important enough to sanction the whole concept, that our father unknowingly died a martyr's death. Now isn't that a lot better than believing it was just the work of a bunch of bigoted, money-grubbing bankers?"

Bennet slowly rose, walked over to the terrace and stood staring out. Then, turning, he approached Forster.

"Tell me, Paul. How did you feel when you learned all this?"

"Sick . . . angry . . . depressed."

"And how do you feel now that you've had time to let it settle in?"

"No better."

"Then how could you want to see those six bastards go unpunished for what they did?"

"I don't," said Forster. "If they were the only ones involved, I'd happily let them go to jail. But I can't accept the entire country having to pay right along with them."

Melissa's smile was less sardonic than sad. "You may as well save your breath," she told her brother. "He doesn't just mouth patriotic platitudes, he believes them."

"I wish I could believe them," said Bennet. "There's little warmth or comfort in cynicism. But I can feel only contempt for a government that could have let something like this happen to a man like David Berenstein."

Robert Bennet looked into Forster's eyes, then shrugged, sorrowful and defeated. "I'm sorry, Paul. Mellie and I love you for what you brought us here this evening. We even love you for your proposed deal. It's just that there's no way I can see us accepting it."

Later, when Robert had left to meet Annie, Melissa threw together a chef's salad in lieu of going out for dinner. Forster found the apartment strangely peaceful, a quiet empty space through which a riot had passed. Yet the small, falsely domestic scene, the mindless act of eating, of simply sitting across a table from each other, was its own kind of refuge. Forster accepted it gratefully. But at one point he felt Melissa's eyes on his face and they made him burn. The suppressed anger in them was that intense.

"What's bothering you?" he asked.

"You."

"Suddenly?"

"It's not sudden. Sometimes it's just harder for me to hide." Melissa lit a cigarette, blew smoke, and looked at Forster through it. "Do you know what it's like to have someone like you tracking us, breathing down our necks, waiting to pounce?"

Forster was silent. At least it was an honest reaction, he thought. She didn't offer many.

"And despite what Robert said before," Melissa told him, "I *don't* love you for what you brought us here this evening. I hate you for it. There was nothing kind in your proposed deal, no feeling or understanding for what it meant to us. It was just another weapon in your hand, a bargaining chip, something to give you leverage to save those six bastards."

"I no longer care about those men. They deserve everything they're getting. But there are millions in this country I *do* care about, who *don't* deserve what *they're* getting. Why is that so hard for you to grasp?"

"Because they're strangers to me, an abstraction. Only those six men are real."

"I can't believe you're that unfeeling."

"And I can't believe you're so self-righteous that you'd become obsessed with unseen millions you don't even know."

"You're the one who's obsessed."

"With good cause."

"Not anymore," he said. "Not since you turned down a

chance to clear your father's name and get a government apology and substantial reparations. Now your cause has been reduced to nothing more noble than empty vengeance."

Her eyes flashed light. "And just you watch us get it."

"Not if I get you first."

They stared at each other. The heat between them could have been sexual. Yet it wasn't. Maybe I'm being too polite, Forster thought, and decided on another approach.

"Who's in this with you?"

Her face closed in. "What are you talking about?"

"I've gone along with your little fantasy long enough. You and Robert could never have pulled off something like this alone. You needed at least three hundred million dollars just to get started, and you've got nowhere near that kind of money. So you had to have some really heavy backing, right?"

"If you say so."

"And certainly no individual would absorb such a loss."

Melissa looked at him over her cigarette.

"Which means you and Robert probably had to sell your idea to some unfriendly government."

"Brilliant!" Melissa's eyes were cold, mocking. "Which one?"

"Russia might be a possibility—yet I can't really see the Soviets as part of this."

"Why not?"

"Because right now they need détente and trade with us much more than confrontation. They'd never risk being labeled the snake in so vile a plot."

Melissa leaned across the table. "Who then? China?"

"No. China's even more eager for our trade and technology than Russia. And I'd also have to eliminate our alleged allies. Not that some of them wouldn't love seeing us fall on our face. It's just that we're all so economically entwined these days that they'd end up being as badly hurt as we."

"You're running out of countries."

"Not quite. There's still all those Third World states that hate our guts. Not to mention the Arabs."

Forster caught Melissa's eyes off guard and held them. They stung like salt. "No, not the Arabs," he said. "You and Robert would never go to the Arabs for money. That's about the only scruple I can see you two having."

"Why? Money is money."

"Not to the children of a Holocaust survivor. It would be a betrayal of your father's memory. And isn't that what this whole thing is about? Your father?"

There were hints of purple and silver in the hollows of Melissa's face. She said nothing.

"So I'm picking one of the Third World countries as your probable backer," Forster said, "one of those miserable little pest holes we've been pouring billions into for years and who hate us because we haven't given them more."

"It must be wonderful to be so all-knowing."

"I'm not all-knowing. If I were, you'd be in jail right now."

"And that would make you happy?"

"No. But maybe just the smallest bit less unhappy than I am with you and some piss-ass, profligate country dumping all over us."

Melissa rose and began clearing the table.

The skirmish had shifted to the living room, with brandy adding to the heat. They sat on opposite sides of the couch, grinding out their cigarettes in a common ashtray. Renoir's misty, pastel-colored woman observed them without change of expression. Melissa's face was cold as she awaited Forster's next attack.

"I don't find you sympathetic anymore," he said. "I did at first. The whole idea of two orphaned waifs pulling off a world-class act of vengeance was irresistible. I could never condone the results, but I could see where you were coming from, be touched by your needs. Now I don't even feel that. Now all you're after is blood."

Melissa was still sitting on the couch. Forster paced in front of the terrace's sliding doors. She watched him in silence. Then she closed her eyes.

"You're wearing me out," she said tiredly. "Why don't you go home and let me sleep?"

Forster continued his pacing; drinking and smoking as he walked. He had stopped counting cigarettes more than half an hour ago—four days' allotment smoked to one-inch butts in a single night. *She's giving me cancer.*

* * *

"I've figured it out," he said. "I know why you and Robert didn't accept my deal."

Melissa had turned off the lamps earlier and lay stretched out on the couch. In the dark, through the glass terrace doors, the moon was a cold stone over Central Park.

"I was wrong," Forster admitted. "I should have known it couldn't be that simple." He approached Melissa where she lay. "You couldn't accept my offer because your backers would never let you. They don't give a damn about your father or the six bankers. All they care about is our continuing disaster. That's what they paid their three hundred million dollars for and that's what they want to go on."

"You're brilliant," she whispered.

It was hard to be certain in the dark, but she seemed to be smiling. After a while he heard her rhythmic breathing and realized she was asleep. He found a summer blanket in a closet and covered her with it. How gentle she looks, he thought. Then he went home.

Forster came awake later that night with the wail of a siren in his ears and no idea whether the sound was real, imagined, or part of an oppressive, already forgotten dream.

Beware, shrieked the siren with the iron tongue of a locomotive blighting the old west. *Greed is on the loose. Run for the hills.*

Yes, but where were the hills these days?

He no longer had the warm feeling of some years ago, the glowing sense that this was the American century and that Americans controlled their destiny. Instead, he felt only a visceral malaise, the gloomy shadow of a half-remembered dream. They had shaped their institutions and systems, and now their institutions and systems were shaping them; disastrously. They were in the hands of dark, grasping forces. The dirty moment had come, the moment he had been warning about, writing about, for years, the moment when moral feeling died, conscience fell apart, and respect for the needs and rights of the helpless collapsed in deceit and avarice.

Listen, he wanted to say. I know we haven't done too well so far. I know we haven't learned anywhere near enough from all that happened. But God knows some of us are trying.

Amen, thought Forster.

The sound of the siren died.
He drifted back into sleep.

In Pontiac, Michigan, Rose Lapitchik was out of bed at six in the morning, had her son and daughter fed and on the school bus with their lunch kits by seven, and was marching on a picket line in front of Pontiac's General Motors Assembly Plant #3 well before the eight o'clock shift was due to start arriving.

Until yesterday, Rose, a thirty-two-year-old divorcée, and the seventy-three other women picketing with her, had been employed at the plant. They had been hired during the past several years in answer to federal lawsuits demanding that women be hired on an equal basis with men. But when General Motors announced the forced layoff of a hundred workers due to the current slowdown in sales, seventy-four of those laid off were women. In response to the women's protests, management claimed they were merely following official union seniority rules of last hired, first fired. Unfair!—cried the women and set up their picket line at the plant entrance. They carried signs that called for an equal chance to work and support themselves and their families. Most were divorced, widowed, or single. Many had children at home who were being fed, clothed, and housed by their earnings.

The first day-shift workers began arriving, and Rose bunched up with the other women to block their entrance. Shapely and attractive, she called out to the men to stand with them. There were no strangers here. They were all members of the same union locals and they all knew one another. It was a clear, sunny morning and the general mood was light, with a lot of laughing and joking as more men arrived and saw what was taking place. Some of the single men and women had gone out together. Others were, or had been, lovers. It was a strange, potentially embarrassing situation.

"Hey, Chuck!" Rose called as she spotted Charlie Baldwin, a recent date, arriving with a couple of friends. "Give us a break. We need help."

Someone handed Charlie a sign and pulled him into the cluster of women blocking the gate. A few men sheepishly joined him, kidding back and forth with the other male workers. So far, no one had gone through. Rose had a good feeling about these people. They were her extended family. She had grown up and gone to school with many of them. They had shared joys and losses. Some had helped her through the dark days of her divorce, had made her feel less alone, less rejected. Her heart swelled with a sense of community. Whatever troubles she now faced, these people would be facing them with her. She wanted to embrace each one. In the best and truest sense of the word, they were Christians.

By 7:45 there were several hundred workers gathered outside the gates, calling to one another, laughing, making wise-cracks. The women, still jammed in a tight knot and physically blocking the entrance, argued and pleaded their case in shrill voices.

"We have kids to support, same as you men."

"Fair is fair."

"Don't throw us to the wolves."

"Stand with us. Stay out a few hours and they'll talk to us."

"We need work, too."

But at 7:50 a lot of men started getting restless and pressed toward the gate. They were worried about their own jobs. They read the papers and watched the news. Talk of depression was everywhere, with more and more comparisons to 1929 being made. Their fathers and grandfathers kept repeating tales of fifty percent unemployment, of men selling apples on street corners, of the dust bowl and the Okies, of troops being set loose with bayoneted rifles on bonus marchers. If they stayed off the job today, if they were branded troublemakers, they might find themselves high on the list of those to be laid off next. There was no doubt that more layoffs were coming. In the past week alone, auto and truck sales had dropped a frightening 42 percent from the previous month's figures. It wouldn't take long for those numbers to be translated into production and employment cutbacks. They were sorry for the women, but they had their own families to worry about. Their wives and children came first.

Still, they felt badly at not being able to support the women. It offended their manhood, their sense of chivalry. All of which added up to guilt, and the guilt quickly turned to anger. How else could they justify what they knew they were going to have to do? So they began shouting at the women.

"Go back to your knitting!"

"Take care of your kids!"

"Get yourselves husbands!"

"You want us to lose *our* jobs too?"

"Take it up with the union, not us!"

"You're making trouble for everyone!"

Their anger grew with their embarrassment. Feeding on itself, it finally took over. It was 7:55, the shift had to punch in at 8:00, and they were still diddling around outside the gate.

A bunch of them pushed forward. The women, standing shoulder to shoulder and six deep across the entrance, refused to give way. The few men who had joined them were caught in the middle and had nowhere to go. Standing in the front rank, Rose Lapitchik couldn't believe what was happening. How had it all changed so quickly? What had become of all her friends, her supporters? Where had all the smiles and laughter gone? In their places, there suddenly were hard, thrusting bodies, brutally shoving aside anyone in their path. An elbow jammed into her breast and she cried out in pain. A shouting, cursing face appeared above her and she tore at it with her fingers. She felt her nails dig in. The face grimaced, the eyes, just six inches away, were pitiless as they glared at her. I know him, she thought. It's Tom Branka. We go to the same church.

Then she heard the screams all around and the shouting. They closed around her. She felt bodies drive into her and the gushing of blood, hers or someone else's, on her face. She saw the vicious swinging of fists, arms, and picket signs, and someone dropping with a cry at her feet. Then she, too, fell, and a tide of bodies swept over her.

The media had been alerted by the women's leadership, and reporters and photographers from the *Detroit Free Press*, the *Pontiac Guardian*, and several local network television affiliates were on hand to cover the brief one-sided confrontation. It was all over in less than ten minutes, with the full day shift at work on time and police and ambulance sirens screaming into the area.

Bruised, bloody-faced, but otherwise unhurt, Rose Lapitchik was defiant as she was interviewed by television and print reporters. "They can't do this to us," she said. "This isn't the Dark Ages. We deserve equal treatment with men. We'll be back tomorrow, and the day after, and the day after that. We won't be stopped."

The next morning almost 1,500 women showed up in front

of the plant. Rose Lapitchik's pretty, blood-streaked face appeared on television screens and the front pages of newspapers all over the country. Working women publicly destroyed their union cards to demonstrate their opposition to archaic, chauvinist seniority regulations. Less than twenty-four hours later, in response to the protests pouring in and a threatened buyers' strike by feminist groups, General Motors rehired sixty of the seventy-four laid-off women; Rose among them. The company announced that the rehiring was in line with its newly formulated policy, in agreement with concerned unions, to follow percentage-of-work-force figures in determining the number of men and women to be affected by any future layoffs. Since female workers currently comprised 13 percent of the Pontiac plant's employee roster, 13 of every hundred layoffs would therefore be women. Feminists everywhere called it a landmark victory.

10

Forster was up at seven and just out of the shower when Annie called.

"Are we friends again?" she asked.

He took a moment to recall their last argument. It seemed far more than two days ago, and far less important.

"I didn't know we'd stopped being friends."

"Good. Then I'll be over for coffee."

She was in his kitchen half an hour later. Her complexion was clear and her eyes were bright. Pouring her coffee, Forster felt like her father.

"What's happening?" she said. "Robert was late picking me up last night. He said he'd had an unexpected meeting with you and Melissa. It sounded serious."

"It was."

Her eyes were anxious, impatient. "Well?"

He told it to her, letting it unfold like some ancient, mythic tale of power and treachery. He welcomed the chance to go over it all, not only Wendell Norton's personal confession of a twenty-three-year-old conspiracy, but also Robert and Melissa's response to his own offer of a deal. The repetition, in the morning light of his kitchen, added needed solidity to both concepts.

Annie shook her head in disbelief. "Did you really expect Robert and Melissa to accept your deal?"

"I hoped. There was always a chance."

"Not the slightest. Only a compulsive dreamer would have bothered to make the offer." Annie considered Forster with the loving eyes of a mother whose child's naïve deficiencies of judgment only endeared him to her more. "How can you understand so little about those two? Nothing in this world is going to stop them from extracting their revenge. And they won't hesitate to

184

dispose of you, me, or anyone else who threatens to keep them from doing it.''

In the apartments above and below, Forster heard the sounds of housecleaning. Inside a wall, the ancient plumbing complained. Here, at least, nothing changed. The building had been coming awake the same way every morning for twenty years. ''I thought you found Robert so appealing.''

''I do. But the more I see of him, the more I become aware of what he is.''

''And precisely what is he?''

''A man who could easily have you knifed. I've looked close and hard into his eyes, love. They're clear and beautiful. But they don't fool me for an instant. I know they can buy me, sell me, and close me out without so much as blinking.''

A cold silence took over, and they sat inside it. It was Annie who broke out.

''Want to know what I think?'' She spoke in even, measured tones, her expression that of someone who has just penetrated a disturbing riddle. ''I think you should drop your investigation. I mean right now. This minute. I say to hell with it. I say to hell with your friend Wendell Norton and those five old-boy bigots he nests with. They don't deserve another minute of time and risk. You no longer have any obligation to them.''

''And what about my obligation to—''

''Don't say it!'' Annie almost shouted. ''I swear I'll throw up in my coffee if I have to listen to one more pious word about the welfare of the country.''

''I don't mean to sound holier-than-thou.''

''Yes you do. You adore the image of yourself as national savior.''

Forster was silent. Was it possible?

''Besides,'' said Annie, sensing a momentary advantage, ''why punish Robert and Melissa for seeking what we now know to be a justified act of vengeance?''

''It's not justified against all of America. Besides, are these the same two people you've just described as my potential killers?''

''If they are, it's because you're driving them into a corner. Tell them you're giving up the investigation and the threat will be removed.''

''You mean we then can all live happily ever after?''

"Why not?"

"If you don't know," he said, "there's no way for me to explain it."

Marty Jennings had his own reaction to Forster's latest report.

"That fits perfectly with what you said a couple of days ago about Bennet and his sister not being alone in this. If they were, they'd have jumped at your offer. Why wouldn't they, when they can see how you're closing in?"

"Who's closing in?" said Forster flatly. "I still haven't a single hard fact that can tie them to anything. All I know is that they did it. Even my feelings about Borman, Harwith, and Stone are still only supposition. And so far, my wiretaps on them have produced nothing."

"That'll come. It's got to. In the meantime I'm increasingly intrigued by your idea of a hostile power backing the whole scam. It's also a little frightening. Maybe you should concentrate on that area for a while. Anyway, think about it."

Think about it, Forster thought later—the patient thinking about the cancer in his liver, the poison in his belly. Maybe a trifle over-dramatic, but the analogy offered a fair picture of his current mood. He felt weary and baffled, weighed down by a thick, nagging anger. Everyone seemed so sure he had the answers. Yet only days ago he himself had been accused of that same sin, that same arrogant certainty.

Maybe he had always known that he was surrounded by people who were not what they seemed, that he was pledged to ideas and loyalties that couldn't stand up to close investigation, that the nature of the world he had chosen for himself had depended on his own naïveté, and when the naïveté was blown apart by truths, his world would go to pieces with it.

Yet this was something he couldn't afford to believe. If he did, then what would happen to the notion of moral choice and the concept of personal dignity and the hope of achieving some small good by taking action? And what would be left without these?

Schmuck! he thought. Stop beating your breast like an old *rebbe* at the wailing wall. Stop waiting for something to happen. *Make* it happen.

Take action.

* * *

He called Castanzo at his Washington number and reached him at once.

"I take it you have nothing new for me," he said when the investigator had recognized his voice.

"Not a thing. But I figure you should have plenty for me."

"Damn right," said Forster, and for the fourth time in twenty-four hours he repeated Wendell Norton's bitter confession.

Castanzo whistled softly. "Beautiful. Fucking beautiful. Have you told the Berensteins?"

"Last night. I also offered them a deal." Forster sketched in the details.

"And?"

"They turned it down."

"Too bad."

"Anyway, the days are going and there's still no evidence," said Forster. "I want to try stirring things up a little. What I need from you is Alec Borman's phone number. It's unlisted."

Castanzo let several seconds go by. "I hope you're not going off half-cocked with something stupid."

"Just give me the number, Guido."

Castanzo checked it out. Then he read it to Forster. The number had the 516 area code of the Long Island house where the Swiss banker was waiting to bear witness for the government.

"I wish you'd tell me what this is all about," said the investigator.

"I don't want to have to listen to you trying to talk me out of it."

"I just—"

"Stop worrying, Guido. If it works, you'll know about it before I do when you pick up the tapes tomorrow."

"And if it doesn't work?"

"Then there'll be nothing to know," said Forster.

Twenty minutes later, he was dialing Alec Borman's number from a public phone on Third Avenue. He had never met the alleged account executive for the six bankers, but had seen news photos of him that showed an innocuous-looking Swiss with a plump face and steel-rimmed glasses, who gazed into the camera with the smiling, open eagerness of a small-town grocer. That was the trouble with today's villains, thought Forster. They didn't really look evil. But perhaps it was this very banality, this ordinariness, that made them so much more dangerous.

The phone was picked up on the third ring, and a man said hello with a distinct German accent.

Forster covered his mouth with a handkerchief to disguise his voice against the outside possibility of a chance, future meeting.

"Mr. Alec Borman?"

"Yes?"

"You don't know me, but I know you. And I know what you've done."

"What? Who is this? What are you talking about?"

"I also know what Katherine Harwith and Peter Stone have done," said Forster. "You've all been made rich by swearing to false evidence. And that's fine with me. I never cared much for those six bastards anyway. I still don't. But I've got to get mine, too."

Forster paused. In the sudden silence, he heard heavy, adenoidal breathing. He had chosen to call Borman rather than Harwith or Stone because he not only judged him the most important of the three but potentially the most vulnerable. Borman had a wife and family, which meant he had more at risk, more to worry about, more to protect.

"If you don't tell me at once who this is," said Borman, "I'm going to hang up and call the police."

"No you won't, Alec. Because if you do, you and your two friends are going to end up in prison. And none of us wants that, do we? So just be patient and I'll tell you what the deal is. Okay?"

The Swiss banker said nothing, but the connection remained unbroken.

"Now you pay careful attention, Alec, because I'm going to say this only once. I'm not going to be greedy. All I'm asking for is a hundred thousand from each of you. That's three hundred thousand altogether."

"You're crazy!" Borman shouted. "A madman."

"If you and the others are foolish enough to refuse," Forster calmly went on, "I'll be forced to send your names to the attorney general, along with documented evidence of everything the three of you have done to destroy the careers and lives of six innocent men. Did you get that, Alec? I said *documented* evidence. This call is just to start you thinking about the idea. You'll hear from me again soon with the details. So long, Alec.''

Forster hung up.

Forster was delivering a lecture early that afternoon to the faculty and students of Columbia University's department of economics, currently meeting in summer session.

It was one of perhaps a dozen such talks he gave each year at various colleges around the country. He had not held a regular teaching job since quitting his post at Yale more than twelve years ago, but he accepted offers as a guest lecturer since this allowed him to be seen and heard as he wished to be seen and heard. You had an idea, a wish, a conviction, and you disseminated it. If you were good enough, if your words grabbed hold, those who heard you were persuaded to feel the same way. In his own case, Forster tried to make it known to thinking audiences everywhere that if the earth deserved to be abandoned, the catastrophe would have to be blamed as much on their fiscal transgressions, as on their moral, venal, and military sins.

Yet today, faced with an auditorium crowded with receptive listeners, Forster had his own small weakness swelling and bulging inside him. He wanted to confess. He yearned to admit he was not nearly as confident and certain as he no doubt seemed, that he had only questions and not a single significant answer in which he truly believed. He longed to reveal to all those attentive faces that he frequently woke in the night with a noise inside his head, that his shrapnel-torn body had never really healed properly or left him free of pain, that when staring into early-morning mirrors he sometimes saw the beginnings of mortality in the circles under his eyes. It was all repressed, of course. This was not his chosen speech. Yet standing up there on the platform in that warm, expectant silence, he experienced a confusing moment when he was not quite sure what to tell them.

Then what *was* he saying to them this afternoon? What solutions was he advocating for their current afflictions? No solutions. Not here, anyway. Here all he could hope to deal with were some of the root causes.

Man was just fundamentally foolish and greedy, Forster told his audience. Metaphysical forces drove him to higher and higher levels of greed. He felt compelled to amass vast amounts of money by manipulation, without actually creating wealth. He felt himself a failure if he didn't make his first million by the age of thirty, then became obsessed to get on with his second. For what purpose? At one moment, he wished to conglomerate every company in sight. The next, he played the newly fashionable game of takeover and divest, making the sum of the conglomerate worth less than its parts. None of it made any sense in terms of goods or services, but it did punch out instant millions for those who managed the finances. Until the breakdown finally came as money was siphoned from productive investment and the country lost the ability to compete with other producers in terms of quality and price.

Forster's Theory.

Clearly enunciated, even-toned, it sailed across the auditorium. In the midst of the surrounding fiscal maelstrom were his audience and he crazy? Sometimes it seemed so, said Forster. America, Europe, the entire world, had created a system of financial markets that ended up controlling the national economies that were supposed to be controlling them, and that even the alleged experts didn't completely understand. If you read all the financial pages, if you listened to all the investment analysts in search of answers, you'd soon run screaming through a maze of madness. For every ten experts, there were almost the same number of opposing positions. And it had been no different throughout history. While experts were still busy diagnosing and trying to understand old financial panics, new ones erupted, and for new reasons. The true experts, the only ones worth listening to, were those brave enough to challenge the old theories, who thought the unthinkable, who created new concepts to deal with new conditions. The hardest thing to do in economics, or in any other field, was to toss away a theory that had been in textbooks and labeled successful. Yet new policies had to be created and put into effect to face the new realities. Today's panics weren't going to be cured by trying to cure the panics of 1907 and 1929 all over again. Today's generation was programming and maneuvering billions by computer, and they were frightened. Maybe they had to be condemned for arrogance, but their elders had to share the blame for their own foolish notion that youth was the new panacea that would bring them their pot of gold. Avarice was not a generational thing. Yet it was fast becoming a national disease. And it could, finally, become terminal.

They gave Forster an ovation when he was finished.

He didn't stay long after the lecture. He usually enjoyed the questions, the student adulation, the coeds with their nubile heat, all moving flesh and shining eyes, the flattering deference of the faculty. Ego food . . . and he was not immune. But he had little patience for it today and broke away fast. It was only as he was nearing the exit doors that he saw Robert Bennet.

As Forster approached, Bennet smiled, made a small mock bow with his head and quietly applauded.

"Bravo," he said. "I wanted to throw confetti and whistle through my fingers. If you ran for president, you'd have every vote in the place."

"Yours too?"

Bennet considered it. "If you were running for chief rabbi, yes. For president, no. Your ideas are wonderful, but they'd work only in heaven. Here on earth, we unfortunately lack the requisite number of angels to carry them out."

"I'm flattered that you took the trouble to be here."

"Why wouldn't I? You're my most dangerous enemy, my greatest living threat. So who could be closer and more important to me than you?" Bennet took Forster's arm and led him out of the building. "Also, with you, I'm in a wonderfully unique and relaxing position. I no longer have anything to hide."

"Want to bet?"

Bennet laughed, the sound bright and vibrant, losing itself quickly in the soft summer air. Students strolled past with their books, jeans hugging like a second skin. The world according to Levi's and Calvin Klein, thought Forster, and was vaguely jealous of the extra years ahead of them.

"Normally," said Bennet, "lectures on economics bore the hell out of me. Not yours, though. You're all fire and brimstone, a true preacher with genuine passion in your voice. Anyone listening knew you meant every word."

"Except you."

"Oh, I knew you meant the words, all right. I just couldn't see any chance for them among our less than perfect species." Robert smiled thinly. "Still, if I had college children of my own, I couldn't think of anyone I'd rather have them listen to than you. Do you know why? Because I know you'd fill them with an excitement, a trembling tenderness for life, a mysterious sense of expectation at an age when dreams are as vital as breath. And if you're wondering how I know these things so well, it's because I never had them.''

Forster saw the gray limousine parked directly ahead. The chauffeur stood beside it, chewing on a cigar. Forster himself had arrived by cab.

"I know how busy you are," said Bennet, "but I was hoping you might be able to spare me an hour or so.''

"You mean right now?''

"Yes. If possible. There's someone I'd like you to meet.''

"Where?''

"Down on the Lower East Side.''

Forster stood looking at him.

"It won't hurt," said Bennet. "I promise.''

"Here we are," said Bennet. They had left the limousine a few streets back and were walking on a narrow side street, just off Delancey Street. Forster looked up at a small, shabby building squeezed between two of the nineteenth-century tenements that made up much of the block. Above the entrance, a weathered sign said YESHIVA KOL VODDEM, RABBI AVROHOM LIEBMAN, DEAN.

"You're taking me to study Torah?" said Forster.

"It might not hurt.''

Joke. Except that Bennet didn't look especially amused.

Inside, a poorly lit corridor ran between classrooms in which Forster glimpsed boys in yarmulkes seated at rows of desks. Forster remembered the aged, dusty smell from his own brief stint in Hebrew school. For years he had believed it to be the odor of God. Maybe it was.

Bennet led him to a cluttered cave of an office at the rear of the building. A man rose from behind a desk, a thin, shrunken scholar wearing a black, ash-dusted suit and a yarmulke, who squinted narrowly at his visitors through thick glasses and the smoke of a cigarette clamped between nicotine-yellowed teeth.

He shook Bennet's hand. "It's good to see you, Robert. It's been a few weeks.'' His eyes shifted to Forster. "This is the friend you told me about?''

"Yes. Paul Forster. Used to be Forstersky, I'm told. Paul, I'd like you to meet Rabbi Avrohom Liebman, one of our more enlightened leaders.''

Forster shook the rabbi's hand, feeling the fragile bones between his fingers. It was only then, looking at him more closely, that he realized the man was no older than he. The aging of piety, perhaps. The rabbi's initial act of greeting was to give his visitors yarmulkes to cover their bare heads. Then, waving them into a pair of shaky, wooden chairs, he settled behind his desk once more.

What am I doing here? Forster wondered.

The rabbi was looking at him. "If you're a good Jew," he said, "why did you change your name?"

"My father changed it."

"He was ashamed of being Jewish?"

"No. He just thought it would help him to earn a better living."

"Did it?"

Forster shook his head. "Not the slightest bit."

"Of course not. The wrath of Jehovah is nothing to fool with." Liebman showed his yellow teeth through the smoke. "And you, Mr. Forster? Has your Anglicized name at least helped *you* earn a better living? Are you perhaps a tycoon like your friend Robert?"

"I'm afraid not."

"Too bad. So what then do you do?"

I search for hard evidence of my "friend" Robert's guilt, thought Forster. But he said, "I write."

There was a flicker of interest. "About the Jewish condition?"

"No. Not really."

"Why not?"

Forster lit a cigarette. "It's not my subject."

"If you're a Jew, it's your subject." Liebman's eyes pecked at him from behind his glasses. "I'll be honest with you, Mr. Forster. I have little patience for assimilated Jewish writers. I've never read anything worthwhile by any of them. Besides, if Jewish writers don't write about the Jewish condition, who will? Moslems and Mormons?"

Forster said nothing. He still had no idea why he was sitting in this acerbic rabbi's office, but he did know it wasn't to defend himself.

Robert broke in. "Paul's an economist, Avrohom. You may have read his books. He also writes for *Finance Magazine*."

"Aah." Liebman's eyes were respectful. "So you're *that* Paul

Forster.'' He frowned reproachfully at Bennet. "Why didn't you tell me whom you were bringing? *Him*, we really can use. What have you told him so far?''

"Not a thing. The poor man has absolutely no idea why he's here. I thought it would be better if you explained.''

The rabbi shrugged. "Why not? It's probably what I do best . . . explaining.''

A half inch of ash dribbled unnoticed down Liebman's chest. He took a fresh cigarette from a pack on his desk and absorbed himself in lighting it. Forster noticed the wall above his head. It appeared to be a faded monument to Russian Jewry. Yellowed clippings and photographs told of trials, persecution, and daring escapes to Israel and the United States. The air of centuries seemed to float off the collection, dim ghetto rooms in forgotten cities, precarious shtetls awaiting the next Cossack pogrom. Yet this was almost the end of the twentieth century. Czarist oppression was long gone, and the revolution was supposed to have brought hope, freedom, and equality for all, Jews included. *Supposed*. So what else was new? thought Forster.

"Have you ever heard of Chai?'' the rabbi asked him.

"You mean the Hebrew letter for life?''

"I mean Chai, the cabal, the syndicate, the cartel, the Jewish mafia, the international conspiracy. Or whatever else it may happen to be called by somebody between his last martini and dinner. Have you ever heard anything about *that* Chai?''

"I've heard rumors, intimations.''

"Did you ever give them credence?''

"No. None at all.''

"Why not?''

"Because I'm neither a plain idiot nor an idiot anti-Semite. Because I've been hearing that pap about an international Jewish conspiracy since I was ten years old. Because nothing really new has been dug up out of that garbage since the *Protocols of the Elders of Zion* first polluted the air at the turn of the century.''

The rabbi seemed pleased by Forster's response. "You see?'' he said to Bennet. "Even to someone of your friend's obvious intelligence, Chai remains a myth. God willing, may it never be different.''

"What are you implying?'' said Forster. "That it's *not* a myth? That it *does* exist?''

"Exactly."

Forster gazed first at the shrunken rabbi, then at Bennet, then at the rabbi once more. "I think you're going to have to work on that one a bit for me."

"Of course." Liebman's yellow-toothed smile managed to appear almost benign. "I intend to explain it. In fact, it's just for that purpose that Robert brought you here this afternoon."

The rabbi went into his explanation. It began with the portentous sound of a mythic talk about a man, a stranger, who walked into his office one day thirteen years ago—because he had read his book *Anti-Semitism Since Christ*—and changed the entire focus of his life. The man was Robert Bennet, and he arrived with a detailed, twenty-page outline of a plan that he handed to Avrohom Liebman and asked him to read. When the rabbi was finished, he just sat there looking at Robert. "All right," he said at last. "So I'm ready to weep. What happens next?"

What happened next, continued the rabbi, was that one evening three weeks later fifteen men were gathered in the library of the Albert Lowenburg estate in Old Brookville, Long Island. Lowenburg himself was the board chairman of Kalimon Brothers, one of Wall Street's prestigious investment houses, as well as a director of seven corporations and three banks, and a ranking officer of the Anti-Defamation League of B'nai Brith. It was upon his personal invitation and urging that most of those present had come there that evening. They had arrived from all over the country, and in wealth, influence, and prestige, were the leaders of American Jewry. But until Robert Bennet was introduced and started to speak, only he, the rabbi, and Lowenburg knew the true purpose of the meeting.

"Gentlemen," Bennet said, "thank you for being here tonight. Unfortunately, you're not going to have a pleasant time of it. But I can't help that. Because what I'm going to show you now, has to be seen."

He then had the lights put out and proceeded to show them film clips bought from American, British, Russian, and German sources. Some had been taken by liberating troops, others captured from the SS before they could be destroyed, still others smuggled out of Russia by several high-ranking defectors. Altogether, they added up to a portrait of evil that few had seen before, or ever would again. And all of it had been perpetrated against Jews.

"For a while," declared Avrohom Liebman, remembering aloud, his face, even now, marked by the memory, "no one seemed able to look at anyone else. Survival guilt. They just sat there blinking, these sleek, well-fed American Jews who between them represented unmeasurable wealth and influence, yet who suddenly found themselves naked in the fire." Liebman got a strong whiff of the fear, could almost feel all that was bright and green draining away. If they lived another twenty years, or even fifty, they would remember that this was the moment that death began.

Then Robert Bennet stood before them again like the angel of death, the rabbi told Forster. "So now you've seen it," Robert said. "And they were all ours. *Landsleit*, every one. Six million. *Six million*," he repeated slowly, letting the two words sift through the large room of the Long Island mansion while the world sat quietly by, not believing, or not caring, or even being secretly pleased. "A limit was broken by the Holocaust. A control is gone. The whole procedure of genocide is now better laid out, better understood. It's no longer just the insane notion of madmen. It's become a workable fact. And unless we want to see it working again, we're going to have to start doing something. So, gentlemen, . . . let's start doing it tonight."

Then the room was quiet, the rabbi told Forster. No one said anything. Yet a message came up out of the silence like the whispering of a forest, and Robert picked it up.

"Those in this room," Robert went on, "weren't picked at random. You were chosen because you're among the leaders in those areas of government, industry, finance, security, and communications most vital to our needs. Together, you represent a power base broad and strong enough to influence most aspects of American life, and thus much of the free world as well. All that's missing is the right operating procedure, and now we believe we have it. For centuries we've been falsely accused of nurturing conspiracies. Now, finally, we're going to actually put one together."

"The next hour or two," said Avrohom Liebman, "was spent outlining details."

An initial revolving fund of fifty million dollars would be established immediately under the auspices of the investment bankers in the group, with further assessments to be levied on the basis of operational needs. The bulk of these funds would be held in numbered Swiss accounts, and working capital kept in a dummy division of Albert Lowenburg's investment company. Operations would originally be confined to the United States, with expansion aboard coming only after a firm base had been established. The entire network would, of course, function undercover. All communications would be coded, and no more than five principals would ever convene at any one time. To assure growth and continuity, the names of additional principals would be submitted for possible approval. Only one overall objective would be recognized: the survival of the Jewish people. To this end, all other considerations and judgments would be subordinated.

There were questions, objections, and doubts when Robert was finished, but none that couldn't be handled. "I learned something about wealth and power that night," Rabbi Liebman told Forster. "Mostly, they make the fear of dying that much greater." Still, three of the group refused to make the necessary commitment and, after pledging silence, were excused.

The remaining twelve stayed and worked together for three days and nights. "Robert and I broke them into four committees," said Liebman: finance, security, government, and industry. The operations of each section were outlined and procedures established. Each committee chose a chairman to represent them on a central governing board, which, in turn, chose Bennet and the rabbi as their own co-chairmen. When the group finally dispersed, they were never again to meet as a complete unit. But from then on, the organization existed. Deliberately left nameless, its unofficial designation did not evolve until sometime later. Curiously, no one was ever quite sure how or when it came about, but Chai it became, and Chai it remained.

"A mystique had begun to evolve about Chai," said Liebman, a suspicion that international Jewry was up to something, was conspiring to act in threatening ways. Even its name had started to be whispered about. It was considered a definite plus, the rabbi felt. A little fear in the right places could go a long way toward achieving respect. For two millennia, Jews had believed the recital of a chapter of the Psalms would do more to affect the course of events than killing their enemies. They had fought the world's evil with spiritual courage and the Bible, and they had paid in blood. It was time, finally, to try rifles and machine guns.

Liebman's explanation was finished.

Now all three men were silent, the long recital hanging about them move heavily then the smoke. Forster's initial shock had passed. He felt weighted down, uncomfortable, deeply confused.

"Why have I been told this?" he asked.

"I'm sorry," said Bennet. "I assumed you understood. We'd like you to join us."

"But why me?"

"Why *not* you? You're a smart, thinking Jew. You're a widely read writer. You're a noted, highly respected economist whose views carry considerable weight. You could be a significant force in pushing public opinion and political action in the right direction."

"You mean the right direction for the Jews, of course."

"For who else?" said Liebman.

"I've never thought that way, Rabbi. I've never written, made judgments, or performed with a strictly Jewish bias in my life."

"Before Hitler, Germany's Jews never performed or lived with a strictly Jewish bias either. But they very quickly found themselves dying that way."

"America isn't Germany."

"Maybe not," said Avrohom Liebman. "Still, in a few hours I'll be conducting a funeral service for one of our teachers, an old *rebbe* who fell asleep in an abandoned shul on Rivington Street while someone burned the building around him. Spraypainted on a wall were the words, Burn Kikes—Not Oil."

The rabbi's eyes peered myopically at Forster's face, a lecturer on pogroms making sure of his audience's attention.

"A brief history lesson, Mr. Forster. Some years ago, three young boys, Jewish civil rights workers from New York, were murdered in Alabama, and the six men tried for the killings were set free despite overwhelming evidence against them. Three weeks later, the released killers were taken from their homes during the night, shot once through the head, and their bodies left on the steps of the county courthouse. Their executioners were never identified. But I was one of them. Does that shock you?"

Forster just looked at him.

"Of course it shocks you," said Liebman. "You ask, how could a spiritual leader, a man of God, sanction the taking of human life? Truthfully, I sometimes wonder myself. I become ashamed. I think perhaps I should give up the calling. How did I get this way? I ask. Yet it's no great mystery. All I had to do was think about babies being thrown alive into the ovens of Auschwitz."

Once more, the three men sat in silence.

"Please understand," said the rabbi. "We don't expect an immediate answer from you. There's obviously a great deal involved. All we ask is that you think it over."

Forster smiled. Suddenly, everyone was asking him to think things over. What choices you got to make these days, he thought resentfully. Between being a victim and being a vigilante, between being killed and killing, between a physical death and a spiritual one.

Avrohom Liebman rose and came out from behind his desk. "Now if you'll excuse me," he said, "I have a funeral to prepare for."

What else? thought Forster.

The gray limousine was waiting on the next block, looking as incongruous as a spaceship would in the crumbling old neighborhood. Forster and Bennet got in, and the car headed back uptown.

"That's some man," said Forster.

"I chose him carefully. There aren't too many like him."

"I don't doubt it. But I find it hard to believe that Chai was your idea."

"Why?"

"Because it's a concept I'd expect from someone obsessed with the Jewish condition, and your only real obsession is your father."

"You're right." Bennet seemed pleased by Forster's perception. "It actually was my father's idea. He used to talk about it all the time. I was only a kid, of course, and he was just talking, but I ate up every word. With all my father had seen and suffered, he remained an innocent, filled with the most outlandish dreams."

"Obviously this dream wasn't so outlandish."

"The way he talked about it, it was. I was ten years old and he was playing Robin Hood . . . wistfully, angrily, a psychological paraplegic, sustaining himself during his more terrible moments by dreaming about a kind of international Jewish mafia, dedicated not to illegal profit, but to the survival of his people.''

Bennet's laugh was self-mocking. '' 'The survival of his people.' Sounds pretty exalted, doesn't it? Yet my original purpose in planning Chai, in getting it started, was much more self-serving. I saw it as my passport into the inner circle of Jewish wealth and influence throughout the world. And, by God, it worked. As Chai took form and grew, so did my career. Yet I never once betrayed Avrohom to further my own ends. And eventually, I came to believe in what we were doing. As I hope you will, Paul.''

It had started to rain, a light summer drizzle that misted over the smoked-glass windows and made the limousine feel to Forster, as it had once before, like part of a funeral cortege.

"Has it ever occurred to you," he said slowly, "that you may be certifiably insane?''

Bennet grinned. "Often. But I didn't think it showed.''

"Just take a look at what you've done here this afternoon," said Forster. "You've actually invited *me*, perhaps the single person in this world who poses you the greatest threat, to join you in yet another conspiracy, one that may well be even more disastrous in the long run than the plot you've perpetrated against the six bankers. Aren't you worried about my exposing both you and the operation?''

"I don't believe you would. Besides, you've nothing to expose but a myth. If you did try, you'd be dead within twenty-four hours.''

Bennet paused to pour them each some brandy from the limousine's elaborate bar.

"And as far as your being my single greatest threat is concerned," he went on, "I think my revelation about Chai was brilliant. Admit it, Paul. Doesn't all this make you wonder a little about me, make you ask yourself whether I truly merit destruction?''

"No. I still can't live with the havoc you're causing.''

Bennet stared off somewhere, his eyes those of a man who hears nothing, listens to nothing but the beat of his own pulse.

"I'll be honest with you," he said softly. "I'm only too well aware of the abnormalities of my life. Sometimes I wonder whether I have any place at all among people with natural lives and goals. I suspect my feelings and judgments because my life has been so extreme. I was once a quiet, shy boy. Then suddenly there was this thing with my father, and my world came apart. It was very brutal surgery. I didn't come out of it whole. I tended to brush aside ordinary motives and reactions and simplify everything savagely. First came my father, then came everything else. I had to ask myself savagely simple questions such as, Is this really what I want to do with my life? Am I willing to go to prison, even die, for what I believe is just?''

Bennet leaned back against the gray upholstery, head raised, gazing through the car's roof as though at a sudden dislocation in the heavens.

"I came to think of myself as marked for a disastrous end, accepted it, and lived my life accordingly. I allowed myself no wife, no children, no friends, no real home. It wasn't that I didn't want or need such things. They just didn't come with the territory. For almost a quarter of a century, I've been fighting a war without rules or armistice. Experience of this kind is deforming. It twists you out of all natural shape.''

Forster concentrated on his brandy. He was considering the question that had been puzzling him for much of the past hour. Did Rabbi Liebman know who Robert really was, and what he had done?

As if reading his mind, Bennet said, "And if you're wondering whether Avrohom and the others in Chai know who my father was, or about my little private vendetta with the bankers, they don't. That one is still all mine. And, of course, yours,''

So he's psychic, too, thought Forster, yet he had no idea whether to believe him.

11

President Hanson felt himself afloat, as in a calm sea or a dream. Making love with his wife was often like that, with their coming together in a quiet mood that was free from vanity and haste to take pleasure. After more than thirty years, there were few surprises left in their bodies. But if much of the early excitement was gone, the warmth and tenderness had grown, along with a sensitivity to each other's needs.

Tonight, fatigue and tension had left Hanson all but dead. At such moments he felt he had no brain left, no ambition, no pride, no hope. Everything appeared to have been placed off somewhere at a great distance. Even his lungs seemed to breathe back only ashes. Yet this one particular part of him remained singularly and gloriously alive inside her, inside this Felicia of his.

My Felicia.

But then there was the intrusion.

The knowledge of it came from outside, with the chill of a frightened little boy who on one particular morning knows the class bully is going to force him into a fight he doesn't want. It made him ill. He had slipped out of her, the shock comparable to an unexpected blow in the dark. He lay back in the unlighted room, feeling his heart clamoring inside his chest.

"I'm sorry." Even his voice had gone bad, as though he had been shouting for days.

"What is it? Are you all right?" Felicia touched his brow, his cheek. "My God, you're soaking wet."

"I'm fine. Stop worrying. I'll be all right in a minute."

Felicia turned on a bedlamp and stared at him. "You look ghastly."

Hanson managed a feeble smile. "Is telling me I look ghastly supposed to make me feel better?"

Felicia had reached for the phone. "I'm going to call your doctor."

"No! Put that thing down!"

Hanson's tone was sharper than he had intended. "If there's anything we don't need right now," he said, "it's rumors about my failing health. That would just about finish things off."

"And you think your dying of a coronary would be better for the markets?"

"I'm not dying of any coronary. My heart is fine. It's what's in my head that's the problem." He took a sip of tepid water from the glass on his night table. "I've decided. I can't afford to wait any longer. I'm giving Falcon the green light in the morning."

Felicia Hanson slowly put down the telephone. "Congratulations."

"What is that supposed to mean?"

"Nothing very terrible. Only that I'm glad all the soul-searching is over and you're finally going to do it."

"I wish I could be as sure as you that it's the right thing."

"It's not just the right thing. It's the only thing. What's your alternative? Standing bravely and stoically in the Oval Office as the dollar disappears from sight? Do you want to be thought of with Hoover as one of our depression presidents?"

"No," said Hanson in a flat voice. "But neither do I want to be remembered as having been the one to set off our final Armageddon."

His wife sighed. "I wish you wouldn't do that to me, Donny. I wish you wouldn't dump on me with a worst-case scenario you don't really believe, just to shake me up."

Hanson looked at her. "Is that what I'm doing?"

"Isn't it?"

"Not consciously."

"Then you truly believe the action you're going to take tomorrow could escalate, lead to something terrible?"

"I suppose if I truly believed that," said Hanson, "I wouldn't be doing it. But isn't it terrible enough that a small number of innocent lives are going to be lost?" The sweat turning cold on his body suddenly chilled him and he put on the top part of his pajamas. "But maybe you're right about my dumping on you. Now that you've shoved it in my face, I guess that's pretty much what I was doing."

"Why?"

Hanson let himself think about it. This was one night on which he didn't want to give his wife any glib answers.

"Because I'm frightened," he told her at last. "And because I love you. And because I need to feel reassured and loved in return."

"Don't you think I love you?"

"Yes. But regardless of how many people I talk to, none of them can make me feel as you do. None of them can make me feel less alone with this."

Felicia was silent.

"I guess that mostly," he said, "I wanted to see you frightened a little, too."

"I'm frightened. More than I've ever been. You can depend on it."

"I'm sure I knew that also. But this is such a damned lonely thing. I had to try to make you show me. I'm sorry."

She took his hand.

"Do you feel that?" she asked.

"Yes."

"What else do you feel?"

He was not sure what she meant.

"What *else* do you feel?" she insisted.

Hanson smiled. "I guess I feel love."

The ripple effect of the stock market crash continued to spread.

The heads of major public corporations, many of whom already were recording paper losses running into millions of dollars, found themselves in a strange, highly pressured situation. With the prices of their companies' shares down 30 to 40 percent since the start of the market slide, they felt called upon to take some sort of action by way of response. Some considered initiating stock buy-back programs to take advantage of the cheap share price. But most thought it wiser to do nothing until they had some idea of where things would bottom out. Yet they had the public relations factor to consider. Nervous executives, employees, and shareholders had to be reassured. Even though it might be better to do nothing at this point, the CEOs and chairmen had to avoid appearing helpless. They had to give the impression they still were in command.

So they jawboned it. They called press conferences. They

arranged meetings with employees. They set up hotlines so worried stockholders could have their questions answered. They emphasized that overreacting to panicked markets would do more harm than good. They admitted that recently granted stock options didn't look so great at the moment and that previously well-funded pension plans were suddenly on the thin edge of things. But they claimed that neither of these problems was life threatening, and that it would be the worst sort of foolishness to start dumping shares at currently depressed prices.

Still, what they didn't do much talking about were the layoffs already made and those planned for the weeks and months ahead. Nor did they say anything about expansion plans being canceled, or buildups in inventories, or purchasing budgets being cut back, or incentive programs being eliminated, or sharp economies being instituted in every corporate area from car rental, to air travel, to carpeting in the executive offices. And what they especially didn't say a word about were the contingency plans being drawn up for dealing with a major depression.

Carpenter & Company, which tracked household investment patterns, estimated that there were a record 50.8 million individuals in the stock market just prior to the crash. In a new estimate released two days ago, the number had shrunk to 39.6 million, and John Carpenter, the company's head, said he would not be surprised if they fell to 25 million before the month was over. He believed that many who got badly scorched over these past, punishing days would probably keep their fingers away from the market for years, if not forever. Although others might very well try again. "Human nature is strange," said Mr. Carpenter. "I think a lot of former investors will never touch common stocks for as long as they live. Yet there's always the greed factor, the desire to make money without actually working for it. For the young ones, the yuppies, the ones who never got hurt in the market before, I think there's a good chance they'll forget about this disaster and get sucked back in again."

Experiences varied. Two weeks before, Bob Handley of Short Hills, New Jersey, had written a great many call options—rights to buy stocks at higher prices—then had gone off on a long-planned trekking trip to Nepal. While he was away, scrambling happily across the foothills of the Himalayas, he lost close to two million dollars.

Henry Abbot, a building contractor in Battle Creek, Michigan, needed two new dump trucks and sold his holdings in mutual funds to pay for them just twenty-four hours before the crash. He made a 60-percent profit on his original investment and was now considered the local financial genius by his family and friends.

Most small investors were not as fortunate as Abbot. If nothing else, the collapse taught them how helpless they were in a plunging market. Thousands and thousands of stockholders weren't even able to reach their brokers by telephone to get information or give them instructions.

"What was most astonishing to me," said Professor Alfred Stiegman, a Princeton economist, "was how many investors had most of their capital in the market yet believed that stocks were way overpriced and dangerously vulnerable. When I asked them why they didn't sell, they always replied that they'd have enough warning of a collapse to be able to get out in time. Now I'm sure they'll never forget how swift and all-encompassing a market crash can be, and how impossible it can become to get out in one piece."

In a Sunday morning television broadcast, Dr. Claude Rodine, a Protestant minister and Chairman of UCLA's theology department, had this to say about the current financial crisis. "For more than a decade I've had a very strange sensation while staying in or passing through our major cities. There are all these soaring office towers where millions of men and women go to work each day and produce nothing more tangible than tens of millions of pieces of paper. The paper may come out of computers, or typewriters, or financial ledgers, or copywriters' folios, or cameras, or layout studios. Their source doesn't matter. What does matter is that they have gradually been replacing our production of *things*. Which means we're spending less and less time, effort, and capital in the creation of actual products, and more and more time, effort, and capital in the sales and marketing of products that are created and produced someplace else. Sometimes it almost seems like a diversion, an entertainment created by society to keep us amused and busy between meals, a kind of large scale Monopoly game played with real money."

"During these past days since the crash," said Dr. Rodine, "I sense a new attitude, a new outlook on the current scene in those I've spoken to. It's more than just a feeling about financial matters, about business. Religion being my field of study, I can't help noting the effect of the crash in this area as well. There's a new sense of disorder, uncertainty, confusion, all of which an unquestioning belief in a Supreme Deity is supposed to protect us against. People feel that if this can happen, anything can happen. They begin wondering what happened to the basics; a good day's pay for an honest day's work. They doubt their new high-tech diversions, their increasingly advanced generations of computers that human rationality can no longer seem to control, the concept that one can really become rich without the grinding, all-out effort of working forty to sixty hours a week for it. They feel betrayed. Suddenly, things are no longer fun.

"Well," said the minister gently, "where has it ever been written that things were supposed to be fun?"

Castanzo called Forster at home, just as Forster was starting to shave. It was June twenty-sixth, the fourteenth day after the breaking of the scandal.

"When do you sleep?" Forster asked the investigator.

"On this case, I obviously don't. Are you alone?"

"Yes. Do you have something for me on Borman?"

"Yes."

Forster's pulses picked up a beat. "Anything that sounds like a breakthrough?"

"Not really. Though you sure as hell got the fucker worked up with your call. Meet me in an hour and I'll give you the tape. I haven't time for a drive today, but since you seem to have gone into business for yourself on this, you don't need me anyway."

"Don't sulk, Guido. We both know I'm nothing, absolutely helpless, without you."

"Sure. Is 8:15 okay?"

"I'll be there."

Forster was waiting on the designated corner as the blue Chevrolet pulled up to the curb beside a fire hydrant. Forster got in, and Castanzo handed him a small package. The investigator's face was dark.

"I don't know what you're planning to do with this," he said, "but I have an unpleasant feeling it's going to be something exceptionally foolish."

"You've got to have more confidence in me."

"I usually do. But not in this. In this, you're starting to act just the slightest bit crazy."

"You can stop worrying right now. I'm too full of fear to be anything but sane."

"You're doing odd things for a man with fear."

Forster said nothing. The early morning traffic crawled past, bumper to bumper. Horns complained. A pedestrian shouted elaborate curses. New York was starting its day.

"Whatever it is you're going to try," said the investigator, "at least let me help."

Forster left the car with his precious package. "You've already helped," he said.

There was only one reel of tape. The section that interested Forster was marked as having been recorded from the home phone of Alec Borman on June twenty-fifth, between 3:07 and 3:16 P.M. As Forster recalled it, he had made his own call to Borman a half hour earlier. The banker had wasted very little time before responding.

Forster put the tape on a machine in his study and ran it fast-forward to the segment he wanted. Borman's first call was to Peter Stone at the New York headquarters of the Securities and Exchange Commission.

"It's me," he said. "Can you call me back from an outside public phone?"

"When?"

"As soon as possible. Now."

"Is something wrong?"

"It does look that way."

"I'll get right back to you," said the SEC lawyer.

The sound-activated tape clicked off.

Then it clicked on.

"All right." It was Peter Stone's voice. "We can talk now. What is it?"

"A man called me a short while ago," said Borman. "He didn't identify himself and sounded as though he was disguising his voice. He said he knew what Katherine Harwith, you, and I had done and had documented evidence to prove it. He said he wanted a hundred thousand dollars from each of us to keep quiet, and that if he didn't get it he would send his evidence to the attorney general."

"Do you think he was bluffing?"

"I've no idea. And I have no intention of putting him to the test."

"We were so damned precise in every detail. What could he possibly have?"

"He has each of our names. That in itself is potentially lethal."

"Have you told Katherine?"

"Not yet. I'll call her next. We're all going to have to get together and talk. We have a great deal at risk here."

"Everything. But I'm not sure how wise it would be to meet. We're not supposed to see one another."

"I know. But we're not supposed to be blackmailed either. For God's sake, Peter! Let's not worry about breaking rules at this stage. Anyway, we'll be careful. How about tomorrow night at nine? Is that all right with you?"

"It'll damn well have to be. Where?"

"There's a place I know on Long Island. It's a clearing in a heavily wooded area near Westbury, not far from my house. Take the Long Island Expressway out to the Glen Cove Road exit, go north to Route 25A, then east for a few miles to Whitney Lane. Turn right on Whitney Lane for a short distance until you see an old crumbling barn on your left. Then—"

"Hold it a minute," Stone cut in. "Give me a chance to write this down. Christ, how infuriating! And everything was going so smoothly. Okay. Now let me have all that again."

Forster listened as the directions were repeated. He was disappointed. He had been hoping to hear some of the conspiracy's details along with a specific tie-in to Robert and Melissa, but had gotten neither. What he did finally have, however, was the elimination of any possible doubt as to Stone's, Borman's, and Harwith's involvement.

"I'll arrive first at 9:50," Forster heard Borman say. "You'll arrive ten minutes later, and Katherine, ten minutes after that. When we leave, we'll reverse the order. Unless Katherine can't make it for some reason. In which case, I'll call you."

"Christ, I don't like this."

"Who does?"

"I just wish I knew who the guy was. You don't have any idea at all, Alec?"

"None whatsoever. All that matters anyway is that he obviously knows. Which means he has the potential to finish us.'' Borman breathed heavily. ''Unless you hear from me, I'll see you tomorrow night at nine.''

The tape clicked off.

When it next went on, Forster listened to Borman call Katherine Harwith at her Virginia home and present her with the same bad news he had given Stone.

''Oh, my God!'' she said. ''I've had recurrent nightmares about something like this happening. I've felt it in my bones. What in heaven's name do we do now?''

''We do our best to stay calm.'' Borman's speech sounded softer, more controlled than it had with Peter Stone. ''It's not the end of the world.''

''Yes it is,'' Katherine said morosely.

''The man simply wants money . . . not justice or vengeance. Which means he's a reasonable person, willing to deal. Life is full of such accommodations.''

''Please. There's not a nerve in my body that isn't shaking. At least spare me your homespun banalities.''

''Forgive me,'' said Borman. ''I was trying to make you feel better.''

''How can we make a deal with this so-called reasonable person? If we pay him what he asks today, he'll just be asking for more tomorrow. There'll be no end.''

''Peter, you, and I are going to meet tomorrow night to talk about it.''

''But we have strict orders not to meet until the trial.''

''I'm afraid we're going to be forced to ignore those orders,'' said Borman, and gave Katherine Harwith the same directions he had given Peter Stone as to time and place.

Forster heard the tape click off, then he ran the entire segment again. He wanted to be sure there was nothing he had missed. Besides, just listening to the three confederates speak helped personalize them, helped make them less abstract in his mind. Although he had known Katherine Harwith for years through Wendell Norton, they had never really gotten past the amenities. The few moments of recorded conversation had at least given him some idea of her emotional state.

As for Stone and Borman, the surprise was the Swiss banker's apparent role as leader. Somehow, considering Stone's long-heralded mixture of brains, youth, and arrogance, Forster had expected him to be the one who would be taking charge.

So what now? Forster thought and settled in with his first scheduled cigarette of the day to consider it.

He needed two things. One was a link between the hired help and Robert and Melissa. The other was detailed evidence of how the conspiracy had actually been carried out. It appeared that he was not going to get either of them by listening to any more telephone conversations, and he certainly was not going to get what he needed in time to help soothe the still-rampaging markets.

It was time for extreme action. The question was, just how extreme was he willing to make it?

The answer came quickly. He would do whatever the situation required.

And if it required the threat of violence?

Then he would threaten.

What about the actual use of violence?

If necessary, he would do that too.

To the point of taking a human life?

This was something else. He did not know. Too, it depended on whose life. Melissa and Robert's? Only if his own head were on the block. And then? he pressed himself. Then, definitely—if sadly.

Having to literally push himself, Forster rose, went into the living room, and opened the cabinet where, four days ago, he had placed the gun left behind by the anonymous intruder. The revolver and attached silencer lay behind a row of books, looking doubly lethal in this innocuous, comfortably familiar place. Forster picked it up, reflexively checked its six loaded chambers, and hefted its weight and balance. It felt solid, re-assuring, and curiously natural against his flesh. Raising the revolver, he squinted along the barrel until front and rear sights were aimed squarely at the head of a small, bronze figurine that stood on an end table. Then he let his finger slowly tighten against the trigger guard.

"Bang!" he said, and half expected to see the tiny sculpted head disappear.

In downtown Detroit, during the early evening of June twenty-sixth, the conditions for riot were ripe: an idle crowd, frustration, ugly rumors. What eventually would precipitate the necessary spark arrived at approximately 8:00 P.M. in the person of Reverend Howard Gilbert, a black Methodist clergyman with strong, highly visible political ambitions. Reverend Gilbert was addressing a rally of his supporters not far from the Cadillac plant off West Grand Boulevard where more than a thousand workers, most of them black, had been laid off earlier that day.

Gilbert stood on the bed of an open pickup truck while loudspeakers sent his voice crackling through the hot summer air and over the heads of those in the crowd.

"How long, brothers and sisters, . . . how long do we have to remain suffering black sheep in a white Promised Land?

"When are we going to stop being the last ones hired when things are going good, and the first ones fired when things turn bad?

"Haven't we had enough of our unblessed president's vision of America, where the rich, white, fat-cat bankers get richer and fatter while the poor black workers get poorer and thinner?

"Where, brothers and sisters, . . . where is the economic justice that's promised to us by the Constitution of the United States and is our God-given right?

"Why must we grow decrepit waiting for our generation to serve its day? Why can't we reach beyond ourselves as our people of the sixties did at Selma and Birmingham, in the sit-ins across the South?''

Reverend Gilbert's string of rhetorical questions soared through the settling darkness, with the crowd responding to each one with the zeal of practiced churchgoers who understand the litany from long experience and draw comfort from their prescribed roles.

"Tell it like it is, Reverend!"

"Right on, Brother Howard."

"That's the true gospel."

It was a pleasant summer evening and the crowd's mood seemed relaxed, almost festive. Street vendors were doing a brisk business in Popsicles, ice cream, and soft drinks, and there were a great many women and children present. Although there were plenty of six-packs visible, and even scattered pints of gin and whiskey clutched in paper bags, no one appeared to be drunk. Nor was there any visible rowdiness. The crowd filled much of a small, urban park, in which there were benches, a scattering of trees, and a central fountain. A squad car with two police officers was parked along the fringe of the crowd. One of the cops was white; the other, black. Groups of teenagers lounged about, bantering.

At 8:15, an argument broke out between two women, one of whose children had taken a Popsicle from the other woman's child and refused to give it back. Within moments, the argument had escalated into a full-fledged fight. One of the women pulled a switchblade and slashed her opponent's arm and chest. There were screams and shouts, and some men got involved as they tried to pull the two women apart. A police whistle blew. The two cops in the squad car radioed for the nearest backup unit. Then they left their car and started toward the expanding trouble.

Reverend Gilbert's voice called for calm through the loud-speakers, but no one appeared to hear or pay attention. The police had managed to reach the bleeding woman and were trying to help her out through the crowd. But most of those present, not having seen what had actually happened, thought the woman was being arrested. Among them was Tom Ellis, a thirty-four-year-old assembly-line worker from the nearby Cadillac plant who had been one of those laid off earlier in the day. Ellis had been drinking heavily ever since finding the dismissal notice in his final pay envelope.

"Hey, what the hell are you guys doin' to that girl?" He heard the woman screaming and saw the blood running. "I swear I don't believe this shit."

Planting himself directly in the officers' path, he effectively blocked their forward progress. Huge and deep-chested, Ellis had muscular arms bulging out of a T-shirt that declared LIFE SUCKS. THEN YOU DIE.

"Get the hell out of the way," said one of the cops and tried to shove Ellis aside. It was the black officer who had said this, but it was to his partner, the white officer, that Ellis now spoke.

"Listen! You got no call to arrest this woman." Raising his voice to a shout, Ellis addressed the crowd. "Hey, we gonna let this copper beat on our little sister?"

Others took up the cry, drowning out the few who had seen what had happened and knew the police were just trying to get the woman to a hospital. The bleeding woman herself, whose name was Marcy Wilson, was faint and said nothing. By the time the distorted version of the incident reached the majority of those gathered in the park, it generally was believed that the police were brutalizing and arresting an innocent mother of three.

The white officer, fearing that things were about to turn violent, drew his revolver and pointed it at Tom Ellis's chest.

"Step aside. We don't want any trouble here. You're interfering with police officers in the performance of their duty."

"Up yours," said Ellis.

The black cop, struggling under the weight of the swooning woman, said, "Don't be an asshole, man. We're just getting this lady to a hospital."

"Bullshit! You ain't getting her nowhere."

Ellis stood there, his anger building. Then he went for the cop with the gun.

He heard an explosion and felt something slam into his chest with the weight of a machinist's hammer. He fell and lay still. The crowd moved in. Marcy Wilson was carried off by some men. The two cops were shot at close range with their own weapons, then kicked and stomped until what remained of their faces no longer resembled anything human. Sirens wailed in the distance. Reverend Gilbert shouted for order until his loudspeakers were torn apart.

President Hanson, when informed in the early morning hours of Detroit's tragic outbreak of violence, was deeply moved and disturbed. However, he tended to blame the calamity less on racial factors than on the heightened tensions created by the current scandal-induced economic crisis. In later confirmation of this view, it was pointed out that Tom Ellis, the young Cadillac assembly-line worker whose shooting by a Detroit police officer was considered to be the spark that set off a night of looting, burning, and violence, had never before been in trouble with the law. Indeed, the fact that he had been fired from his job just hours prior to the incident, and had been angry, depressed, and intoxicated because of it, was undoubtedly the cause of his aberrant behavior in attacking the officer who shot him.

At 8:15 that same evening, well before Reverend Howard Gilbert had started to address his supporters in downtown Detroit, Paul Forster left Manhattan and drove toward Long Island in a rented car.

In his pockets were the .38-caliber Smith and Wesson revolver, with attached silencer, that he had taken from the intruder, and a dark blue ski mask that would cover all but his eyes and mouth. On the seat beside him was the miniature recording device that Castanzo had given him three nights before.

His plan was so simple that it had at first worried him. Forster intended to be at the meeting place that Borman had described to Harwith and Stone well in advance of the three conspirators' scheduled 9:50 to 10:10 arrival times. He would remain out of sight in the heavily wooded assembly area until the three appeared, had their meeting, and started to drive away. When the first two had left, Forster would slip on his mask, quietly approach the single remaining car which, according to the departure schedule, would be driven by Alec Borman, place the muzzle of his revolver against the Swiss banker's head, and get down on tape the answers he needed. If Borman thought he was bluffing and refused to talk, Forster was prepared to pump a bullet through the fleshy part of his leg and let him bleed until he did talk.

Basically simple.

And undeniably brutal. Yet not even in the same league with some of the less-official Vietnamese interrogations that Forster had witnessed.

No Saint Paul here, thought Forster. Not when speed and results were what counted and the alternatives were considered. Remembering the soft, comfort-loving face of the pudgy Swiss banker from his news photos, Forster expected very little self-punishing resistance from the man when it actually came down to it.

Why am I so nervous?

A stupid question, Forster thought. He was nervous because he had a lot to be nervous about. Despite the basic simplicity of his plan, it was still nothing more than a plan and therefore subject to unanticipated vagaries. Many things could go wrong. But mostly, he was nervous because so much depended on the next few hours, and he had to work alone.

It was close to 9 P.M. when he found Whitney Lane going off to the right. He turned onto it, a dark, narrow country road winding between old trees with black, twisted trunks. A bright moon flickered in small, blue patches among the leaves and across the road. Overhead, Forster saw the lights of a plane rising in the sky and heading east from Kennedy. He opened a window and heard the plane's engines, wishing he, too, were being carried off. Coward, he thought. Then he breathed the night air, fragrant with pine and honeysuckle, and felt better.

At 9:11 he saw the old barn on his left, exactly where Alec Borman had said it would be. He drove past it, through a field of high grass and into a stand of pine. He stopped the car, switched off the lights, and tied rags around the license plates. Then he drove forward once more, letting the moonlight pick out his trail through the woods. When he saw a small clearing fifty yards ahead, he eased the Camaro behind a cluster of brush. Then he cut the motor and walked back to the trail he had just left.

The Camaro was invisible to anyone who might be driving past or parked in the clearing. Forster returned to the car. Peering through the windshield and a small opening in the brush, he had his required view of the rendezvous area.

He checked the revolver, taped the miniature recorder to his chest, and placed its mike under his jacket lapel. Then he sat still, listening to the forest sounds. The air was cool, but he was still sweating.

The minutes moved slowly, making him start at every faint, innocent noise. The thought of what he might be forced to do began to disturb him, and he had visions of snakes and demons in the surrounding dark. A sullen, poisonous fire seemed to be burning somewhere. God knew he had shot men before, but never as he might have to tonight.

Tough, thought Forster coldly. Then let the perjuring bastard tell me what I need to hear and it will be easier for us both. Once he had Borman's confession, all the evidence he needed, Robert and Melissa would have little choice but to accept his deal. The greater problem might be getting the Justice Department to agree to an amnesty for them. But that could be managed too. Either the attorney general would go along with it, or Forster would simply withhold the evidence clearing the six bankers. On that basis, it would be no contest.

Or was it all just a little too neat, too pat? Either way, he would know soon enough.

At 9.48 he heard a car engine in the distance. The sound slowly grew louder, and Forster watched for a glimpse of headlights. According to the prearranged schedule, this should be

Borman. Forster peered through the darkness but saw nothing. Then the rumble of the engine died and there were only the night sounds.

Once more, he waited. Except that this time the air and the woods were altogether sinister. Something definitely was wrong, Forster thought.

When it was ten minutes past the designated meeting time, Forster drew his .38 Smith and Wesson, quietly eased himself out of the Camaro, and started toward where he thought the other car might have stopped. He circled through the undergrowth, stepping carefully and lightly, trying to think only of what lay immediately ahead. Which was what? And what had happened to his plan?

There was a flicker of movement in some branches immediately ahead and Forster crouched and whipped his gun toward it. But it was only a bird fluttering on a branch and he continued on. He could feel his heart going very fast and he kept yawning nervously. *I'm too old for this.* Relax, he told himself, or you'll end up shooting at shadows. But he suddenly felt adrift in a dark cavern.

A dry twig snapped behind him.

At almost the same instant, Forster dove forward and to the right, hearing the soft *whoosh, whoosh* of two silenced shots and crying out as one of them tore through his arm. A split second later, he hit the ground.

There was a fluttering sound as a torn branch and some leaves twisted down. Then there was no sound at all.

Forster lay in a patch of brush and weeds. He had seen nothing. The snapping twig and old instincts were the only reasons he was still alive. He lay half on his side, unmoving, feeling the damp foliage beneath him. His left arm and sleeve were wet with blood, but he felt little pain. That, he knew, would come later. If there *was* a later, he thought, and wondered from which direction the next bullet was going to come.

What had happened?

A frightened squirrel, disturbed from his sleep, chattered from a branch directly ahead, then came down the tree trunk, stopping on the way to look at him. Forster saw the squirrel's eyes in the moonlight, and the bushy tail, jerking with excitement. Better beat it, he silently told the eyes, it's getting dangerous around here. The squirrel bounded out of sight as Forster lay quietly in the underbrush, gripping his revolver in his good hand and waiting.

Come on, you bastard. Where the hell are you?

He felt a sudden spasm of pain in his left arm and closed his eyes against it. But this just made him dizzy and he opened his eyes at once. For God's sake, he told himself, don't faint.

It was then that he heard movement. Or sensed it. If anything, it came from directly ahead of him. Then what appeared to be a figure moved out from behind a tree, a black two-dimensional silhouette that seemed to float rather than walk. Forster picked up the glint of metal, which had to be a gun and was pointed right at where he lay. There was still no true sound and it might have been no more than a nightmare image of death itself. Whoever the guy was, he was good. But not good enough, thought Forster, and fired without seeming to move or take aim, fired as naturally as pointing a finger. He got off a full cluster of three shots, got them off so quickly that the silenced explosions might have been a single sound. The silhouette pitched forward into the high grass and disappeared.

"Aah . . ." The sigh was Forster's. *I'm not yet dead.*

He lay where he was for several moments, listening for movement, forcing himself to remain still. Slowly, he pushed himself to a sitting position and probed his wound with the fingers of his right hand. He was lucky. The bullet had missed the bone and passed completely through the fleshy upper part of his left arm. He felt the blood beginning to dry in the webbing of his shirt and thought, Forster the clotter. Nature's law on the full utilization of talent. Maybe that was why his flesh had been punctured so often.

He decided it was time to move, so he crawled painfully forward through the brush, his revolver ready.

There was no need for caution. The would-be assassin lay face down, unmoving. Forster turned him onto his back and felt for a heartbeat. There was none. With great effort, he dragged the body out of the undergrowth and into a patch of moonlight. Then he gazed down into the pale, animal eyes of the same man who had slugged him in his apartment four days ago.

How young he is, thought Forster, and closed the fine, golden eyes for the last time.

He felt no joy, not even in survival. There was too much else involved. His wound, mixed with the pestilent mood drifting out of the wood, were suddenly more than he could accept. For a true sickness seemed to be rising from the night air, something broken and dead, stale, used up, which collected as nausea in Forster's throat and came rushing out. There it goes, he thought, and sent it off, all of it, all of the bile of anguish and the horror of killing and the stink of fears yet to come. He knelt there with his eyes closed, drained, but feeling a rare moment of calm.

All right, he told himself, get on with it. When there's so much to do, even vomiting had to be a form of idleness.

He went through the dead man's clothing and found nothing, no wallet, no identification, no labels, no cleaning tags. Everything had been removed. Professional. Forster's three shots had entered the man's chest in a tight cluster, leaving the entire front of his shirt dark with blood. In one spot a shattered rib broke through in red-and-white splinters. Forster moistened his lips with his tongue and tasted his sickness. The man had been killed by his own gun firing his own bullets, but Forster failed to appreciate whatever poetic justice may have been involved. He recovered the assassin's other weapon from the grass and slipped it into his own pocket. The way things were going, he might need a spare.

Forster sat waiting beside the body on the chance that someone else might be coming. He no longer expected Borman, Harwith, and Stone, but there was always the possibility that the hit man had brought along a backup. Feeling blood starting to leak down his arm, Forster took off his jacket and shirt and knotted a handkerchief tightly about the wound with his teeth and good hand. The bleeding stopped and he put his clothes back on. When ten minutes had passed without anyone showing up, Forster took a tire iron from the Camaro and scraped out a shallow grave behind a patch of brush. Then he dragged the fair-haired man into it. Blotting out all thought, Forster covered him over with consecutive layers of dirt, dead leaves, and branches. *That could be me under there*, said a vagrant voice. Then he went looking for the man's car.

He found it about two hundred yards back along the trail, a black Ford Fairlane with New York plates. An insurance card and two repair bills said the car belonged to a Joseph Scanlon of Queens, but Forster was certain the car had been stolen that evening. No amateur night here.

The keys were in the ignition and he drove the car to the edge of a ravine he had passed a short distance back. Then, switching off the motor, Forster pushed the Ford over the brink and watched it tumble down into the gully. He climbed down after it, broke off some leafy branches, and used them to camouflage the car as well as he could. Let there be a little wondering, he thought, and struggled back up to the trail. When he gazed down into the hollow, the car could not be seen.

Forster returned to the Camaro, uncovered the license plates, and drove away.

He drove with caution, his right hand gripping the wheel, his left hand lying limp in his lap. For the first time since he had heard the life-saving snap of the twig behind him, Forster let himself think about it.

What had happened?

The most obvious possibility struck his brain like a breaking blood vessel. One of the three conspirators had probably discovered a tap on his phone, guessed that their meeting arrangements had been overheard by the blackmailer, figured him to put in an appearance himself, and sent the assassin to put an end to him.

Fine. Except that there was a second possibility. Borman or one of the other conspirators might have been frightened enough to contact Robert and Melissa about the blackmail threat, and the two Berensteins worked out the rest on their own. Reluctantly, Forster favored this second possibility. Just thinking about it brought a groan out of him. Would Robert and Melissa really have been willing to let him be murdered?

God! How naïve and sentimental could he get?

Come on, he told himself. If *he* was hunting *them*, surely they had the right to protect themselves by hunting him in return. Yes, but to want to *kill* him? Particularly, when all he really was trying to push them into was a beneficent deal, one that would not only clear their father's name but grant them immunity. And for this, they wanted to bury him?

Unless—and Forster was eager to grasp at one additional possibility—unless Robert and Melissa had no way of knowing for certain that he was, indeed, the anonymous blackmailer. Or that even if he was, that he himself would be the one to appear tonight.

I need this kind of thinking like I need this hole in my arm.

By the time he reached Route 25A his arm was throbbing and

he was beginning to see white spots in front of his eyes. I'd better get to a doctor, he thought. A hospital, of course, was out of the question. Gunshot wounds had to be reported to the police and he was not about to let that happen. He stopped at a roadside phone and made a call to an old friend.

Twenty minutes later, he drove up to a rambling, white Colonial, not far from Northern Boulevard, in the North Shore community of Manhasset.

There was a lighted coach lantern hanging from a post on the front lawn, and a shingle that read: HENRY GOLDSTEIN, M.D. Forster parked the Camaro in the driveway, got out, and approached the entrance. The doctor evidently had been watching from a window because he had the door open before Forster reached it. Neither man spoke until they were in the examining room at the rear of the house.

"What did you do with Ellen?" Forster asked.

"I sent her for a drive."

The doctor had Forster on a white metal table and was helping him out of his clothing. His jacket came off easily enough, but his shirt and handkerchief-bandage were stuck to the wound and had to be loosened with warm water.

"A drive?" said Forster. "At eleven o'clock at night?"

Goldstein grinned. He was a tall, gaunt man who had extracted uncounted pieces of shrapnel from Forster's body in Vietnam and had manifested an irrepressible affection and sense of responsibility for him ever since. "After thirty-seven years of marriage to me, she knows better than to ask questions."

The doctor studied the two fresh wounds. "You didn't have enough holes in you? Since when have they started shooting you again?"

"Since tonight."

"Who?"

"An obvious professional. Some hired hand. No one I know." Forster gasped as the antiseptic burned through. "Hey!"

"You're lucky. Nice and clean. In and out and not a bone touched. Two beautiful holes." Goldstein gave his attention to cleaning the wounds and the purple aureoles surrounding them. "So how come they're shooting at you? Is it the start of a national pogrom? They're starting to blame the Jews for our latest fiscal problems?"

"Not quite yet."

"You'll let me know when it's about to begin, so Ellen and I can get out in time?"

Goldstein finished the cleansing and stepped back to consider his work, an artist.

"Another few inches in and I'd be saying kaddish for you."

"The man was a bungler."

"So next time he might not be such a bungler."

"At that, you get only one chance."

Goldstein's eyes darkened. "You killed him?"

"I had no choice."

"And you buried him, too?"

"Yes."

"Where he won't be found, I hope."

"Not for a while, anyway."

"How do you feel?"

"Pretty good, considering."

But Forster was not nearly as casual as he seemed. Even as he spoke, he was working to master small spasms in his stomach, and he could almost hear the sound of his blood, rhythmic and quick, washing within his skull.

"You'd better take it easy for a while," Goldstein said. "You may feel good now, but there could be a reaction. Not only physical, but psychological. You did kill a man and you did almost get killed yourself. You're not a twenty-year-old soldier anymore and not nearly as tough as you like to think."

"I don't think I'm so tough. I'm just a survivor."

"Well, please survive a bit more quietly for a few days."

"Sure."

The doctor looked at him. "What the devil are you into, Paul? What have bullets and killing got to do with economics?"

"Academically, nothing," said Forster. "Pragmatically, everything. I doubt if there's been a war since the Crusades that didn't have economics at its base. Money is even more dangerous than ideology and almost as lethal as religion."

"In other words, you're not going to tell me."

"I can't, Hank. Not now, anyway. Maybe when it's over."

"You may be dead by then."

"If I am, then it won't matter anymore."

"You're a real *shtarker*, aren't you?" said Goldstein flatly.

"One of the strong, fearless ones. Unfortunately, that's just the kind that do their dying the youngest."

He worked in silence as he bandaged Forster's arm. "These dressings will need changing."

"I'll take care of it."

"You can't do it alone."

"I'll get someone to help me."

"You're a liar." Goldstein sighed as he scribbled a prescription and handed it to Forster. "Follow these instructions and don't try to be too smart. You could get yourself a beautiful infection."

He brought Forster a clean shirt, helped him to dress, and walked him to the door. As though searching for possible danger, he peered out into the darkness.

"Do you think anyone followed you here?"

"No," said Forster. "The only one who might have is dead."

"Then why don't you stay with us for a few days. I could treat the wound and you would at least be safe."

"I appreciate it. But no thanks."

"Why not? Is the thought of being safe too much of a threat?"

"I can't stay here forever, Hank. Besides, I've got too much to do."

"You can't do it dead."

"You're really hanging the crepe tonight."

"Only because I love you like a brother."

"I know." Forster grinned, feeling his flesh pull tightly against the new bandages. "Man liveth not by self alone, but in his brother's face."

"Sure," said the doctor and embraced him. "And each shall behold the Eternal Father and love and joy abound. But in the meantime, you'd better watch your ass."

And exactly how, wondered Forster dimly as he walked out to the Camaro, am I supposed to manage that?

12

Forster awoke before dawn in the cold sweat of a fever. His arm throbbed with pain, and when he tried to sit up, the room spun in the darkness. He lay back and closed his eyes.

At last, he called the magazine and told the receptionist he had picked up some kind of bug and wouldn't be in for a day or two. Then he took three aspirins and again fell asleep.

He awoke to a ringing doorbell and no idea of where he was. Then he felt the pain and remembered.

"Paul!" It was Annie's voice calling through the door.

Forster rolled over with a groan. Annie still had her key, but there was a dead bolt in place that she couldn't open.

The ringing continued.

"Paul! Open up!"

Sweating from the fever and aspirin, Forster struggled into a robe. Then he stumbled out to the foyer and let Annie in. He barely made it back to bed.

Annie followed him. "What happened to you? What's wrong? When I called the magazine, they said you had a bug or something."

Forster was silent.

"Why didn't you answer when I rang?"

"I was sleeping."

The exertion of going to the door had again made him dizzy and he lay once more with his eyes closed, waiting for it to pass. He could feel sweat cold on his face. Even his robe felt wet.

"Oh, my God." Annie's voice had dropped to a whisper. Her face showed horror; she was staring at the sleeve of Forster's robe. A deep, red stain was slowly spreading. "Paul . . ."

"Easy. Don't be upset. I'm all right. I just had a little accident. Can you help me?"

Annie made an effort to calm herself. "What do you want me to do?"

"Are you going to faint?"

"When have you ever seen me faint?"

"When have you ever seen me bleeding?"

She got some clean towels and a pot of hot water. Then she helped him off with his robe and the bandages beneath. When she saw the wound, her face blanched.

"You've been shot!"

He was able to smile. "Good diagnosis."

She had grown used to the assortment of battle scars on his body, but a fresh wound was something else.

"Don't be so smart," she said. "You can't fool around with this. You've got to see a doctor."

"I saw one last night. It's not as bad as it looks. The bullet passed through. And I'm a great clotter."

"But how? . . ."

"Later."

Forster sent Annie to the drugstore for the gauze, tape, and medication that Hank Goldstein had prescribed. It felt good just knowing she'd be coming back. *Annie.*

Returning with the medical supplies, Annie disinfected and dressed the wound while Forster lay back almost happily, feeling like a suddenly sick child whose mother had just arrived, taken over, and relieved him of all worry.

He kissed her cheek. "Mommy!"

"All right," she said when she had finished. "Now tell me what happened."

He told her the entire story from the beginning—tapes, plans, rendezvous, ambush, shooting—letting it all unfold evenly and without emotion. Annie listened in silence until he was through.

"My hero." She shook her head in exasperation. "How could you do something so foolish?"

"It didn't seem so foolish at the time."

Annie's face went slack. "Ah, Paulie. I told you those two were dangerous."

"You think it was Robert and Melissa who sent the assassin?"

"Who else?"

"There are other possibilities."

"Such as?"

"Harwith, Borman, and Stone, for one."

Annie thought about it. "No. It couldn't have been them."

"Why not?"

"Because you said the dead assassin and the intruder in your apartment were the same man. So he had to be hired by the same people. And Harwith, Borman, and Stone didn't even know the blackmailer existed when the break-in took place. Only Robert and Melissa could have known enough to send the man to both your apartment and the meeting place in the woods."

"Or it might have been Robert and Melissa's backers," said Forster.

"But you're not even sure they exist."

"They have to exist. The only thing I'm not sure about is who they are."

"Why do you refuse to believe it was Robert and Melissa?"

"I don't refuse to believe anything. They're still my prime candidates. But it would be stupid not to keep an open mind."

Annie's eyes were clouded. "I'm frightened for you, Paulie. Whoever tried once is going to try again."

"Not for a while. They still don't know for sure that I'm the telephone blackmailer. In fact, they don't even know whether anyone at all showed up in the woods last night." Forster paused. "The only one who can tell them that is buried. Do you have any plans to see Robert?"

"We're going to a concert this evening." Annie hesitated. "Would you rather I canceled?"

"I'm not opening *that* can of worms again. Besides, canceling at this point would only make him suspicious. Just be careful of what you say. Don't let anything slip out about my arm."

When Annie had left for her office, Forster put through a call to Jim Connery, a lieutenant at NYPD Headquarters and a friend.

"A modest request," he said when they were past the amenities. "Would you please tap your computer and see what it has to say about a Joseph Scanlon of Queens."

"What do you want to know?"

"Whatever you've got."

"Give me five minutes," said Connery. "I'll call you right back. Are you at the office?"

"No. I'm at home."

"Jesus, I wish I had your fucking life. Almost lunchtime and you're still in bed."

Forster lay there, waiting. Had he been thinking clearly, this was the first call he should have made this morning. It bothered him to be functioning so sluggishly.

Connery called back in ten minutes. "This is damned peculiar. We've got no record on your Joseph Scanlon. But just this morning the guy reported his car stolen. A black Ford Fairlane."

Forster hung up with a letdown feeling. Although he'd been certain the car was stolen, there had remained the outside possibility that even a pro might get careless. Now even that small hope was gone.

He kept dozing on and off, though the medication had taken hold and he was comparatively free of pain.

The phone woke him at 1:30. It was Marty Jennings, calling from a crisis conference in Washington.

"What's this business about your being sick?" the editor said accusingly.

"Nothing critical. Probably just a twenty-four-hour virus."

Forster saw no point in going into it long-distance. It could wait until Marty was back in the office.

"Anything new?"

"A few things. But they'll keep."

There was a long silence. "You're sure?"

"I'm sure." Forster could see Jennings's dark look of concern as clearly as if it were on a television screen. "What's going on in our nation's capital?"

"Controlled hysteria."

"Be grateful it's controlled."

"I don't know how much longer it's going to be." Jennings sighed. "I wish you could hurry things along."

"I'm dancing as fast as I can."

It was close to an hour before Forster had his next call. This one was from Melissa.

"Your office told me you weren't coming in today," she said. "I hoped you might be working at home."

As he recalled it, this was the first time she had ever phoned him. Just twenty minutes earlier, he had called the magazine and instructed them to tell any callers that he simply wouldn't be in today and not to mention anything about his being ill. He'd had a feeling that either Robert or Melissa might call. *I'm getting prescient.*

"It's sometimes easier to concentrate here when I'm writing," he said.

"I'm sorry to break in." She sounded curiously stiff, formal, almost awkward in her apology. "But I have to see you."

"When?"

"Right away, if possible."

Forster felt better, but not that much better. He raised his bad arm as a test and winced at the pain. Still, the arm was movable. "It sounds important."

"If it wasn't, I wouldn't ask."

He remained cautious. Bleeding could start at any time at this stage. Yet how could he logically refuse?

"Can you come over here?" he said.

"I'd prefer it. I don't want anyone knowing about this—not even Robert."

Forster gave her his address.

"I'll see you in half an hour," she said.

Forster sat there with a sudden tightness in his chest. She knew about last night, he decided. The call, the sense of urgency, were too coincidental, coming so soon after the shooting. But what was she trying to do? And why the fiction of Robert not knowing about her coming over? Forster doubted that she had done anything in the last twenty years that her brother hadn't known about.

He began preparing for her arrival. Moving carefully, he put on jeans and a long-sleeved shirt that would hide the bandages on his arm. His legs felt strange, as though he were using them for the first time after a long illness. Hank was right. He wasn't a twenty-year-old soldier anymore. As he shaved, his eyes stared back at him from dark hollows. His cheeks were drawn, unnaturally pink with fever, and tiny pearls of sweat beaded his forehead.

Terrific.

Forster policed the apartment, getting rid of the gauze, medication, the blood-stained robe and bedsheets, and anything else that might hint of a wound. He would have liked a drink, but he doubted that it would go with whatever antibiotic Hank prescribed. His mood was such that he was ready to believe Melissa capable of anything. In response to this last, he actually went so far as to stick one of his recently acquired .38s inside his belt at the small of his back. Then he pulled his shirt loose and let it hang out over the gun.

What was he expecting her to do, shoot him herself? His near panic disgusted him. Still, he left the revolver where it was.

Melissa arrived just half an hour after her call. She was still apologetic over disturbing him. Even her smile seemed forced, uncertain. Forster had never seen her so obviously disturbed. Unless this, too, was an act. At this level, he felt his suspicions beginning to cripple his judgment. Not everything she was about to tell him was going to be a lie. Before she had even begun, Forster felt himself immobilized.

She pecked his cheek, then looked around as he led her into the living room. "This is where you used to live with Annie?"

"Yes."

"It looks like home. I've never lived in one place long enough for it to resemble anything like this. Whatever I do, I always end up feeling as if I'm living in a decorator's salon."

She slowly circled the room, taking silent inventory—books, paintings, pieces of memorabilia, well-worn furniture.

"May I get you a drink?" he asked.

"God, yes. Vodka on the rocks."

Forster prepared two drinks. They looked identical, but one was pure water. He gave the vodka to Melissa and they sat down at opposite ends of a couch, an empty cushion between them. She took a moment to light a cigarette before she spoke.

"This isn't easy for me. And in a moment, you'll understand why." Again, she paused; this time for a drink. "The point of all this, my intruding on you and you stiffly sitting there, waiting to reject whatever I have to say—the point is that if you don't give up your investigation at once, you're going to be"—she hesitated—"forced to give it up."

"Is it really that hard for you to say murdered?"

"I don't even think that way."

"Your sensitivity surprises me."

Melissa said nothing, but two round spots of color appeared high on her cheeks.

"What do you think?" Forster asked. "Is there any chance of my giving up the investigation?"

"I'd like to hope there might be."

"Yes, but what do you really think the chances are?"

"Not very good."

"How about none at all?"

"Yes."

"Then what have you come up here for? To shoot me yourself?"

"You couldn't believe that."

"What I've come to believe, is that everything is possible."

"Even *that*?"

He couldn't quite get himself to say it, but he didn't have to.

"How sad," said Melissa.

They sat silently drinking. The afternoon sun slanted in, growing a small yellow garden on the faded oriental rug that had once been Annie's pride.

"It's sadder than you know," Forster said, and reaching behind him, he plucked the revolver from under his shirt and laid it on the coffee table. "This is how I prepared for your visit."

Melissa stared at the .38 as if it were a new breed of snake.

"Now empty your purse," he told her, "and maybe we can start talking about why you're really here."

"And if I refuse?"

"Then I'm afraid there's nothing left for us to talk about."

Melissa's stopped-up anger fired the room. Forster could almost feel the heat. There was even an instant when he felt her ready to swing the bag at his head. He had only to close his eyes and the violence would start. Then the moment passed and without change of expression she opened her bag, turned it upside down and let its contents spill onto the cushion between them. There was no weapon, just the usual assortment of articles that women carried. Forster picked them up one by one and put them back in the bag.

"All right," he said. "Go ahead and talk."

"I know what you're thinking, but Robert and I had nothing to do with what happened last night. We didn't even learn about it until late this morning. We were furious when we found out. We don't operate that way, Paul."

"Who does? Your silent partners?"

"I can only talk about Robert and me. Right now I'm just gratful you're alive."

"Why?"

She stared blankly at him.

"Why should you be grateful I'm alive?" said Forster. "Unless you enjoy the prospect of my sending you to prison."

"You keep singing that same song. You're not sending me to prison. You need evidence for that and you'll never have any. That's why, apart from everything else, the attempt on your life was so stupid. It was unnecessary." She sighed. "And in answer to your question, I'm grateful you're alive because whatever you think of me, I've never come close to being responsible for anyone's death—directly or indirectly—and I certainly don't want to be responsible for yours."

A curious, closed-in look came onto her face, and she paused. It was a long pause. The silence went on so long that Forster could hear a ringing in the air.

"Which brings me to why I'm here," she said at last. "I came to tell you what you should have been able to figure out for yourself by now—that if there's been one attempt made to kill you, there'll be more. So for God's sake, don't just hang around here waiting to be hit. Go someplace. Disappear for a while. And make sure you don't tell anyone where you are."

"Except you, of course."

Her look turned vapid. "I can understand your not trusting me, but don't be ridiculous. I came here to warn you, to get you to burrow in somewhere safe. How can that possibly hurt you?"

"I don't know," he said flatly. "But I figure that somehow, in some way, it's got to."

"Ah, you're impossible." The anger seemed to drain from her. "You make me wonder why I bothered to come at all."

"Why *did* you?"

Melissa pursed her mouth as though adding up an expensive bill. When she spoke, her voice was soft, without pretense.

"I came because I felt you were worth saving. And I haven't felt that way about many. I didn't want you throwing your life away foolishly."

"And Robert?"

She frowned.

"On the phone, you said you didn't want anyone knowing about your coming here—not even Robert."

"I changed my mind about that. I told him."

Forster believed her. It couldn't have been otherwise. Which was probably why she had decided to admit it. Axiom—what you can't logically justify, what's a bad lie to begin with, is best conceded.

"He had no objection?" asked Forster.

"None. I knew he wouldn't."

"How could you know?"

"Because I know my brother. And he had told you about Chai. For me, there could be no clearer sign of how he felt about you."

Forster drank his ice water. It numbed his palate. *I'm a dying leaf waiting to fall from a tree, and these two are waiting with me. But they're growing impatient. They're trying to help me fall.* Yet he had no idea what their plan was. The only thing he felt he knew for certain was that it somehow involved getting him out of his apartment.

"You and Robert humble me," he said, although the inflections in his voice made the words noncommittal. "I apologize for my ugly suspicions."

Melissa's smile was mocking. "Don't overdo it. At best, you're unconvincing." Her smile faded as she considered the .38 on the coffee table. "Would you really have used that on me?"

"Only if you left me no choice."

"There's always a choice."

"Like between living and dying?"

Melissa shrugged.

"In that case, I'd have used it."

She thought about it. "Maybe I'm being foolishly sentimental, but I don't think so."

"Don't bet your life on it."

"I doubt that I'll have to." Melissa finished her drink, put her cigarettes in her purse, and rose. "I hope you're going to do the smart thing in this."

Slowly, deliberately, Forster rolled up his sleeve and showed her the bloodied bandage. "I'll do the smart thing. If I'm ever tempted not to, this'll change my mind."

Her face went slack. "That's from last night?"

"Yes."

"I'm so sorry. But please . . ." She left the thought unfinished.

At the door, Melissa paused before leaving. She tried to smile, but it didn't quite come off. She had that look of sad, naked exhaustion that's shared by sex, grief, and total physical exertion. Then she turned and walked down the corridor to the elevator.

Forster went to the living room window and studied the street far below. There was a thin scattering of pedestrians. Cars were parked bumper to bumper at the curbs. The little traffic in motion, moved slowly.

Moments later, he saw Melissa emerge from the building, cross the gutter, and walk east toward West End Avenue and Broadway. She walked quickly, purposefully, as she did all things. Forster doubted whether she was even capable of strolling. As she passed along the line of parked cars, a tall, thin man in a light, seersucker suit got out of a black sedan and followed her. When she stopped for a traffic light at the corner of West End Avenue, the man stopped beside her, and they stood waiting together for several moments. Then the light changed to green, Melissa continued east across the avenue, and the man turned around and went back to the sedan. Forster stood at the window for a full ten minutes watching the car. It never moved. Nor did the man inside it.

Forster checked the car and its lone occupant at fifteen-minute intervals for the next hour. He tried using a pair of high-powered binoculars on the chance that he might catch a glimpse of the man's face, but the viewing angle was too high and all he was able to make out was a faint trail of cigarette smoke rising steadily from the driver's window. Once, however, as the sun was hanging low over the Palisades, the man did get out of the car to exercise his legs, and Forster saw his face. It was no one he had ever seen before.

The phone rang shortly after six o'clock.

"How are you feeling?" Annie asked.

"Much better."

"I'm coming over to feed you and change your bandage."

"I appreciate it, but please don't bother."

"It's no bother. I want to."

"I managed to change the dressing myself," Forster lied, "and I had the deli send me some dinner."

"Then I'll come over and just fuss over you and let you see how worried I am."

He smiled. "You're being an exceptional former wife, but all I really need right now is sleep. In fact the phone just woke me. It must be the medication. I feel drugged."

"You're sure there's nothing I can do?"

Forster watched the smoke rising from the black car. "I'm sure." It suddenly occurred to him. "What time is your appointment with Robert?"

"He's picking me up at seven-thirty. You can imagine how much I'm looking forward to going to a concert with *him* tonight."

"Just be careful of what you say."

The line was silent for a moment.

"Paulie, I'm suddenly scared half to death."

"Nothing's going to happen."

"I'll call you in the morning."

"Not too early." He had already begun making his plans for the night.

When it had been fully dark for half an hour, Forster made a final check of the car through his binoculars and saw the glow of the tall man's cigarette. They evidently planned to keep the surveillance going all night. He packed a small bag and, as an afterthought, the second revolver he had picked up beside the body of the man who had shot him. The assassin's original weapon, he already had in his belt. *I feel as though I'm going to war.*

He rode the elevator down to the basement. Then he left the building through a rear service entrance, climbed over a chain-link fence to the back areaway of the adjacent apartment house, and exited onto Riverside Drive. He was just around the corner from where the man in the seersucker suit was quietly smoking himself to death. Parking was banned on the Drive, but there was a steady stream of traffic as well as a few pedestrians. Street lamps threw cold, blue shadows. A breeze came off the river, and Forster felt it ruffle the ends of his hair. The sky was clear and star-laden.

He walked over to Broadway. Then he headed south for half a dozen blocks before picking up a cab and continuing in the same direction. He saw no one at his back but changed cabs three times just to be sure. In the Soho area, he paid off his last cab, walked three blocks north, and finally stopped before a converted loft building on Broome Street. He stood on the sidewalk for several moments studying the passers-by. Then he entered the empty lobby and used a key to unlock and start a self-service elevator that took him to the fourth floor.

When he left the elevator, there was a steel door facing him along with an open stairway. Using a second key that was attached to the same ring as the first, Forster opened the steel door and entered the studio-loft of an artist friend who had taken a free-lance job in Paris for a month and left him the keys for an emergency.

He guessed this could be called an emergency.

About forty miles northeast of Laredo, Texas, on a dark barren stretch of Route 59, Hank Deacon had his huge, eighteen-wheel cattle rig rolling along at a steady sixty-five when he saw yellow warning lights flashing in the distance. Oh, shit, he thought, and glanced at his watch. It was 3:25 A.M., he had a good four hours yet to Houston, and he was running late as it was. What he didn't need was another road problem. He already had gone through one detour outside of Laredo that cost him twenty minutes, and a second delay would throw him off entirely.

Behind him, the cattle shifted and complained softly as he began braking. There was a crescent of moon, but it threw little light and the road stretched off darkly across the plains on either side. As Deacon drew closer, he saw that the flashing lights were attached to a road barrier. A couple of pickups were parked on the shoulder, and some men with shovels and the orange, Day-Glo bibs of a road repair crew stood beside them. Deacon tried to peer past the barrier to find out what was wrong with the road, but he saw nothing.

A uniformed Ranger appeared in the truck's headlights and waved Deacon onto the shoulder. When the rig was parked, the Ranger motioned Deacon out of the cab. As he stepped down, a man came out of nowhere and pointed a rifle at him. A bandana covered all but his eyes.

"Just take it easy and do as you're told, son, and you'll be fine," he said.

Deacon swallowed hard. "I don't believe this shit. You guys
really gonna rustle cattle?"

The man remained silent. Deacon glanced at the others and
found them in motion, moving quickly. They also suddenly had
bandanas covering their faces. As did the man in the Ranger's
uniform.

"Hey, come on—I'm—" Deacon began, but was cut off by
the rifle butt against his back.

"Just shut up and watch, son."

Deacon heard the thump of hooves. Turning, he saw four
horsemen trot out from behind a stand of mesquite a few hundred yards off to the right. They, too, had bandanas covering
their faces. When they reached the rig, several of the other men
attached an unloading ramp to the rear and prodded and
whooped the cattle from the trailer. Then the four horsemen
took over and drove the cluster of lowing cattle off the road and
onto the plain. The rifleman prodded Deacon to follow after
them.

The trucker moved as though in a daze, feeling himself part
of a dream. It made no sense. He had been hauling cattle for
more than ten years and thought he had run into just about every
kind of craziness around, but this was a new one for him. With
the price of beef falling through the cellar, who would even *want*
to steal cattle? It was almost as crazy as wanting to steal oil.

About three hundred yards from the road, Deacon saw a bulldozer standing beside a large, freshly dug pit that was around
one hundred feet long, twenty-five feet wide and four feet deep.
An incline sloped down into it at the near end. The other three
sides were straight-walled and piled high with earth. Maneuvering the small herd like the expert cow hands they clearly
were, the masked horsemen drove the cattle down the incline
and into the ditch, where they milled about while the bulldozer
blocked all retreat with the piled earth.

Then three men with rifles walked to the edge of the pit and
began firing down at the cattle. They squeezed off their shots
slowly, taking careful aim at each steer's head, then moving on
to their next targets. It was all done very efficiently, with just
the cracking of the rifles and the grunts and lowing of the cattle
to break the quiet. No traffic passed on the road. Nor did any of
the men speak. There was only the deep, blue darkness, a sliver
of moon and a few lighted cigarettes.

They're crazy, thought Deacon. I've fallen into the hands of a gang of madmen who get their rocks off by killing perfectly good cattle and might even end up killing *me*. He thought of making a run for it but knew he wouldn't get ten feet. Finally, he just stood there, watching the methodical slaughter and wondering how he had gotten so unlucky.

When the last steer had been shot and lay still in the ditch, a layer of lime was spread over the carcasses. Then the bulldozer went to work piling the excavated earth back into the mass grave. A few men helped out with shovels. From start to finish, the entire operation had taken no more than half an hour.

The rifleman marched Hank Deacon back to his rig. "You can be on your way now, son. Just do us one small favor. When you get to Houston, go straight to police headquarters and tell them what you saw happen here tonight."

Deacon stared dumbly at the pale, squinty eyes above the bandana. "You mean *everything*?"

"That's right. Everything."

"But what's this all about?"

"Beef, son—a fair and decent price for beef."

It was all on the ten o'clock network news that morning. For hours, partial reports had been drifting in from various locations throughout the west and southwest, but it wasn't until ten that the full picture emerged. In all, 217 shipments had been stopped in nine states, and the cattle slaughtered and buried. The total loss came to slightly over ten thousand head of prime beef. Additionally, anonymous messages to newspapers and network newsrooms promised that unless the nation's giant meatpackers and supermarket chains immediately raised the prices paid to cattle ranchers back up to where they had been prior to the recent crash, the slaughter would be repeated at regular intervals until the resulting beef shortages alone forced up the going rates.

The message writers claimed they didn't want to be unreasonable. They understood that the nation's markets were going through a period of turmoil. But they found it impossible to survive a situation that saw them being paid less for cattle than it cost to feed and market them.

"We refuse to be punished and destroyed," declared one of

the more thoughtful of the messages, "for venality and greed in which we never took part. What has happened in this country is that our financial system has become totally separated from the realities of day-to-day living. Beef has always been and continues to be one of those realities. If necessary, we'll bury our cattle rather than have them stolen from us."

On the Chicago Commodities Exchange, the price of beef leaped its daily allowable limit within minutes from the time the news flashed across the tickers.

Admiral Payson's breath was bad again. He could almost taste it as he swallowed. The coded message from the chief of Naval Operations had come in less than three hours ago and changed the condition of his stomach, his blood pressure, and his whole outlook on life. It was daylight, with the Mediterranean stretching off in the sun and glinting like the purest of sapphires. Yet the admiral felt as though he, his flagship, the might of his entire fleet, was suddenly sailing to some baleful rendezvous in the dark.

Something bad was waiting for them, though he had no real knowledge of what. He couldn't see or even envision it. But his senses told him it was there, bringing him one of those anxieties that made it a dangerous act of balance simply to breathe. Something hurtful was out there gathering force, and they were getting closer to it. His radar reported no ships, planes, or missiles, yet he had a sense of oppression. Payson felt vile, and it was the message from Washington that had done it.

The admiral, a lean, hard-faced, graying man, stood alone at the starboard side of the battleship's bridge and squinted toward the sun and the horizon, seeing nothing of either. Several of his officers glanced at his back from time to time, but knew better than to approach him in his present mood. He was tough, iron-assed at best, and he currently was far from his best. Those officers senior enough to be privy to the contents of the top-secret dispatch that had come in from Washington that morning were as puzzled and concerned as their commander, but it was the curious intensity of the admiral's reaction that disturbed them even more.

The communication itself was less than reassuring. All leaves were canceled as were the training exercises scheduled for the weeks directly ahead. In addition, a long-planned good will mission to the French Riviera by several of the fleet's smaller battle units was put off indefinitely. Fuel and ammunition were to be checked and brought to full combat status. It represented the highest state of readiness short of an outright declaration of war. The officers reflected on the implications of the sudden, unexpected situation. None of them could come close to guessing the truth about what had become known, to only that select few in Washington, as Operation Falcon.

Admiral Payson did not even try to guess. Intuition was more to his taste.

The admiral gave some orders to the senior watch officer and left the bridge.

Out on the forward deck, alone at the rail, the purity of the air left him breathless. There was no hint of stain on the water, which stretched off, unbroken, to the horizon. Its color was deep and clear, its smell pungent with life. A vast, unseen action was going on below. Yet, thought Payson, death watched.

"I wish we were going home," he said aloud.

But now the president, his commander-in-chief, was inexplicably sending him, and every man with him, into war.

Some of the medication that Hank Goldstein had prescribed for Forster's wound must have indeed contained a strong soporific, because Forster had been settled into his friend's loft for no more than an hour when he fell into a deep sleep.

He awoke to silence, a bright morning light, and the head of an old man staring at him, one-eyed, from a tall studio easel. The eye was a pale, glittering blue that caught the light of a window and threw it back like chipped glass. The other eye, the blind one, gazed out of a milky pool. Forster's unknowing host, Isaac Becker, had a morbid eye.

He rose from the couch and drifted about the cool, high-ceilinged loft with its exposed pipes, rotting floors, and collection of canvases hanging from and leaning against the walls. His arm was stiff and hurting, but was no worse than yesterday. Nor was there any sign of fresh blood on the dressing. He showered carefully, keeping the wound dry, and took his medication. Fever and infection were not included in his plans. He found some eggs, instant coffee, and stale bread in the refrigerator, and put together a quick breakfast. When he finished eating, he was ready to start.

Whoever it was out there, he would make come to him.

A brief concern that he had failed to consider was the telephone. If Isaac had had it disconnected before leaving for Paris, there would be complications. But when he picked up the receiver, he heard the dial tone.

All right.

His first call was to Annie's apartment. He knew she would be in her office, but he wanted to leave a message on her machine.

"Hi, darling," he said when her recording had given him the signal to speak. "Just didn't want you worrying in case you called, got no answer, and thought I'd died. I'm really feeling much better. In fact, I'll be working at Isaac Becker's studio for a few days. Take care and I'll be in touch."

Forster then called Annie at her office.

"Where the devil are you?" she said. "I called twice and got no answer. Were you unconscious or just not answering the phone?"

"Neither. I'm at Isaac Becker's loft. I'll be staying here for a few days while he's in Paris."

"What for?"

"I just thought it might be smarter to disappear for a while."

There was a long pause.

"I have the extremely unpleasant feeling," Annie said slowly, "that things are even worse than I thought."

"The only reason I'm calling is so you won't worry about where I am. Nothing has changed."

"Do Robert and Melissa know where you are?"

"Definitely not. And if you happen to speak to either one of them . . . or to anyone else, for that matter . . . you don't know either. As far as you know, I'm still in my apartment. Understand?"

"No. I don't understand a thing."

"Good. Let's keep it that way for a day or two. If you need me, I'm at 555-8837. But don't call unless it's an emergency."

"Oh, Paul . . ." Annie sounded miserable. "Have you got your medicine? Who's going to change your bandage? Is there anything there for you to eat?"

"It's okay. I've got everything I need."

Forster said good-bye and hung up.

His third and final call was to Marty Jennings, who was due back from Washington that morning.

"I'm on to something, Marty. I can't tell you anything now, but it looks to be a lot more than either of us ever expected. I probably won't be in for another day or two."

"You mean the virus was just a gambit."

"Yes."

"I feel better. I knew you couldn't be like everyone else. You didn't answer your phone early this morning. Where are you calling from?"

"Isaac Becker's studio. The number is 555-8837. But don't call unless you're bleeding."

"What's going on?"

"When I can talk about it, you'll be the first to know."

"You're sure you're okay?"

"I'm terrific."

"I think you're a fucking liar."

"If you've got to be a liar, that's the best kind to be," said Forster and gently put down the receiver.

With all three hooks baited and in the water, he settled in for the several hours of waiting it probably would take to know whether he had gotten a nibble. They would have to be consummate fools not to have tapped at least one of the three numbers he had called, and fools they definitely were not.

He began checking the loft, which was just one huge, unbroken expanse with partitions separating the living, sleeping, and dining areas from the central work space. There were two fire exits as well as the steel door through which Forster had entered. The fire exits were secured with dead bolts and police locks that could not be opened from the outside. The entrance door was fitted with an ordinary commercial spring lock that could be picked open in a minute by any competent professional. It also had a dead bolt that Forster slid open.

Then he went over his two revolvers, both courtesy of the dead assassin. There were three unspent cartridges left in one revolver and four in the other. He left them divided that way. He placed the first weapon in his belt and the second one behind a couch pillow.

Then he sat down on a scratched bentwood chair and stared back at the one-eyed old man on the easel.

Time dragged. His arm began to ache, reminding him to take

his pills. He stared out of the big loft windows. It had started to rain, a soft summer drizzle that drifted against the glass and ran down in tiny rivulets, blurring the outlines of the soot-stained buildings across the street. Weather had never played much of a role in his life, but he wondered now what effect the wet skies might have on what lay ahead. Still, the air in the studio smelled pleasantly pungent with the odor of Isaac Becker's oils and turpentine, and if there were demons in the heavens, they made no entrance here.

It was early evening, and he was on the edge of dozing again when a soft tapping at the door brought him out of his chair in a rush. He drew the revolver from his belt and moved quickly and silently to the wall beside the entrance door. There was another, heavier tapping at the door and a man's voice called, "Hello? Anyone home in there?"

Barely allowing himself to breathe, Forster stood there, poised and waiting.

"Mr. Becker?" called the voice more loudly. "This is Andy, from maintenance. There's a problem with our main drain. I'm going to have to turn off your water for a few hours."

Forster carefully drew back the hammer of his revolver. He heard the scratching sound of a key being fitted into the door and worked from side to side. Then the lock clicked, the door slowly opened, and a man came in behind a leveled automatic.

Forster rammed the muzzle of his .38 against the back of the man's neck. "Don't move."

There was the soft, sibilant sound of air being sucked in. That was all. "Now you can drop the gun," said Forster.

"It may go off if it hits the floor wrong." The man's voice was calm, reserved, and carried a slight Boston accent. "May I flick the safety on?"

"Yes. But very carefully."

The automatic clattered to the floor; Forster kicked it into a corner. Then he shoved the gunman into a chair and sat down on the couch, facing him. "Who are you?"

"Call me Max."

He smiled as he spoke, a balding, middle-aged man whose steel-rimmed glasses and dark, pinstripe suit gave him the look of a moderately successful accountant. His eyes were dark and as flat in expression as an Oriental's. But his smile was impressive, because it so clearly was that of someone who had learned to smile through losses.

"I need some questions answered, Max. You can do it the hard way or the easy way. It's up to you."

"You've got the gun, Mr. Forster. I suffer no death wish. Ask your questions."

"You were sent here to kill me?"

"Nothing personal. I've enjoyed reading you for years. But a job is a job."

"Who hired you?"

Max sighed. "Unfortunately, I don't have the answer to that."

"Come on!"

"I'm not stalling. I absolutely don't know who hired me. I almost never know. It's all done via the telephone these days. It's for our mutual protection. If something goes wrong, neither of us can identify the other."

"I haven't time for bullshit. You have ten seconds to give me a name."

"Shooting me won't get you what I don't have. Please consider the logic of what I'm saying. Despite my embarrassing failure here this evening, I'm the best in my field. I'm a specialist. I work only for a select clientele who demand discretion, efficiency, and no complications. They call in their instructions via a public number, never identify themselves, and leave full, cash payment, in advance, at a predetermined drop. It's a system that functions on mutual need, not trust."

The sonofabitch is telling the truth, thought Forster, and wondered what he was supposed to do with the Boston killer now that he had him. If he turned him loose, he'd simply come right back after him.

Coldly amused, Max was watching him, radar to radar. "You really have no idea how to handle me, do you?"

"There's always the police," Forster said.

"Not for you. I don't know what you're involved in, or why my client wants you dead. But if you were able to go to the police you'd have gone to them long before I ever arrived."

Max sighed. "What you really should do is shoot me. But of course you won't. You're obviously too civilized for that."

"Wishful thinking."

The gunman's smile was still there, brighter than ever. He gave a brush to the lint on his sleeve, let his hand follow through in a broad, sweeping stroke and knocked the revolver free of Forster's grip, across the floor, and under the stove. Instantly, Max was out of his chair and sprinting for the automatic that Forster had kicked into a corner. Forster went after him, his adrenaline pumping. *Schmuck! You're dead if he gets that gun.*

He left his feet in a flat-out dive that carried him halfway across the room before he landed like a beached porpoise. But his momentum sent him sliding far enough across the floor to grab Max's ankle and hang on. The pain left the wound in his arm and ran riot through his body. A kick caught his head with enough impact to jar him loose from Max's ankle. Pulling free, Max went for the automatic once more.

Forster was up and right behind him, but something took over the gunman then, perhaps some instinct that said the odds weren't quite good enough, for he suddenly decided to get himself out of there while he still had the chance. Turning, he dashed for the door instead of his automatic.

Forster picked up the gun, flicked off the safety, and went after him. But Max was part way down the fire stairs and out of sight before Forster even reached the vestibule. Forster started down the stairs after him, then stopped. What did he expect to do? Chase the man through the streets, gun in hand, firing as he ran?

Painfully, Forster climbed back upstairs to the loft. This time he locked the dead bolt behind him. It was only as he was sitting on the couch once more, that he thought of the revolver he had left under a pillow for an emergency. Not good. He should have remembered it earlier. Still, he wasn't dead. So there was hope.

He left Isaac Becker's studio half an hour later. If Max himself didn't return, someone else undoubtedly would. Forster carried one .38 stuck in his belt, the other, in his inside jacket pocket. He tossed Max's automatic down the first open sewer he passed.

Frank Reilly left McGinty's Bar and walked west on Twenty-fourth Street toward his parked car. A hazy moon hung low over the New Jersey Palisades and the masts of a freighter rose above its pier at the far end of the block. It was a warm evening and the SEC lawyer had his jacket off and his tie loosened. It had been another draining day and even his usual stop at McGinty's had failed to refresh him. He felt tired in a way he had never been tired before. Although he knew it was more the emotional strain than the physical, the net result was exhaustion. And he saw no prospect of it changing anytime soon. Certainly not until the banker's case was tried, settled, and part of history—and maybe, he thought, not even then.

Reilly was at the point where he considered his life divided into two separate areas—Before the Case and After the Case. In his mind, the words were capitalized. Nothing had been the same for him since the indictments—not in the office, not at home, not with the women he saw, not with friends, not with strangers who approached him in restaurants and on the street to offer their thoughts on the subject. Reilly had known it was not going to be easy for him, but had never expected anything close to this. The hostility was overwhelming. It was almost as though *he*, not the six bankers, was responsible for what was happening to the country. It was *he* who was head of the SEC's investigative branch. It was *his* division that had come up with evidence upon which the Case was built. Meaning, had it not been for *him*, the economy, the country, the world at large, would still be happily spinning along. During the darkest of his moods, he came close to believing it himself.

Lost in his thoughts, Reilly walked past his car and had to backtrack fifty yards. Then he got in, pulled away from the curb, and stopped for a traffic light on Ninth Avenue.

Something cold and hard pressed against the back of his neck.

"This is a gun," said a man. "Don't look in the mirror and don't turn around."

Reilly stiffened at the wheel. A hand reached over his shoulder and angled the rearview mirror upward. "No hassle," he said. "My wallet's in my back pocket."

"Shut up and do as I tell you," said the voice. "Turn down Ninth Avenue and make a right on Twenty-third to the river. Then head uptown for three blocks to Twenty-sixth. You got that?"

"Yes."

"Do it."

The light changed, and Reilly followed the man's instructions. He hoped he wasn't a trigger-happy junkie and that all he wanted was money. The fact that he was trying to hide his identity was a good sign. There were mostly factories and warehouses in the area, everything was closed for the night, and the streets were empty. Reilly turned uptown under the West Side Highway and slowed as he approached Twenty-sixth Street. The gun was still pressed to the back of his neck.

"Pull in between those two bulldozers."

There was construction going on in the area and machinery was parked in the center of the road. Reilly stopped the car, facing piers and the river. There was the sound of traffic on the roadway overhead.

"What do you want?" he asked.

"My job . . . my money . . . my future," said the voice. "Everything you've taken from me."

Christ, another one, thought Reilly. "You've got the wrong guy, mister. I don't even know you."

"But I know *you*. You're the bastard who's pissed up everything. I don't blame those six bankers. So they're money hungry; they're greedy. Who isn't? Yet nothing they did hurt a soul 'til you blew the whistle. But *you* sure as hell hurt plenty. And for that, I'm going to put a hole in your head."

Reilly felt the sweat break out across his back. He was frightened but not surprised. Considering the calls and letters he'd been getting, he was amazed that something like this hadn't happened sooner.

"I was only doing my job."

"Come on, Reilly. You're not stupid. You're an SEC lawyer. You understand things about the economy that I'll never understand in a hundred years. But even I could have figured out the kind of earthquake those indictments were going to set off. Why the hell couldn't you?"

Reilly stared straight ahead through the windshield. The sweat was on his forehead now and running into his eyes. "What did you expect me to do? Bury the evidence and let them go on spitting on the law? I couldn't do that."

"You self-righteous prick!" The man's voice rasped harshly. "Why couldn't you?"

"Because I took an oath to—"

Something exploded across the back of Reilly's head. I'm dead, he thought, and saw red rain. But he had just taken a gun butt.

"Don't give me that oath shit. You got some kind of deal with God? You just had to be a big man, and to hell with the rest of us. All you cared about was getting your goddamn picture in the papers."

"No." Reilly's head was spinning, his voice a whisper. The lights of cars sped by—front and back. "I swear. Even if I'd wanted to bury the evidence, I couldn't. Too much was involved. Too many knew about it."

"But you didn't *want* to bury it. You wouldn't have buried it no matter what. *Would* you?"

Reilly licked his lips and opened his mouth, but nothing came out. *He's really going to shoot me. I'm going to die in the front seat of my car like a Mafia hood and no one will ever know who did it.* The gun hit him again and he slipped sideways against the door.

A hand grabbed his collar and yanked him straight. "*Would* you?" insisted the voice.

"No," the lawyer whispered. "I wouldn't."

"Sure." The man hit him again, this time for just the pleasure.

Reilly felt a light going out somewhere inside his head and fought to keep it alive. If he had to die, he didn't want it to be for the wrong reason. That seemed insanely important. "But it wasn't because I wanted my picture . . . in any . . . goddamn paper."

"What then?"

"To keep . . . those six fucking money barons . . . from crapping all . . . over . . . me."

"That's all?" The voice sounded disappointed.

"Hey . . ." Reilly concentrated on not passing out. "What . . . else is . . . there? . . ."

Then there was a giant explosion that took off the back of his head, and the wavering light went out.

He awoke lying across the front seat of his car, staring sideways at the dashboard lights. I'm alive, he thought, and wondered what was coming next. When he was able to lift his head, he peered into the rear of the car and found it empty.

14

The human soul has more faces than I will ever begin to imagine, thought Forster, and I will never get to know even the smallest fraction of them. Did someone like Max, who actually took pride in his work, also enjoy the luxury of a soul? Did it simply come with the territory, or did it have to be earned?

Forster wished he knew. Or at least that it might be possible for him to learn. He was learning other things, so why not that? Tonight, for example, he had found himself learning to enter a new realm of reverse thinking, in which right became wrong, and wrong turned out to be only what ended up getting you killed. He also had learned that it was quite possible to sit face-to-face with a hired assassin, talk with him, and find the conversation to contain more clarity and logic than many of the intellectual discussions that had bored him over the years. Finally, he had the feeling that before the night was through, he was going to learn even stranger things than these. That is, if he lived.

Driving another rented car, a gray Cutlass, Forster already had traveled over much of the same route he had covered two nights before on his way out to Old Brookville. This time, however, he was heading straight for Alec Borman's house. There was no more time for subtleties. Two attempts already had been made to kill him.

Once again he turned off the Long Island Expressway at Glen Cove Road and headed north. His plan was little different from that of the other night, when he had hoped to pressure Borman into a detailed confession, except this time it was likely that Borman's wife would be present. Forster didn't like it, but could see no way of avoiding her, not if the action was to be carried out tonight.

For the second time in forty-eight hours, he turned east on

Route 25A, but this time he continued on past Whitney Lane for several miles until he came to Route 107. Then, following the directions he had once gotten from Castanzo, he drove north for about five minutes, then right on Chicken Hawk Road until he saw house lights through the trees. He pulled off the road and parked in the shadow of some privet hedges.

The earlier rain had stopped, and there was a moon and stars, blue-and-white points between clusters of leaves. A fluid suddenly came into Forster's eyes, clear but distorting, and he wiped it away with a handkerchief. God, he despised what he was about to do! If you finally became what you did, what did this turn him into?

Forster put on his ski mask, checked the revolver in his belt and the miniature recorder taped to his chest, and left the car. It was shortly after ten.

The house was a white, shingled Colonial. There were coach lanterns on either side of the entrance and lights were on in several of the downstairs rooms and in one of the upstairs bedrooms. Two cars were parked in the driveway; Forster had no idea whether they both belonged to the Bormans. If there were guests, nothing could be done until they left.

Moving across a shadowed stretch of lawn, Forster crouched among some shrubs and peered through a living room window. The lights were on, but the room was empty, as was the dining room when he crossed over to another window and looked in. Circling to the rear of the house, he stared into the kitchen, feeling like an unsettling mix of voyeur and cat burglar. No one was in the kitchen either, although there were unwashed dishes in the sink.

Forster was tempted to take off the ski mask, but didn't. Although the conspiracy's principals knew who he was, he doubted that they had passed the information on to Borman, Stone, and Harwith, and he thought it best to leave it that way. An anonymous gun always carried more threat. Economists might depress people, but they frightened no one. And if nothing else, it was important that he be able to scare the absolute hell out of Borman.

The only remaining room on the first floor was the den, and when Forster looked in, this, too, was empty. The Bormans were upstairs, and there probably were no guests. The kitchen window was open, and Forster cut away a section of screening with his pocket knife and climbed through. He stood there in the kitchen, listening, his gun in his right hand. He heard no voices, no radios or television sets, no squeaking of floorboards beneath someone's feet. The house was quiet.

Planting his feet with care and listening after each step, Forster left the kitchen and began climbing the stairs to the second floor. He moved in an aura of pain and fatigue. A light was on in what appeared to be the master bedroom, and he headed toward it, the .38 extended before him, his feet soundless on the carpeting of the upper hall. He paused for a moment at one side of the open doorway. Then crouching slightly, he whirled into the room.

Alec Borman and his wife lay side by side fully clothed on the double bed, each of their pillows soaked with blood. Mrs. Borman had been shot through the back of the head, her husband, through the right temple. A nickel-plated revolver was in Borman's hand. Both bodies were still warm, but Forster could feel no pulse. A soft groan came out of him. Closing his eyes, he saw a fall of red velvet rain, brilliant as blood. My God! he thought. The sonofabitch is going to kill all three of them.

The knowledge arrived in an instant of calm as absolute as the silence you hear in a snow-covered wood on an icy winter night. *Call Stone.*

Using a downstairs phone, he got information and called Peter Stone's number in Manhattan. When there was no answer after ten rings, he left the house at a dead run. Moments later, he was speeding toward New York.

The concept had hit him whole, but now he worked it through, step by step. The calm was still with him, making everything so clear he could all but see the images and hear the imagined dialogue as Max dashed out of Isaac Becker's studio and found a pay phone somewhere.

The client would have to be furious and a little desperate. Forster imagined him having to switch over to his contingency plan. It could be days or even weeks before Max could fulfill his contract on Forster, during which time there would be a good possibility that Forster might get to any of the three key witnesses in the scandal, put on enough pressure to squeeze out the truth, and destroy everything. The logical step was therefore the elimination of the three most vulnerable links in the conspiracy's chain . . . Borman, Stone, and Harwith.

With Borman and his wife already disposed of, Forster figured that Stone had to be next. Since Katherine Harwith lived way off in a suburb of Washington, Max would in all probability be keeping her for last.

Forster wished he knew how much of a lead Max had on him. Since the bodies on the bed were still warm, they couldn't have been dead for long. He had the Cutlass up to seventy now and was watching for police cars, yet even if he went to ninety, he still couldn't beat Max to his next target. His only hope was that Stone would be someplace other than in his apartment when Max arrived there. It was close to midnight, but there was always the chance that Stone might still be out. Gripping the wheel, Forster's knuckles were white.

He was on the Queensborough Bridge when he heard the wail of sirens in the distance. They went through him in an icy blast. Forster stormed the Cutlass up Third Avenue.

The avenue was blocked at Seventy-third Street by two police cars. Forster double-parked and walked the rest of the way toward the high rise where Peter Stone lived. There was a crowd of people in the street and faces at windows. Forster pushed through the crowd in time to see a green body bag on a stretcher being loaded into an ambulance. There were pools of blood in the gutter and trails of red footsteps. Men and women stood about in small groups, talking and shaking their heads. Forster saw two cops taking notes as they talked to a uniformed doorman. When the cops had finished their questioning, Forster went over to the doorman.

"What happened?" he asked.

The doorman was enjoying his celebrity. "A high diver. Dove right off his terrace. Thirty-second floor. Damndest thing you ever saw. Split his head like a fucking cantaloupe." A grimace, intended to demonstrate horror, showed mostly delight.

"You knew him?"

"Sure did. Lived here for three years. A real young hotshot. Government lawyer. Who'd expect something like this from a guy like that? I mean he had it made. Picture in all the papers. You must have seen it. He's the one nailed those six crooked bankers." The doorman mopped his face with a handkerchief. "Jesus Christ! The guy had everything to live for. Must have been on something. Damned shame."

Forster walked away. Every pulse in his body was hammering

and his mouth tasted of ashes. He had thought himself prepared, but there was no preparing for this. It was as if something deadly had been grated into his bloodstream. Then a warning bell sounded somewhere in his brain and he took hold.

What he had to think about now was Katherine Harwith in Alexandria, Virginia.

It was nearly midnight, and when he called La Guardia he learned, without surprise, that there were no further flights to Washington that night. Which meant that Max would be driving, just as he himself would have to do. Except that Max, having close to an hour's lead, would be impossible to catch.

Armed with a pocketful of change, Forster got Katherine Harwith's number from information and put through the call. This isn't going to be easy, he thought, but what choice do I have? A sleep-fogged voice answered on the fifth ring.

"Katherine?" he said.

"Yes. Who is this?"

"This is Paul . . . Paul Forster. I'm sorry to have to call at this hour, but something important has come up."

"Paul Forster?" She was still struggling for comprehension.

"This is serious. Are you awake? Do you understand what I'm saying?"

"What is it? You sound strange." She was fully awake now, her voice alert and cautious.

"Just listen to me. Alec Borman and Peter Stone were murdered tonight. And the man who killed them left New York less than an hour ago to do the same to you. Now what I—"

"Where in heaven's name are you?" Katherine cut him off, her tone brusque and suspicious.

"At a pay phone in New York."

"Did Wendell put you up to this? Is this one of his nasty little tricks to try to trap me into something?"

"Katherine, please! Listen to me for a minute." Forster heard his voice rasp with frustration. This was exactly the reaction he had anticipated. Being Wendell Norton's friend made him instantly suspect. "This has nothing to do with Wendell. You should know me better than that. You're in very real and immediate danger. The man who murdered Borman and Stone will be at your house in less than five hours."

The line was silent and Forster could feel Katherine's hesitation. They had always gotten along well. She had liked and respected him. He was counting on that now.

"Maybe I'm crazy, but I trust you," she said. "What do you want me to do?"

A bead of sweat slid down Forster's face. "Get dressed and get out of the house. At once. Drive over to the Holiday Inn just east of the George Washington Parkway and wait for me at the far end of the parking lot. If I can hire a plane, I'll meet you there in two hours. If I have to drive, it'll take about five. But I'll be there. Wait for me. I'll answer any questions later. All right?"

"Why am I doing this?"

"Because you want to live."

Forster hung up and fumbled through his wallet. He found the dog-eared business card of the Eagle Flying Service, consisting of a single plane and its owner, and called the home number printed beneath the office listing.

"Yeah?" growled a hoarse voice.

"Paul Forster, Frank. Are you sober enough to fly me to Washington?"

"Shit, man, if I was sober I couldn't fly. When do you want to go?"

"Right now."

"Meet me at the hangar in forty minutes."

The flight to Washington's National Airport took just under an hour. But then there was the problem of getting a car, since all the rental booths were closed for the night. Finally, a mechanic friend of Frank's agreed to lend Forster his Trans Am for an even two hundred.

He took the George Washington Memorial Parkway all the way to Alexandria. He had been to Katherine Harwith's house several times over the years, so he knew the area. The Holiday Inn was less than five minutes from the parkway. Circling the parking lot, he saw Katherine sitting in a red Audi and pulled up beside her. He took a deep breath. A small part of him had half expected her not to show. Just seeing her felt like a victory.

Forster left his borrowed Trans Am and slipped into the Audi beside her. "Hello, Kate."

She was wearing jeans and a short-sleeved blouse—a slight,

attractive, still youthful woman who looked closer to forty than
the fifty she probably was. Her face stared back at Forster, de-
void of makeup but provocative, pretty, even though concerned.
And for the first time Forster felt a true sense of what she must
have been able to do for Wendell over the years. They sat facing
each other on the front seat of the car in the dark lot. Still, the
stars and a patch of moon did offer their own faint visibility
while Katherine's tilted, aristocratic nose, sensitive to mood as
the antennae of a cat, aimed itself at the undefended space between Forster's eyes.

"Borman and Stone are really dead?" Her voice was dull,
flat, with a mixture of fear and disbelief. But the question was
purely rhetorical. She knew the answer. "What happened to
them?"

Forster told her. Katherine sat listening, not quite looking at
him, hugging herself with both arms as though chilled.

"Oh, God," she whispered. "What I've gotten myself into
. . . what I've done."

Forster was silent.

"How much of all this do you know?" Katherine asked.

"Almost everything."

"I suppose it was Wendell who asked you to start digging?"

"Yes."

"Of course," she said coldly. "Your dear friend and men-
tor."

Forster left that one alone.

She stared off at the other cars across the hotel parking area.
"I appreciate your warning me, but in the long run it's not going
to change anything. If they want me dead, I'm as good as dead
right now."

"Not necessarily."

"I can't hide forever."

"You won't have to. Not if things work out as I hope." Forster
glanced at the dashboard clock. "Do you trust me?"

"I'm here, aren't I?" she sighed. "Anyway, what choice do
I have?"

"Not much."

"What do you want to do?"

"I want to get Max—the man who's coming to get *you*."

"What's the point? They'll only send others."

Forster was already planning ahead. "No they won't. Not if

we handle things right. Anyway, let's start with Max. He should
be at your house in less than an hour, so let's get back there and
set things up."

"What things?"

"I'll explain on the way," said Forster. "We'll go in my car.
Leave yours here."

It was only a ten-minute drive from the Holiday Inn. Katherine
lived on a winding country lane with the houses spaced far apart
and no sidewalks or streetlights. Her house was completely dark
as he drove past it and parked about two hundred yards away.
On either side of the road were clusters of pine broken by
stretches of open field.

They left the car and walked back to Katherine's house, a
modest, single-story clapboard with a wraparound country porch
and a gracefully angled roof. Wisteria grew in front and the
smell of honeysuckle sweetened the air. Katherine unlocked the
door and they went inside.

"Don't put on any lights," Forster warned.

Enough light filtered in from the sky for them to move about
without difficulty.

"Where's your bedroom?" he asked.

It was at the rear of the house, and Katherine led him to it,
her movements quick, awkward, nervous. "Are you absolutely
sure you want to do this?"

"Yes."

"It's so dangerous."

"We're the ones in control. The odds are with us."

"But you said he's a professional killer."

"He's also human," said Forster.

"You're sure this is the only way?"

"Would you rather go to the police?"

"You know I can't do that."

"Then it's the only way."

Setting up the scene like a stage director, Forster arranged
some pillows and blankets under the covers of Katherine's bed.
Then he set an old costume wig, scrounged from the attic, where
the figure's head would be. In the darkness, the form appeared
to be a sleeping woman.

"That should do it," he said.

"You must loathe me. Why are you doing this for me?"

"We need you alive. And I don't loathe you."

"How could you not?" she said miserably. "I loathe myself." She was close to tears, but fear seemed to have rendered her arid.

Forster took her out through the rear door and settled her a hundred yards back into the woods. "No matter what you hear or think you hear," he said, "I don't want you coming back inside until I call you."

"And if you never call me?"

"If you don't hear anything in the next hour and a half, go to a neighbor's house and phone the police. But don't worry. It won't come to that."

Forster left her, looking forlorn and deserted, behind a pile of brush.

Returning to the dark house, Forster switched on a small night lamp in the entrance hall. Then he eased himself through a glass door leading from Katherine's bedroom to a rear terrace, where he had an unobstructed view of the bed. With everything in order, he drew the revolver from his belt and waited.

Again there were just the night sounds and the patches of black woods and the open, moonlit fields. Washington was just a short drive across the Potomac, but might have been part of an alien, long-forgotten land. Forster kept checking his watch until it was 5:14. After a while he heard a car drive quietly by the front of the house. A few moments later, he heard another car pass. Neither car stopped. Then for a long time he heard only the hum of insects. He wondered when it would start getting light. For a moment he stopped staring into the bedroom and looked at the pine trunks behind the yard. Wisps of mist rose about them. Then he turned back to the bedroom once more and thought of nothing.

"Good morning, Mr. Forster."

Death touched the back of his head in the form of a gun muzzle and he had a new vision of the abyss. Blackness opened before him; he prepared for the fall. Still, he instinctively started to turn.

"Don't even think about it," said Max. He took the revolver from Forster's hand. "Now let's go inside. This damp is murder on my arthritis."

In the bedroom, Max switched on a lamp and gazed coldly at the makeshift dummy under the covers.

"You may turn around now," he told Forster.

In the soft lamplight, Max looked as fresh and well-groomed as he had back in the Soho loft. And in between then and now, thought Forster, he had murdered three people at two locations, then had driven more than three hundred miles to murder a fourth. Now he stood at ease in a Virginia bedroom, casually pointing an automatic pistol at another intended victim. Forster blessed the man's need to communicate. If he had any weakness, this was it. Indeed, Max's compulsion to talk was probably the only reason that Forster was still alive. *Wrong. I'm alive because he needs me to tell him where Katherine is.*

"I should be put out with you," said the assassin. "By escaping me in New York, you made me appear incompetent in the eyes of my client. But it's all turning out for the best. I'm simply winding up with three additional assignments."

Forster felt as though he had slipped off the lip of all sanity. The murdering sonofabitch not only looked like an accountant, he talked like one.

Max adjusted an intransigent shirt cuff. "All right, where did you put our Miss Harwith?"

"Where you won't find her."

"Oh, I'll find her. You should know that by now. But I'd rather not waste a lot of time looking. There's always the chance she might go to the police, and my client wouldn't care for that. So I'm going to offer you a deal. Tell me where she is and you're home free as far as I'm concerned."

Forster just looked at him.

"Why not?" said Max. "It's nothing personal with me. I work by the job. If I finish with Miss Harwith today instead of a week or a month from today, I'm that much ahead."

The stink of death came from Max. When Forster swallowed, he tasted copper pennies. Slowly, he sat down on a straight, wooden chair, arching his back in sudden pain and reaching behind him, pressing with both hands for relief.

Max pointed with his automatic. "Back problem?"

"Tension spasm."

"Relax, I just offered you a deal."

"It doesn't make sense. Why would you let me go?"

"Because as I understand it, once Miss Harwith is gone, my client no longer has reason to feel threatened by you. So what would be the harm in letting you live? Particularly if my client thinks I never caught up with you.''

Forster sat there, grimacing, massaging his back as he thought through the deal. ''Why the hell not?'' he finally grunted. ''Dead, I'm not worth shit.''

''Congratulations. An intelligent decision. We're both better off.''

Forster started to rise, slowly, tortuously. It was as though a fear had broken loose in his body along with the pain. Was an invisible club really beating at his back? Forster looked at the assassin, holding his eyes with what might have been an appeal for mercy. It was as if Max had only to say, *Let's stop all this— it's gone far enough*, and they could become friends. But Max's eyes were cold, glacial. Then, like a terminal patient whose faculties were leaving him one by one, Forster's right leg gave way as his back appeared to go into spasm. He fell backwards, coming down hard against the edge of his chair, toppling it over and collapsing with it, both he and the chair hitting the floor together in a tangle of legs. Forster rolled with the fall, a moving blur to Max who was standing there and staring. But he never saw the gun in Forster's hand until it exploded.

There were two shots. The first tore through Max's neatly arranged breast pocket handkerchief. The second bullet entered his left cheek and lifted the upper part of his skull. He was dead before he struck the floor.

Forster got up and looked at him. Sucked in backward upon the gouge of the bullet, Max's face had the look of an old man— sly, toothless, reminiscent of pain. Yet something about the dead assassin seemed to grin, too, with a clown's deep gloom, as if he had found pleasure even in death.

Automatically, as though it were now a newly conditioned part of his survival instinct, Forster returned his .38 to where it had been before—tucked under his shirt at the small of his back. Then he went to get Katherine.

''Do you know him?'' Forster asked. ''Have you ever seen him before?''

Katherine shook her head. Her face wore an expression of cool, thoughtful reserve as she stared at the body on her bedroom floor. She seemed to cling to the expression the way a woman might cling to a very fine piece of jewelry that is too precious to sell despite her need.

"Are you all right?" he asked.

She nodded. But her lips tightened, her chin trembled. Forster gently sat her down in a wooden rocker beside the bed.

"Is he dead?" she said.

Considering the nature and location of the wounds, there seemed little need to feel for a pulse. But Forster felt for one anyway, as a human gesture. Then he went into the living room, returned with brandy and fed it to Katherine.

"My God," she said softly. "If it wasn't for you—if you hadn't called me, if you hadn't come here—I'd have been the one lying there."

"Well, you're not. He is. So think positively."

"Think positively?" Her voice was flat, her face riddled with despair. "What is there for me to think positively about? If Alec and Peter are dead and they want me dead, too, then I'm as good as finished right now." Her eyes were drawn compulsively to the assassin's body. "What am I going to do, Paul?"

"You can change your name and spend the rest of your life running, or you can tell me everything you know and let me handle it from there."

"What does 'handling it from there' mean?"

"Once I have all the facts, all the details, I'll be able to neutralize those who want you dead."

"I take it that neutralize is your euphemism for being sent to prison."

"Yes."

"And what will happen to me? Will I be neutralized too?"

Forster considered it. "No. You'll be clear. I promise to tell nothing until I get a written statement of immunity for you."

"Why would you do that for me?"

"Because without you, I'd have nothing to take into a court."

Katherine sat rocking in her chair. "All right," she sighed.

"Good." Forster felt a provisional sort of calm begin to take place somewhere inside him. "The first thing we've got to do is get rid of Max. There must be no hint that he was here."

It required a particular discipline to be thorough. Enclosing the body in a pair of large plastic bags, Forster carried it out to the stand of pine in back of the house. Then he dug a deep hole, a sudden rage giving added strength to his arms as he thought of Robert and Melissa. How much of all this had they known, maybe even planned? Then confusion and doubt softened his anger. There were still too many unknowns.

When he returned to the house, Katherine had finished scrubbing the bedroom floor. There was the burning smell of ammonia and not a sign of blood. But Katherine's face carried its own mark. "I've got to shower," she said.

She looked better when she returned. Forster got the brandy and they sat over it in the living room, survivors just escaped from the jungle.

"Bless you for being able to shoot like that," she said. "Where did you learn?"

"Vietnam."

"I guess some good comes of everything." Katherine held out her hands and studied the tips of her fingers, which were trembling. "God, look at me."

Forster saw the sky beginning to lighten in the east. "Time is important. If you feel you're able, I think we'd better get started with this."

"I'm all right."

"I'm wired with a recorder," Forster told her. "When I switch it on, just start talking. I want everything. How you, Borman, and Stone became part of the conspiracy. Who approached you. What your motivations were. The outside forces involved. Things like that. Speak as naturally as you can. I'll interrupt from time to time when I need specific answers, but this is your story and that's how I want it coming across. Okay?"

Katherine nodded and took a sip of brandy. "Lordy . . . Lordy," she whispered. "All right. Switch on your machine. I'm as ready as I'll ever be."

Forster pressed the button on the recording pack.

"You've gotta help me, Joe," said Virgil Langer. "There's nowhere else I can turn."

Joe Needham looked at the pained face of the man sitting across his desk and thought of how many times he had heard the same or similar words during the past week. As president of the Farmer's Bank in Cherokee, Oklahoma, Needham was the appeal of last resort for every customer already turned down by his lending officers for a new loan or an extension on an overdue one. The whole county had been pressured by falling land values, low crop and beef prices, and a top-heavy burden of debt long before the present fiscal crisis. But the total collapse of the commodities markets in recent days had sounded the final bell for many marginal farmers and ranchers who, until then, had just barely been hanging on. Virgil Langer was one of them.

"I'm sorry," the banker said. "The good Lord knows I feel for you. How could I not? I've known you all my life. But there's nothing I can do anymore. You're forty-two thousand dollars overdue now, and things being as they are, you'll be even worse off next month."

Langer's eyes fluttered behind the steel rims of his glasses. He was a lean, sun-wrinkled man whose brain refused to accept what his ears were hearing. "What the hell do you mean, there's nothing you can do? You're president of this damn bank. All you've gotta do is say I've got an extension."

"It's not that simple. We've got so many bad loans on the books now, that we're teetering on the edge of insolvency ourselves."

"And extending my forty-two thousand dollars for another six months is gonna send you over the edge?"

"We have to start holding the line someplace."

"I haven't missed a payment till now in twenty-seven years. You're sending my life's work down the drain. Start holding the line with somebody else, not me."

"You know it's not only you. We've had to foreclose on five spreads in the last week alone." The banker leaned back in his chair and unbuttoned his jacket and shirt, exposing a dark undergarment. "Ever see one of these before?"

Langer stared blankly. He seemed unable to focus his eyes, a blind man seeing nothing but his own despair.

"It's a bullet-proof vest," said Needham. He opened his desk drawer and took out a pistol. "And this is a .38-caliber revolver. You know why I've got these? To protect me from my friends and neighbors. After thirty years behind this desk, isn't that a great way to have to go to work in the morning?"

"You think I'm gonna shoot you?"

"I don't know. You might. You or some other customer whose life's work I have to send down the drain. We got a bulletin from the Farm Credit System the other day. They said these were dangerous days and extra security had to be used. Two loan officers have been shot in Abilene, a bank president was knifed in Lake Wilson, Minnesota, and near Omaha, where the land and machinery of foreclosed farms were being sold, the auctioneer showed up with a pair of shotgun-toting bodyguards. That's the climate these days.''

Langer had stopped listening halfway through the banker's discourse. He was too deep inside himself to be held by anything outside for more than a few seconds. "You know me. I'm not one to whine. I do the best I can and take what comes. But I'm a good rancher. This got nothing to do with how I manage my place. I just need a little time for beef and wheat to get back where they were."

"They may never get back where they were."

"They got to. This whole country won't be worth cow shit if they don't."

"That could happen, too."

"You don't believe that."

The bank president slowly buttoned his shirt, his fingers not quite steady. "If I can believe I'm sitting behind my own desk in a bullet-proof vest, I can believe any damn thing at all. I looked at the bank's books this morning and I swear I almost puked."

"All I need is six months, Joe."

"Six months won't help you. You owe too much." Needham sighed. "You'd have been okay if you hadn't bought those last three hundred acres a few years ago. It's those extra payments that broke your back."

A muscle twitched in the rancher's jaw. "It was you who told me to pick up that land."

Needham finished buttoning his shirt. Then he carefully put the revolver back in his drawer.

"You remember," said Langer. "I was sitting right where I'm sitting now. You said that parcel was too good to let go and that you'd work with me on the payments. In those days you people were pushing us all to take out bigger and bigger loans, to buy more land, more machinery. Every lousy banker in the county wanted to lend me money. Beef and wheat were high and you said it was going higher, and that expanding was the only way to take advantage of it. You remember that, Joe? Or maybe you've forgotten."

Needham sat considering the pistol in his open drawer. It was true, he thought. With cash pouring into their vaults, they'd had to get the money working for them. Still, the farmers had been as greedy as the bankers. Nobody ever had enough. Everyone always wanted more. But then, who had expected this?

"You're a responsible man," the banker said. "I didn't have a gun to your head. You bought that extra land because you wanted it, because it seemed a pretty damned good investment at the time. So don't go dumping it on *me*."

"Somebody's sure gotta dump it on you. What about those five places you foreclosed last week? How many of *them* did you push to buy land and machinery they couldn't make the payments on?"

Needham closed his desk drawer. He had a dozen possible answers to Virgil's accusations but he didn't like any of them. And the worst of it was that Virgil was right. But who could have anticipated this kind of drop in prices? Certainly not he, and not any other banker he knew. Yet, ironically, it was those six top bankers who had set this whole chain reaction in motion.

"We're farmers and ranchers," said Virgil. "We know beef and wheat. That's all. When it comes to money, we go to our friendly, neighborhood banker. Money's what *you're* supposed to know. So when you tell us it's right to buy more land, more machinery, we listen. We trust you. Now you say we were wrong to listen? To trust you?"

"We make mistakes too, Virgil. We're not God."

"You're God to *me*. You're taking my land, my work, my whole life. I'd say that's pretty Godlike." Slowly, tiredly, Langer rose. "And there's no use your wearing that fancy vest with me. If I'm gonna shoot any part of you, it'll be your fucking head."

15

It was just a simple country living room, but to Forster there was a mood in the place as exact as the moment of entering some dark royal confessional.

Could it really be only seventeen days?

Despite her nervousness, Katherine spoke quietly, almost matter-of-factly as she began a tale that started close to five years ago in Basel, Washington, and New York, and ended with the arraignment of the six bankers in a crowded federal courtroom. The basic facts were plain enough. Katherine, Borman, and Stone each received five million dollars for their respective roles in the conspiracy, with Robert Bennet himself doing the actual recruiting.

"I don't know anyone other than Robert," said Katherine, "who else could have handled all three of us with such artistry, choosing each of us because of our backgrounds and positions, cultivating us as personal friends over the years, learning about our psychological, professional, and personal neuroses, and finally being able to sense that we all would be amenable to his proposition when he got around to presenting it to us."

Katherine paused and looked at Forster. "Since you've spent time with Robert, I'm sure you can appreciate his talents. What he finally doesn't know about a person isn't worth knowing. With Alec Borman, he knew the motivation would be pure and simply the money, that irresistible five million in cash. With Peter Stone, he very quickly saw that the money wouldn't be nearly as important as the notoriety he could achieve by uncovering and breaking the financial scandal of the century. And with me, of course, he had the perception to utilize the vengeful spite of an aging, discarded lover."

Tears appeared in Katherine's eyes, seeming to begin in some tightly knurled pit of grief, then rushing down her cheeks. "God, look at what I've done," she wept. "Look at what I've turned into. I've loved only one man, Wendell, half my life. I'd have done anything for him. I was a decent, moral woman, a loyal American. And look at me now. I've helped destroy the only man I've ever cared about. I've done untold damage to my country and millions of innocent people. I've just barely been saved from being murdered by a professional killer. And now I've got to go into hiding or be murdered by someone else."

Katherine put her face in her hands and gave herself up to anguish.

"I'm sorry," she said at last. "I should do better than that."

With effort, she regained composure.

"Understand," Katherine continued, "as Wendell's trusted personal secretary and administrative assistant, I was privy to just about everything in his life—who he knew and saw, where he went and when, what he did or planned to do. So when it became necessary to falsify his movements, meetings, phone conversations, correspondence, and records to establish his guilt, I was in the perfect position to do it. I also set up close enough personal ties with the five other bankers' chief assistants, for them to let me know whenever their bosses were involved in the financing of particularly large mergers or takeovers. I'd then pass on to Alec Borman—as the bankers' alleged Bahamian account executive of record—all the necessary details, so he could buy stock in the companies involved for the phoney code-named accounts of the six bankers."

Katherine's voice, growing softer as she spoke, finally faded off into silence.

"What about Peter Stone's part?" Forster asked.

Katherine gazed into her brandy glass as though it were a crystal ball projecting calamity. "I gave all the same details to Peter that I gave to Alec. With that information, it was simple enough for him to establish the incriminating trading patterns in the takeover stocks that he'd supposedly discover later, during his investigation for the SEC. In a single six-month period, he picked out unusually heavy trading volume just prior to the Standard Corn merger, the International Airlines deal, the takeover of United States Can, and the tender offer for Filmways Cable." Katherine grimaced. "Easy enough to be brilliant under those conditions. But Peter also made contributions of his own by giving all of us involved in setting up the trades—Robert, Alec,

Melissa, and myself—a direct pipeline into the more subtle of the SEC's investigative procedures. Which allowed us to adjust our own techniques accordingly."

"Just for the record," said Forster, "when you referred to Robert, Alec, and Melissa, were you speaking about Robert Stone, Alec Borman, and Melissa Kenniston?"

"Yes. I was."

Forster listened with interest, but there were no real surprises. He had figured most of this out for himself. He simply needed everything confirmed and set down in the voice of one of the conspirators. What he really was waiting to hear had not yet come.

Kind as a mother, he fed Katherine another drink and said, "Now let's hear about the heavyweights."

Her eyes widened slightly. "You know about them, too?"

"I know they exist. I know Robert and Melissa didn't have three hundred million of their own to invest. I know they're the ones who probably had Stone and the Bormans killed and tried to kill us as well. The only thing I don't know is who they are."

Katherine smiled. "Strike a bargain with the devil and the devil will collect."

"Does your devil have a name?"

"How about Hassan Motomedi?" said Katherine.

Forster stared at her. "Are you telling me that Robert and Melissa actually went to the finance minister of Iran for their backing?"

"Exactly."

"Then maybe you can explain how the son and daughter of a Holocaust survivor could possibly have allowed themselves to go to a bunch of hate-mongering Shiite butchers for help?"

"They didn't want to go to them, but they had no other options. It was either the Iranians or no one. In fact they may even have enjoyed the poetic justice involved."

"Bullshit!"

Katherine was watching him curiously. "Why are you so angry? If you'll take a moment to think about it, you'll realize that all Robert and Melissa actually were doing was using the Iranians for their own purposes. Under the circumstances, it was quite reasonable."

Reasonable, thought Forster as he rose and went over to a window because it suddenly was impossible for him to sit still.

He stared out at the gray beginnings of dawn, but saw only blackness.

Robert and Melissa had picked their silent partner well, he thought, and could feel his stomach turn with it. But now the Iranians obviously were taking things into their own hands. Then why not their own assassins? Because, naturally, there must never be any visible connection to Iran.

Forster returned to Katherine. "Okay, give me the rest of it. I want details—specific cases. You mentioned a few before. Let's hear about the International Airlines deal and the takeover of U.S. Can—who was involved, where you picked up the information, what you did with it, who said what to whom."

"I can't give you exact dates and figures without checking the records."

"Approximations will do. We can be more precise later. All I care about right now are procedures, channels of information, and timing."

Katherine closed her eyes and sat rocking gently, a fiscal medium contacting her special spirit world of common stocks, tender offers, and junk bonds. But when she finally began, her voice was flat, even, matter of fact, her eyes level, her manner brisk, efficient, and not without its own fine layer of professional pride. Whatever she had done, it said, had been done well, without bungling, and surely some credit had to be given for that. Forster, listening, was prepared to give nothing.

"I first learned about the International Airlines deal when I was in New York one weekend last September. I was having lunch with Ellen Barstow—Pete Farnham's administrative assistant at Chase. Ellen was red-eyed and exhausted from weeks of overtime and batteries of lawyers—whom she despised on principle as arrogant nit-picking vultures who made the simple complex and the complex undecipherable. She found one lawyer, Tom Hammond, especially offensive, and described the hours of extra work his wrangling had caused the bank these past days over a large loan agreement. 'How large?' I asked. When she told me it was well over two billion, I had all the information I needed."

Katherine's smile was sardonic. "Since I knew Tom Hammond was International Airlines' general counsel, and that International had been considering a tender offer for its own stock to prevent a possible takeover by Republic Steel, the rest wasn't hard to figure out. I called Alec Borman in the Bahamas that night and he began buying International common at the opening on Monday.''

''For whom?'' Forster asked.

''Allegedly, for all six bankers' coded accounts at the Bank Streit. Starting at eight dollars a share, Alec bought about fifty thousand shares a day for four days running and ended up with a total of two hundred thousand at an average price of eleven. The following week, Republic Steel put in an unfriendly take-over bid of sixteen dollars a share and International countered with its tender offer of an even twenty. The bidding moved up-ward from there and ended a month later with International's final and successful tender offer of twenty-six, giving the bank-ers' combined accounts a net profit of close to three million.''

''Please give us the full names of the bankers allegedly in-volved.''

''Alfred Loomis, Pete Farnham, Bill Boyer, Hank Ridgeway, Tom Stanton . . . and, of course, Wendell Norton.''

''How did Peter Stone come into this at the SEC?''

''I simply kept feeding him the details as we went along—the number of shares Alec bought, the dates of purchase, the prices paid. Then I gave him the same reports when the shares were sold. With this information it was easy enough for Peter to set up his SEC records in reverse, and pretend to have plucked the trades out of the computer as suspicious in timing, volume, and profits. Then he'd allegedly trace them first to the Bank Streit, and then to Alec Borman as the executive handling the six coded accounts involved, and finally to Farnham as the original source of the information.''

Forster lit a cigarette and blew smoke. How simple all this made the full act of betrayal seem. ''And the U.S. Can take-over?''

''I was in Wendell's office one day when Citibank's Tom Stan-ton called. Federated Hardware had just asked for a three billion line of credit for what he described as a possible acquisition, and Citibank was a little tight on cash at the moment. Stanton wondered how Wendell felt about the deal in the light of current market conditions. By the time I'd finished listening to Wen-dell's side of the conversation, I'd learned that U.S. Can was Federated's projected target, that their common stock was cur-rently quoted on the Big Board at about thirty dollars, that its book value was estimated at close to seventy-five dollars a share, and that Federated was prepared to chase the stock as high as fifty in order to get working control."

"And Wendell discussed all this with you sitting right there, listening?"

Katherine's laugh was bitter. "Wendell had no secrets from me. You should know that. He trusted me implicitly. And for more than twenty years I gave him no reason *not* to trust me." She looked long and hard at Forster in the yellow lamplight. "Now I've given him reason."

"Anyway," she went on, "Wendell told Stanton he judged the three billion a good risk, considering the companies involved, and couldn't see why Citibank shouldn't go ahead with the deal."

"Which the bank did?" prompted Forster for the record.

"Yes."

Katherine's eyes had turned remote. Her thoughts were suddenly elsewhere.

"And?" said Forster.

She stared blankly at him.

"What did you do then?"

"The usual," she said. "I called Alec Borman with the information and he took the required market action."

"Which was specifically what?"

"He bought about a hundred thousand shares of U.S. Can at an average price of thirty-two."

"For the same six coded accounts you mentioned earlier?"

"Yes."

"And then?"

"Alec sold the shares two months later at an average price of forty-seven when Federated Hardware acquired its controlling interest. The combined profits in the six accounts from the trade was more than a million and a quarter."

"And Peter Stone's part?"

"The same as I described in the International Airlines deal. He received all the details of purchases, sales, share volume, and account numbers for his investigative records. Plus Tom Stanton's name as the source of information."

"Would you say you used the same general procedures outlined in these two cases in all the deals in which the six bankers, named earlier, were allegedly involved?"

"With variations—yes."

"To the best of your knowledge," said Forster, "did these same six men actually profit from or know about any of the trades carried out for the coded accounts that allegedly belonged to them?"

"No."

Forster went on a while longer with what was finally reduced to routine technical detail, all the bits and pieces needed to complete the puzzle and lend authenticity to the main body of evidence. He taped everything because it would all be essential somewhere along the line, but he had lost the heart of his interest. He already had heard what was important to him, the Iranian connection, and he was still angry and disgusted with it. He also was impatient, the way a dying man is impatient when he feels death come up like a shadow and is anxious, finally, to just slip inside and get it done.

At last, switching off the recorder, he felt like an overaged scholar, finally graduated from a special university of the damned whose every book, every course of study, he has memorized and sucked dry.

They sat there, the sudden silence a weight on their wills. Watching Katherine, Forster once more saw her eyes turn remote, her thoughts suddenly appear to be focused elsewhere.

"What is it?" he said.

She looked at him.

"What's bothering you?"

"Really, Paul."

"I don't mean the obvious."

"Considering what the obvious is, it doesn't leave much room for anything else." Her face was brooding. "Actually, I was just thinking about your reaction to Hassan Motomedi and the Iranians. I must admit I didn't feel too differently when I finally learned about them. I didn't care much for the idea of their involvement either."

"You didn't know about them from the beginning?"

"No. At first I thought it was only Robert and Melissa. Then when I started estimating the amount of money needed, I knew there had to be others behind them. It bothered me. I wanted to know everything. I didn't want any surprises later. My whole life, whatever future I had left, was hanging on this deal. I refused to have people knowing about *me*, if I didn't know about *them*. I told Robert I'd drop out unless I knew everything.''

"That's when he came up with Motomedi?''

Katherine nodded. "But too easily.''

"What do you mean?''

"He didn't put up enough resistance. I had the feeling his arguments were specious, token. He almost seemed prepared, even pleased, to concede me Motomedi to keep me from pressing further on something darker.''

"Like what?''

She shrugged. "I haven't the faintest idea.''

"What could be darker than Motomedi and his Shiite cut-throats?''

"Nothing as far as I'm concerned. I despise everything they stand for. But Robert and Melissa obviously feel differently. With minds like theirs, who knows what new breed of devil's disciple they've got hidden away somewhere, pulling the strings.''

Her voice drifted off as all interest went out of it. "Anyway, it's just a feeling I've had. More to the point, what happens now?''

"Now we put you where they won't be able to find you. Do you know someone living not too far from here whom you can trust?''

"What about a hotel?''

"They're too easy to check.''

"I have a friend in Bethesda. She lives alone.''

"Will she ask a lot of questions?''

"She may. But I don't have to answer.''

"Call her up.''

Katherine left the room and returned moments later. "It's all set. She said she'll be glad to have company. She didn't ask a thing.''

"Good,'' said Forster. "Pack a bag and I'll drive you over.''

"Take me to my car and I'll drive myself.''

"No. I don't want your car parked in the neighborhood. We'll have to leave it at the Holiday Inn.''

Dread darkened her eyes. "I'm suddenly scared to death.''

Half an hour later Forster left Katherine off in her friend's drive-way. "Don't leave the house,'' he said as his final warning.

"And don't speak to anyone until you hear from me. Don't even call *me* because there'll probably be a tap on my phone."

He watched as she entered the house, a small, delicately made woman carrying a suitcase that seemed much too big for her.

He returned his borrowed Trans Am to Washington's National Airport. Then he rode the ten-thirty shuttle back to La Guardia. The recording pack was still taped to his chest.

In the Judean hills, not more than an hour's drive from Jerusalem, General David Yaacov, recently returned from Washington, was being updated by a group of the Mossad's senior field officers on their current state of readiness relative to Operation Falcon. The briefing was held in a small, whitewashed cottage nestled within the boundaries of what appeared to be a hill village, but which was actually a high-level intelligence installation. None of the officers were in uniform and they sat about informally, in straight chairs, facing General Yaacov. The place was sparsely furnished, all but bare other than for the chairs, a desk, and some giant cactus plants, as stark and forbidding as the surrounding landscape. The air smelled of disinfectant.

It was Major Avrum, the demolitions officer, who was speaking, a dour, hatchet-faced man with a flat voice and manner that seemed never to have been tempered by humor.

Yaacov stopped him. "We're limited for time this morning, Major. Just give us the essentials."

"Yes, sir," said Avrum. "Just a few additional points about the kind of explosives we'll be using in the bombing of the American embassies in London, Paris, Bonn, and Rome, and their consulates in Damascus, Cairo, and Beirut. It'll be a special type of high-density charge, a mixture of A-1 and K-2, which are usually used by Libyan terrorists in their more powerful car bombs. We're going to detonate them by remote control, with their placement set up with particular emphasis on the equipment-survival factor. Which means there has to be enough deliberately malfunctioning equipment involved so we can make sure of the survival of certain key parts. These parts, of course, must be clearly identifiable as having originated in Libya."

"Excellent, Avrum," said Yaacov and cut the major off before he had a chance to editorialize on the facts. He turned to the other officers in the room, two colonels and a captain, and received each of their reports in order. To this point, everything seemed to be on schedule in all seven of the cities involved. The two known Libyan terrorists, Abu Gamal and Bayed Shanti, whose bodies would later be found within the compounds of the bombed embassies in London and Paris, had been taken into custody within the past several hours. As a possible emergency backup, two additional Libyan nationals also were in the Mossad's hands should they be needed. There had to be unmistakable evidence of Libya's involvement in and responsibility for all seven bombings.

When the room was at last silent, General Yaacov looked at the almost shockingly youthful faces of his four senior officers. "I want to be sure you've got this absolutely straight," he told them. "I want no mistakes about what we're getting into and why."

They sat facing him in the harsh, unsparing light of a nearly barren room in an ancient, biblical land.

"There's nothing that says we have to do this," Yaacov told them. "This is one of those rare moments for Israel when we're not in an official state of war with anyone. We're in this because I volunteered us to be in it. Not because I was afraid we didn't have enough troubles of our own, but because I'm an Israeli who will never stop being grateful to America and Americans. I know there are others among us who feel differently, but this is the way *I* feel."

The general gave them a moment to think about it.

"I bless Americans in my prayers each night," he said, "in the same way I curse Germans. Just know and remember this, and make sure that every man under you knows and remembers it too. If anything goes wrong, the Americans had no part in the operation. We take it all. There's to be no connection whatsoever to the United States. Our official line, our *only* line, is that we simply were trying to counteract growing sentiment in Congress for the sale of advanced weapon systems to some of the more moderate Arab states. By bombing American installations in Europe and the Middle East, and making it appear to be the work of Arab terrorists, we hoped to forestall any such action. That's the line every man is to live with, and should it become necessary, it's the line that every man is to die with."

Yaacov paused. "Are there any questions?"

There was some stirring but no one spoke.

"All right. You all know what to do." The general smiled for the first time. "And may God be with you, because you can be damned sure not many others will."

It was past noon by the time Forster was in a cab, heading for Manhattan. Although he hadn't slept in more than thirty hours, he had not even come close to dozing on the plane. Too many thoughts, too many emotions, were churning in his head. In the cab, an air of impending hurricane seemed to hang over him.

He went straight to his bank and left the recording pack in his safe deposit box with his will and other documents. Then he found a phone in the upstairs lobby and called Jennings at the magazine.

"For once in your life just listen and don't ask questions," he told the editor. "There's a good chance your phone is tapped. I just want you to know I'm okay and onto something. I'll be in touch when I can."

"But—"

"No buts," said Forster and hung up.

He called Annie at her office, but she was off at a meeting and her secretary wasn't sure when she would return.

"May I take a message, Mr. Forster?"

"Just tell her I'm fine and to stay happy."

The secretary giggled. "You're very thoughtful for an ex."

"It's much easier when you're an ex," he said.

Certain that his apartment building was being watched, Forster checked into a third-rate hotel on West Twenty-eighth Street. He felt like a soldier in enemy land. There must have been hotplates burning in nearby rooms, because there was the high, peppery smell of Hispanic cooking, an odor of garlic, pigs' guts, and assorted spices that tore at the nose and throat membranes without mercy. But there was a bed, a lock on the door, and the reassuring certainty that no one would consider looking for him here.

He stripped down to his shorts. Then placing one of his two revolvers under his pillow and the other beside him on the bed, he closed his eyes and tried to sleep.

The past thirty hours paraded through his brain like the mutilated corpses of a battlefield. Some of the corpses were real— the two Bormans, Peter Stone, Max—all dead in the same cause. But there was also Melissa, Robert, and Katherine, along with

Hassan Motomedi and his Iranians, and these were nowhere near dead. After a while he was able to lose them, one by one, until only Melissa was left. He had no idea what to do with her.

Finally, he slept, but kept waking in a sweat, the memory of some vague terror clogging his throat, his hand grabbing for the .38 beside him. When he woke for good, it was dark and close to midnight.

He washed in a rust-stained sink, dressed, left the hotel, and took a taxi to Melissa's building.

The doorman knew him, but he still had to be announced, so Melissa was waiting for him in the corridor outside her door. Although it was near one o'clock and she was wearing a robe, she apparently had not been asleep because her makeup was still on.

Her face was concerned, questioning, possibly even a bit fearful. All of these expressions fleetingly passed by. But she took him inside without a word and kissed and held him. Holding her in return, Forster was filled with an unreasonable hope. We might still be all right, he thought confusedly.

Melissa pulled back to consider him, top to bottom, an anxious taking of inventory. "Are you all right?"

He nodded.

"The wound is all right? No infection? No fever?"

"The wound is fine." He had all but forgotten about it.

"You shouldn't be here, you know. They might have someone watching the building."

"I didn't see anyone."

"When they're good, you don't see them."

He shrugged. "Are you ready to talk to me about them?"

"You know I can't do that."

Something sagged inside him. "It's all right. I know who they are. I know everything."

She stared at him as if enough concentration would stamp her features on his eyes for all time.

"I was hoping you'd be the one to tell me," he said. "But I guess that was foolish. Get dressed. We're going over to visit Robert. We have to talk."

"Talk about what?"

"About the three of us. About what I've learned. About what I'm going to do about it."

"I don't know what you think you've learned, but—"

"Put your clothes on, Melissa."

"Don't treat me like this. Don't brush me aside as if I were nothing."

Forster just looked at her.

"I have a right to know what happened."

"No you don't. As far as I'm concerned, you've stopped having any rights at all."

"Paul—"

"Just get dressed. There isn't much time."

Coldly furious, Melissa turned and went into the bedroom. Forster followed, then watched as she picked up a telephone and started to dial.

"Whom are you calling?"

"Robert."

"Hang up, please. I'd rather he didn't expect us."

She went right on dialing.

Forster bent, grabbed the telephone wire, and ripped it out of the wall.

"Have you gone crazy?" she said.

Her face had turned pale. Forster had never seen her afraid like this. Was he really so frightening?

"How much do you know about what's been happening over the past eighteen hours?" he said. Then he shook his head. "No. Don't bother answering that. I wouldn't believe you anyway."

"Do you believe I feel anything at all for you?" She said it so softly that he barely heard her.

"I don't want to even think about that."

"What do you want to think about? Shooting Robert and me? Is that what's on your mind?"

All he could do was look at her, seeing her sudden paleness, and the way her hair drooped over one eye, and the two openings in her robe, top and bottom, that exposed more of her body than he was able to deal with comfortably at that moment.

"When you held me before," she said, "I felt two revolvers between us. Is that what we've finally come down to?"

Forster raised his hand in a futile gesture of denial. It dropped of its own dead weight. "All I want right now is to talk to you and Robert. I'm not shooting anyone. Just get dressed.''

This time she did as he asked. Then they left the apartment.

Melissa stood staring at him in the elevator.

"What's happened to you since I saw you last?"

"A lot."

"And you're not going to tell me what it is?"

"I'll tell you, all right. But not until we're with Robert."

The doorman got them a cab and they rode toward Sutton Place in silence. It was only a short drive, but Forster could feel Melissa glancing at him throughout, searching his face for reasons, explanations. Then giving this up, she just stared coldly out the window.

It was close to 2:00 A.M. when they reached Robert's fortieth-floor duplex, yet he greeted them as matter-of-factly as if they were arriving for a long-scheduled luncheon appointment. Dressed in designer slacks and a sports shirt, he showed neither surprise nor concern as he kissed Melissa, shook hands with Forster, and led them into a high-ceilinged living room that seemed to draw the Queensborough Bridge, the East River, and much of Long Island City inside it. Forster had never been in the apartment before, but it was what he might have expected, an urban luxury that carried the blank intensity of the Stock Exchange.

"What can I get you two night owls to drink?" Robert asked, as though just staying with the amenities would somehow insure proper decorum.

"Nothing for me," said Forster.

Melissa just shook her head.

The tone of the meeting was set.

Forster sat down facing a giant picture window. Was there still some small hope? He did not think so.

Robert just sat waiting. He had enough poise, enough confidence, enough inner serenity, to be able to do that. Well, thought Forster, now it's all mine.

"To begin with," he said, addressing them both, "I know everything. I know who was in this with you, who gave you your backing, why they gave it to you—everything. The fact that it disgusts me is beside the point. It's enough that they, and possibly you, tried twice to have me murdered, tried to have Katherine Harwith murdered, and did, in fact, murder Peter Stone and Alec Borman and his wife.''

His eyes flat with the furies, Forster pressed on. ''Katherine put every detail on tape, which I've hidden safely away. But I still can't begin to understand what sort of creatures you are. I've always felt for your need to avenge your father. I've even empathized with it. But the rest of your chamber of horrors is beyond me. And how you could have coldly set me up to be murdered when—''

''Stop!'' Melissa's cry cut him off. Her face was pale. ''Don't you dare talk to us like that! If we wanted you dead, you'd have been dead a long time ago. Wasn't I the one who warned you to go into hiding?''

''Sure,'' said Forster. ''But with a man parked outside my house to either pick me off along the way or else find out where I was going and finish me there.''

''No! I put that man there to watch out for you, to protect you from those animals.'' Melissa chewed her lip. ''God, you're infuriating.''

Forster just looked at her.

Robert finally spoke. ''Everything you feel is understandable. But Melissa and I aren't violent people. Maybe we should have been. Maybe we should have just had those six bastards shot for what they did to our father. But we didn't. We operated within the system. We simply did to them what they did to David Berenstein. We despised having to use Iran, but it was them or nothing. Maybe that's where we made our big mistake. At least that's how it suddenly seems to be turning out.''

Bennet gazed directly at Forster. His face looked drawn, its hollows deep. A barren landscape. ''The fact is, I've been trying to reach you for several hours. I've something to tell you that not even Melissa knows. Thank God you finally showed up.''

''What are you talking about?'' Forster turned to Melissa for a possible hint, but her expression was blank.

''I got a call earlier from Ibrahin Zahedi,'' said Robert, ''the deputy director of Iran's secret police, who's been over here giving us all trouble. He's the one who put out the contract on you, and when that failed, decided to protect Iran's interests by killing Borman, Stone, and Katherine.''

Robert abruptly rose and went over to the window, as if to study the Queensborough Bridge.

"It makes me sick to have to tell you this," he said over his shoulder, "but the gist of Zahedi's call was that he'd picked up a hostage just in case his hired assassin failed to eliminate Katherine. And the hostage he picked up was Annie."

Forster sat there—mute. Robert turned to face him, as though an odor of violence had suddenly erupted from his skin. Then Forster was out of his chair, gun in hand.

"You sonofabitch! I'm going to blow your fucking head off!"

Indeed, the silencer on Forster's revolver was jammed so hard against Robert's forehead that the surrounding skin had turned white. Forster could feel his own heart pounding. I'm either going to kill him, he thought, or I'm going to break apart and die myself. Robert's face looked red to him, then white, then red again. Slowly, Forster lowered his revolver.

"My God," he whispered.

"I know what this has to be doing to you," said Robert, "but I swear I had nothing to do with it. I happen to care about Annie, too."

They stood staring at each other.

Forster turned to Melissa. He had the sensation that vital parts of him were passing through a tunnel and were never going to come out. The gun in his hand was trembling so violently that he was afraid it might go off by itself.

"I didn't know, Paul." Melissa spoke so softly that Forster could hardly hear what she said.

He made a soft, dry sound in his throat. "Get her back," he told Robert.

"I can't."

"What the hell do you mean, you can't? This is your goddamn show, isn't it?"

"Not anymore. Not since we brought in the Iranians." Robert's voice was bitter. "Right now there's no way I can even reach Zahedi. He's smart. Knowing how I'd feel about this, he didn't leave me any number or address. So I have to wait for *him* to get in touch with *me*."

"When will that be?"

"If Zahedi doesn't hear from his hired gun by early morning, he'll know he's been picked up or stopped by you. That's when he'll call me. That's when I'll be expected to contact you and make a deal for Annie.'' Robert poured himself some brandy from a cut-glass decanter. ''What happened to Zahedi's man, Paul?''

''What he deserved to have happen.''

Melissa's eyes were wide. ''You killed him?''

Forster nodded. Robert was looking at him curiously, and Forster stared back at him, at the glinting luster of his skin, at the something so sharp and spare in the bones that in comparison, most men's faces were soft, sleek blobs, unkneaded dough. His eyes, shadowed now, were so dark with silent hurt that Forster, in a sudden swell of fury, would have liked to stick pins in them to teach him about real pain.

''And I'm putting you both on notice,'' he said. ''Whatever happens to Annie, the same thing is going to happen to you.''

They waited for Zahedi's call.

It was certainly the strangest of waitings, with the three of them closeted together in the vaulted living room, and the light-strung Queensborough Bridge their silent warder. As if by tacit agreement, no one left the common ground except to go to the bathroom. Forster's revolver remained either in his hand or in his belt. Not that he was worried about a possible attack. He was, after all, the only one who could tell them where Katherine and the tapes were.

But poor Annie.

His thoughts about her were controlled at this point, but the concern and rage were still intense. And she had gotten into this to help and protect *him*. A particular irony there, but he was in no mood to dwell on it. All he felt was a cold, killing rage, and this disturbed him. He was going to have to think quickly and clearly in whatever lay ahead, and the only thing that anger ever did for him was cloud his brain.

Once, looking at Melissa, Forster had a sense she had traced a line across his eyes, a begging for him not to see and examine her too closely. Or if he did see, a hope that he would understand. Or failing even that, a pleading not to pass judgment. And how was he supposed to answer *that*? There seemed to be a new sound somewhere in his head, and something violent was loose inside him. But he held it with a delicate calm and made himself stare hard at Melissa's face. He had never seen her more lovely. It was the truth. Her hair was alive, her skin aglow, her eyes windows to a palace. But most of all, she had a splendor at a time when few could have managed it. And for this alone, he could have hated her.

Briefly dozing near dawn, he dreamed he saw Robert's eyes seeking their own jeweled cities. But the odor was that of a heated gallery in a zoo, and Forster felt a high pinch of pain as if fangs had dug into him. Still, Melissa was no part of it, and the only sound he heard come out of her was a groan.

16

He awoke to the ringing of a telephone.

Robert, still on the couch, groped for the receiver and picked it up on the fourth ring. Forster and Melissa silently watched and waited.

"Yes?" said Robert, then listened grimly as the caller went on at some length.

"I know all your reasons," he said at last. "They don't mean a damn to me. That woman is not to be touched. I've been assured by—"

Apparently interrupted at the other end, Bennet sat listening once more. His face had turned pallid, a mottled pink beneath his tan.

"Forster's right here," he said. "He came after me in the middle of the night. He blamed me for all your killing." Robert listened a moment longer, then beckoned to Forster. "Zahedi wants to talk to you."

Forster took the phone.

"Since I haven't heard from our mutual friend, Max," said a deep, distinguished voice with just the barest trace of an accent, "I must assume he's dead. Correct?"

Forster swallowed dryly. "What do you want?"

"Just Katherine Harwith. I don't know whether you've forced some sort of confession from her. But even if you did, it's legally worthless without her supporting testimony. So Katherine is really all I want from you. Do you follow me?"

"Yes."

"Comply with this demand and Mrs. Forster will be released unharmed. Refuse, and a small portion of her person will be delivered to you by special messenger. Continue to refuse, and the procedure will be repeated until you change your mind."

"Tell me something, Zahedi," said Forster softly. "At what

point did you abandon all normal human behavior and turn into an animal?''

The Iranian didn't even hesitate. "I can tell you exactly, Mr. Forster. It happened the same day your American-owned shah's police showed me my mother, father, and two sisters, hanging by their mouths from four large fish hooks like so many naked carp.''

At that moment some part of Forster's soul felt as though it were trapped and drowning in sewage.

"I promise you Miss Harwith won't be harmed," said Zahedi. "She'll simply be kept incommunicado until all this has become irrelevant. Then she'll be released.''

I'll bet, thought Forster. "I want to speak to my wife," he said. Somehow, at that moment, it would have seemed denigrating to call her his ex-wife.

"Of course. One moment.''

Waiting, Forster avoided looking at either Robert or Melissa. He was afraid of what might be showing in his face. So he just stared out of the giant duplex window, seeing the sun burning through the early mists over the East River and Long Island City.

"Paul?" It was Annie's voice but she sounded very far away. "Are you all right?''

"Terrific," she said flatly. "Except that I'd like to kill myself for doing this to you.''

"You're sure they haven't hurt you?''

"I'm fine, I'm fine. This Zahedi is so polite I could vomit. He'd cut my throat and apologize while doing it." She paused. "I think they're very serious about this;" she said, and suddenly it wasn't quite her voice.

"Don't worry. I won't let them hurt you. Whatever they want done, I'll do. You're my Annie, aren't you?''

"I don't deserve to be," she whispered. "Ah, Paulie, why am I such a fool?''

Across miles of wire, they somehow managed to touch. Then Zahedi was back on the line.

"You've got what you want," Forster told him. "Let's make the arrangements.''

It was not at all simple. There were details and guarantees to be thought out, discussed, then accepted or rejected. Both sides had their own needs and fears. Forster had to be certain he didn't relinquish Katherine before Annie was safely in his hands, and the reverse was true of Zahedi and his hostage. A leaden anxiety seemed to have settled in Forster's stomach. He was trying to think, plan, be clever, and cover every possibility of disaster as he went along. But this was all new to him and there were no second chances.

While at his back, watching, listening to every word he said, were Robert and Melissa. He had many reasons to resent them all that moment, but most especially because they were winning it all right here as he stood helpless and alone in the loser's circle. He sometimes had wondered why certain of the very elderly and infirm—sick, weak, a hopeless burden to those saddled with their care—still clung desperately to their last joyless days. But he had some small understanding of it now. Because there was a great blob of the coward's poison deep inside him that was ready to do anything at all—lie, cheat, damage, kill, sacrifice hope, honor, sanity—if there was even the smallest chance of getting Annie out of this. Yet all that was left for him to do was deal with Zahedi.

Finally, the arrangements were worked out. The deal was to be consummated at eleven o'clock that night in a large, densely wooded park area outside of Bethesda, Maryland, that was close to where Katherine was staying. It was a place that Forster himself knew about, had selected for both its isolation and accessibility, and which he had described in detail before Zahedi accepted it.

Zahedi said, "I believe we have it all, Mr. Forster. But please, for all our sakes, I hope you're not going to try anything clever. It won't help any of us. Until eleven tonight, then."

There was a click as the Iranian hung up.

Forster continued to hold the phone. Putting it down meant having to deal with Robert and Melissa, and there was not a part of his insides that didn't churn at the thought. Because it undoubtedly was one or both of them who had conceived of the whole obscene idea of taking Annie hostage. They were the ones who were aware of Annie's importance to him, who had seen the kind of irresistible leverage she would offer. His instinctive reaction had been correct when he jammed the muzzle of his gun against Robert's forehead.

Forster put down the phone and faced them both.

"Here's how it's going to be," he said, and spent the next five minutes describing the details of the little pas de deux he had choreographed with Zahedi. He spoke quietly and without visible feeling. It was the manner of a man who, having suffered a great personal loss, was so exhausted, so drained of emotion, that some significant part of him already had died.

Robert said, "I appreciate your arranging for Melissa and me to be part of this."

"I didn't do it for you. I just wanted to be sure that if anything went wrong with the exchange, I could get my hands on you fast."

Forster heard a ship's horn from the river. The sun had broken through the mist but everything was still tinged with gray. Wanting to bring his fists to his forehead in frustration, he gazed out of the window instead.

At 8:50 A.M., Melissa and Forster left the apartment and went their separate ways, having arranged to meet Robert at 5:00 that evening for the drive to Maryland.

Forster stopped at a phone on First Avenue and called Jennings at his office.

"Take down this number," he told the editor, "and call me right back from an outside phone."

"What's happening?"

Forster read off the number on the phone. "Just call me," he said and hung up.

He stood there, studying the parked cars and the passers-by, and the traffic moving slowly uptown. There was no practical reason for him to be under visual surveillance at this time, but he kept a careful watch anyway. Exactly seven minutes after he called Jennings, the telephone rang and he picked it up.

"It's me," said the editor.

"Are you out of the building?"

"I'm two blocks away, on Madison Avenue."

"Okay, listen to me," said Forster and briefed his friend on all that had happened.

Jennings listened without interruption.

"Now comes your part," said Forster, "so stay with me. Who do you know at the FBI? Preferably someone high up."

"Is the deputy director high enough?"

"How well do you know him?"

"Well enough for most purposes."

"Good. Because you're going to have to put this whole thing

on a personal basis. I want no second guessing from some agency Neanderthal. I want done only what I'm about to tell you should be done. Do you have your notebook with you?''

''Yes.''

''Then take down these details. Katherine Harwith is staying with a Linda Gilbert at 186 Deepdale Road in Bethesda, Maryland. I want seven agents at that house no later than nine this evening. They're to be six male and one female. The men can range from average to medium-tall in build, but the woman *must* be small, delicately made, and fair-haired—like Katherine.''

Forster paused to study several men walking by on First Avenue.

''Now I'm going to give you exact directions for getting to our meeting place from Linda Gilbert's house,'' he said, and outlined roads, turns, distances.

''Slow down,'' said Jennings. ''I don't have shorthand.''

Forster slowed his speech, wondering whether his entire plan was overly ambitious and beyond his means to carry out. A blueprint for disaster? Yet he cared even less for the alternatives. Still, by the time he finished telling Marty the last of the details, a new chill of uncertainty was sweeping through him.

''How do you feel about this whole setup?'' he asked the editor.

''I'd feel a lot better with a few dozen agents staked out in the woods around the clearing.''

''So would I. But Zahedi's too much of a pro not to have the area checked out in advance. So please, Marty. Don't you or anyone else try to outsmart me.''

''Don't worry about it. Good luck.''

Forster hung up. Then he went home for the first time in three days.

He spent a long time in the shower, toweled off, and changed the dressing on his arm. The wound was healing well. Then he lay down and tried to sleep because he wanted to be fresh for whatever lay ahead that night. But he might just as well have tried to fly across the Hudson. Sleep refused to come. I may never sleep again, he thought, and got up to pour himself half a tumbler of bourbon, although it was not yet noon and he was still on medication.

When his drink was finished, he started to pour another, then

changed his mind and decided to have lunch instead. He opened
a can of clam chowder and scrambled a couple of eggs, eating
directly from the pot and pan to avoid having to wash dishes.

From the center of the kitchen, he considered the possible
directions he could take. The refrigerator hummed efficiently
and the pilot light of the stove gleamed its small blue flame. He
stood there for several moments, feeling the silence of the apartment about him, picturing its separate rooms. When he finally
left the kitchen, it was without particular destination. Bare-
footed, he walked more heavily than necessary, taking some
small comfort in the sound of the floorboards yielding to his
weight and the apartment carrying at least that human sign.

He was in the foyer when the house phone rang. Some part
of him knew, even before the doorman made the announcement,
that Melissa was on her way up.

When he opened the door they just stood looking at each
other. Forster could feel the full weight of his blood.

"Would you like me to leave?" she asked.

"It might be better for us both."

Her eyes widened, but she didn't move or speak.

"What do you want?"

"To talk."

"We've nothing more to say to each other."

"Yes we do."

Her fingers were clasped like spikes. She must have come
straight from her office because she was dressed for work, a
beautiful, urbane woman with a pale, tensely drawn face.

"What's the point, Melissa?"

Still, she stood there until he made a small, helpless gesture
with his hands and stepped back. Melissa came in and closed
the door behind her.

They sat on the same couch they had shared on her first visit.
Forster offered her no drink, no conversation, no encourage-
ment. He wanted her to speak her piece and leave.

"I don't care whether you believe me or not," she began
softly, "but there are certain things I have to say. And I want to
say them before tonight, because I don't know what's going to
happen." She closed her eyes to gather her thoughts. Then she
looked at Forster once more. "I don't blame you for the way
you feel about me. I deserve it. Not because I planned or even
knew about this thing with Annie, but because I *should* have

known. I knew Zahedi. I knew the Iranians. I knew what they were, what they were capable of. I just didn't want to accept it. All I cared about was what they could do for Robert and me. And for that, I'll never forgive myself.''

Forster gazed at her and saw worlds whirl past and darken her face.

''For as long as I can remember,'' she said, ''I've walked in strange places. The ground was always soft, treacherous. I never felt safe. I never knew when I'd fall through. So I was always protecting myself. That's an explanation, not an excuse. There is no excuse for much of what I've done and allowed to be done. I know I never fooled you about that or about what I was, and you didn't fool me for long either. But there were still moments when we came near to feeling something good, nearer than I've ever let myself come with anyone before. And for that, at least, I'm grateful.''

Melissa rose. Her eyelids were pink.

''That's all I wanted to tell you,'' she said and left.

Forster sat there, unmoving: *I'm a pillar of salt.*

Later, he dressed with care for the night ahead. At one point, tying his tie, he almost felt like an aging matador going through his ritual preparations for a final confrontation. Except that there was neither the history nor the tradition of the bull ring, only the threat. He tucked one of his two revolvers inside his belt and slipped the other into a jacket pocket. He hoped he wasn't going to have to use them, but didn't even consider leaving them behind.

He took a final look around the apartment. He had left lights burning in one of the hallways and the bathroom, and he switched them off. There was the faint scent of Melissa's perfume in the living room and he stood there for a moment breathing in. Then he went to meet her and her brother.

17

It was an especially humid night, but the limousine's air conditioner, working as smoothly and silently as its engine, kept the temperature at a comfortable level all through New Jersey and Delaware and then deep into Maryland. Indeed, Forster felt encased in a dove-gray vacuum that sealed out all unpleasantries as part of its five year or fifty-thousand-mile warranty. With the chauffeur absent, Forster sat up front beside Robert, who was doing the driving, while Melissa sat alone in back. The seating arrangements had been Robert's idea. Seeking possible significance in everything, Forster assumed Robert wanted to keep watch on him; the feeling was mutual. The long ride itself had started off to the accompaniment of Brahms tapes, followed by Chopin and Mozart. And what was the possible significance in *that*?

Forster felt himself heading out to the end of a string that stretched all the way back to New York. He could almost feel it getting ready to snap. Still, they were moving west and slightly south into a blazing sunset, into a sky so vast, so filled with brilliant color, that it couldn't help but touch him with its promise.

There was little conversation. The music was enough to ease them through the heavier of the silences. Passing the outskirts of Aberdeen, they ran into an electrical storm with rain driving across the windshield in sheets and stabs of lightning turning the landscape blue. The wind was bad, like a hurricane's blast that comes off the sea and rips long stretches of beach. Forster pressed back against his seat, ready to start sniffing for brimstone. For he had a sudden burning hatred of what lay ahead for all of them. Even if it went well, there was going to be pain. Then the wind and rain died, and they drove out of the storm into what remained of the sunset.

* * *

They were the first to arrive. The limousine glided into the area like a long, gray ghost, its engine barely audible, its finish gleaming under a full moon. They parked at the edge of a large grassy field surrounded by trees. Robert switched off the headlights but left the engine and air conditioner running. The dashboard clock read 10:52.

Forster turned toward Melissa. Alone in the rear, she seemed very much apart from everything, a hitchhiker in a hearse. Moonlight rendered her face luminous. She should be in diaphanous veils, frolicking about the glade, he thought. Instead, she sat stiff and frightened in the backseat of a limousine, clutching a purse with a gun in it. Forster hadn't seen the weapon, but he knew it was there. Somehow it pleased him. He felt it lent a certain symmetry to things, a balance of unseen forces that reduced an otherwise unfathomable world to its essentials. He could almost feel his life simplifying, its separate parts coming together.

In what? A final explosion?

A car's headlights flickered through the trees, broke into the clear, and came to a halt about fifty yards away. The lights went off and two men got out of the car. At the same time, Forster left the limousine. The three of them moved quickly about the area, checking among the trees and underbrush. They did their work separately, not speaking or making contact, three silent searchers in an equally silent wood. Evidently the rainstorm had passed this way earlier, because the grass and bushes were still soaked, and Forster's light-toned suit was soon marked by dark, wet patches. He circled to a depth of about a hundred yards, probing the brush with a long stick he had picked up and scanning the lower branches of trees for possible sharpshooters. He discovered nothing. Neither did the other two men, and they returned to their respective cars.

"You can give them the all-clear," Forster told Robert.

The limousine's headlights flashed on and off and the other car returned the signal.

An instant later Forster started toward the center of the clearing, leaving Robert and Melissa in the limousine. At the same time, he saw Annie get out of the other car, accompanied by an average-size man in a dark business suit. Zahedi, Forster thought. Then he had a good look at Annie and felt himself go soft inside. Stepping delicately through the wet grass in high-heeled shoes and a pale blouse and skirt, she might have been walking down Fifth Avenue on the way to her office. Which probably had been where she was heading when Zahedi picked her up. Her hands were not tied, but Zahedi was holding her arm in the polite yet proprietary manner of a possessive husband.

The two men who had done the searching earlier followed at a distance of perhaps fifteen yards. They were clearly professionals . . . Americans, from the look of them. Both were of medium build and moved with the easy grace of athletes. One wore a white, short-sleeved shirt and jeans. The other had on a dark blue polo shirt and tan chinos. Each man carried an automatic in his right hand.

Zahedi spoke first. "Good evening, Mr. Forster. We're lucky. We avoided the rain."

They all stood ten feet apart.

Forster was looking at Annie. She stared back at him with a clear, luminous look, some frightened creature with huge eyes. "Are you all right?" he asked.

"Yes. I'm fine."

"They didn't hurt you?"

She shook her head and despair passed her like a wind. "I'm just so sorry I had to cause you all this. You'd have had it made without me. I've ruined everything."

Forster was still watching her face. Her skin kept her intact, but the nerves beneath seemed to do things on their own. One group wept, another was furious, a third cluster was simply stricken dumb.

"If you're satisfied, Mr. Forster, I suggest we move along to the next segment of our arrangements."

Forster really considered Zahedi for the first time. Had he expected to find himself looking at some ultimate cynosure of evil, the pleasant-faced man standing opposite him would have been a disappointment. But he had learned differently. Evil in real life breathed no fire, wore no devil's horns. Most often it came in banal packages. In this case it happened to be a curly-haired Iranian with graying temples, full, dimpled cheeks, and the friendliest of smiles.

He took a sheet of paper from an envelope and handed it to Zahedi. "Here's where you'll find Katherine Harwith and the directions for getting there. It's just a five-minute drive from here.''

Zahedi motioned for his two men to join them. Robert and Melissa left the limousine and took up their own positions about twenty feet behind the group.

"Who else will be at the house?" Zahedi asked Forster.

"No one. The place belongs to a widowed friend, who's off on vacation and left Katherine the key. Your men should have no trouble making entry. Just be sure they understand Katherine's not to be hurt.''

"I've already instructed them.''

The Iranian gave the directions to the man in the jeans and white shirt. "I'll expect you two back in about twenty minutes. No speeding. Carelessness at this point could be disastrous.''

The men left without a word. A pair of programmed pistols, thought Forster, and watched them walk back to their car and drive off.

Then, like a repertory company of trained actors, everyone else took up their assigned positions. Zahedi gallantly laid his jacket on the wet grass at the foot of a giant elm for Annie to sit on. He and Forster then separated and moved about twenty feet apart. Robert and Melissa remained off to the left.

Everything seemed to be going exactly as planned, yet Forster felt curiously little confidence in the ultimate result. He couldn't quite believe he actually was outmaneuvering these practiced conspirators, these masters of treachery and deception, these deliberate planners of past, present, and future murders. He had a sudden sense of almost being forced, against his will, to do exactly what they wanted him to do, as if the mood of the wood itself, even the air, were his enemies. Which was pure neurosis, of course, and he knew it. Still, he felt as though he had drawn himself, and Annie with him, into some bleak, all but inextricable situation in which Zahedi, Robert, and Melissa were managing to push him further and further again, like the devil's own hunters tracking their final victory.

Then the moment passed and he was nowhere but in a verdant, woodland glade, with a bright moon overhead and everything smelling sweet and clean with the recent rain.

Zahedi's car returned exactly seventeen minutes from the time it had left the clearing. Forster watched as it circled the area then stopped at a totally different location from where it had been parked before. Not only was the car now much closer to those waiting, but it was facing them from precisely the opposite direction. It took Forster a moment to realize that both of these factors were deliberate. The car was parked closer so that the three agents would have less distance to walk as they approached. And coming from their present direction, the moon would be behind them, casting their faces in shadow. Forster's respect for the FBI soared.

A woman and two men emerged from the car. From where Forster was standing, they looked so much like Katherine Harwith and Zahedi's two pistols (one wore tan chinos and a navy shirt, the other, jeans and a white shirt) that for an icy moment he was sure something had gone wrong. Then he saw that the woman was not nearly as slender as Katherine, and knew better. The woman's hands were behind her back, as though tied, and the two men were on either side of her. They walked quickly across the clearing, the moon lengthening their shadows before them. The only sound was the whisper of grass about their feet.

Just a little more, thought Forster, and they'll be close enough to draw. His own hand was inside his jacket, gripping the butt of the pistol in his belt. Zahedi's face was relaxed, easy, seemingly concerned with nothing. Robert and Melissa looked almost bored. Annie, the only one of the group seated, might have been on a solitary nocturnal picnic, a lonely lover in a bucolic setting.

The three advancing agents were no more than about twenty to thirty feet from Zahedi. *Now*, thought Forster, do it *now* or he'll spot you for sure.

They did it.

Suddenly all three stopped walking and had guns in their hands. One revolver was aimed at Zahedi, another at Robert and the third at Melissa.

Forster drew his own weapon. "Don't anyone move."

No one did. The surprise was so complete, so stunning, that for several beats none of the three seemed to understand what was happening. But it was mostly Robert that Forster was watching. Yet what could he possibly do now? If anything, Robert simply was gazing back at him with a vague half smile, as though to say, I didn't think you had it in you.

Neither did Forster. Not even now.

It was then that the machine gun opened up.

The chattering came from somewhere out of the surrounding wood, and even as Forster ducked low and began zig-zagging toward Annie, he saw one of the FBI agents take a hit and go down. The other two dove for the ground and began firing at Zahedi, and Robert. *Oh, Christ,* thought Forster. Reaching Annie, he half ran her, half dragged her deep into the brush. Behind him, he heard the firing still going on . . . the sharp, individual crack of handguns mixing with the heavier bursts from the automatic weapon.

He pressed Annie flat between two bushes. "You all right?" Her face a pale blur in the darkness, she nodded.

"Stay right here," Forster told her. "No matter what you hear, don't move. I'll be back for you as soon as I can. I've got to get that machine gun." He took out his second revolver and pressed it into her hand. "If Zahedi or Robert finds you, just point this thing and squeeze the trigger."

He circled back toward the sound of the automatic fire, making certain he approached it from what would be the rear. Branches clawed at his clothing slowing his movements. There was still firing going on, so he knew that at least one of the agents had to be alive and functioning.

At a distance of sixty feet, he caught his first glimpse of the machine gun's muzzle flash. It came from fairly high up in a tree overlooking the clearing. Forster edged closer and found an opening through the leaves of the tree's lower branches. Then lifting his revolver and aiming carefully with both hands, he squeezed off a cluster of four quick shots.

There was no sound of a cry, but an instant later a man and a submachine gun came crashing to the ground. The man appeared to be an American and was dead. The submachine gun was an Uzi, an Israeli weapon recognized as among the best in the world. Forster found a fresh ammunition clip in one of the dead man's pockets and clicked it into place. A Jewish gun, he thought, and wondered if he would ever be able to appreciate the irony. Then he pushed through the brush to the edge of the clearing.

All shooting had stopped in the glade.

Forster peered out from behind a tree trunk. The one female and two male agents lay unmoving in the grass with the special awkwardness of the newly dead. Melissa was on her knees and bent over Robert, who was on his back and obviously wounded. Zahedi, a revolver in his hand, was crawling brokenly toward them, like a squashed bug. Before Forster even realized what was happening, the Iranian stopped crawling and fired twice at Melissa and Robert without any apparent effect. Melissa did, however, stop tending her brother long enough to glance up and see where the shots had come from. Still on her knees, she picked up an automatic from the grass, calmly aimed at Zahedi's head and blew part of it away. Then she bent over Robert once more.

About to start toward them, Forster hesitated as some undefined instinct held him back. Too much was happening that he didn't understand. A chill passed by him like the beat of a dying heart. Gripping his newest acquired gun, he stayed where he was, cold yet sweating. His mind kept slipping in and out of focus, finding and losing direction, circling itself like an explorer lost in snowy wastes. On a summer night there was a blizzard inside his head. Why had Zahedi been shooting at his two partners? And why had Melissa killed him with as little apparent thought or emotion as she might have given to stepping on a cockroach? Forster vainly sought answers from behind his tree.

Moments later, he saw Melissa walk over to the gray limousine, and drive it to where her brother lay. Robert apparently had lost consciousness in the interim, because Melissa was struggling with dead weight as she tried to tug and lift him into the back of the car. Forster glanced once more at the four bodies in the clearing; a moonlit charnel house. Then he hurried back to where he had left Annie.

"It's me," he whispered, approaching through the brush. "It's all right."

White faced, she held him. "Thank God! What happened?"

"I'll explain later. Right now I have to stay close to Robert and Melissa. More FBI should be here in minutes. Don't come out 'til you hear them."

He was gone before she could protest.

Melissa had lifted Robert into the limousine and was about to get in herself when Forster returned. He watched her in the moonlight, hoping the agent who had driven Zahedi's car back had left the keys in the ignition. If not, he'd have to lose precious seconds going through the dead man's pockets.

There was the sound of an engine starting and the limousine glided away in the darkness. The survivors, thought Forster coldly, and dashed across the clearing for Zahedi's sedan.

The keys were in the ignition.

Not putting on his lights, Forster drove after them. His eyes picked out Zahedi and the three FBI agents as he left. The fifth body, the machine-gunner he had shot in the woods, was out of sight.

Forster drove through a veil of quiet that dimmed the hum of his car's engine. A ground fog folded into the road and placed red aureoles around the taillights of the limousine in the near distance. Few cars were moving at this hour and it was easy enough to keep the limo in sight. Melissa had been heading mostly west and north on two-lane country roads for perhaps fifteen minutes, and Forster had the feeling she was not going much farther. She'd have been using one of the big interstates if she were.

So where was she going?

Forster couldn't even venture a guess. He only knew where she was *not* going, which was back to New York—and where she *should* be going but didn't dare go, which was to a hospital emergency room. Unless Robert was beyond such help. If he was unconscious at this stage, it didn't look good. Forster had seen enough gunshot casualties to know the signs. If you didn't die from shock, you died from hemorrhage.

He saw the two red taillights turn left, and moments later he did the same. The road dipped low, and the fog was heavier here. Forster simply followed the double red glow. With his head out the window to see better, he could all but sniff out the sour rot of blood in the air. His knuckles were white on the wheel and he felt something close to nausea. There suddenly were too many new mysteries and he saw no hint of solutions. Katherine Harwith had spoken of something dirtier than the Iranians, some incipient breed of devil's disciple pulling invisible strings; but even she'd had to admit it was nothing more than a vague feeling. Although that feeling was precisely why he was here, driving through fog on strange back roads. Because if someone of importance did exist, where else would Melissa be running at this moment for help and instructions?

The road became narrower and moments later the limousine's

lights swung to the right and into a driveway. Forster pulled onto a grassy shoulder and cut the motor. He saw an entrance lantern and the lights of what had probably once been a farm house, but was now just a modest country retreat. The limousine must have been expected because a man appeared almost immediately. He spoke briefly to Melissa, then helped her lift Robert out of the car and carry him into the house. From where he sat, Forster could see no more. He grabbed the Uzi and left the car, hoping there were no loose dogs around. He stopped to listen for growls or barking. There were only the crickets.

He circled the house at a distance to avoid the front lantern and saw no other houses. Approaching from the right, he came up on the side of the living room. Lights shone from a pair of open windows, and Forster heard Melissa weeping. He crouched behind a row of bushes and peered inside.

Robert was lying on the couch, with Melissa kneeling beside him. His eyes were closed. The front of his shirt and jacket were stained with blood. His face was totally white and had an expression of utter exhaustion, as if he had been sentenced to carry a load of bricks uphill all his life. Forster had only to look at him to know he was dead.

Then Forster looked at the man who had helped carry Robert into the house. He stood with his back to Forster, a tall man whose straight, almost rigid bearing seemed curiously familiar. A moment later he turned his head and Forster saw his face in profile. He saw yet he didn't seem to see. Because he was looking at Wendell Norton.

The shock sent Forster to his knees in the dirt. Then it reached into his gut and sent his nerves into riot. At that instant, simply seeing Norton there and understanding no part of it, he felt himself all open, raw depths. If he had a brain, the best of it had to be gone. It felt near to an extinction.

He took hold. There had to be a reason. There was a reason for everything. Not for this. For this too, he told himself and looked into the room once more.

Norton stood there, silent and unmoving, as Melissa wept. Once, he half started toward her, but changed his mind. When Melissa finally regained control and rose from the floor, he poured her a glass of vodka. Then he brought in a sheet and covered Robert where he lay. Forster had not heard either of them say a word.

"Lord, Lord—what a disaster." Melissa spoke at last. Her voice was hoarse from crying, her face flushed and tear streaked, but she had gained a measure of composure. "Poor Robert. How senseless. To have come so far, and then—this."

Norton sat down with a large snifter of brandy. He was partially facing Forster, but his eyes were on Melissa. "What went wrong?"

"Everything. Though I'm not surprised. We were in trouble from the minute Zahedi started killing people. Then he really finished us off by taking Annie hostage." Melissa's eyes drifted to the bedsheet and welled up once more. "Imagine. Paul thought Robert and I were responsible for all that. At one point, he was ready to shoot us both, and who could blame him?"

Forster breathed heavily. His lungs were foul. But where the devil was Wendell in all this?

"What happened at the exchange?" said Norton.

"Paul must have called in the police or the FBI. Instead of Zahedi's two men and Katherine coming back to the clearing, we got three agents dressed to look like them. When they drew guns, a machine gunner opened up from the woods where Zahedi must have hidden him, and all hell broke loose. When it was over, the three agents were dead, and Zahedi and Robert were close to it."

"Zahedi was still alive when you left?"

"No. I shot him," said Melissa.

Norton considered her. "Why?"

"Because he'd begun firing at Robert and me."

Norton grunted, his face dour. "We're better off without him. What happened to his machine gunner?"

"I heard a cluster of pistol shots in the woods, then the sound of something crashing down. I figure that was Paul's work. It was the last sign I had of him."

"And Annie?"

"Paul ran her into the woods when the shooting started. I'm sure she's all right."

"That was it, then?"

Melissa nodded.

"You're certain no one followed you here?" said Norton.

Melissa looked at him with glassy eyes. "Who was there to follow me?"

"Paul."

"The only thing he had on his mind was Annie. And he had no car."

"What about Zahedi's car?"

"He wouldn't have had the keys."

Norton rose and refilled their glasses. When he returned, he kissed Melissa. "Christ, I'm devastated about Robert."

Melissa's chin trembled.

"Other than for that," said Norton, "we came out of this mess reasonably well. At least Paul and Katherine are alive and still able to turn in their evidence."

"You'll forgive me if I can't exactly jump for joy at the moment."

"I'm sorry, darling." Norton sighed. "I'm far from unaffected. You know how much Robert meant to me."

On the edge of breaking up once more, Melissa took refuge in her vodka.

Forster, watching them, listening to their words, felt all that was clear and rational in him draining away. Only confusion and betrayal remained. Something appalling had been done to him, but he had no idea what, how, or why.

He rose from the dirt. Then, carrying the Uzi on its sling about his neck, he circled the house to the back door, cut a hole in the screening and entered the kitchen. He could hear Wendell's voice as he moved quietly and quickly from the kitchen, to the center hall, to the entrance to the living room.

Melissa saw him first.

Her face showed no real change of expression. Perhaps grief had frozen all inflection. But Forster sensed an attention there as their eyes met, and perhaps a hint of something more, undefined yet clearly present.

Norton, following her eyes, turned.

"Paul!" There was no question about *his* response. His cheeks went pale, his mouth dropped, and a flush of fear almost seemed to come off the air about him. When he tried to lift a hand in greeting, it dropped of its own weight. He stared at the Uzi dangling from its sling and appeared fixated by it. Then grabbing hold somewhere inside, he reconstituted himself out of sheer will. "Thank God you're all right. Melissa was just telling me how—"

"Stop it!" Forster cut him off. "I know what Melissa was telling you. I've been outside the window for ten minutes."

The banker's lips worked briefly before there was any sound. "You've got to let me explain."

"I intend to. That's the only reason I didn't shoot you through the screening. So I can hear you explain. My sanity depends on it. For a moment, kneeling in the dirt out there, I was sure I was mad." Forster paused. "I'm not really crazy, am I, Wendell? You really are here with Melissa, aren't you? You really did say all the things I heard you say, didn't you?"

Norton stood as though anchored to the floor. He stared at Forster. "You're wrong if you think I—"

Forster took two short, quick steps and hit him. It was unpremeditated, a looping right-hand punch that caught Norton high on the side of the jaw and sent him stumbling back into a chair while his drink exploded against the floor. Forster could feel himself shaking. He wanted to hit him again. But he knew if he did, he'd never be able to stop.

"No more bullshit! One more lie and I swear I'll blow your fucking head off!" Forster felt as though he had forgotten how to breathe. He gulped air to keep his rage from choking him. "What the hell have you been doing to me? What kind of sick game have you been playing? What's this thing you've had with Robert and Melissa? You sonofabitch! I want it all!"

Slumped in the chair, Norton gazed blankly at him. A deep red patch showed where he had been hit. "I need a drink," he said.

Melissa rose and poured him another brandy. Then without a word, she sat down once more. To Forster, she seemed only mildly interested in what was happening. It was the sheet-draped body of her brother that appeared to hold the heart of her attention. Was she expecting a second Resurrection?

Forster pulled over a chair and faced Norton. Melissa was off slightly to his left. The room itself was nondescript, impersonal, a random mixture of undistinguished odds and ends thrown together without affection or history. It had the temporary look of a rented place, and Forster guessed that was exactly what it was. But rented for what purpose? Surely not as a confessional.

"Go ahead," he said. "Talk."

Norton glanced at Melissa as if to check out her reaction, but she wasn't even looking at him. Then he stared briefly at the machine gun hanging from Forster's neck and resting against his chest. It seemed to provide the necessary incentive. But when he did start talking, it was slowly, reluctantly, as if each word were a separate weight on his will. His tone, however, carried a mix of ice and steel. And his eyes, when they touched Forster's, were equally cold.

"I suppose the best place to start," he said softly, "is with the Berenstein tragedy and the two orphaned children who were its legacy. Despite what you may think, I never took my part in that calamity lightly. I wore my guilt like a hair shirt I couldn't take off. It was part of my skin. To the point where I carefully kept track of Helen and Arthur—or Melissa and Robert, if you prefer—wherever they happened to be living."

"Why?" Forster cut in. "Did you do anything to help them?"

"A bit here and there. Not too much at the beginning. And always anonymously, of course. How could I admit my guilt? But later, after they ran away from the Abelmans and disappeared, I felt worse than ever. I had visions of terrible things happening to them, and all of it finally roosting on my conscience. So I hired a private investigator, had them tracked down and one day confronted them with who I was."

"This is all true?" Forster asked Melissa.

She nodded.

Jesus, look whom I'm asking, he thought. "Go ahead," he told Norton.

"Initially, they detested me, poured out their years of frustration and childish hate. I bowed my head and accepted it all, including their poor, banal vow of vengeance. I was penitent, humble, patient. I explained the tragedy to them in human terms. Unfortunately, I told them their father was guilty as charged, and I and the others on the Malcolm Commission were only doing our duty by sending his case to the U.S. Attorney's office for prosecution. I told them their father's suicide was all too real and tragic, but was more a result of his years of suffering in the camps, of personal despair, than of the jail term he received."

Melissa made a small sound that was probably a laugh, but sounded more like a groan.

Norton barely glanced at her. "All three of us now know that David Berenstein was innocent, but that's after the fact and another story entirely. Although I can't deny that it added to my remorse, to my need to somehow make amends through his orphaned children. It all seems ugly and twisted, sitting here tonight. But my motives were better than that."

"And your colleagues on the Commission?" said Forster. "They knew nothing of this?"

"Nothing. This was all mine, my private act of atonement." Norton looked at Melissa who was staring fixedly at a fine crack in the wall. "In any case, I gradually won them over. I was very persuasive, very warm, very caring. I helped them with the new identities they'd chosen, with money, advice, education, with whatever they felt they wanted in their new lives. I became their secret godfather. Not even my wife knew they existed. I suppose it was a little like playing God for me, a chance to mold two very exceptional youngsters into my own alter egos. Though they really weren't always so malleable. Especially Melissa, who turned out to be the less-easily controlled, the real maverick of the two."

Pausing for a drink, Wendell once more sought and failed to reach Melissa's eyes. Forster noted that a change had come over him. It was obvious that he was warming to his story, perhaps even enjoying its telling. Who, after all, had he ever been able to tell it to before? And to an egoist like Wendell, thought Forster, that had to be frustrating.

"And when Melissa began growing into a dazzling young woman," Norton continued, "she was even harder to handle. She listened to nothing. That was when she ran off to marry that pervert, Luckner, in San Francisco. Still, she did finally walk away from him with an even ten million, which was all she was after in the first place. Conversely, Robert was easier to deal with. He admired what I represented, what I could teach him and do for him. He was a brilliant and ambitious youngster. It was gratifying to open my world to him. I know it's a cliché, but he was almost the son I never had."

"And Melissa?" said Forster. "Was she the daughter you never had?"

Norton was silent.

Melissa asked, "Would you like me to answer that, Wendell?"

"If it'll make you happy."

"Nothing'll make me happy. But I do think this one is mine." She looked evenly at Forster. "Poor Wendell. He was trying so hard to be a nice, virtuous Daddy Warbucks. And how did I pay him back for all his conscience-soothing benevolence? By coldly seducing him when I was sixteen. For which he's never really forgiven me.'' Her eyes, like twin gunsights, swung towards Norton. "Have you, love?"

His face locked and shuttered, the former Fed chairman said nothing. Forster, considering the two, was almost beginning to feel they despised each other.

"So you see," Melissa told him, "I never did allow myself to be the daughter Wendell never had. Nor did I ever completely leave him alone. I evidently had a need to keep reminding us both of who we were, and this was my way of doing it. Lord knows I've never been a daughter to him. We were both much too carnal for that.''

No one spoke and Forster could all but feel a quiver in the air. Melissa rose to pour another drink. Then she picked up her purse, took out a crumpled handkerchief, and sat down once more.

Forster motioned impatiently at Norton with the Uzi. "How does all this fit into the scandal?"

"You told me to start at the beginning, and Robert and Melissa were the beginning. It was they who inadvertently inspired the whole idea. When I finally won them over, they told me about their scheme to set up everyone on the Malcolm Commission to avenge their father. Extraordinary. They had everything worked out perfectly—down to the last detail. Of course they'd reached the age where they finally recognized the idea as an adolescent fantasy that no sane person would ever dream of actually attempting.''

Norton's eyes gave a hint of new life.

"After that," he said, "the scheme became our private little game, a stimulating exercise in market psychology and economics that the three of us would occasionally enjoy. We'd make computer projections of numbers, percentages, the effects of the imagined scandal on national currencies, on stocks, bonds and T-bills. We'd project budget deficits, trade balances, and index trading in options. Then each of us would describe how we'd handle the panic if we were sitting in the Oval Office. In essence, our little entertainment came about as close to simulating the real thing as one could get without actually doing it. Until one day a thought occurred and the whole idea suddenly became more than a game to me.''

Forster sat unmoving, the Uzi across his chest like a sleeping dragon. He felt he was listening to the ultimate diabolic tale, yet he knew that every word so far was true. Melissa, having withdrawn once more into her grief, was silently weeping as she stared at where her brother lay.

"But why?" asked Forster. His anger had drained off for the moment, leaving a residue of confusion. "I don't understand your purpose in all this insanity. *What did you want?*"

Norton looked surprised. "I'm sorry. I somehow assumed you'd know. But of course how could you? I haven't really told you anything yet." He smiled, but it was the smile of a man with a nerve-ripping toothache. "I wanted what I've been wanting for more years than I can remember, what I still want, what's undoubtedly been the single major ambition and frustration of my life. I wanted to be president of the United States."

Forster could do no more than stare at him. *My God! What happens in one lifetime.*

"I've shocked you," said Norton. "Yet I wonder why. You, of all people, should be able to understand. You've known me for more than twenty years. Time and again I've heard you call it a national tragedy that someone with my background and proven capabilities couldn't even get a shot at the nomination. You once published an article in which you said, 'When is our sleeping American electorate going to wake up and realize that the country's true economic destiny is never going to be fulfilled until it finally gets around to putting its most resourceful and creative financial thinker into the White House, instead of just one more political sycophant with a smile?' You see? I've memorized every word. It couldn't be said more succinctly. Do you remember when you wrote that, Paul?"

"Yes."

"I assume it's a concept you still believe."

Forster nodded.

"And do you also remember when you assured me that I was by far the best man you knew for the job, but that I'd never have a prayer at it unless the country was sliding into economic chaos, and I had to be called to save it?"

Forster could only stare at him.

Norton breathed deeply. "Well, I've done it. I've managed to help slide the country into economic chaos. And when I'm called to save it, I promise you I'll manage to do that, too. God knows it's not the way I'd have chosen to do it, but it finally became the only way available to me."

Feeling himself dangling like a body in the wind, Forster struggled to make sense of it. "Then it was *you* who set yourself and the others up to be indicted and touch off the panic?"

"Only from behind the scenes. It was Robert and Melissa who did the actual work, who hired Katherine, Stone, and Borman for their parts in creating the false evidence, who got the financial backing from Motomedi. Robert and Melissa were the only ones who knew my part in it."

"Then, of course, you got me," said Forster, numbly pushing it to the next step, "to take on the investigation that would eventually clear you and turn you into our national savior."

"I'm deeply sorry about that. I hated having to deceive you, having to presume on our friendship. But I knew you'd get the job done. As you finally did."

"And almost got myself killed three or four times in the process."

"I apologize for that too. But that was all Zahedi. He was worried about your closing in on the evidence and he simply got out of hand. I'm also terribly sorry about his picking up Annie and the whole of that tragic business tonight."

Forster glanced at Melissa and found her still too far inside herself to reach. "And how do you plan on apologizing to Robert?"

Norton quietly sipped his brandy and Forster took a badly needed moment to compose himself. What's wrong with me? he thought. I'm allegedly the sane one. I'm the one holding the gun. Yet that's not how I'm feeling.

"Do you know how many lives this insane adventure of yours has cost so far?" he said at last. "And when I start trying to add in the incalculable financial loss and anguish suffered by untold millions, all deliberately set in motion to feed your incredible ego, I have to worry about my own sanity and judgment almost as much as yours. Because I have to ask myself impossible questions, like how I could have cared for, admired, and respected you for more than two decades, yet not have known what you were really like? And if you weren't always the abominable madman you've turned out to be, when did the change take place and why couldn't I see it? And if you were able to deceive me as easily as you did, might I not have in some way contributed to that deception myself?"

There was real pain in Forster's eyes. "For God's sake, Wendell! How *could* you?"

"How could I?" It took effort, but Norton met Forster's gaze. "If you want the truth, it wasn't easy. Lord knows I didn't start out with this in mind, but this is where I've ended up. And don't imagine I take it lightly. I've done a lot of thinking about it, about the reasons I'm here, and I don't really like any of them—certainly not in retrospect, not considering the cost."

Compulsively, Norton's glance absorbed the omnipresent body on the couch and the solitary mourner beside it.

"But do you know what years of frustration can do to a man? Do you know what it can do to principles, standards, ethics, all the best in you? Finally, you lose it all. Finally, there's nothing left but the thing you've been wanting half your life but know you're never going to get. Not unless you're willing to do something so heinous, that just thinking about it chills your blood."

"Yet you did it anyway," said Forster dully.

"Yes. Because once you've edged up to it, once you've actually started, it doesn't seem all that evil. That's the insidious part. A dream can be a dangerous thing. You have this idea and it's exciting just thinking about it. I can't tell you the wonderful, floating feeling I had when the concept first hit me. Ironically, it was all Robert and Melissa's. If they hadn't tossed it in my lap I'd never have conceived of it in a million years. But once I had it, once I started thinking of it as more than just an adolescent fantasy that we'd turned into an amusing game, it became all mine."

Norton looked despairingly at Forster. "I know only too well what you think of me and I don't blame you. But we all have our collection of miseries. Sometimes the lights go out inside us and we can accept just so much darkness. I reached for what I wanted in the only way left for me. Call it obsession. Call it iniquity. Call it madness. Call it whatever you like. I still wanted the presidency badly enough for all normal judgments of right and wrong to pale beside it."

The banker turned his head slightly and a tracer of light from a lamp seemed to touch his face with hope. "Then you rationalize, of course. You tell yourself that in the long term the country will be better off, regardless of the temporary, the more immediate damage you've done. And it's not that hard to accept, because you know exactly what has to be done and you know you can do it.''

"You really got yourself to believe that?''

"Yes.''

Forster withheld comment. There were still things that puzzled him and he needed answers more than philosophical discussions after the fact.

"What if Zahedi had succeeded in having me killed?'' he asked. "How were you planning to clear yourself and the five you had indicted with you?''

"We had videotapes prepared as a possible backup. Only Robert, Melissa, and I knew they existed. They show Katherine, Borman, Stone, and the Iranian finance minister, Motomedi, discussing the details of the conspiracy with any references to Robert and Melissa edited out. If needed, the tapes and additional evidence would have been mailed to the attorney general.''

"Then Motomedi would have been indicted as the mastermind behind the whole conspiracy?''

"Precisely.''

"With Katherine, Borman, and Stone also paying up?''

Norton shrugged. "They're hardly deserving of concern.''

"And Robert and Melissa?''

"They'd have been clear, of course. We made certain there was no hard evidence to tie them into anything. And nothing that you or anyone else might have said to the contrary would have been anything more than hearsay in a courtroom.''

Forster glanced at Melissa to find her staring at him, her face as set and hard as a death mask. She had stopped crying but her cheeks were wet, her eyes red, the lids swollen.

"There's no logic to insanity,'' he told her, "but I can at least see what Wendell hoped to accomplish by this. What excuse did you and Robert have?''

Shaking her head, Melissa just stared hopelessly at him. Once, Forster saw her lips start to move, but no answer came. Norton, sipping his brandy, watched them both and said nothing. The room was like an empty space in which a death had occurred. Robert's body, though covered by its sheet, remained in plain sight and marked everything. Gripped by the moment, Forster would not have been too surprised to see Robert suddenly sit up with his usual wry smile and join the discussion.

Norton said, "It's time we talked practically, Paul. What's done is done, and unfortunately there's no bringing back the dead. So we may as well start making our plans from here."

Forster blinked several times, a man waking from a nightmare only to find the worst of his nocturnal demons still facing him. "Do you really think I'm going to let you get away with this?"

"Again, I can't blame you for the way you feel." Norton spoke gently, as to the newly bereaved. "But neither can I see you punishing me at the expense of the entire country. Because that's exactly what you'll be doing if the truth of all this is ever made public. Just imagine the effect of this latest and worst-yet breach of trust on our already crumbling markets. Having the country's six top bankers indicted for insider trading was bad enough, and that was supposed to be just simple venality. To expose the chairman of the Federal Reserve, the high priest of the sacred temple itself, as having deliberately plotted and set off this economic earthquake for strictly political purposes would be to shake the foundations of the republic."

A faint nausea drifted through Forster's lungs. It was, of course, a convincingly outlined worst-case scenario by a super salesman. But it was not impossible.

"On the other hand," Norton continued, "if you're sensible enough to act on reason rather than emotion, you'll end up with everything you set out to achieve when I first asked you to take on this investigation. Motomedi and Iran will be exposed as having conspired to demolish the American economy, I and the other bankers will be cleared of all charges, confidence and trust in the dollar and the financial community will be restored, the markets will soar back to where they were before the scandal broke, spending and factory orders will pick up, laid-off workers will get back their jobs, and the American Dream will take its rightful place in the heavens."

"And you'll be rewarded by being elected president?"

"I hope I'll finally get my shot at it. And if I do, we both know I'll do as well as any and better than most."

"I did once feel that way about you," Forster admitted.

"And not now?"

Forster could do no more than look at him.

"I'm the same man I always was," said Norton.

That's probably true, thought Forster, but I never knew about it. He abruptly stood up because it suddenly was impossible for him to sit there an instant longer, looking at this stranger who had been his close friend for so many years. Needing a drink at that moment about as badly as he could remember, he poured himself some of Norton's brandy.

When he returned to his chair, Norton was considering him carefully. The banker seemed weary and regretful, a bitter, aging man, not quite so certain and impervious as he had appeared a moment ago.

"You're not going to be able to do it, are you?" he said.

"Do what?"

"Act on reason rather than emotion."

"Did you think I would?"

"Not really. But I did have some small hope. For both our sakes."

Forster peered long and consideringly at his brandy. He missed the searing anger of half an hour ago. He even missed the confusion that had come after it. Now, with everything explained and clear, there was only a dull ache and the futile wish that none of this had ever happened. Then he glanced up and looked into the small, dark muzzle of an automatic.

His first instinct was to reach for the trigger of the Uzi, still resting against his chest on its sling. But at a distance of five feet, Norton would have had three rounds pumped into him before he could ever get the gun straightened out and into action. So Forster just sat there holding his drink. He had no idea where Norton's gun had come from. It might have been under his seat cushion or in his pocket. As Forster recalled it, he had never bothered to search him. *Stupid.*

"Melissa, take his gun," said Norton. "Carefully. From behind."

Melissa, sitting off to Forster's left, appeared frozen.

"Melissa!" said Norton.

This time, doing as ordered, she moved behind Forster's chair and lifted the Uzi's leather sling over his head.

"Now move back a few feet," the banker told her.

Forster heard her feet slowly shuffle on the bare, wood flooring. I'm in trouble, he thought. But far more than fear, he felt a hard, contemptuous disgust for himself, for his carelessness in having let this happen.

Incredibly, he heard himself laugh.

"What's so funny?" Norton asked.

"I keep forgetting. Never underestimate your enemy."

"I'm not your enemy. It's you who've made yourself mine. I can't tell you how sorry I am it had to turn out this way."

The crazy thing was, thought Forster, that he probably *was* sorry. So much for regret.

There was silence between them and Forster could feel his own death as clearly as if it were an attachment on his nerves. Wendell had no alternative but to get rid of him. Once he did, he was free. The irony of it was, the sonofabitch *would* make a superb president. He had all the necessary requirements—cunning, treachery, pragmatism, ego, pathological ambition, and a total absence of the restraints imposed by God's Commandments.

"I just want you to know," said Norton, somehow compelled to explain, to justify, even to a dead man, "that if everything had gone as I'd planned, you'd have gotten whatever cabinet post, or any other appointment, you wanted."

Norton allowed himself the faintest of smiles and Forster thought, if I'm going to make a move, I'd better do it now. But he had a moment when he remembered Max facing him with a gun, and Max's predecessor buried in a Long Island wood, and all those others lying in a Bethesda wood, and his will was all but gone. He looked deep into that glitter of recent death and could hear its song. *Come on,* it was saying. *It finally happens to everyone so it can't be that terrible. And haven't you had enough of all this degraded clowning anyway?* Then the rational part of his mind said angrily, *Schmuck! How can you let him get away with this?*

Forster felt his legs tense under him, tremble slightly, and start to uncoil. Watch his eyes, he told himself, not his gun. But he was only part way out of his chair when the shots went off, filling the room with their sound as he braced for the impact. He half sensed the blast from the explosions roll over him and he breathed the acrid smell of the powder. But he felt no hit and he kept going, pushing off hard with both legs and covering the distance between them in a single leap. Norton and the chair went over backwards under him.

Struggling for position, Forster groped for the gun before Norton could squeeze off another shot. *How could he have missed me at five feet?* Then he looked down and saw Wendell's eyes boring into and through his own. He also saw that a small section of his friend's forehead was missing. Breathing heavily, Forster lay there like the ascendant partner of two lovers. A sick spasm lifted from his stomach and touched his brain. Only inches away, the broken face beneath his seemed to be trying to tell him something. *What?* Numbly, like someone truly rising from the dead, Forster rolled to one side and looked up at Melissa.

She stood a short distance behind his chair, holding the Uzi and staring at Norton where he lay. Part of her face had the look of a child touched by angels. The other part might have belonged to the devil. For the barest of instants Forster had the icy feeling that it was him she had been shooting at, but had missed in her rush to get off her shots and hit Wendell instead. He was half prepared to grab Wendell's automatic and dive for cover the moment she swung the Uzi in his direction. Then she looked at him and he knew better.

Forster got up and gently took the machine gun from her hands. She offered no resistance.

"I'm grateful, but I don't understand it," he said.

She sat down where she had been sitting earlier, picked up her drink, and gazed once more at her brother's body. But whatever grief she had shown before, appeared to be gone. An icy void had taken its place. Forster preferred the grief. What she had now was a snake pit.

"Why did you shoot him?" he asked.

"For a lot of reasons."

"Such as?"

"Why are reasons so important?"

"They help preserve the soul."

"Do you really believe that nonsense?"

"No," he said. "Though I'd sometimes like to."

She brooded over her drink and said nothing.

"I'd also like to believe that at least one of your reasons might have been to save *me*. Or am I being naïve?"

"I'd definitely say you're worth saving."

Forster looked at Melissa to see if she was mocking him, but he saw only the void. Then he watched as she went over to where Norton lay and forced his eyes closed.

Still kneeling beside him, she said, "If he killed you, he'd have had to kill me too."

"Why?"

"Because I'd have been witness to your murder. Also, I'd

have been the only one left who'd be able to tie him to the conspiracy. And knowing Wendell, I doubt that he could have lived with that for long.''

''But weren't you lovers?''

Rising, she considered Forster with something near to amusement. ''What has *that* got to do with anything? Besides, once I learned the truth about what he and the others actually did to my father, I never could feel the same about him again. Imagine lying to us all those years. And he knew how I felt. Which was another reason he couldn't have trusted me.''

The full weight of the night's events seemed to hit her again. She gasped a bit and chewed her lip. ''God, I feel alone. What happens now? Are you going to have me arrested?''

Somehow, the question itself was enough to anger him. ''Hey, come on. You just saved my goddamn life. What do I look like?''

She considered him for a long moment before she answered. ''Someone I wish I could have known about twenty years ago.''

Something, a sudden thickness, clotted in his throat.

''I'm not a cop, Melissa. Get out of the country for a while. At least until things quiet down. I should have enough credit going to buy you forty-eight hours.''

''They're going to be asking you a lot of questions.''

''Let them ask. I'll have more answers than they'll know what to do with.''

They stood staring at each other.

''I never wanted you hurt,'' she said.

He knew that now—finally.

She kissed him and his heart, if it was his heart, seemed severed from him, as in those nights before he knew her. He breathed deeply and felt a woe come riding in with the night air.

''I'm not complaining,'' Melissa whispered. ''All things considered, I know I'm getting off very easily. It's just that I suddenly feel so—cheated.''

She went to the couch, drew back the sheet, and briefly embraced her brother. ''Please take good care of him. He was all I ever really had.''

Forster's last glimpse of her from the porch was of a slender, delicately made figure fading into the mist. When the limousine had driven off, he went back into the house to call Marty Jennings.

Four hours later, while it was not yet daylight, Forster was in an upstairs study of the White House, offering his devil's fable to the president and attorney general.

Epilogue

At four o'clock in the afternoon of July second, the twentieth day of the crisis, Martin Alcott, the White House press secretary, called an emergency press conference to say that the president would appear on national radio and television at nine o'clock that evening to make an important announcement to the American people. When pressed for some hint as to subject matter, Alcott refused to comment further.

Although business had ended for the day on the New York and American Stock Exchanges, there was instant reaction on the West Coast, with all sorts of unfounded rumors swirling, and trading having to be halted in many of the more volatile issues. In light of the current economic crisis, the president's scheduled announcement was generally regarded to be among the most anxiously awaited in recent history.

"Ladies and Gentlemen," said a White House spokesman at precisely 9:00 P.M., "the president of the United States."

With the presidential seal as a backdrop, Donald Hanson looked pale despite his television makeup. But his eyes were steady as they gazed into the camera, and his voice, when he began to speak, was firm and sure.

"Fellow Americans," he said, "it's with a full and happy heart this evening that I'm able to report the withdrawal of all civil and criminal indictments against Wendell Norton, Alfred Loomis, Tom Stanton, Henry Ridgeway, Peter Farnham and William Boyer—six of our nation's foremost financial leaders. As of several hours ago, the Justice Department has officially declared them innocent of all charges.

"Because of the classified nature of much of the material surrounding this important case, I'm not free at this time to discuss many of the details. What I can tell you, however, is that the unfortunate indictments of these six men were the result of a carefully orchestrated conspiracy, designed and backed by a hostile foreign power and carried out by certain individuals for personal gain. It was this criminal conspiracy that resulted in the appearance of illegal acts by the parties in question and gave rise to widespread doubts as to the viability of the American economic system.

"Now," declared the president, speaking slowly and carefully, "with this fortuitous uncovering of the truth, it is hoped that these doubts, totally unjustified to begin with, will be quickly dispelled. Faith and trust have long been the precepts that have inspired America's greatness—faith in our future and trust in those chosen to serve our national interest. In time of need, neither of these qualities has ever failed us. I'm grateful—I'm sure we're all grateful—that this has once again proven to be so.

"God bless you and good night."

Several hours later, all regular network programming was once again interrupted—this time, for a news bulletin announcing the death of Wendell Norton in an automobile accident. Few details were as yet available, it was declared, other than that the former Fed Chairman had apparently lost control of his car on a Maryland road, plunged into a ravine, and died instantly in the resulting explosion and fire. According to the bulletin, it was uncertain whether Norton had been informed of his being absolved of all guilt in the banking scandal prior to his sudden, tragic death.

At the White House, the Hansons were preparing for bed when they heard the bulletin come over the radio.

"So that's the official version," said the First Lady quietly. Knowing the truth, she sighed. "I just thank God that's the end of it."

The president said nothing.

She looked at him. "It *is* the end, isn't it?"

"Not really—not until we see the markets' response to the news. It should be positive, of course. But just how positive and for how long, is something else. A great deal of damage has been done. It may not go away overnight or by itself."

"Does that mean you haven't canceled Falcon?"

"I can't take that chance—not yet. Too much preparation has

gone into it. Once it's scrubbed, it won't be easy to revive. I'll see what happens. I still have a little time.''

Arthur Berenstein, aka Robert Bennet, was buried early the next morning among the converted potato fields of Suffolk County, Long Island. Because of the circumstances surrounding his death, it was officially labeled a vehicular accident, like Norton's, and news of it had not been made public. Forster was the only mourner present. Melissa, having followed Forster's advice, was already out of the country. So that at sometime after 9:00 A.M. on July third, Forster stood beneath an azure summer sky and watched the casket of the man whom he had wrongly suspected of trying to have him killed, and who had ended up being killed himself, lowered into the earth.

He had arranged to have Avrohom Liebman officiate. Considering Robert's long and close association with the rabbi, it had seemed only fitting. Now, doing his prescribed job, Rabbi Liebman recited the mourner's kaddish. ''*Yisgadel v'yiskadash sh'meh rabbo. . . .* '' And Forster repeated it after him, a five-thousand-year-old prayer for a thirty-nine-year-old man. Forster guessed it was about as good a prayer as any and better than most.

''May the father of peace send peace to all who mourn,'' chanted the rabbi, ''and comfort all the bereaved among us.''

''Amen,'' whispered Forster, but expected neither peace nor comfort.

The funeral party of two drove back toward New York together.

''He's going to be sorely missed,'' sighed the rabbi. ''I can't begin to tell you how much.''

Not by the American people thought Forster. But he said, ''I know.''

''No you don't. You couldn't. Not unless you'd been part of what we've been doing all these years.''

The shrunken scholar peered at Forster through thick lenses and cigarette smoke. ''Have you made your decision yet about us, about Chai?''

''I'm afraid I can't join you.''

Liebman's prematurely wizened face looked more morose than usual. ''May I ask why not?''

''I just don't believe in vigilance committees.''

"Not even for the survival of your people?"

"I can't accept the idea that the survival of the Jews is in Chai's hands. If it is, we may as well kiss each other goodbye right now."

The rabbi sadly shook his head. "I pray you're not soon proven wrong."

Forster gazed out at row after row of small houses with pridefully tended lawns. They slept, neat, weathered, and hopeful under their safe American sky. "If I am, I'll call you."

Economists, of course, had their differing views as to the underlying causes of what had come to be known as simply The Panic, as well as to how the clearing of the six bankers was likely to affect conditions when the markets resumed trading after the holiday weekend. But it was just the president and a handful of top government officials who were privy to the truths that lay hidden at the heart of the crisis—and then, only after Forster's three stated conditions had been met.

First, he had told the president and the attorney general, Katherine Harwith would have to be guaranteed full immunity from prosecution for any and all illegal acts of her own while involved in the conspiracy to falsely incriminate the six bankers.

Second, evidence would be presented from other sources attesting to the fact that these same six bankers, while serving on a federally appointed commission more than two decades ago, did knowingly indict and send to prison an innocent man, thereby destroying not only the man's own life, but the lives of his wife and two children. No punishment would be demanded at so late a date since this would serve no positive national purpose. But in all fairness, a public statement had to be issued by the Justice Department testifying to the victim's innocence and admitting the terrible wrongs perpetrated upon him and his family. Also, suitable reparations would have to be paid to his single surviving heir.

Third, Forster had declared, this aforementioned heir, Helen Berenstein, aka Melissa Kenniston, though having played a major role in the banking conspiracy, would have to be allowed to leave the United States for however long she chose and promised immunity from extradition and prosecution. Which had to be considered only just, inasmuch as without her having taken action as she had, Forster himself would have been dead, Wendell

Norton would have been alive, and his entire personally planned conspiracy would have gone undetected.

With the pure platinum Forster had in his pocket to sell, all three stipulations were quickly accepted.

At 10:00 A.M. on July fifth, while it was still the afternoon of July fourth in New York, in Melbourne one of the first of the world's markets was about to open since news of the six bankers' innocence broke. The Australian market quickly signaled the euphoria to come. On a catwalk high above the growing excitement on the trading floor, uniformed "chalkies" swiftly sketched stock prices on a huge green board. All prices were rising.

At 9:00 A.M., in Tokyo's new Kabutocho exchange building, cautious joy predominated among the more than two thousand dealers as they tried to estimate the kind of reaction that would be taking place on Wall Street later in the day. Meanwhile, the Nikkei Dow Jones index of 225 traded stocks did its own celebrating by rising 423 points.

In Hong Kong at 10:00 A.M., traders in red waistcoats on the Hong Kong Stock Exchange floor did business in a frantic rush as the Hang Seng index of 30 stocks leaped a startling 142 points in the first hour of trading. By noon the index was up 357 points, its largest morning point gain ever.

London, 8:00 A.M. A backlog of buy orders had accumulated over the weekend, and brokers were at their desks earlier than usual to prepare for the expected buying binge. A manager for Prudential-Bache's London branch gathered his traders together for a pep rally. "This is going to be our biggest day ever," he told them. "We're going over the top!"

In New York, the next day at 9:00 A.M., the New York Stock Exchange was not yet open, but in Merrill Lynch's trading room some of the firm's brokers were perspiring at their telephone consoles as they stared at rows upon rows of several hundred blinking buttons.

New York, 9:30 A.M. The Big Board opened. At the bell the Dow was already up 72 points. In the next thirty minutes, 57 million shares were sold. At Shearson, Lehman, Hutton several blocks away, glowing green figures on computer consoles traced the market's rise. "It's a second Fourth of July!" exulted Trader Mark Kinnear.

New York, 10:30 A.M. In the first hour, 163 million shares had been traded on the Big Board alone—an average day's entire volume. The Dow had jumped another 38 points, up a total of 110.

In San Francisco at 7:30 A.M., Henry Anker, an insurance broker, was listening to radio reports of the soaring market as he drove to work. Anker turned off the highway at the next exit and phoned his broker with orders to buy Texaco and General Motors. The broker read off the jumping quotes on the two stocks. By the time Anker's buy orders were in, he had paid an additional 2 points for each.

New York, 11:45 A.M. The first substantial bout of profit-taking had hit. After having risen 278 points, the Dow had dropped 103 in the past thirty minutes. Which was not unexpected and caused little concern. "Every market needed its period of correction," said the cliché mongers. "Nothing went straight up or straight down."

New York, 12:30 P.M. The Dow had continued to fall and had now given back 187 points of its early gain. Long lines of people were again forming to take their turns in the New York Stock Exchange's spectator gallery. Voices were quieter on the trading floor below. There seemed less joy.

Washington, 12:30 P.M. In the Oval Office, the president watched the deteriorating rally with growing concern. He had a call put through to the NYSE chairman. "What do you think it means?" he asked. "It's hard to tell at this point," the chairman said. "Every rally runs out of steam, Mr. President, but this one seems to have died a little early. If it doesn't revive soon, it could mean a reassessment of the good news and another sell-off."

"God forbid."

"Let's hope He's watching, Mr. President."

Chicago, 1:00 P.M. The Standard and Poor's 500 trading pit at the Chicago Mercantile Exchange was quiet. One could breathe the uncertainty. The trades that were made were volatile, way out of line. Trading at the futures pit ordinarily moved up or down in ticks of from five to twenty dollars a contract. Now it was moving in ticks of two hundred and fifty to one thousand dollars.

At the New York Stock Exchange at 2:30 P.M., another rally attempt had failed, sending the Dow into a tailspin. By the time it leveled out, the entire morning gain was gone and the index was 23 points into minus territory. At Prudential-Bache, broker Tom Neal paused amid the worried calls from his customers. He took off the button pinned to his shirt and stared at it for a moment. It said DON'T PANIC. Then he pinned the button back on his shirt and took his next call.

Washington, 3:30 P.M. White House Spokesman Martin Alcott, instructed to say a few calming words to reporters, said in grim jest, "I would like to open our news conference by leading you all in prayer."

New York, 3:40 P.M. When there were no further rally attempts, computer program trading in stock index futures kicked into gear and accelerated the selling. By the 4:00 P.M. closing bell, the Dow had turned its early celebration into a 217 point rout for the day.

At 4:30 P.M. President Hanson had Treasury Secretary Gaynor and the interim Fed chairman, Howard Bloom, sitting in the Oval Office. He looked at their faces and found them as dour as his own.

"I don't understand it." Hanson spoke softly, calmly, as he did when he was most disturbed. Controlling his voice helped him control his emotions. "We couldn't have announced better news if we'd invented it ourselves, and look what happened. Why?"

Neither man rushed to answer. White House convention demanded pondering. Too quick a reply could be considered shallow.

Bloom finally said, "If you'll forgive an aphorism, Mr. President, nobody who has been on a falling elevator and lived through it, ever gets on one again without being nervous. It's going to take time to rebuild confidence. No single announcement can do it."

"But why a further fall?"

"Disappointment," said Bloom. "Failed expectations when the rally ran out of support. Which isn't unusual in a market fueled more by hope than reality. It's an insane system and it scares me half to death. Only one in five households invest in the market, but stocks still regulate every damn thing in this country—from jobs, to spending, to bonuses, to pensions, to confidence in the whole economy."

Gaynor cleared his throat. "I've been speaking to investment people all afternoon, Mr. President. The whole idea of a conspiracy is frightening to them. It indicates a vulnerability, a lack of control at the top. It makes them wonder what can happen next that they don't expect or know anything about." The treasury secretary's restless eyes swept the room. "But it's obviously more than just that." he said glumly, "We seem to have entered a whole new world lately in which a government even as powerful as ours can be held hostage by the financial markets. The truth is, we really don't know what we've created. It's high-tech, and it's transnational and more powerful than anything we could ever have imagined."

The president's face showed nothing. Yet at that moment he felt claw marks on his chest and an oppression close to strangling in his throat. "Then from what you're both telling me, we're no better off now than we were before the bankers were cleared. And perhaps worse off if this fear of further conspiracy is really so."

"It's impossible to gauge these things in advance, Mr. President," said Bloom. "We'll just have to wait and see."

You wait, thought Hanson. I've just run out of time.

At 2:18 A.M. London time, on July sixth, a black sedan drove slowly into Grosvenor Square and stopped a short distance from the entrance gates of the American Embassy. It was a quiet night with a soft rain falling and heavy ground fog. A few red double-deckers were moving, along with a scattering of high-roofed cabs and private cars. In the embassy itself, lights indicated some late-working personnel. An armed marine guard was visible at the entrance, and a Bobby in rain gear patrolled the square nearby.

A man got out of the black sedan. He was picked up almost immediately by a van that then continued across the square and disappeared down a side street off to the left. A young couple with their arms about each other got off one of the double-deckers and walked slowly in the same direction the van had taken. The Bobby, who apparently had just noticed the parked sedan, began strolling toward it. He was still about a hundred yards away when the explosion erupted.

There was a cracking roar and the entire square flared bright orange. It would be determined later, from the force of the blast, that there had been close to two hundred pounds of dynamite packed into the sedan. Thirty seconds after the explosion, while shattered sections of the American Embassy's façade were still falling, the van returned to the square. A body and some broken metal parts were dumped about a hundred yards from the crater where the sedan had been. After several moments, the body appeared to explode with a small curious blast of its own. But by this time the van had disappeared once more.

Hours later, when the police had identified the body as that of Abu Gamal, a long-sought Libyan terrorist, and the broken pieces of metal were determined to be parts of an explosive device of known Libyan origin, there was little doubt as to who was responsible for the bombing.

With the five-hour time differential, news of the London bombing reached the president at shortly after 10:00 P.M., Washington time. It was followed, at approximately half-hour intervals, by similar reports from Paris, Bonn, Rome, Damascus, Cairo, and Beirut. As planned, Bayed Shanti's body was discovered outside the embassy in Paris, where he allegedly had been shot by a guard.

Hanson made no attempt to sleep that night. Along with waiting for everything else, he was waiting for the casualty reports. He was prepared, yet he was not prepared. *How could you prepare?* They came in one by one—so many dead here, so many there, so many maimed, so many missing, so many that were just bits and pieces. Yet they were only numbers. All very remote, all very impersonal, all very modest, really, as such catastrophes were judged. As world events went, they were just an insignificant business. In the total human experience, they were a few specks of sand. Or so he told himself.

He recalled a moment of his last meeting with General Yaacov. The Israeli, seeing how deeply affected he was by what lay ahead, had looked at him. *"Hazak, v'ematz,"* he said, which was the order, Yaacov explained, God gave to Joshua and which meant "strengthen thyself."

Good advice.

Yet it was only the beginning.

Seventy-two hours later, during the early morning of July ninth, the United States Seventh Fleet took what was described as limited reprisive action against the State of Libya for the criminal bombings of its embassies and consulates and the ensuing loss of innocent lives.

It was not intended to be, nor was it, a lengthy or large-scale military operation. Despite Colonel Qaddafi's repeated vows to fight to the death, all effective resistance collapsed in less than four days. By that time, the Seventh Fleet's air strikes had destroyed 70 percent of Libya's tanks and planes, and the marines were in control of all communications and strong points.

President Hanson had viewed the operation as if it were little more than some sort of distant theatrical performance. Though it was perhaps no different for him than for most of the ranking naval and marine officers of the Seventh Fleet. Sitting in the White House and watching the videotapes relayed from the combat zone, he could see tank columns, miles away, maneuvering in dust. Bombs dropped from planes as tiny as insects, their wings bright as they caught the sun. Then he heard faint explosions and saw puffs of smoke. All very abstract, far away, and safe.

Afterward, the cameras moved in with the marine infantry and he saw the burned out tanks up close, along with the Libyan dead. If you didn't know about such things, you might not have even known what they were. In the sun, the faces blackened. The bodies swelled. Huge arms and legs cooked in the heat. The dogs ate cooked men. It was a genuine war. The press was there, correspondents from the wire services and networks. The great numbers of Libyan dead impressed them. The whole world respected killing, thought Hanson. There were hundreds of vehicles driven off the road, sunk in the sand—tanks, trucks, personnel carriers, all smashed, exploded, burned. But the main theme was really the dead, bursting out of their greenish brown uniforms, giving off their special stink that you didn't have to smell to know was there. In the blazing desert, they were the one thing you were forced to take seriously.

Watching her husband's face, Felicia Hanson said, "There's no law that says you have to memorize every last detail."

"Yes there is."

"It had to be done," she told him. "You said yourself it was the only way."

"I just hope to God I was right."

* * *

At first it didn't seem so. The world's financial markets' initial reaction to news of the attack was to sell off—as they usually did in such cases. The markets hated surprise. It frightened them. And there was always the added fear of possible escalation. How would the Soviets respond?

As it turned out, predictably.

Like a conditioned reflex, Moscow condemned the Libyan incursion as a dangerous threat to world peace and another example of American imperialism at work. Too, there was the usual rhetoric in the United Nations, unswervingly divided along rigid, geopolitical lines. But once the obligatory overreactions were out of the way, and quiet diplomatic assurances were given that the United States' actions in Libya were limited, temporary, and no more than a long-overdue lesson that terrorism would never again go unpunished, things settled back into their customary propaganda grooves.

Colonel Qaddafi, of course, kept screaming of Libya's innocence in the seven bombings of American installations, but no one believed his hysterical truths any more than they had ever believed his equally hysterical lies.

The markets, meanwhile, had begun to move according to their own lights. Once the original shock was out of the way, the reassessments started clicking into gear as neatly as programmed trading patterns. The defense stocks were the first to get a play, with heavy-industry cyclicals close behind. No one expected a major war. But a war psychology was suddenly on the loose, and this was even better for projected defense appropriations and recipient contractors than a war itself with its lower profit margins. In the international currency markets, the dollar benefited from an initial surge followed by a more modest but steadily upward trend as fiscal support from America's allies and trading partners grew.

At home, young men swarmed into military recruiting offices as a wave of patriotism swept the country. Stars and stripes decals began appearing on auto bumpers and windows. Commentators spoke of a new restored grass-roots pride in all things American. A new spirit of leadership was seen in Washington with the emphasis on strength and hope rather than fear and guilt. The postscandal sense of panic faded as the absolution of the bankers was viewed in a more logical light. If their alleged guilt had shaken the country's faith, should it not follow that their proven innocence would restore it? The logic had been there with the president's first announcement of their guiltlessness, but there had been too much fear to sustain it. Now the fear was gone.

The president, with a fine sensitivity to the prevailing mood, kept the marines in Libya longer than originally intended. Merely their presence was proving to be an effective reminder for the country and the world. *DON'T TREAD ON ME.* The implied warning worked in unexpected areas; not the least of which was Iran, where the ayatollahs and their Shiite terrorists had literally been getting away with murder. Now, with Washington having actual hard evidence that Iran was interfering in America's internal affairs, murdering its citizens and conspiring to destroy its economy, the ayatollahs, showing their first-ever public sign of caution, took special pains to disavow any official knowledge of, or part in, the conspiracy. To further emphasize this fact, Iran's highest court tried, convicted, and publicly executed the country's minister of finance, Hassan Motomedi, for having taken unauthorized action that was in no way compatible with the principles and peaceful intentions of the Islamic Republic of Iran.

I did it, thought Hanson, *and it worked.* Which didn't mean there weren't still moments of doubts. Yet why? Wasn't it his job as president to preserve the common good? And hadn't he helped preserve America as a lush, air-conditioned garden where honest toil was nourishment, people lived in Hamburger Heavens, and the skies were not cloudy all day? Maybe. But his job also sent him down mean streets. It too often tore away the bright red-white-and-blue wrappings and exposed the maggots beneath. Everyone had their own private landscapes, but his was a grotesque blend of ice cream sundaes and sudden death, brass bands and dirty secrets. Many of those who peopled his turf dared shake a fist at the land of opportunity, and refused to be grateful. Worst of all, they betrayed the ultimate trust. Hanson suppressed a sigh. They were betraying it still.

One night Annie appeared at Forster's apartment, the same apartment they had shared as man and wife, with a suitcase in her hand.

"I thought I'd just try staying for a few days," she said. "I thought it might not be too bad an idea to see what happens. That is, if it's all right with you.''

It was all right with Forster.

At times, he still thought of Melissa. Part of it was unavoidable. Reparations for the false imprisonment of David Berenstein were being discussed and he was occasionally consulted. Also, she had taken to dropping him wry little messages on picture postcards from various parts of Europe. But he thought of her quite apart from that. How could he not? She still perplexed him, still filled him with the same sense of wonder he had felt when she was no more than an old research file on his desk. She had cynically used him. Yet she was the one who had finally offered him deliverance.

Melissa.

Nothing of his original obsession was left. The last hint of that had died when he peeled her open and found Wendell lurking inside, gazing out at him. Yet her legacy of pain, the anguish of her beginnings, remained real, untouched. She had suffered. It was this that had moved him, that moved him still. The rest of her was all illusion, lies that she made up as she went along. He regretted the loss of her determined grace with the truth uncovered. How much more splendrous if she and Robert had *really* been fixated on avenging their father, had *really* flown above their private darkness all these years. As we all sought to fly, he thought. That endless struggle for faith, for exaltation. This was what she had promised. And it was all a lie.

About the Author

Norman Garbo is the author of many highly popular works of suspense fiction. He lives with his wife and family in Sands Point, New York.